Praise for Tamara Morgan's
Confidence Tricks

"This book is a lot of fun with a great hero... The caper spirit, Asprey's irrepressible nature, and the smart exchanges carry the story..."

~ *Dear Author*

"*Confidence Tricks* is an entertaining and enjoyable book that will have you questioning your morals."

~ *Guilty Pleasures Book Reviews*

"This was just flat-out fun... Full of dry humor with an ending I didn't see coming, I recommend *Confidence Tricks* to any romance reader looking for an unusual hero and heroine that will keep them laughing."

~ *RR@H Novel Thoughts*

"I'll start by saying I adored this book. It made me laugh and the hero made me swoon."

~ *Smexybooks*

"*Confidence Tricks* is truly a fun and sexy ride with an appealing hero and an amusing heroine who knows how to kick ass."

~ *The Bookpushers*

Look for these titles by
Tamara Morgan

Now Available:

Games of Love
Love is a Battlefield
The World is a Stage

Confidence Tricks

Tamara Morgan

SAMHAIN
PUBLISHING

Samhain Publishing, Ltd.
11821 Mason Montgomery Road, 4B
Cincinnati, OH 45249
www.samhainpublishing.com

Editing by Linda Ingmanson
Cover by Angela Waters

First Samhain Publishing, Ltd. electronic publication: February 2013
First Samhain Publishing, Ltd. print publication: February 2014

Dedication

For Alexia Reed, who pretty much made this book happen. Asprey is all yours.

Chapter One

The stiletto heel pressed against his jugular had yet to break the skin.

It was a small comfort—Asprey's only one at the moment. Gravel dotted painfully into his cheek and temple, and his arm hung limp at his side. Only a few cords of fiery, razor-edged nerves seemed to connect the bones of his shoulder to the rest of him, and every movement was a clear reminder that he lay completely at the woman's mercy.

That was, if she had any.

"I think maybe we should give the lady her necklace back," Asprey offered, his words a little raspy since several handfuls of the grit from the road had made their way into his mouth. "I've never been partial to pearls anyway."

Asprey couldn't see much other than the tires of his Ducati and the sprawl of the ground before him, but he could hear Graff's muttered curse. It was a short trip from there to imagine what his brother looked like at that moment, his nostrils all flaring and irate as he held a shotgun to the woman's date.

"Don't listen to him," Graff said. "All you have to do is let my incompetent accomplice go and we'll be on our way. It's that easy."

A sharp pain as the stiletto dug deeper indicated retreat wasn't going to be as easy as Asprey had hoped.

"How about I call the police and let them decide who's going where?" the woman asked.

That, at least, didn't strike fear into Asprey's heart. Cell phone reception was impossible up here—it was why they'd picked the location. Just a few hundred yards up from the highway by virtue of a dirt path that few people knew about and even fewer tried to navigate, they were hidden away in the perfect place for a quick robbery. That was the plan, anyway.

Force the car up the path. Point a shotgun. Demand the jewels.

It was hard to tell exactly where things had gone wrong. If Asprey had to guess, it was when they'd assumed their target's girlfriend, a platinum blonde in a tight black dress, would react like every other woman in the world with a gun placed squarely in her face. A few tears, a little hysteria. Possibly a can of mace hidden in her purse.

Not so with this one. When Graff had ordered her to hand over her necklace, a string of pearls set with diamonds and boasting an estimated twenty-thousand-dollar value, she'd launched some sort of ninja attack. That was the only way to explain it. One minute, Asprey was reaching out a gloved hand to take the necklace. The next, he was about to be impaled on the end of a high heel.

Hence the stalemate. And the pain.

"How about I blow your boyfriend's head off instead?" Graff countered.

Even though Asprey knew his brother would do no such thing—there weren't even any bullets in the gun—the words sent a shiver down his spine. On a good night, Graff was an asshole. On a night like this, in the middle of being bested by a hundred and twenty pounds of finely crafted femininity, he was right up there with political dictators and the people at animal shelters who put kittens to sleep.

"How about someone lets me stand so we can work this out like calm, rational adults?" Asprey interrupted, keeping his tone light and pleasant. He'd always been that way—the more intense a situation got, the less concerned he appeared on the surface. It drove Graff crazy. "If it helps, I'm pretty sure you've dislocated my arm. I don't pose much of a threat."

"Maybe you should just let them have the necklace," a third voice added. "It's not worth anyone's life." The voice belonged to Todd Kennick, their target for the night. He was currently pressed up against the side of his dark blue Mercedes, Graff's gun between his shoulder blades.

"That's some pretty sound advice." Asprey tried swallowing, but the lump throbbed painfully as it moved past the shoe's point. "We wouldn't want anyone getting hurt. Would we...Natalie?"

At the sound of her name, the woman started, and Asprey couldn't help a feeling of triumph from swelling inside him. Okay, so he wasn't much of a hand at robbery, as the current state of affairs indicated, but the legwork ahead of time—predicting patterns—was kind of his thing. He knew where his victims would be and when they would be there. He knew where they lived, what they read in the bathroom, how they took their coffee.

He also knew when they gave ridiculously overpriced pieces of jewelry to gorgeous women who dressed like they were one step away from the pole. Todd Kennick, forty-eight-year-old finance executive, was that man. And Natalie Hall was that woman.

"How do you know my name?" Natalie's voice was cold, but the stabby heel loosened a little, putting Asprey even more at ease. He was even able to turn his head enough to look up the expanse of her calf, all sleek muscle and smooth skin. *Ninja legs.*

"Who are you?" she added.

"Some call us highwaymen. Some call us gentleman thieves," Asprey said. He turned even more and managed to smile up at her, just inches away from a glimpse at the goods. "But if you move your leg a little bit to the right, you can call me anything you want."

"Oh, gross," she muttered, shifting her body just enough to close off his view. "You're kidding, right?"

"I never joke about women's underwear." *Wait. That didn't come out right.*

From across the gravel lot, he heard Graff's exaggerated sigh and the cock of the shotgun—equal signs that his brother was losing patience.

"Natalie, please," Todd cried, obviously feeling the pain of a cold ring of metal against his spine. "He's going to kill me. Give them what they want. The necklace. The car. *Anything.*"

Asprey didn't like to judge a man based solely on how he reacted in situations like this. He'd seen far too many guys lose their shit on the wrong side of a gun to believe anyone appeared in their best light when confronted with their own mortality. The big ones always cried; the rich ones offered to buy their way to salvation.

This Todd character, though—he had to be the worst. For all the man knew, Asprey planned on kidnapping his ninja girlfriend and selling her on the black market. Yet all his heroics were directed at saving his own ass, at getting the gun pointed anywhere but toward himself.

This Natalie woman could surely do better. They were practically doing her a favor here.

"I'm begging you." Todd's voice rose.

"But my necklace," Natalie protested, frowning down at Asprey. "I...I love it."

"For Christ's sake," Todd cried. "I'll buy you another one. I'll buy you three more. I don't understand why you're acting like this."

Natalie must have decided three necklaces were worth it, because her heel finally pulled away. Asprey scrambled to his feet before she could re-invoke the Force or launch another stealth attack. His arm hung useless and throbbing at his side, but he was at least able to back away a few steps, angling himself behind his motorcycle. No way was he getting anywhere near that woman again—not while he couldn't fight back.

"So, I'm supposed to hand it off, just like that?" Natalie asked, looking back and forth between Asprey and the necklace. It was clear which one she liked better. "To robbers?"

"Crazed robbers," Asprey added helpfully.

A brief flash crossed the woman's face as she took one last, longing look at the necklace. She wanted to fight for it, Asprey could tell. He felt similar pangs all the time—usually for his downtown loft apartment with the voice-activated control panel, or Ruby, his sweet little three-passenger Cessna Corvalis.

God, he missed that plane.

But common sense won out—it always did. Asprey had given in when the real cost of that kind of luxury became clear. The Natalie woman gave in when Graff warned her one last time to give it up or risk Todd's untimely and gruesome death.

Resigned, but clearly unhappy about it, she moved toward Asprey with an almost feline slowness, the necklace in her outstretched hand. Now that he thought about it, she was a lot like a cat, all sleek on the outside, her long, bouncy hair and tight clothes clearly designed to encourage heavy petting. A slightly snaggled front tooth and oversized brown eyes added a touch of humanity—but the *claws*. As Natalie got closer, she narrowed those eyes and tensed, as if she planned on lunging at him again.

Asprey held his ground, but just barely. Best not to forget the claws.

"I'm losing my patience," Graff growled.

Asprey offered an apologetic smile. "He's hypoglycemic. We really should get this moving."

"Is this supposed to be some kind of good cop, bad cop thing?" She was almost within arm's reach now. "I'm not scared of you, you know."

"No worries," Asprey replied. "I'm scared enough of you for the both of us."

A laugh—strangled and almost against her will—escaped Natalie's throat. She jiggled the necklace, all those pearls and diamonds shimmering even though they had only the feeble Puget moon to go by. "Fine. Take it. Go buy drugs or fund a yachting excursion around the world or whatever. I hope you enjoy it."

Asprey didn't move. He was normally a confident man, the kind who walked into a room without hesitating, the first one to jump from a moving car or take a bite of a decorative pepper plant on a dare. But this woman disarmed him with her beauty and ninja skills.

"This isn't a trick?" he asked.

"You're the ones with the guns, the face masks and an impeccable sense of timing," she said, her voice so low they were the only two who could hear it. "You tell me."

"We just want the necklace."

"Funny thing, that." She threw the jewelry at him with so much force it hit his chest and bounced uselessly to the ground. "So do I."

It seemed as good a time as any to get the hell out. As carefully as he could, Asprey squatted to retrieve the string of pearls, not once losing eye contact with the woman, hoping it would be enough. It seemed dangerous to be down near her legs again without some kind of safety net.

There was no way Asprey could ride his motorcycle out of there with just the one good arm, so he and Graff moved quickly. He slipped the necklace into his pocket and nodded once. Wordlessly, and with an understanding bred of several months of robberies, he and Graff switched places. The scene was silent save for Natalie's careful breathing and the crunch of their feet as he and Graff took their places.

Asprey slid into the driver's seat of their unmarked black van while Graff hopped onto the bike, making sure to keep his shotgun trained on the couple the entire time. He tossed the gun into the open door of the van at the last minute, and Asprey pushed the automatic sliding door button so that it came to a neat close.

And Graff had mocked him for adding that feature. Said it smacked of soccer-mom ambitions.

The two engines of their getaway vehicles roared into action as one, filling the air with the sound of motors gunning and men gratefully escaping the scene of the crime. Fire pokers stabbed at Asprey's useless arm as he tried to steer, his left hand crossing over to shift the van into drive. It was going to hurt like hell to put that shoulder back into place—especially since the hospital was out of the question. Chances were he'd have to ask Graff to pull it back in for him, and of all his brother's virtues, gentleness wasn't the one that most often sprang to mind.

At least we have the necklace.

Say what he might about inferior medical care and gravel in his teeth, that counted for something.

Asprey cast one last look in the rearview mirror as he sped away. Half of him expected the Natalie woman to be hanging on to the undercarriage or calling on the powers combined, but she simply stood watching them go, hands on her hips, something very much like vengeance contorting the beautiful angles of her face.

Poppy's hands moved quickly as she began extracting the more than fifty bobby pins that held her wig into place. Even though darkness seeped through the underground parking garage—even more so since she hid behind the open trunk of her ancient Ford LTD—she swore she could see blood on the ends of at least a few of the pins.

Six hours was about as long as she could stand having the heavy, blonde hair manacled to her head—and according to her watch, she'd about doubled that today.

Masked crusader bastards.

She hadn't exactly planned to be sitting in a police station for several hours, recounting a watered-down version of the night's events and wishing she was anywhere else.

"Yes, Officer. Two men, both of them large and intimidating, threatening to kill Todd at every turn."

"No, Officer. I didn't attack the man. At one point, the robber fell and hurt his shoulder, but I'm just a woman. What could I have possibly done to make that happen?"

Tears had helped. Tears and Todd's version of the story, which skewed things decidedly in his favor. She wasn't sure if he actually *believed* he was the hero of the day, saving her from raping and pillaging and all that, or if he was choosing to ignore that brief moment when his supposed girlfriend, a slightly empty-headed yoga instructor named Natalie Hall, kicked a man's ass and threatened to end his life in a whirlwind blitz of bones and body parts.

It doesn't matter. All that counted was that she was home, Todd didn't think any less of her for putting her own brand of street fighting to good use, and, with any luck, her plan could continue moving forward with just a few slight adjustments.

She grabbed one of the baby wipes in the trunk and scraped away at her make-up, which had streaked black and tan over her face as she'd faked hysteria. She scrubbed harder when the ancient church bell down the street from the apartment complex rang two ominous notes, a clear sign of how late it had grown.

Her game face removed, she turned her attention to the rest of her façade. She extracted the silicone cutlets from her bra and slipped off her heels, tossing the dangerously tall shoes deep into the gym bag she kept stashed in the trunk. It would have been a huge relief to take off the Spanx that vacuum-packed her body into a seamless collection of curves, but the night was already way too far gone. An oversized sweatshirt hid the low plunge of her dress, and tennis shoes—which she had to shove painfully over three new blisters on each heel—rendered her expensive black minidress almost unnoticeable.

It would have to be enough. Hopefully, Bea would be fast asleep and fail to notice that Poppy was hours later than promised, looking like a woman making her way home from the undeniably worst date of her life.

"Don't you dare make a sound," Bea whispered as Poppy let herself in. The apartment was dark save for the flickering lights of the television, whose flashing pictures urged them to buy a complete suite of James Earl Jones DVDs. "Jenny is finally asleep, and I will end the life of anyone who wakes her before eight o'clock tomorrow morning."

Relief shouldn't have been Poppy's first emotion at seeing her friend completely bedraggled and unkempt, but it was. Four months of cohabitation, and she never remembered how much motherhood drained a person.

"Rough night?" Poppy asked. She stepped carefully over Jenny, an almost-two-year-old bundle of heat, currently spread out all over the living room floor in what might have once been a fort but was now a tangled mess of blankets and exhaustion. "She always looks so sweet when she's sleeping."

Bea rubbed her eyes, spreading mascara over the tattoo that extended from the corner of one eye to her hairline, all shooting stars and pink skulls. It wasn't the most maternal look in the world, but it matched Bea's general aesthetic of shorn black hair and colorful highlights in an alternating pattern of blue and green. Her sweats also hid several other tattoos, most of them of naked fairies and wolves howling at the moon.

They'd been young. They'd had a friend with a mobile tattoo parlor, rolling through the late-night streets to the cheerful clang of an ice cream truck's song. They were lucky that tattoos were the only thing Bea had caught.

"I swear, Poppy—it's almost inhuman, how she acts when bedtime rolls around. It's like she'll eat my soul if I show a hint of weakness."

They both looked down and watched as the little girl's chubby, roseate cheeks quivered and blew out in the pattern of deep sleep that only children enjoy. Poppy was just about to offer all kinds of nonsensical compliments when Bea cleared her throat. It was a serious sound—one Poppy wasn't all too keen on hearing at the moment.

"You got two phone calls today," she said.

"Oh, really?" Poppy feigned unconcern. "Did you write down the messages?"

Poppy bent to scoop the little girl up and tuck her into her converted toddler bed that sat squeezed in Bea's bedroom between the dresser and a futon. Things were tight in the apartment since Poppy had moved in—a burden she felt keenly, but Bea had insisted that her home would always be Poppy's. The apartment was just one part of a long line of atonements Poppy hadn't asked for and didn't want.

When she reemerged from the bedroom, it was to find a much more alert Bea looking up at her. "The messages weren't hard to remember. The first one was from your parole officer."

"Nancy? That old battle-ax?" Poppy waved her off. "She's always trying to butter me up. The last time I saw her, I believe the exact words used to describe me were, and I quote, 'a black hole of common sense.' I think she meant it as a compliment."

Bea wasn't amused. "She wants you to call her back in the morning. And you have to stop treating this like it's a joke—"

"How many times do I have to tell you?" Poppy leaned in and planted a kiss on Bea's cheek. It was sticky and tasted of apple juice, clear evidence that bedtime really had been as rough as it looked. "Don't worry so much."

"If you want me to stop worrying, then explain why the second phone call was from Jared."

Goddamn him. She'd told her fence—the guy who was supposed to sell her necklace—not to call her at home. Or to call at all, actually, but taking hints had never been his strong suit.

"I'm sure he just wanted to chat about the good old days," Poppy assured her. "You know how bad Jared is about taking a hint. I get the feeling he thinks we're going to pick up where we let off. You know, now that I'm a free woman and all."

Bea drooped—all of her, from the tired lines of her face to the solidly packed muscles of her body, which also fell in line with her general bad-ass appeal. Or what used to be her bad-ass appeal, anyway. Bea was officially out of the game now. Motherhood had forced early retirement, transforming her from a free-wheeling sidekick to this benevolent, maternal creature Poppy barely recognized anymore.

"You promise it's not anything else?" Bea stood, her eyes traveling the length of Poppy, finally taking in the miniskirt-in-a-wastebasket look she had going on. "You're not doing anything *illegal*?"

"Of course not," Poppy lied smoothly. The less Bea knew about her current activities, the better it was for all of them. Besides, it wasn't totally wrong, what she was doing. Lots of young, attractive, falsely blonde women dated older men to try to get them to buy expensive jewels. She was a little more intent on her goals, that was all.

She planted her hand firmly on her friend's back and pushed her in the direction of the kitchen. "Everything is fine, I swear. I just find it difficult to stay inside for long periods of time. Whenever I turn around, the walls are a little bit closer, the air a little bit harder to breathe. I needed to get out."

That, at least, wasn't a lie. Even though the air outside had cooled to about forty degrees, she pushed open the window above the sink, letting the night air waft in with the tangy promise of rain. Small spaces had never bothered her before, but these days she couldn't even stand in a closed gymnasium without feeling an overwhelming rush of panic. She needed windows and doors and the absolute certainty that she could walk away at any time.

"Want some chamomile?" Poppy asked, changing the subject.

"I wish you'd let me thank you," Bea said quietly. She settled onto one of the yellow vinyl kitchen chairs and ran a finger along the edges of a Dora the Explorer placemat. "Ever since you got out—"

"Stop right there. I don't want to hear another word on the subject, okay?"

"Poppy..."

Poppy clanged the teapot in the sink as she filled it with water, making as much noise as possible extracting the mugs and bags of tea. The last thing she wanted to do right now was get into a soul-searching discussion with Bea about the choices they'd made.

Why beat a dead horse when you can make some damn fine dog food and leather jackets out of it? It wasn't hard to imagine Grandma Jean standing in the kitchen with them, spouting her usual crass wisdom.

"There's no reason, Bea," Poppy said, her voice firm. "Regrets and apologies don't mean anything. If I could go back, I'd do it all again."

"And you're sure you aren't in any trouble?"

Oh, she was in trouble, all right—but not over anything Bea could control. Poppy's biggest problem right now was that those two robbers had somehow known who she was—or at least who she was with the wig on and her breasts out. That meant she was being watched, and that her activities weren't going unnoticed.

There was no way those men were there by accident. And there was no way she could just let that necklace go.

Todd was *her* mark, dammit. She wasn't going to sit back and let him get poached by a pair of ham-fisted men in masks. Girly masks too—not some cool Zorro swatches of fabric, but velvety masquerade things. All that had been missing were some feathers and a cape, and it would have been a ticker-tape parade of mockery.

"I'm good," Poppy said, a smile firmly on her face. "I promise."

The kettle screamed then, and Poppy poured Bea her favorite calming tea. Thankfully, her friend was too tired to do much beyond lifting the steaming cup to her lips.

"Sit down," Bea murmured. "All your energy is making me antsy."

"I'm just going to do the dishes." Poppy surveyed the mountain of pots and pans—most of them crusted over with baby food and macaroni and cheese—and pushed up her sleeves. In times of trouble, Grandma Jean had recommended elbow grease. Personally, she'd always preferred a hearty bout of hand-to-hand combat in the Pit.

These days, she'd take whatever she could get.

Chapter Two

"Someone has breached the perimeter," Asprey announced, pulling a pair of binoculars down from his eyes.

Graff looked up from his book. "You make it sound like we're in the White House or something. It's probably a salesman or a Girl Scout. Get rid of them."

Asprey ignored his brother and peered back through the window, which faced the runway leading up to the massive hangar they called home. This was definitely no salesman or little girl. The woman was still far enough away that he couldn't make out all the details, but a smallish pair of jean shorts, bright teal cowboy boots and a flowy white blouse didn't seem like standard attire for hawking Avon or vacuum cleaners.

"She's on foot," Asprey added, searching around for a parked car or bicycle. Located as they were at the end of an abandoned airport, the only other way to get to the hangar was by teleportation. They weren't exactly on the bus route. "Why would anyone walk all the way out here?"

Graff slammed the book in his lap that time. "I don't know, Asprey. Why don't you go out there and ask? I know it might seem foreign to you, but I'm actually working over here."

"Fine," Asprey returned. "I'll forcibly remove our visitor." He set the binoculars aside and gently rotated his shoulder. It still hurt like a bitch—he'd gotten their younger sister, Tiffany, to pop it back in two nights ago, but she'd been less of the ministering angel he'd been hoping for and more like a gleeful spectator.

"Man up, big brother," she'd said as he lay on the ground and she lifted his arm over his head. Bones and joints weren't supposed to go that way, he was sure of it. *"According to Graff,*

the woman could have done a lot worse to you. He said she went easy. I bet she thought you were cute."

"*Laugh it up, Tiffany,*" he'd replied. "*It's easy for you to judge from the safety of your Internet cocoon back here at the lair.*"

At least he thought that was what he'd said. His memories were rendered slightly hazy, what with the bone-searing pain and all. He might have just been screaming.

And now he had to hold his arm at a weird angle for days, moving around like a baby bird and praying there'd be no call for any sudden movements. Experience and multiple dislocations had taught him to avoid a sling—sucking it up and getting back to life were the best ways to make the recovery period ten times shorter, mostly because the muscles grew too stiff otherwise.

"Need some help?" Tiffany didn't glance up from her computer, set up along the far wall of the hangar on a long, faux-wood table like the kind housed in school cafeterias. "I'm just about done with this code."

"Sure," Asprey said. "Why don't we put you in charge of security? You can intimidate all incomers with your stature and overalls."

That got her to look up. Tiffany promptly stuck out her tongue. "I can't help that I'm short. And it's called a romper."

He laughed. "I can't remember the last time you did anything even approaching romping." For as long as he could recall, Tiffany had been attached to technology like her USB cord was some kind of umbilicus. She had the translucent skin tone and caffeine addiction to prove it.

"Can you please stop being an idiot for five minutes and go take care of our problem?" Graff asked.

"I was about to." Asprey used his stiff movements to exaggerate a swagger. "Do you think I should do slick mobster or Texas Ranger?" When Graff didn't answer right away, Asprey swiveled on one leg and pretended to pull a gun out of a holster. "Texas Ranger, I think. That thar woman won't be able to resist the ol' Asprey charm."

Graff sighed and got up from his chair, gently adjusting it so he faced the opposite direction of the door. Asprey made a face. His brother never appreciated his talent for accents. His brother never appreciated him, period.

As he passed, Asprey ran his hand over the upholstery of his brother's chair. Soft, buttery yellow silk rippled under his fingertips.

"Don't. Touch. Louis," Graff said through his teeth. "Unless you wash your goddamn hands first."

Asprey leaned down and licked the chair, careful to duck when the heavy leather tome his brother had been reading sailed past his head. He covered his laugh with a tsking noise. "Didn't you say that book was a first edition? You should be more careful."

And then he practically skipped away before Graff threw something heavier—like a hammer or one of the steel katanas they'd recently acquired. The only thing he could be sure wouldn't be thrown was Louis, their authentic eighteenth-century Louis XV chair. It was Graff's prized possession, his baby.

It was also the only piece of furniture in the entire twelve-thousand-square-foot hangar, if you didn't count a few folding chairs and the worktables heaped with Tiffany's computers and the bulk of their stolen goods.

Asprey thought about grabbing one of the shotguns leaning against the wall by the door, but changed his mind at the last minute. It was early afternoon, and the woman traveled alone. Chances were she'd gotten lost or had a flat tire somewhere in the vicinity. Even he couldn't botch this one up.

As the woman drew nearer, Asprey leaned against the corrugated metal exterior of the hangar and donned his most disarming smile, squinting into the rare patch of sun. The shorts she wore were as infinitesimal as distance had promised, and she carried a red jug in one hand, a clear sign that her tank was empty and she was in need of a little assistance.

"Do I detect a damsel in distress?" he asked as soon as she came within earshot.

One of the woman's brows rose, but she didn't say anything, so Asprey took her reticence as an invitation. In addition to the world's smallest shorts and her odd choice of footwear, everything about her attire was eccentric and playful and invited perusal. Her hair was a short tangle of loopy brown curls, and there were a few brightly colored feathers worked in, dangling over her shoulders and making it look as though she might take flight at any moment. She looked to be in her mid-twenties, fresh-faced and glowing with the exertion of hiking all the way to their quiet, secluded hiding place.

But it was the legs he kept going back to. This woman obviously worked out.

"Are you done?" she asked, using the toe of her boot to scratch the back of her calf.

"Sorry," he said, not feeling nearly as sheepish as he should have, given the situation. He blamed months of sleeping on a mattress next to Graff in their makeshift apartment in the office above the hangar. All that stuff in the movies about dashing thieves and women being wooed by his outlaw ways were a crock. He couldn't remember the last time he'd been on a date, let alone near a pair of legs like that.

"So...what can I do for you?" he asked. She wasn't a very forthcoming visitor, that was for sure, content to stand there trying to stare him into a state of discomfiture. Good thing Asprey was impervious to the disdain of others. As the least impressive and most likely to screw up member of his family, that sort of thing came standard. "Are you running on empty?"

"Only temporarily," she said. "I was hoping you might be able to help me get on track again."

Her smile, crooked and mocking, seemed familiar. His awareness of it was more of a visceral reaction than a mental one, all warm and tingly and a bit like he was about to be strapped to a chair and given intense dental work without Novocaine.

"So I was right?" he asked, ignoring the feeling. "About the distress?"

"This place *was* hard to find," she agreed, setting down the red jug. "But I hate to disappoint you...I don't need anyone to rescue me."

"Oh, really?" Asprey asked. "Then what brings you all this way?"

"You do," she said, her eyes meeting his. They were large and brown and seemed to be on intimate terms with him.

Asprey's mind immediately started flying through all the women he'd slept with in the past year, searching for eyes like the ones facing him. He tilted his head a little. Would he call those scorned eyes? Irate eyes? You're-a-jackass-and-I'm-going-to-kick-you-in-the-face eyes?

"If this is a staring contest, you really suck at it," she said, breaking into his thoughts. "You've blinked like twelve times."

"House rules—blinking is allowed. I have very dry eyes."

"That's odd," she said, breaking into a wide smile and flashing her teeth, complete with a strangely charming turn to the tooth in the front. "I don't recall your eyes being very dry. In fact, there was a moment there when I was pretty sure you were crying."

It took a moment—a much too long moment he would later regret—before Asprey realized what she meant, before *those* legs and *that* smile finally registered in his brain. He only got one step back before Natalie did some strange sort of tuck-and-roll maneuver to get behind him, and she had his bad arm in her clutches before he was able to do much more than draw a breath.

The familiar feeling of fire and ice, alternating in a kind of primitive torture, shot up his arm. She didn't pull hard enough to pop his shoulder back out of the socket, but his poor muscles had already had their fill that morning trying to eat breakfast. And that was just Cocoa Puffs.

"Okay, okay, okay," Asprey cried, bending awkwardly to try to reduce the amount of pressure. "Spork! I cry spork!"

She released some of the tension on his arm but didn't back away. "You cry spork?"

"It's my safe word," he managed. "You know—functional yet innovative? I hate to brag, but I've been told I'm a little of both."

Her laughter was warm on his neck. "For a miserable thief, you're kind of funny."

The compliment meant far more than it should have, given the circumstances. "And for a killer ninja-spy, you're incredibly attractive."

"Flattery will get you nowhere." She turned them so they faced the door to the hangar. "All sporks aside, are you going to invite me in, or am I going to have to storm the castle?"

"It's Natalie, right?" He didn't wait for an answer. "Our home is yours. Please, come in. We might even be able to offer you tea."

"That's better," she said but didn't let go. "You guys packing in there?"

"A little," he lied. *Do the katanas count?*

"How many of you?"

"Counting me? Three." He wished there was some way he could warn Tiffany to get out. Graff could handle himself, but neither one of them had ever wanted their younger sister to get involved in all this. Unfortunately, Tiffany made her own rules—she always had. If Tiffany had a bad first day of high school, she went ahead and tested out of the whole thing. If Tiffany wanted access to her trust fund a few years before she turned twenty-four, she starved herself until a cashier's check was placed in her hand. And if Tiffany wanted to hack into computer databases to help them plan the perfect crimes, there was nothing he and Graff could do to stop her.

They'd tried. And she'd somehow gotten the power company to shut down all their electricity until they caved.

"Okay, then." Natalie pulled closer, her breasts firm against his back as she whirled them both to face the door. He'd become little more than a human shield—and found it strangely erotic. Physical force and boobs had that kind of effect on him. "Let's go say hello to your friends."

"By the way," he couldn't help adding, "I like your hair better this way. It suits you."

She paused but didn't speak.

"And I would have eventually known you were the woman from the other night. You smelled like strawberries then too."

"How cute. Is this where you tell me you love strawberries?"

"No," he said truthfully. "I'm deathly allergic."

Her body shook with laughter. "Thanks for the tip. But I'm not kidding—I will snap your arm if you try anything funny."

"I'll try not to." He groaned as she reached around to pull open the door. "But I feel I should warn you, I'm naturally hilarious."

"I can tell," she murmured, her lips against his ear. He suppressed a shiver—of fear or excitement, he couldn't quite say. With this woman, he suspected the two emotions were inexorably combined.

They moved through the door as carefully as individuals in a hostage-like situation could, with plenty of noise and Asprey swearing twice. The first time was because he caught his foot on the doorframe, sending a jolt of pain down his arm. The second was because Natalie noticed the shotguns by the door and picked one up.

Since Graff had turned his chair the other way and Tiffany was plugged into a pair of giant padded headphones, their entry went unnoticed. It didn't help that Graff assumed everything Asprey did was a failure of epic proportions, so not even the sound of the admittedly girly squeal he let out when Natalie yanked on his arm was sufficient to pull Graff out of his belligerent funk.

"Uh, guys?" he called when it became clear Natalie was waiting for him to say something. "Hello? We have a situation."

"Did you get rid of the Girl Scout?" Tiffany asked. She swiveled in her chair, her arms shooting up the moment she saw the woman with the gun.

"Not exactly," Asprey said.

"What do you mean, not exactly?" His brother took his sweet-ass time getting out of the chair and turning to face them, but Asprey at least had the satisfaction of noting the exact moment when the details became clear. Graff's face turned red, then purple, and then he moved in front of Louis, as if to shield the chair from any of the crossfire.

"What the fuck is wrong with you?" Graff wasn't talking to Natalie. "You've got to be kidding me right now."

"He's not kidding, and neither am I," Natalie said coolly. She released her grip, tossing Asprey a few feet into the room. He sank gratefully to his knees, using his good hand to gently realign his arm in front of him. Stupid arm. Stupid Graff for dislocating it in the first place. Sure, they'd been seven and twelve at the time, and the rope swing they'd built over the bay had been a feat of epic proportions that made them famous among their peers even to this day. But *still*.

Poppy cocked the shotgun and pointed it at Asprey, ushering him back toward Tiffany and Graff.

"I'm going, I'm going," he muttered. "But that shotgun isn't loaded, so you're wasting your time."

"Goddammit!" Graff yelled. "Why would you say that? You just gave away the one advantage we had here."

"How is this my fault?" Asprey yelled back. "I told you there was a breach in the perimeter, and all you did was sit there, making sweet love to Louis and forcing me to do all the work. As usual."

Tiffany let out a giggle. "You are kind of obsessed with that chair."

"What happened to the Texas Ranger?" Graff spat back, ignoring their sister. "I thought you had a plan."

"I *did* have a plan. But plans sometimes go wrong—no one knows that better than you."

"Oh, sure," Graff muttered. "Bring that up again. Like I'm the one who—"

"Uh, guys?" They both turned to find Natalie watching them, her arms crossed over her chest. She'd given up the shotgun, but that didn't make Asprey feel any better. If anything, it made him more nervous. She probably had machine guns for nipples or something freaky like that. "Are you two almost done?"

"You want the necklace, don't you?" Asprey asked. "She's the woman from the Kennick job, Graff. She changed her hair."

Graff balled his hands into fists. "I cannot believe you just used my name. You are officially the worst criminal on the face of the planet."

"Actually, I might agree there." Natalie reached into her jean shorts. Asprey had just enough time to maneuver himself in front of Tiffany before her hand re-emerged...holding a brown leather wallet. A very nice brown leather wallet, worn to the kind of supple softness it took years to perfect. His good hand immediately went to his back pocket.

It was empty.

"Is this the residence of Asprey Manchester Charles, six feet tall, one hundred and eighty pounds?" she asked. "Isn't that cute...you're wearing the same too-tight vest in your picture. Do you always dress like you've just been kicked out of a wedding?"

Well, shit. "How did you get that?"

She smirked, her lips pulling at one side and looking far too appealing than seemed fair. "I picked your pocket the other night—right before you hit the ground. You really should check the organ donor box on your ID, you know." She shook her head and tossed the wallet on the ground before kicking it toward him. "It can be really hard for a family to make that kind of decision on their own."

"I'm going to fucking kill you, Asprey," Graff growled. "You listed our secret hideaway as the place of residence on your driver's license?"

"It's outside city limits," Asprey explained. "The licensing process for the bike is easier out here."

Natalie laughed. It was strange—when she made a sound like that, all throaty and warm, it was hard to imagine her taking a blade to their throats or stealing all their worldly possessions.

But he didn't put it past her.

"So what do you want?" Graff asked, his hands still up. "The necklace? Money?"

"Both of those sound great," she said. "But first, I think we should all sit down and have a little chat."

"I wouldn't tell you anything even if you ripped off both of my brother's—" Graff began.

"Done," Asprey intervened. He turned to Graff. "What? It's easy for you to play fast and loose with my body parts. You're not the one in desperate need of painkillers right now."

Natalie looked back and forth between the two of them, a bemused expression on her face. "You guys are for real. This isn't some crazy joke. You're this bad at it."

"You have no idea," Tiffany muttered. She pulled the headphones up over her ears and turned to the computer. In any other hostage-like situation, this would have been a perfect opportunity to alert the authorities via email or send out a plea for help in Morse code or something. Not Tiffany. She was probably uploading viruses into the FBI website or, as she called it, a regular Tuesday afternoon.

"Did you still want that tea?" Asprey asked, standing and brushing dust from his clothes. Like it or not, they were in this now.

And he liked it. God help him, he liked *her*. He couldn't remember the last time he'd had this much fun.

"You don't have anything stronger?"

Asprey laughed. They could probably all use a drink right about now. "How do you feel about scotch?" He motioned at one of their tables of loot. "I've got a sixty-four-year-old Maccallan over there that recently sold at auction for about thirty grand."

Natalie's jaw fell open. "That you stole?"

Graff's voice rumbled, but Asprey ignored him, striding over to the table of goods and grabbing the bottle with a flourish. "It's single barrel."

"I was wrong," she said, her face breaking out in a grin. There she was again, unassuming and almost benign. She grabbed the bottle and inspected it, taking off the top and giving it a tentative sniff. "I guess maybe you guys aren't as bad at this as I thought."

Chapter Three

"This tastes like regular scotch." Poppy frowned into her glass, swirling the amber liquid. "It should be illegal—the way those high-end companies try to pass this stuff off as something it's not."

Asprey coughed heavily, not stopping until the youngish-looking woman, Tiffany, poured him some more of the alcohol. They'd pulled a few folding chairs and one hugely ornate yellow throne into a circle in the middle of the airport hangar, making it feel cavernous and informal at the same time. It was like an Alcoholics Anonymous meeting, except instead of drinking coffee and divulging life stories, they were swilling scotch that cost more than a kidney and sharing a mutual distrust that had her adrenaline pump set on high.

It felt *good*. There were guns and stolen goods and one palpably angry man, and all Poppy could think was how happy she felt to be a part of it all.

"Look—I'd love to sit here and chitchat all day," the brother, Graff, drawled, looking full of neither love nor chitchat. "But can we get on with this?"

It was clear they were all siblings, now that she could see them in the full light of day and no one hid behind a face mask. Graff was obviously the oldest and meanest of the bunch, but both men had the same dark hair, defined facial features and signature dimple right in the middle of their chins—those dimples that always looked incredible on a man and made women look like John Travolta in drag. Tiffany had been spared the chin, but her long hair was a similar dark hue and she had the same bright, intelligent blue eyes that never seemed to stop dancing.

Graff's hair was shorn and brusque, his movements much the same way. Asprey, on the other hand, with his long, lean torso and well-tailored clothes, could only be described as languid—of movement, of meaning, of purpose. Except when he smiled, which he did often, revealing deep laugh lines.

She straightened. Smiles were not her objective here.

This was about the job—not the strange way Asprey made it seem as though life were one big joke and she was seconds away from hearing the punch line. Good-looking men who laughed in the face of pain weren't a good sign.

Her ability to inflict pain was one of the only advantages she had in this world. She wasn't about to give it up that easily.

"I want you to tell me about Todd," she said, directing her attention to Asprey. Based on her reception so far, he seemed the most likely to tell her what she wanted to know. "More specifically, why were you after the necklace?"

The brothers shared a glance that spoke volumes and in a language she understood well. *Don't tell the common folk any more than you have to.* It was something she'd heard far too often in her twenty-five years of existence.

"I'm not stupid," she pointed out, frowning at her glass, now half empty. She should probably lay off the liquor if she intended to get out of this with the information she needed. Setting the glass on the concrete floor, she added, "That job was planned down to the last detail. You knew we were headed out to Le Petit Âne for dinner and that I'd be wearing the necklace. You had our arrival timed to the minute and knew how many of us would be in the car. You also planned to hold us up miles from help, which gave you plenty of time to get away."

"Well, we *are* thieves," Asprey said. "I've heard that getting caught tends to result in unpleasant consequences."

You have no idea. With his fancy shoes and polished speech, Asprey was the last man on earth who knew what it was like to live in the same room as your toilet. She ignored him and went for the one thing that bothered her more than anything else. "More importantly, even though you took the necklace, you didn't even glance at Todd's diamond tie pin."

33

"Fake," Asprey said confidently. Graff growled low in his throat. "What? The tie pin was a fake, Graff. I could tell from where my face was planted in the ground."

"Sorry about that," Poppy said, not meaning a word.

Asprey obviously knew it. He inclined his head a little and grinned, giving her a glimpse of the raw scrapes just underneath his stubble. It was sexy stubble, all dark and masculine and the right texture that would graze against her skin but not scratch it.

She forced herself to focus about a foot above his head. She did *not* get involved in the middle of a con—no matter how cute the other players were. That was the first rule.

She leaned back in her chair and crossed her legs, happy to note that Asprey's eyes followed. He obviously didn't play by the same rules, and that was fine. The control in this situation was all hers. "So you're not just crappy thieves. You're crappy thieves with a clear target and the ability to appraise jewelry. What gives?"

"We're not telling you anything," Graff bit off. The man had a serious chip on his shoulder. "You're lucky we don't load that shotgun and blow your pretty little head off."

"And you're lucky I haven't turned you over to the police," she returned. "This isn't my first time invading enemy territory. I left this address and a written statement about the theft with my friend. She won't hesitate to turn them over if I miss our pedicure this afternoon."

It wasn't true, of course. Bea would be devastated if she had any idea what kind of situation Poppy was placing herself in right now.

"Oh, I like this woman," Tiffany murmured.

"This can't be happening," Graff grumbled. A look of defeat crossed his brow. It was irritated and ominous and filled Poppy with a sense of pure elation.

"What exactly is your problem?" she persisted. "If you ask me, I've been nothing but nice to you. I gave you the necklace when it was clear I could have walked away with both it and your brother's head under my arm."

"Hey now!" Asprey called, though it was said with a good-natured undertone. Was the man never ruffled? "I was being a gentleman. I *let* you win."

Poppy ignored him and held up her fingers, ticking off the rest. "I told the police some stupid story about being scared and not remembering anything about the robbery when I could have just as easily turned you over. I came all this way—on foot—to return the wallet. And instead of blasting this place open and stealing everything you have on clear display, which, by the way, is a really stupid place to keep it, I'm sitting here, willing to negotiate. This old chair is really uncomfortable. Did you steal it too?"

Graff's eyes brightened dangerously, and he pressed his hands on either leg as though preventing himself from strangling her right then and there. Poppy made note and moved closer to the edge of the chair. She might have the situation well in hand right now, but there was no telling how quickly things could change.

Never let your guard down. That was rule number two.

"Don't mind Graff," Asprey said, laughing. "He hates everyone. Especially women who are smarter and stronger than he is."

Poppy arched a brow. "Flattery?"

"Truth," he said firmly. "Now. Since you, as you so delicately put it, have been the soul of conciliation, what can we do for you?"

"Why Todd?"

Asprey opened his mouth, but Graff interrupted. "He's rich."

"So?" Poppy shifted so she faced the other brother. Now that Asprey had pointed out his brother's hatred of women, she could see it. It was in the predatory way he moved, the way his smile twisted off at one end as if it were almost painful. A man with that kind of look was dangerous.

It wasn't very feminist of her, but Poppy would be the first to admit that a large portion of her success in any con situation was thanks to the innate reserve most men carried against harming a woman. It was a reserve composed of equal parts deference and disbelief. Deference to her vagina; disbelief that said vagina was anything but a handicap in life.

If Graff saw her as a real threat, that definitely changed the balance of things.

Poppy sat up a little straighter. "There are lots of rich men in Seattle. Many of them richer than him. Why Todd?"

"He's rich *and* he wastes his money on low-class pieces of ass like you. That good enough?"

"Graff," Asprey warned.

"Oh, he can be a dick all he wants," Poppy offered. She stared at Graff, her whole body tense. "As long as he gives me back that necklace. It was a gift, and I'm feeling very sentimental about it. You know how women can get over gifts, all emotional and unstable."

"I won't do it."

She rose to her feet, careful to make slow movements across the cracked cement floor, both threatening and nonthreatening as the heels of her favorite boots made echoing clicks. "Oh, I think you will. Look—I respect the gig you've got going here. You obviously put a lot of time into your fledgling criminal career, and I'm all for reaping the rewards of the work you do. I'm no narc, and I promise not to ask any questions about this giant pile of stolen goods—provided you comply. I've put more legwork into Todd Kennick than you have, and I want that necklace back."

Graff snorted. "Legwork? Is that what you call it?"

"Jesus, Graff." Tiffany shook her head, an apology in each movement. "At least she's being polite about it."

"Thank you," Poppy said, though his words didn't rattle her. Poppy had long subscribed to the sticks-and-stones motto. Words couldn't hurt her...but Todd *had.* "I need that necklace.

All I want is a single string of pearls, and I'm out of your life forever. It's that simple."

The three siblings shared a look then, and it was the first time Poppy felt that maybe she was out of her element coming here like this. There was no malice in their look—no antagonism or furtive moves toward the artillery near the door. It was almost regret, like the situation was out of their hands and luck was out of hers.

"What?" She looked back and forth between them. "What are you not telling me?"

Asprey winced. "The thing is..."

Even Graff softened a little, if that term could be applied to a creature made of stone. "We *could* give it to you, but it's not going to do you any good."

"What do you mean?" Even though she couldn't fence it for full value, her ex could get her at least ten thousand. She'd probably even be able to sell the diamonds and pearls piece by piece, if it came to that. "I'm discreet. I have contacts. It's not like I'm going to saunter into the nearest pawn shop and see what I can get for it."

Asprey stood and moved to the nearest table, plucking the necklace from an ivory jewelry box that looked worth a fortune by itself. "I wasn't lying when I said I can appraise jewelry. This necklace? It's a fake. Unless the grand plan is to wear it to a costume party, you're headed for disappointment."

She took the proffered item, her fingertips just grazing Asprey's. The contact made him flinch—and it made her shiver.

Stop it. This was neither the time nor the place to start losing her head.

"How do I know you're not lying?" she asked, looking closely at the pearls. "You could be trying to trick me."

And they'd have good success—she had no idea what to look for. She could pass most forgeries off in a con, pull in a few thousand dollars and leave her mark with a bad case of buyer beware, but appraisals and evaluations had never been her area of expertise.

"It's not a trick," Asprey said. He handed her an eyepiece, one of those owlish-looking things jewelers always stuck in their eyes.

She hesitated before taking it. If she directed her attention to the necklace, she'd be letting her guard down in a clear violation of rule number two, something she never did unless absolutely necessary. "Stand on the other side of the table first," she commanded, angling herself behind it.

Asprey placed his hand over his heart. "You wound me. I thought we were becoming friends."

"I'll tell you what. We can be friends when I'm safe at home with twenty thousand dollars in my purse. I'll even make you cookies. How's that sound?"

He winked. "Consider it a date."

Winking? Honest-to-goodness winking? Not even Todd tried something as hokey as that...and yet...Asprey actually looked charming while he did it.

That had to be another trick, part of the whole tight-pants-tighter-vest-rolled-up-shirtsleeves-hipster-hottie thing he had going on. Men weren't normally that good-looking and perfectly put together as they lounged about empty airport hangars. It was unnerving.

She stared him down until he moved to the other side of the loot table. Graff arrayed himself by his brother's side, arms crossed in full-on militant mode.

"If it helps, I can vouch for him," Tiffany called. She hadn't gotten up from her chair, opting instead to pull out some handheld device and scroll through the screen. She peeked up through the hair that had fallen in her face. "I'm really sorry if we took a necklace that was supposed to be yours. But if my brother says a piece of jewelry is a fake, it's a fake."

It was oddly sincere.

Asprey grinned sheepishly. "It's kind of our thing, if you can't tell from the names. You could say we were born to it."

"The names?"

Tiffany laughed. "Maybe you can help us settle a bet. Asprey thinks he got the worst of the lot. I say no one should have to be saddled with a name like Tiffany."

Poppy's confusion must have shown on her face, because Asprey's dancing eyes met hers. "Graff Diamonds. Asprey of London. Tiffany & Co." He offered her a one-shouldered shrug. "We're a Cartier short of pure, unadulterated pretention."

"Those are your real names?" And she'd always thought being named after an opiate was bad.

Graff gave a slight bow. "Unless you need us to jot down our social security numbers next, can we please move on?"

It was enough for her. Poppy put the eyepiece to her eye and looked at the necklace. "Okay. What am I looking for?"

"The texture of the pearl—what do you see?"

She glanced up. Asprey had adopted a professorial tone, but instead of making him look more arrogant, as she'd expected, the aura of command suited him, made him more natural.

She focused on the necklace in her hands, unsure what she was supposed to say. "It's white and swirly. Exactly like a pearl."

"Look closer. What does the surface look like?"

She compressed her lips and tried again. "I don't know—it almost looks grainy, maybe like a newspaper picture?"

"Exactly!" Asprey cried, obviously pleased. "What else? Do you see any imperfections?"

She looked closer. Honestly, she wasn't qualified for this—and if his goal was to make her feel stupid, it was working. "Not really. It looks perfectly round."

"That's another big clue. Real pearls tend to have one or two flaws when under that kind of magnification. Even at that level of quality. Go ahead—run it over your teeth to feel how smooth it is. That one is clearly a fake."

"Really? It's that easy?"

Graff rolled his eyes. "Any more secrets you want to give away, Asprey? How about the combination to our safe?"

"You guys have a safe?" Poppy asked.

"It's in the back—strictly for practice." Asprey laughed. "So there you have it. Fake necklace. You still want it?"

Not really. Something about the way they looked so apologetic made her believe them. She'd known enough criminals in her lifetime to recognize real sincerity when she saw it—it came with pity that softened the hardest edges. It showcased regret and inefficacy wrapped up in one sad smile.

Funny that those were attributes she'd come to value in a person.

Poppy dropped the necklace to the table, taking in the rest of the contents with renewed interest. If the necklace Todd gave her was a fake, she'd need an alternate stream of income. There were some pretty impressive pieces over there.

She was about to pick up a silver cigarette case engraved all over with tiny horses when realization came at her from the side. "Wait just a fucking minute!"

Asprey dropped into a crouch. "What?"

Graff burst out laughing. "Always such courage, little brother. Way to impress the lady."

She ignored them, her mind whirling around the one person for whom pity and regret were dirty words. "You know what this means, don't you? Todd gave me a fake necklace as a gift."

No freaking way. That man had enough money to buy his own island in the United Arab Emirates—threw hundred dollar bills around like they were crumpled receipts. For weeks now she'd been giving him the runaround, playing hot and cold, bold and shy. Her pinky finger practically sagged under the weight of him wrapped so firmly around it.

"I can't believe he wouldn't sacrifice a few thousand dollars to give me a real necklace."

"Well, technically..." Asprey began, but Graff reached out and smacked him on the back of the head before he got very far.

She let them fight, though it was more of a brotherly tussle than anything else, Graff being extra careful not to jar Asprey's shoulder as they circled and danced. Let them kill each other, for all she cared. She had problems of her own. Big ones. That necklace was her ticket, the down payment on the long con she'd been planning for months.

If she'd wanted to scam Todd before—*and she had*—the urge now magnified about a hundred times. Except she had to find the money somewhere else. She could try the angling-for-jewelry gambit again, but the asshole would probably just pull the same stunt with another fake.

What she needed was a guarantee.

She narrowed her eyes. What she needed was a partner. *Or three.*

"Are you guys almost done?" she asked, inserting a false note of irritation into her voice. "I'd love to sit here and watch you demolish one another, but since that worthless piece of crap necklace isn't going to fill my empty wallet, I need to make alternate arrangements."

"You never did tell us what you need the necklace for," Asprey said, stopping the fight as suddenly as Graff had started it.

"What can I say?" she asked, showing her hands like an old-time shell man. "I'm a grubby gold digger."

Asprey's gaze flicked over her, and he shook his head. "Nope. I'm not buying it. I know lots of grubby gold diggers— and they don't moonlight as killers for hire. The worst of their sins is lying about their age."

She quirked a brow. "Exactly how many gold diggers do you know?"

Asprey rolled his eyes toward his brother. "I'm not sure. Graff—what would you say? Do you think the Nesbitt twins count?"

Poppy smothered a laugh as Graff let out another low growl of irritation. He obviously didn't know when his brother was baiting him.

"Fine," she said, capitulating. If she wanted their help, there would have to be at least a little transparency. "You caught me. I'm not a gold digger, and I'm not the least bit interested in the Nesbitt twins. But I *am* after Todd's money."

"Then I'm truly sorry we couldn't be more help," Asprey offered.

"Oh, but you can be," she replied, squaring to face him. Pulling in partners she barely knew wasn't the best idea of her life, but it wasn't the worst either. *Definitely not that.* These guys had resources and no qualms about traversing the wrong side of the law. That was quite a few points in their favor right there. "I'd like to make a proposition."

"Now you've skipped gold digger and gone straight for call girl."

She laughed. "That's not exactly what I had in mind. But you're obviously criminals of a sort, and ones who could use a little help. No offense."

"None taken."

Graff frowned. "Speak for yourself."

"It just so happens that Todd has a slight gambling addiction that makes him ideally suited for my line of work," she ventured. Might as well get it out there. "In exchange for your services setting up a slightly rigged poker game, I'd be happy to...whatever. Fight, lie, cheat, steal. I'm flexible."

"No," Graff said, at the same time Asprey licked his lips and offered, "We're in."

Tiffany looked up from her handheld device. "I guess that makes me the tiebreaker."

Poppy had met a lot of strange criminals in her line of work, but this family had to be the oddest. It almost felt like she'd wandered onto the set of a movie, and they were all here to play a part before going home to normal, crime-free lives.

Except for, you know, the table of ill-begotten goods.

"I'll tell you what," she offered, playing her hand conservatively. "You take some time to think about it, discuss the idea amongst yourselves. I can give you a few days, but I need an answer soon."

"And how will we find you?" Asprey asked. "Do you answer to a bat signal?"

She laughed. This guy was cute. "I'll be in touch."

With that, she turned on her heel, exposing her back to them as she raised a hand in farewell. It was a gesture of goodwill, letting them watch her go. Not many people got that privilege.

And she was so pleased when they didn't try to stop her that it wasn't until she'd hiked the two miles back to her car that she realized she never asked why, if Todd's necklace was so clearly a fake, they'd bothered stealing it at all.

Chapter Four

"Great class," Poppy said warmly as she handed out towels and bottles of water to her students. They looked like they needed it. Most of the first-timers in her self-defense aerobics class had taken her before for yoga, and they expected the same kind of experience—languid stretches, abdominal tightening holds, the typical om-nom-namaste stuff that bespoke green tea and holistic dentistry.

What they got today was something a little bit closer to Poppy's preferred type of activity. Hand-to-hand combat. Elbow torques and roundhouses and scissor kicks. *Real exercise.*

"I'm not going to be able to walk for a week," one woman complained, though she had a sweaty, post-workout sense of satisfaction going on. She took one of the waters gratefully. "That was really intense."

"It's a nice way to work out your aggression," Poppy agreed.

Unfortunately for Poppy, a similar sweaty, post-workout sense of satisfaction wasn't hers to enjoy. Her employment at In the Buff, a twenty-four-hour gym that catered to a suburban crowd, was grueling at best. She still had to make overpriced protein smoothies at the juice bar, looking perky and rested in a pink sports bra and her blonde wig, for another six-hour shift.

Poppy Donovan was an ex-con legally required to disclose her criminal record and file her place of employment with her parole officer...which was why In the Buff had hired Natalie Hall, whose falsified paperwork made her hesitant to demand better hours. As long as they didn't ask any questions, neither would she.

"Aren't you looking gorgeous today?" a smooth male voice called, pulling Poppy's attention toward the front desk. She forced herself to smile as she bounced over to greet Todd, clad in gym pants and a tank top as he prepared to sweat buckets on one of the treadmills.

"Hey, doll," she cooed, leaning in for a quick peck. "Make sure you stop by after your workout for a shot of wheatgrass, 'kay?" She liked to make him a special cocktail laced with chasteberry. The herbal supplement had been used to subdue the sex drives of monks for centuries—which made it ideally suited for her purposes. She liked keeping Todd interested, but not *too* interested. The last thing she needed was to drop-kick her cover because he couldn't keep it in his pants.

He nodded and puffed up, clearly loving the attention, as she knew he would. She'd gotten the job here solely as a means of tracking him. It didn't take any master training in Confidence Tricks 101 to know that the best way to gain a man's interest was to be a yoga instructor at the gym where he exercised. It had taken all of two hours to get him to ask her out on a date.

Because Todd worked out, his body was fairly trim, if built a little like a pit bull, and there was a firmness to his jaw that denoted power. Other than a slightly bulbous nose signifying his excesses, he wasn't half bad.

In another lifetime, she might have called him handsome.

In another lifetime, however, she would have kept him far away from her grandmother and none of this would be necessary. No lying to Bea. No master criminal plans. Just her and a respectable life, all laid out like a flat plain, each step plotted and planned and perfectly safe.

She fought a shudder—not because Todd leaned in for another kiss, but because the only thing that scared her more than facing another two years in jail was a lifetime of respectability. It might be a different type of imprisonment, but the bars were there all the same.

"I've been missing you something fierce since that awful robbery the other night, you know. I was beginning to feel afraid you didn't want me anymore." She stuck her lip out in a pout and ran a finger along the side of his face, grazing her fake nail—a Natalie staple—against his jaw. "You aren't going to cancel our date for next week, are you? We're still on for lunch?"

His eyelids slipped down, supposedly sultry, mostly so he could concentrate on her cleavage. "Of course we are. Unless you want to come over tonight, that is. There's a fight on cable—I've got quite a bit riding on Cracker Black Jack, and didn't you say you put a little down on the match? We could watch it together, order in, maybe fool around a little..."

Her fake smile widened until it felt like her exterior was going to splinter. An evening eating greasy Chinese and betting on a pair of middleweights as they bashed each other's faces in was something she would normally love.

As long as it was with any other man on the planet.

"That sounds wonderful, but I have this thing at my parents' house," she said. "I know I've mentioned them before. Maybe you could come and meet my family?"

Todd mumbled something about giving her a call the next day and practically ran in the direction of the elliptical machines. She watched him go, laughing at how easily he was manipulated. *Men.* Criminals or scam artists or respectable doctors—they all fled at the mention of home.

By chance, she glanced over a few minutes later, catching a glimpse of Todd as he stood outside the pool area, chatting up an elderly woman who came into water aerobics three times a week by order of her physical therapist to recuperate from the second of two grueling hip replacements.

It took all Poppy had not to vault over the desk and deliver a roundhouse kick to Todd's face as he slipped the woman a business card, full of smiles and lies. She could practically hear him giving the pitch, promises of investments and payouts and retirement funds that couldn't go wrong. The kind of promises a woman in her condition needed to hear.

Another day, another victim.

Too bad Poppy refused to acknowledge that word. If there was one thing this life had taught her, it was that avoiding victimhood had nothing to do with steering clear of risks or ceasing to live. In fact, it had a lot to do with the opposite.

So this was her, taking risks. This was her, living.

This was her, getting back the eighty thousand dollars Todd Kennick stole from Grandma Jean just months before she died.

Asprey toyed with the stem of his glass, enjoying the play of light in his '84 Chateauneuf du Pape. It wasn't exactly the vintage he'd have chosen to set off the notes of a take-out hamburger and fries, but they *were* on a budget.

"What the hell is wrong with you?" Graff fell into the chair across from him and grabbed the bottle. He took one look at the label and smacked it back on the table. "Please tell me this is one of your empties filled with grape juice."

Asprey purposefully held the glass to his nose, inhaling deeply and swirling the rich red liquid. "The rustic chestnut notes really bounce off the playful cherry in this, don't you think?"

"We're supposed to be cutting back, Asprey. We sat down with Tiffany and agreed—no expenses unless they're necessary for the job. It's not right to rely on family money now that we know where it's coming from."

Asprey took a deep drink before giving up. Three sommelier classes and it still all tasted the same to him. "Relax. I swiped it from the cellar at Winston's house. Took a whole case, actually. He loves this stuff."

"Oh." Graff sat up a little straighter. "In that case, pass the bottle, will you?"

Asprey grinned. He could probably pass off a theft of the Mona Lisa as long as he said he took it from their older brother, Winston. So far, they'd furnished almost their entire living space above the hangar with odds and ends they'd taken from him. Said furnishings didn't amount to much, but since they'd all felt it was better for Tiffany to stay at her apartment to keep up a cheerful front and to stay safe, he and Graff could pretend it was a debauched bachelor pad, minus any of the good types of debauchery.

They currently sat around the massage table from Winston's office, which functioned quite nicely as their dining room table. Other effects included a polar bearskin rug and five versions of the exact same espresso machine, which, no matter how many times Asprey stole it, Winston replaced. His favorite, though, was the bright Kandinsky painting they used to cover up the moldy patch in the wall—he'd had his eye on it for years, and the bright blocks of red and blue could always be counted on to lift his mood.

Asprey liked to think their home was a work in progress. Graff liked to think it was one step closer to vindication.

In a way, they were both right.

If Graff were any other human being, the food and wine would have mellowed him out a little, made him less likely to throw one of the espresso machines into the wall. But Graff was far from ordinary, and feeding him was like giving fuel to a chainsaw-massacre enthusiast. He grumbled the entire meal, his topics ranging from Natalie the Pickpocket to the teenage punk who'd flipped him off on the road that afternoon.

"By the way," he growled. "I've got a few new locations we can look at tomorrow."

"New locations for what?"

"Don't play dumb with me. That charming-idiot routine might work on everyone else, but you and I both know it's an act. We can't stay here in the hangar anymore. Not after you fucked it all up—"

Asprey listened to the rest of Graff's monologue with a negligent ear. Once upon a time, Graff had been a lawyer—one of those overblown ones who was almost all for show. His brother could talk for hours, driven only by the sound of his own voice and the accumulation of spittle at the corners of his mouth.

Graff had always been the uptight one, the one most likely to erupt in anger over an overlooked detail or tiny hitch in their plans—and he had the blood pressure medication to prove it.

Even as kids, his tendency toward irate anal-retentiveness had been evident. You didn't touch his collection of Transformers, lined up in a perfect row on his desk. Asprey had done it once, and he still had the capped tooth to show for it.

"Stop worrying so much," he said when Graff was done. "Natalie's not going to turn us in."

"I don't want to take any chances," Graff said tightly. "For all we know, she's a federal agent."

"She's not."

Graff gulped back the coffee and crushed the cup in one fist. "Would you stop being flippant for five seconds? There's a good chance you blew the entire operation. I know this is all one big joke to you, but we've worked too hard and too long to throw it away on a pretty face."

Not just pretty.

Asprey knew pretty. He saw it all the time, grew up with it, played with it, definitely enjoyed it. What that woman had was something much more intriguing than beauty, something that made him sit up and pay attention with the kind of urgency that had eluded him for years.

Mystery. An enigmatic magnetism. The kind of complexity that accompanied a painting by a master, where a lifetime of close examination could never yield all the clues.

Of course, Graff saw none of that. If he made a decision not to acknowledge something—be it a universal truth about the world or the value of a fellow human being—it might as well have been crafted of invisible ink. "We're getting closer, Asprey. We've got one job left and we're done. Then we can go home again."

You can never go home again, Asprey wanted to quip, but the words rang uncomfortably true.

He sat back and propped his feet on the table, careful to keep any of his thoughts or regrets from showing. "Nah. She'll be back."

"That's what I'm afraid of."

"We knew going into this that it wouldn't be easy. It's *crime*, Graff. If you didn't want to get your hands dirty, you shouldn't have played." Poor, straitlaced Graff. Even though the robberies had been his idea, every day was a struggle with his conscience.

"Our hands were already dirty, Asprey," Graff said quietly. "That's why we're playing at all."

Asprey didn't reply. Nothing he could say would help. He'd tried—a thousand times, he'd tried, but any attempt at justifying their past only made things worse. Guilt and Graff shared a symbiotic relationship. It was just the way of it.

So Asprey focused on shuffling through the files in his lap, scouring the hacked emails Tiffany had accessed for their next and final target, a wealthy real-estate developer's daughter who lived in downtown Bellevue. The woman, Cindy VanHuett, didn't divulge much in her written correspondence beyond an impeccable attention to grammar and punctuation. Which meant, of course, that Asprey would have to spend the next week or so doing reconnaissance.

The thought didn't exactly fill him with joy. Recon was not what the movies had led him to believe. There were no high-speed chases or gangsta rap soundtracks playing in the background. Most days, it involved sitting on a dirty park bench pretending to drink the same cup of coffee for twelve hours straight.

It would be a hell of a lot more entertaining with someone like Natalie helping him out. Maybe they could sync their watches, designate a convoy, stake out overnight. *The fun stuff.* Graff never let him have any fun.

"What are you doing later?" Graff asked suddenly, tearing Asprey from a particularly entertaining thought about how two attractive people might keep one another company on a long, cold night spent watching for suspicious activity.

"I was thinking about slipping into a hospital and stealing some medical supplies," Asprey answered easily. "If we're going to be working with Natalie, I figure we can use them. Any requests? Maybe some compression hose? You're always saying your feet get cold."

Predictably, Graff ignored him. "I need you and Tiffany to do a quick errand."

That was interesting. If Asprey never got to have any fun, Tiffany was practically a prisoner to tedious, behind-the-scenes work. "Oh, yeah? What do you have for us? Gun running?"

"Don't be stupid," Graff muttered. He tossed his car keys on Asprey's lap, sending the rest of the paperwork flying. "I was afraid you were going to insist on seeing this Natalie Hall thing through. That's why you're going to find out everything you can about her."

"Oh yeah? Shall I consult my crystal ball?"

"No. You should consult Tiffany's. She planted a GPS tracker on the bottom of Natalie's boot."

Asprey dropped his feet and stared at his brother—at the face so like his own but with a kind of deep-seated edge that came from decades of self-loathing. "I didn't say you could do that."

"And I didn't know I needed your permission. I don't trust her, Asprey, and that's just the beginning of our problems if that woman intends to poke her nose around. Find out what you can—and then we'll talk."

Chapter Five

"You know, you can't go around bugging people even if Graff says it's okay." Asprey pointed at the GPS tracker in Tiffany's hands. She watched the movements on the screen with a kind of cool detachment as she sat cross-legged on the floor of the hangar, her back against the wall. "I don't know if you've noticed, but he's kind of like a scary dictator the entire world wants to oust."

Tiffany got to her feet and moved the small black device out of his reach. "If that's the case, then what does that make us?"

Asprey chose not to answer that question. Self-reflection always had a way of conjuring up a prickly sense of unease, which was why he avoided it whenever possible.

"Besides—we bug people all the time," Tiffany added. "You even peek through their windows at night, which, if you ask me, is ten-thousand times creepier. Why is it you're just now developing a conscience?"

"Because Natalie isn't one of our targets." And because slipping a GPS tracker on the bottom of her boot when she wasn't paying attention seemed like the fastest way to be on the receiving end of another ninja takedown.

"Does that mean you don't want to come with me to check out where she lives?" Tiffany asked. "We have a location."

Asprey didn't even blink. "I'll get my things."

The drive took longer than he expected, taking them through the city center to South Seattle, where the buildings got closer together and increasingly touched by disrepair with each block. Their black Lexus—obviously Graff's, since it oozed lawyerly respectability—grew more conspicuous with each block too.

"Are you sure this is the place?" he asked as he parked the car in front of an abandoned apartment building that had enough particleboard nailed up in place of windows it probably should have come with a hazmat warning.

"Not that one." Tiffany pointed across the street. "The one with the big gray mailbox out front."

The second building made him feel only slightly better. It looked as though it had once shared a contractor with the lawsuit-waiting-to-happen they'd parked in front of, but at least all the walls looked solid and the graffiti was spelled correctly. A few plants and open windows indicated life went on inside, though Asprey wasn't willing to take any bets on the quality thereof.

"You think this is where she lives?"

Tiffany undid her seat belt. "I assume so. It's where she's been parked for the past few hours."

"Wait—you're going in?" Asprey checked her with his hand. "What if she sees you?"

"Relax, Asp. I'm only going to run up and check the mailboxes. Hopefully, we can find a piece of mail that tells us which apartment is hers, maybe even a birthdate or place of employment. You know how this works."

It was logical and easy, and Asprey hated how much sense it made. This was how it started—the reconnaissance. They usually had the full name and basic contact information for their targets, but the foundation was always the same. Build a dossier, fact by fact. Run the complete background check. Invade people's bank accounts and closets full of skeletons without them ever knowing.

It hadn't really bothered him when it was strangers they were dealing with, especially since their mission had always been one of, if not good, at least a Hippocratic tendency toward doing no harm. But Natalie...

"I don't know about this."

"You don't have to. You are neither the heart nor the brains of our operation, brother dear." Tiffany checked for bystanders and, seeing none, pulled open the car door. Before she dashed across the street, she poked her head back in and added, "I've always wanted to say that."

Asprey watched as she scanned quickly over the mailbox. Using some kind of magnetic gadget that was able to turn cheap locks from the outside, she began at the top row and systematically opened each one, giving the contents a quick scan before moving on.

It was taking too long, and Asprey didn't like sitting uselessly by while his younger sister took her sweet time examining each envelope. It was stupid of them to come here. It was stupid of him to let Tiffany put herself in harm's way. When she paused and double checked the contents of one of the lower boxes, stealing a startled look at Asprey as she did, he pushed open the car door, ready to come to her aid.

Before he could plant his feet on the ground, the apartment's front door swung open and a man in nothing but a leather jacket and boxer shorts emerged, his attire speaking volumes about this gem of a place Natalie called home. But Tiffany shut the final door and said something that had the guy smiling, saving them both from a likely pounding.

"Well?" Asprey asked as she slid back into the car.

"That was a close one. I'm not nearly as good at lying as you are. I had to tell that man I liked his fringe."

Asprey made a face as he started the car and pulled away from the curb. "Please tell me you meant the kind on his jacket and not in his hair."

"I don't think he cared either way. He said I have pretty eyes."

"He probably wanted to string them on a necklace," Asprey murmured. "You're not going back there—and I find it hard to believe a woman like Natalie lives there. What did you find?"

"Oh, not much. Just that Natalie Hall isn't actually Natalie Hall. We've been played, brother."

"No way." He sneaked a peek at his sister, being careful to keep one eye on the road. What he could see of Tiffany—a smile that was slow and lazy and signified all kinds of mischief—didn't bode well for what was to follow. "How can you be sure?"

"First of all, there isn't a Natalie Hall on anything in that mailbox."

"So? Maybe it's a slow mail day."

"Or maybe, just maybe, her real name is Poppy Donovan, a woman who lives with a roommate named Bea Lewis and is woefully behind on her electric bill."

"Poppy, as in light, floral and sweet?" *That woman? No way.*

Tiffany tucked the magnetic lockpick in her pocket and sat back, her feet up on the dashboard. "Unless you can think of someone else who subscribes to *Mixed Martial Arts Sports Magazine* and orders wigs from an online retailer, I'm pretty confident we've got our girl."

Asprey couldn't help but laugh. Graff's arteries were going to burst when he found out just how much trouble Natalie—no, *Poppy*—was going to be.

Tiffany cast him a sidelong look. "In case you're interested, there was also a catalogue for Victoria's Secret in there."

His mouth went dry. Of course there was.

"When she finds out that we've been spying on her, you do know she's probably going to kill me, right?" Asprey asked.

"Probably using her MMA moves," Tiffany agreed.

Hopefully in the lingerie.

Chapter Six

"Nuh-uh. No way. Not under any circumstances."

Asprey studied his brother calmly, the pair of them facing off in the middle of the hangar, only one of them looking as though a thundercloud had landed on his face and was systematically jolting him with one-point-twenty-one gigawatts.

"So what you're saying is...no?"

Graff's mouth turned down at the corners. "I'm glad this is so amusing for you. But in case you missed the part about having an ex-con stalking our movements, this is pretty much our worst nightmare come to life."

"Maybe it's *your* worst nightmare," Asprey countered. "You know how I feel about clowns."

"I mean it." Graff said. "It was bad enough when that Natalie-Poppy woman was some kind of crazed gold digger asking us to run a poker scheme against Todd Kennick. But you saw the files Tiffany pulled up—that woman served two years in King County Adult Detention for third degree felony breaking and entering. She isn't messing around with this stuff, Asprey, and she knows who we are. We can't risk a partnership. We can't even risk her coming around here. She's a liability."

"You said the same thing about me once."

"You're family," his brother protested, as if that was all the explanation required.

"So what do you propose we do?" Asprey's patience, usually such a solid, immovable thing, was beginning to crack. "Do I take her for a swim with the fishes? You want to strap her to Louis and torture her with a marathon of *Cops* reruns until we're done?"

"She likes you," Graff said, his eyes not quite meeting Asprey's. "Can't you talk her out of it?"

"Sure. That should be easy." Asprey adopted a light tone. "'Gee, Natalie—it sure is swell of you to ask us for help. But we're a set of judgmental pricks who only look out for ourselves. By the way, your case files were really interesting. Would you like to murder me while I sleep?'"

Graff studied him intently. "Fine. How about this—why don't we just offer her the twenty thousand dollars for the necklace and cut the strings? Everyone knows that paying a blackmailer is worse than giving in to terrorists, but I don't see what other choice we have."

"You do realize you just compared a perfectly nice woman to international extremists."

"Just do it."

Asprey stared at his brother for a full minute, waiting for a break in that rough exterior. It didn't come.

"If you insist. But I'm going to do a little recon *my way* first. And I reserve the right to withhold payment if I find anything that might end up working in our favor."

"You have a way?"

"Yes, Graff," Asprey explained with a smile. "It's called the Not Being an Asshole method. You should try it sometime."

Poppy might not have ever noticed the man on the corner if not for Jenny's newfound love of squirrels.

"I swear, if Mike the Slumlord doesn't come fix the locks on these windows soon, I'm going to call the city and have them come condemn these buildings." Bea pulled her daughter away from the family of fluffy-tailed rodents that lived on their second-story stoop—as well as the rickety window that opened out onto said stoop at the slightest toddler touch.

Bea blew a raspberry on Jenny's little stomach, which protruded over the top of the cutest ruffly pink shorts ever, and both mother and daughter squealed in delight. "And you know I can. Remember the time I got them to shut down that Irish pub for twenty-four hours so we could convince that skeezy bartender he wanted to come away with us for the weekend instead?"

Poppy remembered. They'd taken him for almost a thousand dollars—guys who had a habit of slipping roofies into female patrons' drinks at closing time were an easy mark for the threesome scam. Set the scene with the tale of a friend's Jacuzzi condo free for the weekend. Add two parts willing females. Let it set just long enough to firm—pun intended—before asking for money to buy party supplies like cocaine and ecstasy. Take the money and run.

It wasn't their best work, but it did the trick.

"Do you miss it?" Poppy heard herself ask, the words slipping out before she could stop them. "The planning, the adrenaline high..."

"Me?" Bea's glance was shrewd. "No. We had some good times, but the cost was too high. You know that better than I do. Why? Do *you* miss it?"

Poppy shrugged and returned her attention to the window—more specifically, to the dark figure on the corner, a long trench coat and fedora obscuring him from view even though it was the middle of the day. It seemed safer to focus on the creepy predator outside than to admit to Bea that being in the middle of a heart-thumping, quick-thinking con was the only time Poppy felt truly alive.

She'd rather manipulate people than forge actual human bonds. What kind of a person did that make her?

"I'm going for a walk," she announced, pushing to her feet.

"You want company?" Bea asked, although it looked like she already knew the answer to that question.

"No thanks." Poppy made a beeline for the door. "There's a ton of duct tape in the junk drawer, though. That should hold the window for a while."

At least long enough for Poppy to get the Kennick job done, cash in hand. Her first goal was to move Bea and Jenny somewhere safer, somewhere gunshots didn't ring in the night like the chiming of the church's bells. Then she would see about that whole fresh-start thing.

A life of respectability worked for everyone else—surely they'd still have room for her after all this was done?

"I was wrong when I said you suck at crime. You're even worse at stalking."

Asprey had seen Poppy approaching from across the street and, other than a momentary urge to turn and flee, was rather proud of standing his ground. "Maybe I *wanted* to be seen. Did you even consider that possibility?"

She came to a halt in front of him, arms crossed, one eyebrow raised in disbelief. "So...you're standing on a street corner in a trench coat because you're seeking attention? Please tell me you're wearing pants."

He couldn't help a grin from spreading across his face. This might not be the way Graff would go about things, but forgive him for taking a little joy in what he did. "I'll admit this isn't my finest disguise. But if you knew how long I've been tailing you, I think you might revise your earlier statement. Recon is the one thing I can actually do."

Contrary to his expectations, she didn't smile. With a predatory step forward, she jabbed a finger his direction, and her normally large, expressive eyes narrowed. "Let's get one thing straight if we're going to work together. I don't care if you can make yourself invisible or spy like you once belonged to the CIA. You don't come here. Ever."

Now that was interesting. "You came to *my* home."

"It's not negotiable, Asprey."

He studied her carefully. It was hard to imagine how someone almost a foot shorter than him, wearing leopard-print shorts and the same teal cowboy boots from before, could have such powers of intimidation. But the powers were there, and so was she. He stuck out a hand. "Fair enough. But in return, can

59

we at least go somewhere to talk? There have been…developments regarding your proposition."

"Graff would rather eat the feathers in my hair than help, wouldn't he?"

Asprey snorted. "He has a few concerns."

Poppy rattled off an address down by the waterfront and asked him to meet her there in thirty minutes. Almost as an afterthought, she grabbed his sleeve before making her way back across the street. "Have you really been following me that long?"

As in, had he watched as she paid a visit to a parole office downtown this morning? Or been there when she tossed on a wig and spent six hours as Natalie Hall at a gym he knew firsthand was patronized by Todd Kennick?

"Nah," he lied. Better to ease into that sort of thing. "Besides—even if I had, I can promise you that your secrets are safe with me."

She let go and shook her head. "That shows what you know. My secrets aren't safe with anyone."

They met at a place called Dinghies and Donuts. Asprey took one look at the faded, wood-paneled interior and the waitress with nicotine stains on her fingers and almost fell into a swoon.

"This place is perfect." He held up two fingers when the waitress cast a wary and tattooed eyebrow straight up to her hairline. "Your corner booth, please. My colleague and I require privacy."

"Real subtle," Poppy muttered. She nudged him out of the way and followed the waitress toward a semi-private booth farthest from the door. "You might as well wear a sign around your neck that says Aspiring Criminal Overlord."

"You picked it. I would have been just as happy at Denny's."

They slid into the seats as the waitress overturned two brown ceramic cups. "You kids want coffee?"

Poppy widened her eyes and gave a warning shake of her head.

"You might as well bring the whole carafe," Asprey said warmly, rubbing his hands together. "We're going to be here awhile."

"You gonna eat?"

This time, Poppy kicked him under the table. *Point taken.* How bad could the food possibly be?

"We'll let you know," he said.

"If I'd have known you were going to act like a kid at his first coed party, I would have suggested somewhere else," Poppy said. "This place is good because almost no one comes in. Ever."

"Plan a lot of crimes here?"

"You could say that." Poppy watched him for a moment before settling into the cracked maroon vinyl. "But believe me when I say there's a reason this place is usually empty. If you order eggs, expect to be sick for at least three days."

Before he could respond, the waitress came by and unceremoniously dumped a carafe of coffee on the table. Asprey thanked her and poured himself a cup, but Poppy put her hand firmly over the top of hers. "I'll resort to the creamers if I get thirsty."

Considering the way the coffee appeared to have lumps as it moved through the spout, Poppy seemed to have a point.

"My brother used to buy this brand of creamers by the crate," Asprey said, rolling one of the little tubs between his fingers. He could also do a pretty mean coin-roll knuckle, but he drew the line at impressing women with sleight-of-hand tricks. Everyone had standards. "He said they made the best White Russians."

"I have a hard time imagining Graff clinking a glass of vodka with the girls. He strikes me more as a swilled-straight-from-the-bottle type."

"Not Graff—Winston."

"Winston? As in Harry Winston Jewelers?" Poppy grabbed the creamer from his hand and held it aloft. "There's another one of you?"

Crap. Discretion had never been Asprey's strong suit. He covered his slipup by taking a generous gulp of coffee, which burned the inside of his mouth and all down his throat—but not because of the temperature. His eyes watered. "What is this stuff made out of? Napalm?"

"I think they wash out the pot with bleach after each use."

He coughed heavily, taking the creamer she offered in one hand and biting the bottom so he could suck it down, shotgun-style. By the time his eyes had cleared enough that there was only one of her laughing at him from across the table, she seemed content to let the subject of Winston drop.

"So what is the deal with Graff?" she asked, resting her head on both hands, elbows propped on the table. When she did that, she looked young—her actual age, which he'd been surprised to find was only twenty-five. If half of the facts they'd compiled about her were true, there had been a hell of a lot of life shoved into those twenty-five years. "Are you guys in or out?"

"We're hovering somewhere in the middle."

She frowned. "You're either in or out. Don't waste my time."

That seemed a fair response, given what he knew about this woman. But as it was his first foray into attempting to buy a person's silence, he preferred to step lightly. Everything came with a learning curve. "What if I were to make this easy on you?"

She didn't budge.

Fine. They'd do it the obvious way. "We can pay you for the necklace," he finally said. "No questions asked, no trade of services required. All we want is a promise that you won't go to the police."

"You want me to keep my mouth shut? That's what this is about?" She didn't sound happy, and a deep furrow in the middle of her forehead seemed like a sign of impending doom, like a tornado siren or the four horsemen galloping by. This was the last time he was letting Graff talk him into anything.

"Yes?" he tried. "Like the real gentleman we are?"

She hesitated. "How much?"

He tried not to let his disappointment show. Yes, Poppy Donovan-slash-Natalie Hall was a criminal. And yes, she could probably kick his ass with both hands tied behind her back. But there was more to her story—and he wished he could have a little more time to hear it.

"Full market value. Twenty grand."

"You have that kind of money here? Now?" She cast a furtive look around.

"Well, not on me," Asprey said with a laugh. "Not even this trench coat is big enough to hide those kinds of rolls. But we *are* sorry about getting in the way of your—relationship, shall we call it?—with Todd Kennick. This is our way of making amends. Let us do this for you."

She got to her feet so quickly he was sure he must have missed something. With what could only be described as a disgusted look, she dropped a few dollars onto the table and headed for the door.

"Wait!" Asprey jogged to catch up. He grabbed her wrist and pulled her back, her whole body whirling and coming to stop against his, like they were dancing and about to do a dip. If he'd have planned better, he'd have done just that, taking advantage of her proximity to prove that loving was just as effective as fighting.

As it was, he'd have to be content that he still had all the connective tissues in his joints. "You didn't give me a chance to explain."

She didn't pull away, just tilted her head up so her gaze—sharp and to the point—met his. "Explain what? Excuse me if I don't jump at the chance to be bought by a group of inept thieves. If you didn't want to work with me, you could have just said so."

Nothing about this woman made any sense. According to the arrest records they'd creatively accessed via one of Tiffany's backdoor programs, she'd turned herself in to the police about two and a half years ago, walked right into the police station as though she hadn't a care in the world. There was no resistance, no attempt to delay the proceedings. She'd provided a written confession of her guilt in exchange for a sentence of two years.

Took the easy way out.

So why was she refusing the easy way now?

The waitress made an irritated noise and pushed her way between them, breaking the hold.

"So, what? You're just going to walk away?" Asprey asked.

"Yes." But she didn't. Instead, she softened a little, her shoulders coming down about an inch. "I don't want your money, Asprey. I mean—I do, obviously, since I asked you guys for help. I can't set Todd up without a cash infusion, and I've invested too much time in him to give up. Since you guys are already, ah, comfortable with bending the law a little, having you on the job would make a big difference."

Asprey was not immune to such flattery. "I *am* rather handy in a pinch."

The look she gave him voiced an entire stadium full of doubts. "But I'm not going to turn you guys in—if you don't want to help, there's no need to buy me off. I might be a con woman, but I'm not a bad person."

"I never said you were."

"You implied it, and where I come from, that's ten times worse."

"Let me imply this," he said, knowing as they came out that the words didn't make any sense. He didn't care. It suddenly seemed important that *he* make this call. They needed a partner, and so did Poppy. All the rest of it—the pesky details of her criminal record, Graff's objections—weren't nearly as important as making her part of their team. "Graff doesn't trust you, but he barely trusts *me*, and I've known him for twenty-eight years. And Tiffany doesn't care one way or the other."

"And you? What do you think?"

He stuck his hand out and waited for her to shake it. "I think I'd like nothing more than to see what we can do for each other, you and me. We've got ourselves a deal, Poppy. Welcome to the Charles family."

Poppy.

He didn't realize he'd used her real name until she left— and by then, it was too late to recognize that the glittering look in her eyes hadn't been the natural feminine appreciation he'd been going for.

In fact, he'd have said it was a declaration of something much more dangerous.

And Lord help him, but he couldn't help but feel that was *better.*

Chapter Seven

"Hey, that guy's cute." Bea peered over Poppy's shoulder at the computer screen. "Is he some kind of movie star or something?"

Poppy closed the laptop and faked a smile. *More lies.* "Yeah. He's in that new romantic comedy. We should go see it one of these weekends."

Given the hectic whirlwind of their respective schedules, Bea at work slinging coffee to the masses, Poppy falling further into the rabbit hole of her own folly, movies were far from a realistic option for the two of them. That was good. It meant Bea would never get a chance to notice that Asprey Charles very clearly wasn't playing opposite Katherine Heigl in yet another cheesy chick flick. No—he was far too busy slipping past her careful cover, getting under her skin until she felt so hot and itchy not even a cold shower could completely get him out of her system.

A smarter woman would use this opportunity to retreat. Forget the necklace. Forget the partnership. Running the opposite direction was her best option if she wanted to come through this unscathed.

Too bad Poppy had never been known for her common sense. The Charles family—rich, illustrious and all over the Internet—was hiding something. And she wanted to know what.

"I'd like for us to go to a movie," Bea said. "Or you could whisk me away to a bar where I can pretend, for just one night, that I'm not responsible for the life of another human being. It'd be fun. We could talk."

The fake smile stretched wider. Poppy would rather watch a Katherine Heigl movie. "Sure thing, Bea. Soon."

"You're leaving again, aren't you?" Bea stepped back to allow Poppy enough room to get up and slip her feet into a pair of perilously high heels.

"Oh, you know," Poppy said lamely, trying to ignore the undeniable mixture of grief and accusation in Bea's voice. "I've got to go see Nancy down at the prison-away-from-prison."

"Didn't you see her yesterday? And why would you dress up to visit your parole officer?"

Poppy shrugged, as though she didn't care that she was responsible for the heavy sadness that weighed on Bea's once strong shoulders. She didn't want to sit and rehash the past, and she wasn't about to admit that she was elbows-deep in research for a con. It would break her friend if she knew Poppy had gone back on her word.

"I thought a nice pencil skirt might blow the old ball-and-chain away for a change. She thinks I might be sending the wrong impression to potential employers when I wear jean shorts."

"I thought you called her a battle-ax."

"She's that too." Poppy laughed and squeezed Bea's hand. "You need to stop worrying about me. I know it's hard for you to understand, but I'm *fine*."

"A person doesn't lose two years of her life and walk away unscathed. I don't care how much you pretend otherwise. You can't just bury yourself in"—she waved her hand—"whatever this is and pretend it's all okay. I wish there was some way I could repay you."

Enough.

Poppy didn't bother with the fake smile that time. She was tired of thinking about jail, tired of talking about rebuilding her life. Action was so much more effective than sitting around and examining her feelings. That was why she'd learned to fight in the first place. Did a girl with no future and a single-wide trailer she shared with her grandmother cry into her prepackaged, Salisbury steak dinner, or did she go out and find a sparring partner to work out those emotions?

This girl chose the latter. She always would.

"I'll be home late," Poppy said. "Don't wait up."

Before she could think the better of it, or before guilt yanked her back inside their apartment, a colorful mess of baby blankets and too much furniture, she headed out the door.

Her destination, a downtown Seattle office building that rose an impressive fifty stories in height, overlooked City Hall. After finding a parking spot in a garage offering exorbitant daily rates, she twisted her hair into a quick bun. Some nonprescription glasses might have added a nice touch and helped her stay on the down low, but she'd already reconciled herself to the possibility of being recognized. She was here to gather information, sure, but she was also making a statement.

What that statement said had yet to be determined. But as she glanced at the building directory, which included a square plaque announcing Charles Appraisals and Insurance up on the thirty-third floor, she rather thought the statement might fall somewhere along the lines of *lying rich boys better watch out.* They knew where she lived, her real name and who knew what else about her. She was simply leveling the score.

Before Bea had interrupted her at the computer, she'd discovered a few fascinating tidbits about the Charles family— namely that they owned a jewelry-and-art insurance firm that had been in operation for more than a hundred years. Jewelry. Art. Money. Incredible good looks—that one hadn't been hard to miss. More than a few newspaper clips had depicted one of the Charles men with his arm around a well-endowed woman.

It didn't take a genius to realize that their family business and their thieving activities were somehow linked. The question was, *how* were they linked? And what did it have to do with the fake necklace they'd taken from Todd?

The elevator was out of the question for obvious, claustrophobic reasons, so Poppy was forced to take the stairs to their floor. Thirty flights in and she was about ready to chuck the shoes all the way down to the bottom of the stairwell. Yet another reason why rich people sucked—if they hated small spaces, they'd pay a therapist to talk their problems away.

Poppy's people walked instead. At least the calf workout was nice.

She paused for a few seconds once she reached the correct door, straightening her skirt and underwear, which had both ridden to unfathomable heights during her ascent.

The floor she stepped out onto wasn't in any way remarkable, at least not as far as upscale downtown Seattle business real estate went. It was all glass surfaces and sparkling stainless steel, which extended about a hundred feet in the distance, where rows of individual offices fit together like pieces of a Tetris game. Each individual office was walled in with glass, giving the place an eerily fish-tank-like atmosphere.

"Can I help you?" a cheerful woman chirped from behind the reception counter. She looked a bit like Poppy's version of Natalie, except this woman's hair was a more natural shade of blonde, and her well-tailored suit looked infinitely more comfortable than Natalie's Spanx-lined monstrosities.

"I'm not sure," Poppy said truthfully. "What can you tell me about this place?"

The woman's eyes widened in surprise, but she was much too professional to toss Poppy out on her rear. "We-ell, I guess that depends on what you want to know. We're an insurance firm dealing mostly in art and jewelry, with some high-end furniture and heirlooms passing through. We also do valuations and appraisals—usually for the items we insure, but also for private clients. Did you have something you wanted appraised?"

"You mean...like a really old, ugly yellow chair or something?"

The woman's eyebrows flew that time, and she reached for her phone. "Do you *have* a really old, ugly yellow chair?"

Her hand stayed in place on the receiver as she waited for Poppy's answer. Poppy was dying to know who she'd call—if maybe Graff was on site and required immediate notification of any and all hideous pieces of furniture for acquisition, or if it was some kind of code word that would get her into the elite back offices—but she wasn't quite prepared to put that particular question to the test.

"Not on me," Poppy joked. "I actually work upstairs. I've always been curious about this place, so I thought I'd stop by. Oh, I'm sorry—I'm being so rude. The name is Veronica. Veronica Maxwell. It's lovely to meet you."

She extended a hand. The receptionist gave it a wary glance before accepting it.

"You know, now that I think about it, I *do* have some family jewelry that might be worth looking at. If I wanted to make an appointment, who would I be seeing?"

The receptionist handed her a card. "Matthew Gibbons is our client services specialist. All initial consultations go through him. I'd be happy to set up a time for you to chat."

"Gibbons, Gibbons..." Poppy pretended to think. "I thought the company was run by the current generation of the Charles family?"

"It is," a voice said smoothly at her back. "But then, you already knew that, didn't you?"

She turned slowly, knowing full well that when she finally reached the other side, she'd be face to face with her favorite Charles sibling.

Asprey was, as she suspected, standing behind her. What she didn't expect was the three-piece suit, his signature vest this time layered under a tailored black jacket, and a vibrant blue tie the exact color of his eyes knotted around his neck.

"What a surprise to see you here," he said, meeting her eyes with a challenge. "I expected you next week at the earliest."

She was betrayed into a laugh. "What can I say? I like to keep a man on his toes. I hope you aren't disappointed."

His eyes deepened in color. "How could I be, seeing you?"

Poppy found it suddenly difficult to breathe. She would have liked to blame the sensation on a delayed reaction to the stairs but suspected it had more to do with how good Asprey looked in that suit, the close-fitting cut accenting the strong shoulders and lean build she never knew she found attractive in a man.

She flashed him a dazzling smile, doing her best not to let the intensity of his gaze melt her into a puddle. "Does this mean you'll give me the grand tour?"

"It means I'll give you anything you ask." He turned to the front desk. "It's okay. We go way back. I'll take Ms., ah..."

"Maxwell?" the receptionist asked with the kind of smirk that made Poppy wonder if she wasn't the first woman Asprey was on intimate terms with whose last name he didn't supposedly know. "Veronica Maxwell?"

His eyes flashed, humor and something more. She knew what he was thinking: yet another fake name, another lie to sort through. Between them, they had a dazzling array of falsehoods, all laid out like a street vendor and his glittering Rolexes. "Yes. I'll show Veronica around."

"Do you want me to tell your brother that you're in?"

"No." As if realizing how sharp he sounded, Asprey smiled and moderated his tone. "I'll check in with Winston later."

Not Graff—the other one. The one I'm not supposed to know about. Poppy allowed herself to be led away from the receptionist's desk, but only because Asprey's hand fell firmly to the small of her back as they walked.

That part of her was what she and Bea had once coined the x-spot, that one location on a woman's body where all bets were off. It was different on everyone. For Bea, it only took a kiss planted on the soft spot inside her elbow. For Poppy, it was a palm flat against the lowest part of her back. The second a hand landed there, she had a hard time moving her legs anywhere but apart.

And his hand is still there.

"Are you going to tell me what you're doing here, or do you want me to start guessing?" he asked congenially, moving her past the fishbowls toward the back of the building. People answered phones and looked busy in that general, office-like sort of way, but they were little more than a blur in her periphery. *Fingers, palm, thumb.* She barely noticed anything but the pressure of Asprey's hand.

"I've got some theories, if you'd like to hear them," he added.

She couldn't resist. "I came all this way. I might as well."

"Let me see... You're attempting to plant a pint of strawberries in my office desk hoping I'll cave to an untimely death?"

"Would that work?"

"Probably not." He flashed her a brief smile. "My hours here tend to be erratic at best—not nearly enough exposure to the allergens to do any lasting damage. This may come as a surprise to you, but I'm not much for punching a clock. I prefer to set my own hours."

"Imagine that," she murmured.

They stopped in front of a frosted-glass door, the kind with the vertical wobbly lines that looked like they belonged in a detective movie. Asprey's hand finally lifted away from her back as he reached for the door.

She let out a breath she didn't know she'd been holding.

"Well, if it's not strawberries, then you've either taken up a recent interest in estate appraisals, or you Googled us."

She couldn't help a laugh from escaping as he ushered her into the room. "Can you blame me? I had no idea I was taking up with such a famous family—did you really get to meet the President when he came here for that college graduation speech?"

"That was a long time ago." He frowned. "I was just a kid."

Not his favorite subject, then. Noted and stored. "Besides," she added, brightly this time, striving to give nothing away, "I wanted to see for myself what kind of digs you hail from."

"These kind of digs." He gestured widely. "Feel free to contain your excitement. I know I do."

She glanced around, following the path of his arm. Containing her excitement wasn't difficult—like the rest of the floor, it was all chrome and glass, very little to interest the eye or break up the monotony. At least there were nice, big windows overlooking the cityscape. The natural light did wonders for her anxiety at being trapped indoors. "I thought you guys appraised art."

He bowed slightly. "Among other things."

"Then why don't you have any hanging on the walls?"

Asprey pulled out a chair and motioned for her to sit. "Winston—our oldest brother, who I'm sure you looked up online—redid the offices when he took over the company about ten years ago. He likes the modern look. Says it gives us a competitive edge in the insurance business."

She sat directly on the desk, unwilling to continue doing his bidding now that the Hand of Persuasion had been removed. It proved tricky, swinging her body up there with the skin-tight pencil skirt and jacket holding all her parts confined, but it took Asprey a full twenty seconds to remove his gaze from her crossed legs, so she counted it as a success.

Well, a semi-success. Between the skirt and her own carefully angled limbs and that damn three-piece suit he wore, there was a whole lot of pressure building up downstairs. She shifted slightly. Best to keep her thoughts above the waist for now.

"So, have you found what you're looking for?" Asprey asked, drawing closer. He was making it very difficult to keep *anything* above the waist. "If I didn't know better, I'd say you didn't trust me, coming here like this."

"Oh, I trust you," she said coolly, "as much as I trust any man who looks better in a pair of pants than I do."

"And I trust you," he replied, taking another step toward her, "as much as I trust any woman who pays that much attention to my pants."

She let out a soft laugh, but the sound was cut short when Asprey's hands came down on either side of her legs, bracing against the desk and almost embracing her. Whose bright idea had it been to start talking about pants? Her gaze slipped down, almost of its own accord, and when she brought her eyes back up, Asprey captured her mouth with his.

There were some things a woman could anticipate about a man just by looking at him—how soft his lips might feel on hers, how expertly he might deepen a kiss before she had a chance to draw away. But nothing could have prepared her for the *intensity* of it. This man might play at being a thief, and he might wear the pretty-boy stamp with pride, but with a kiss like that, Poppy didn't dare to doubt his virility. Or his ability to use that virility to achieve his own ends.

It was that good.

She scooted closer to the edge of the desk, suddenly filled with the need to feel more than just Asprey's mouth against her, but he chose that moment to pull away, clearly in total control of the moment.

"What was that for?" she asked, breathless but compelled to fill the intimate silence that lingered between them. "Are you trying to distract me from the fact that you and your brother and sister are millionaire art thieves?"

"No." He flashed his teeth, fully aware of his charm and its effect on her. "I did it because you were checking out my inseam."

She let out a sound—half snort, all laugh. "If there's one thing you should know about me, it's that I don't get involved when I'm on the job. I don't care how good you look in a tie. If this is going to work between us, the focus has to be on Todd and whatever racket it is you guys are running here. No funny business. No kissing. No..."

His hand moved up to straighten his tie, and she could have sworn he was preening for her. "You like my pants *and* my neckwear? If I didn't know better, I'd say you're the one trying to distract me."

"No such thing. My life is an open book."

"Bound in human skin, maybe. And I'd hardly call failing to mention you're a con woman with a criminal record 'open'."

The room spun, taking her with it. She slid down from the desk, her feet hitting the ground, heels wobbling, legs not far behind. "So you know about that too?"

"I'm also quite adept at Googling things." His lips turned up at the corners in a half grin. "Well, that's not quite true. Tiffany may have had to, ah, secretly access some county files. But the impetus is the same. You don't trust us."

"Of course I don't," she said sullenly. She shouldn't have been surprised to have her secrets unraveled so quickly. It wasn't like it would even take that much digging—public records were public on purpose. But for some reason, it had been nice showing Asprey a clean slate, as though she wasn't just some two-bit, trailer-trash, blue-collar-criminal. "I guess this means our arrangement is off? Having an ex-felon on your hands is probably a bit much for a pair of fancy boys like you."

He leaned in, and for a moment, she thought he was going to kiss her again. She didn't lean into it, thank goodness, but neither did she pull back.

She needed to work on pulling back.

"As far as I can tell, Poppy Winifred Donovan." Her name rolled intimately off his lips. "The only difference between me and you is that I haven't been caught yet."

Odd how one sentence—kindly worded—could pull her heart up into her throat like that.

"The name suits you, by the way."

"It does not. I was named Poppy because my mom watched *The Wizard of Oz* the day I was born. Believe me—it could have been worse. If I'd been a boy, I would have been named Tin Man."

"Tin Man might be the only name in the world worse than Asprey," he admitted. "Though if I'm being honest, my name is the least of my family burdens."

She took a deliberate look around her. "Yeah. It seems real tough being a Charles."

He didn't respond right away, following the path of her gaze before shaking himself off. "I will admit to being curious, though. Third degree felony breaking and entering doesn't seem like you."

"Stealing expensive family heirlooms doesn't seem like you either. Let's call it a draw."

Asprey was still leaning in too close for her comfort. His voice low and—dare she say it?—serious for once, he added, "This whole situation isn't what you think."

"How do you know what I'm thinking?" she replied. *She* didn't even know that. Whatever the Charles family was up to, there was more to the game than she realized at first, especially since their pawns seemed to be theft and fake necklaces and a multimillion dollar company they happened to own. *And* the ability to kiss away all of those concerns in a matter of seconds.

It was definitely a much deeper game than she was used to playing.

"It doesn't matter," Asprey said. "Whatever you're thinking, it's wrong."

"So tell me." She ran her hands up either side of his vest underneath his suit jacket. It was a caress as much as it was an exploration—and she found exactly what she was looking for. "Is this business some kind of a front or laundering scheme? Is this how you move the goods you steal?"

"I wish it were that simple, but it's not my story to tell. You just have to believe that we're not criminals."

"Well I *am* one—you've seen the case files for yourself." She held up his wallet, giving it a friendly waggle. "Is this where you offer me even more money to keep my trap shut?"

"What the...?" He felt for the pockets of his vest and laughed. "You know, it doesn't work if you keep giving me my wallet back."

She tossed it into his waiting hands. "I'm sorry. I didn't know we were actually out to harm one another. I thought we were proving who had the upper hand."

So far from capitulating that she had, in fact, won that round, he flashed her a dazzling grin and appeared as blithe as he had when she'd been seconds from cutting his throat with a two-hundred-dollar shoe. "If you wanted to frisk me, Poppy, all you had to do was ask."

She didn't want to frisk him. She wanted to *frazzle* him—if only for a second.

"And about the money," he continued. "*Would* you take it? I mean, now that you know who we are, how much we have...?"

"You mean because you probably make more money in one hour than I see in an entire year—you think that's why I came up here? To see what else I could get from you?"

He inclined his head slightly.

"No, Asprey. I wouldn't do that."

The door swung open then, pulled and stopped suddenly, as though the person on the other side didn't expect it to be unlocked. Poppy immediately tensed and squared to face the door. Asprey, much more in command of himself, smoothed his jacket and appeared, as he always did, as though nothing could touch him.

"Winston," he said, nodding once. "What a nice surprise. I hoped to see you today."

Even if Asprey hadn't said his brother's name, Poppy would have been able to tell in an instant that he was part of the Charles line of command. He was chiseled of the same classic stone and boasted the same signature features, from the sweep of dark brown hair peppered tastefully with gray at his temples to the damned chin dimple that made them all so deliciously masculine.

But while Asprey exuded easy charm and Graff's scowls had etched permanent lines into his face, Winston demonstrated a palpable aura of extravagance. His suit made the most of broad shoulders and a stomach given to the early signs of a paunch, and a quick assessment of his fingers showed that they were a little on the plump side. Fat fingers were a dead giveaway. They signified a man with a lot of salt and red meat in his diet, not a whole lot of exercise outside of pumping a few weights once or twice a week. Definitely no cardio, and not enough water to wash out the amount of red wine and bourbon he probably guzzled like it was Gatorade.

He was, in short, the exact type of man the old Poppy would have singled out as a target for a con. He had money and obviously liked it enough to want more of it, excess and greed wrapped up in one tidy package.

That was the third and final rule of the game. In order for a con to be successful, the mark had to be willing to plunge into his or her own brand of vice. Not only were money-hungry benders of the law a lot less likely to pursue legal avenues when they found out they'd been scammed, but she liked to think it restored the karmic balances a little.

"How generous of you to take the time to come into work today," Winston said drily. Even his voice carried that rumbling baritone Charles inflection. "You can imagine my surprise when Tracy at the front desk mentioned you'd come in." He turned to acknowledge Poppy standing there, his gaze running up and down her body with an ungentlemanly flick. "I guess now I know why. Using your nominal vice president title to impress your lady friend? Not very original, Asprey. And a bit desperate, if you ask me. Sweetheart, if you know what's good for you, save yourself a heap of trouble and go home. Anything Asprey has to offer you is due to nepotism and nepotism alone."

Poppy didn't have to be looking at Asprey to see how his brother's words affected him. She'd seen him suffer several insults at Graff's hands, throwing them back at his brother almost effortlessly, deflecting even the meanest with a laugh and a smile. But she heard a sharp intake of breath and felt the desk shift backward slightly, as though he were gripping it with the kind of intensity that might shatter the glass into a thousand pieces.

No way. Not on her watch. It was time to restore the karmic balances.

"Well, you're kind of an asshole, aren't you?" she returned pleasantly. "How do you know I don't have a huge box of jewelry in my purse I'm looking to have insured? Is it the boobs? Do you say that to every woman who walks through the door?"

Behind her, Asprey let out a barking laugh. He used her momentary outburst to recover his cool, moving to her side and making the introductions. "Veronica, this is my brother and the president of Charles Appraisals and Insurance, Winston. He's also, as you correctly assessed, a bit of an asshole. Winston, this is Veronica Maxwell. She owns an art gallery up in Vancouver."

Oh, I do, do I? Apparently, the eldest Charles sibling wasn't to know of the real relationship between them. The game, it grew in complexity—and so did her desire to keep playing.

Poppy stuck her hand out. "I'd say it's a pleasure, but I'm afraid you might take me at my word. Should I save myself the trouble and head home?"

Winston took her hand and shook, but it was obvious from the wild look in his eyes that he was struggling to find a way to backtrack. "I, ah, apologize for my comment earlier. Totally out of line. It's a private argument between my brother and me that I shouldn't have mentioned."

"Winston doesn't approve of my lifestyle," Asprey offered by way of explanation. "He finds me frivolous."

She turned to him, trying to make out his meaning without giving anything away. "And by lifestyle you mean...?" *The tendency to rob people of their most prized possessions?*

"Mostly that I went to art school instead of business school," Asprey said. "He prefers crunching the numbers over actually appreciating the pieces that come through here. But he's also jealous that people actually *like* me."

There was an obvious challenge between the brothers, but there was also quite a bit of subtext. All was not cozy in Charles-town.

"Since we're all here," Asprey added, "I should probably mention that Veronica has just signed an exclusive deal with the executor from the Roget estate. Her gallery is going to handle the dissolution of the entire Warhol collection they've accumulated over the years."

As he spoke, Asprey's tone was clipped and professional—and sent shivers down Poppy's spine. Stern, commanding Asprey was kind of hot.

"The Roget estate?" Winston's already heavy brow drew closer. "But I thought they were deep in probate."

"They are," Asprey said. "Hence the need for a third-party gallery to step in. Isn't that right, *Veronica*?"

"Absolutely," she said warmly. She had no idea what they were talking about, but she had the feeling Asprey needed her to be on his side for this. So she would. "And I naturally thought of Asprey, first thing."

"We go way back," Asprey confirmed, his eyes twinkling. "She once tried to stab me with her shoe."

"If you're going to tell the story, tell it right," Poppy returned, finding it hard to avoid his humor. "Asprey took something of mine—something I very much wanted to get back. My shoe happened to be the nearest weapon at hand. That's all."

"Shall we set up a meeting?" Winston asked, ignoring their banter. "I'd love to talk more about—"

"I'll take care of it, Winston." Asprey's voice was firm.

"I prefer not to work with assholes," she added. "If I can help it, anyway."

Asprey laughed. "And I believe Veronica said something about needing to get to the airport soon."

"But I can call my secretary right now—"

"She has to go."

"I have to go!" Poppy said brightly. No one would ever accuse her of missing her cue. "I wish I could say it was nice to meet you, Winston, but it's obvious your brother got all the personality in the family. Asprey...until we meet again."

Feeling a handshake was the best way to go in this situation, she extended her hand. He studied it carefully before finally deciding to clasp the appendage lightly in his own, bringing it to his lips as though he once again wore the black mask, all gentleman thief and highwayman to the core.

"It's been an enlightening day for the both of us," Asprey murmured, pressing his mouth softly against the skin of her hand. The room seemed to swell and shrink in succession, her body undergoing some dramatic flushes along with it. "Thank you, Veronica."

It was her turn to pause, to watch him carefully, looking for clues.

But there weren't any. He was thanking her for preserving their charade, for playing along.

As she murmured a few more pleasantries and made her way out of the office door, she had to stop herself from turning back and telling Asprey he had nothing to thank her for.

She liked playing along. She liked their game.

And even though all the rules told her to drop this man before things got any more tangled, she was eager to find out what happened next.

"I'll say this about you, Asprey." Winston showed few signs of leaving Asprey's office, lingering near the windows, presumably watching the little people come and go. "You might not be the hardest-working employee here, but you're personally responsible for bringing in at least a third of our female clientele under the age of forty."

Asprey forced himself to smile and leaned back in his chair. Although he hated that the entire office had been remodeled in the sleek metals that Winston favored, the chairs were both flexible and comfortable. "We all have our strengths. Mine just happen to rest below the belt. Was there something you wanted?"

Winston turned to face him, his eyes clouded. Older than Asprey by fifteen years and worn with the worries of running a forgery scam for half that long, Winston was the poster boy for what Graff would become if he didn't learn to relax. In fact, there was the telltale redness on the tip of his nose, as though he'd spent a considerable amount of time rubbing it.

Their father had done that too. Whenever he'd been stressed out or working long hours, Manchester Charles could be seen at his desk, pulling at the tip of his nose with worry.

The sight of it was almost enough to make Asprey feel bad for all the anxiety they must be causing Winston. *Almost.*

"We had to pay out another claim this week."

"So I heard," Asprey replied, lifting his feet so they rested on the desk. He grabbed a hacky sack that he always kept in his top desk drawer and started tossing it negligently into the air. "I do read the memos you send me from time to time."

"That's the third one this month alone—all of the items stolen, and all of them by the same men in black masks. It's like they're leaving a calling card."

Asprey switched hands, tossing the ball even higher. "I can't imagine what this world is coming to, Winston. Masked crusaders? In this day and age?"

His eldest brother let out a snorting sound that belonged on a creature with cloven hooves. *Not too far off, actually.* "Laugh it up, Asprey, but you won't like it when the company has to start liquidating assets to cover the costs."

Asprey swung his legs down and pretended to look outraged—which wasn't too far of a stretch. He'd always known Winston would eventually target Ruby with his greed. He just wasn't ready for it yet. "My plane?"

"Technically it's company property. I don't have a choice. People aren't buying or selling art these days, which slows our business down quite a bit, I've got claims piling up in the millions now, and it's getting harder to..."

"Harder to what?" Asprey asked, struggling to keep his voice flat.

Winston got to his feet. "It's nothing. You wouldn't understand—what with all the flitting in and out of here like work is some kind of party. And where is Graff? I haven't seen him in months."

That's because Graff is a ticking time bomb. Asprey might be able to face Winston and pretend to be his normal, carefree self, but Graff's frown was a permanent fixture these days. One wrong twitch and his whole head was bound to go off. The closest he got to the place was having breakfast every morning at a restaurant across the street. He said he liked to keep an eye on the place—and on Winston—if only from a distance.

"Last I heard, he was in Hawaii, nursing his wounded pride."

"Hawaii?"

Asprey pulled an innocent face. "Don't look at me. You're the one who won't let him help run the company—what did you expect? You know Dad always intended for you two to be partners."

"Yeah, well, Dad didn't exactly leave things in a good way, did he?" Winston raised his voice, clearly losing his calm.

"Nope, I guess not."

"I do appreciate you landing the Roget estate," Winston ventured.

"It's not landed yet," Asprey warned. The last thing he needed was for Winston to go nosing around that account. It *was* a real estate, and it *was* in probate, but it would take the total sum of a five-minute phone call for Winston to realize Asprey had been lying about Veronica.

"If you see Graff, tell him the offer still stands."

Asprey pretended to look thoughtful. "Do you mean the offer to let him bail the company out in exchange for yet another nominal title with no real power, or do you mean the offer to 'bury his goddamned tightfisted morality somewhere you won't ever have to see it again'?"

Winston lifted up his finger, pointing it at Asprey like he was about to mutter yet another ineffective and blustery curse. But all he said was, "You've always taken his side in things. Always."

Asprey shrugged into his coat jacket and gestured with his head, indicating he was on his way out. "That's because no matter how many times Graff might act like a dick, his motivations are in the right place. How many of us can say that?"

Not me, that's for sure.

"Now if you'll excuse me, I have a hot date with a cool blonde, and I don't intend to miss it."

Winston moved out of the way, letting Asprey by. "I bet you do." He paused, calling after him, "You know, I sometimes think that being you must be the nicest thing in the world. You don't care about anything or anyone, do you?"

"You know me," Asprey said, his face almost cracking with the effort it took to remain unconcerned. "Always there for a good time—and never for anything else. You should try it sometime, Winston. You're looking a little rough around the edges."

Chapter Eight

As predicted, the reconnaissance portion of the VanHuett job made Asprey long to stab a fork into his eyes, if only to alleviate the boredom for a while. He'd gone with birdwatcher for this particular stakeout, which meant he could carry binoculars through the park without attracting too much attention. Unfortunately, it also meant he had to pretend to be interested in birds.

They chirped. They flew. He had yet to find anything else remotely interesting about them.

He settled onto a rock that provided him with a view of both an elm tree at its full leafy height and the apartment building he needed to watch. Thanks to Tiffany's handiwork accessing the mainframe of the firm where the woman worked, he had a copy of her daily schedule and a list of contacts for all the people she chatted with on Facebook, in addition to more concrete facts like place of residence and birthdate. Still—there was only so much paperwork could tell a person.

Asprey subscribed to the old-school method of recon, where *real* groundwork trumped technology. Sure, there was something to be said for the flash and bang of Tiffany zipping through the web to pull out private and eerily personal information, but that didn't tell them who Ms. Cindy VanHuett really was. *This* was where he learned how punctual she was or how predictable her actions were, how likely she was to be swayed by a friendly face or an emergency distraction fabricated in the heat of the moment.

Asprey was good at this part. Maybe Graff thought he was wasting his time out here, but his brother also thought that Asprey's art history degree was as effective as underwear worn outside the clothes with a matching cape. Graff's perspective was slightly skewed in favor of pragmatism.

But the watching had worked with Poppy, and so far, things with Cindy VanHuett were looking equally good.

At just thirty-six and with a trust fund that put Asprey's to shame, Cindy could have easily been flighty and unreliable, keener on parties and shopping than punching a time clock. Not Ms. VanHuett. She worked in her father's real estate development firm every day until six. She came home with a bag of takeout, which it took her about an hour to eat and enjoy before she came down to walk her wheezy Bichon through the park.

He'd even stopped her on his last visit to ask the time. Polite but cool, she was clearly more interested in matching her dog's sweater to her own than chatting up handsome strangers. After she took exactly three turns around the park, it was back home by eight, when she presumably settled in for the night.

Not an exciting life, but Asprey wasn't about to complain. Now that they could count on Poppy's help, it was just a matter of finding the right moment. The painting they were after hung a whopping eight feet by ten in her twelfth-floor apartment, and the trick to getting it was finding a way in—and out—of the guarded building undetected. So far, Cindy hadn't proven herself very open to persuasion.

"That is the ugliest sweater I've ever seen in my life," a female voice said, drawing up beside him. "Like the yarn was dragged through mud before someone decided to knit with it. And what is with the binoculars?"

"I'm being inconspicuous." Asprey turned to take in the sight of Poppy standing over him, her mouth crooked in a smile. Today, she'd opted for a short skirt that seemed to be made entirely of baby pink feathers, topped with a shredded AC/DC T-shirt and a cropped leather jacket. The same teal cowboy boots from before also graced her feet.

Inconspicuous was going to be difficult if she was planning on sticking around.

"You look like a serial killer," she offered. Without waiting for an invitation, she plopped next to him on the rock. "Seriously. If I looked out the window and saw a guy with a Mr. Rogers sweater staring at me with a pair of laser rangefinder binoculars, I'd skip the police and go straight for my gun."

Asprey looked over her with renewed interest. There was only one place he could imagine she could conceal a weapon under a skirt like that. "You carry a gun? Thanks for the warning."

"Well, not lately," she admitted. "That was many lifetimes ago."

"I see." He lifted a hand to her cheek. "You're a woman of many mysteries. I don't suppose any of them have to do with the giant glob of red paint under your eye?"

"What?" She scrambled to wipe the offending item off, smearing it into a kind of cheerful war paint under her eye. Leaning to wipe her fingers on the grass, she added, "It's make-up. Blush."

"Hold still."

He wrapped one hand around the back of her neck and forced her to look up, surprised to find how warm she was to the touch. Or maybe he was just cold from sitting and waiting, inert for so long. "No sudden movements," he warned, softening his words with a smile. "My shoulder is finally back to normal."

"Maybe you should keep your hands to yourself, then." The words carried a hint of a threat, but she didn't pull away. Before his brain—or his instincts—could think better of it, Asprey used the wide pad of his thumb to wipe at her cheek. Her face grew red, but he couldn't tell if it was from his touch or whatever dye was in what she called blush but was clearly paint.

He hoped it was his touch—God, how he hoped that.

"What are you doing here?" he asked when he was finished, reluctantly drawing away. "Not that I don't love the company, but you're kind of blowing my cover."

"Your cover sucks—it's even worse than the trench coat."

"And yet my question remains."

She tucked strands of hair and feathers behind one ear. "Graff told me to come get you."

That sounded relatively...sane, especially considering he'd left Graff pacing circles around Tiffany, promises of fratricide spewing from his lips. To say he wasn't exactly delighted with the way Asprey handled things was an understatement. "Oh? You two have a nice chat?"

"Let's just say I think you exaggerated your family's willingness to agree to this arrangement of ours." Her gaze flicked over him, stopping briefly at his crotch before finally settling on his face. "It makes me wonder what else you might have been overselling."

The challenge of it was too much to let slide, stakeouts and the folly of public displays of affection notwithstanding. Letting his binoculars fall to the ground, he wrapped one arm around her, the other gripping the back of her neck, his thumb tilting her chin to meet his. It was a short kiss but a good one, designed to show her that of all the things Asprey bragged about—*this* was not something he failed to deliver.

He pulled away abruptly, before she could do more than yield underneath him, the soft parting of lips all the sign he needed to know his point had been made.

But when he took in her face, flushed but just as impassive as ever, he was forced to concede that when it came to sharing a kiss with this woman, he was the one who stood on shaky ground. "Nothing?"

The corners of her mouth lifted. "I never said you couldn't kiss."

Damn. Poppy took this round.

A blur of movement out of the corner of Asprey's eye pulled his attention away. The man in a dark suit entering the apartment building—he looked familiar in that general business man sort of way, but it was hard to place him. *Definitely worth looking into later.*

Poppy noticed and shifted her attention with him. "Do you need to stick around a bit longer? I can go."

"I thought you said Graff sent you to get me."

"He did, but I'd happily go back there and tell him he's not some king of old who can order his peasants around. If you think for one second that man can intimidate me, you have no idea who you're up against."

He tried for a joke: "Those prison matrons must be pretty tough." But the words fell flat of his goal. She'd only been out four months. *Too soon?*

"Among other things," she said, shifting so that she faced him. Her brows drew together. "Look—you and your family obviously have a different approach to this than I do. I don't appraise jewelry or own a multimillion dollar company or have huge computer systems set up in my home office. I don't plan big heists, and I don't rely on shotguns to get results. It's just me and the con. It always has been."

"This is about me wearing vests, isn't it?"

She laughed and flashed her crooked smile, eyes opening wide as though her own amusement caught her off guard. "You have freakishly good posture too."

"I'll take that as a compliment."

"I guess I can't stop you."

"You aren't all that bad, you know." Asprey turned all of his focus on the woman next to him. There was no use pretending he was interested in the apartment building anymore. "You haven't turned us in yet. You saw our enormous table of bounty and, like the truly noble human being you are, asked no questions about where it came from. You're willing to help us, and you don't even know what it is we're asking."

"Oh yeah. I'm a real stand-up citizen," she said drily. It was obvious she didn't believe it. She got to her feet and extended a hand. "Should we head back to the hangar? I'd like to get started with Todd as soon as possible. Every day we wait is a day I have to spend making googly eyes at him at the gym. It's not my favorite thing."

Asprey laughed and let her help him to his feet. "What *did* you say to Graff to finally get the ball rolling on this, anyway? I've been working on him for days."

She beamed at him, leading the way out of the park. "That was easy. I told him the truth about Todd Kennick."

Chapter Nine

"When you say you're good at poker, do you mean you can play five-card stud with your accountant, or do you mean you can *play poker?*" Poppy warily eyed the way Asprey held the deck of cards. "Todd's no card shark, but he knows his stuff. He once lost his speedboat to the Yakuza."

Asprey cut the deck cleanly on Tiffany's computer table, lifting his arm to reveal an ace poking out the sleeve of his old-man sweater. "There's no need for insults. No one has ever invited me to play with the Japanese underground, but I'll have you know I've been barred from every reservation casino within a two-hundred-mile radius."

"That doesn't speak very well of your technique."

"Not my fault. I have very large hands." He held them up as if to demonstrate. They were an odd combination of masculine and girly, his thumbs wide in all the right places, but with the kind of soft skin that belonged to someone who didn't regularly plunge his hands into the dirty dishwater.

"Besides, cheating at cards isn't really my thing," he added, eyes glinting. She gulped and forced herself to look away. Asprey Charles was the last man in the world who needed his ego stroked. It was already at full attention and dangerously close to poking her in the eye.

"Oh? Is cheating too dishonest for the likes of you?"

"Don't get me wrong," he bragged, his chest puffing with misplaced pride. "I can count cards with the best of them. But actually getting in there and messing with the deck during gameplay? Not my style. I'm better at providing a distraction."

No kidding. It had been a long time since she'd met a man with the ability to disarm her with just one laugh—and that was more dangerous than she cared to think about. Laughter was one step away from camaraderie, which put her on that dangerous and slippery slope toward friendship.

They all knew what came after that.

"So how is this going to go down?" she asked. "I told you Todd's weakness is gambling—and I've been setting him up for weeks to believe I might be able to make a high-stakes game happen. If I want to take him for the full amount, that's where he needs to be hit."

"And that's exactly where we'll hit him." Graff took the seat opposite Poppy—far enough away that he was out of arm's reach, but still keeping her squarely in view. She nodded once, showing her understanding.

She hadn't been lying when she said telling Graff about Todd had been the tipping point in moving things her direction—but that didn't mean she liked the guy any better. He was too drunk on his own power, too much the master of the situation. There were very few men in this world who used that kind of power wisely, and she seriously doubted he was one of them.

Asprey set the deck of cards aside. "You never did tell me what it is you have against the guy."

"He's a crook," Poppy said. "He might look like an upstanding financial broker, but in addition to the regular work with his firm, he runs a side scheme that purposefully tanks investments that are then rerouted to his personal account in the Cayman Islands."

Asprey's eyes widened. "And you know this for a fact?"

"No. I overheard it at the nail salon." She placed her palms face up on the table, her way of showing a clean hand. "Of course I know it for a fact. He targets older investors, gaining their trust and then crushing all their retirement plans to fund his gambling addiction."

Asprey let out a low whistle. "You've done your homework. Tiff didn't uncover any of that stuff when she dug around in his records."

"There's no reason why she should have come across anything out of the ordinary." Poppy wasn't without pride as she told him what she'd learned from piecing together files lifted out of his home office and a visit to the Securities Exchange Commission in a deceptively secretarial suit and glasses. "He accesses the money only after it's been laundered through his firm and put into accounts that fail on a spectacular level. In the eyes of the SEC, all is right and tight in his world—he has no more complaints lodged against him than any other financial broker, and everything always comes back clear. It's only the unfortunate investors who pay the price."

"A crook," he said, echoing her previous words. But then he added, his eyes crinkled at the corners as he appraised her, "How exactly is that different from being a con woman, if you don't mind my asking?"

Those were fighting words. She shot back in her chair, her hands grasping the table for support. "Because I don't steal from people who can't afford it, that's why. I con people like *you*, Asprey, not the homeless man on the street corner looking for someplace warm to sleep. Besides, who are you to be casting stones? You've got enough loot in here to enjoy three lifetimes of luxury."

Asprey spread the cards out in front of her. He'd somehow managed to get all the suits matched up and in order, and they unfolded in a clean, colorful line. "Fine. One deceitfully rigged poker game coming right up."

Poppy looked to Graff. He was the unknown in all this, the wild card, as it were. "And you're absolutely sure you're on board? This is something you can handle?"

Graff bowed his head in a slight nod. "I told you. I don't necessarily like it, but we can play our part if you play yours."

Her part was pretty straightforward. It had taken all of twenty minutes during their first date for Poppy to discover Todd's weakness. He loved cards. He loved boxing. He loved racehorses, greyhounds, a pair of mangled cocks, or anything else that pitted one being against another in a game of chance.

He was also greedy as all get-out. On their second date, she decided to let it slip that sweet little Natalie Hall had once worked as a cocktail waitress at the Tea Room—a falsehood he'd accepted with a hungry glint in his eyes. It hadn't really been surprising. All along the west coast, the Tea Room was synonymous with the underground gambling world, big money and high stakes. Todd might have first asked her out for her body, but he stuck around for what lay underneath the surface—the chance at getting his foot in the top-secret back door with some real players.

She fully intended to deliver.

"I know what I'm doing," Poppy said. "But this game goes down my way—you understand? In order for a con of this magnitude to be successful, we have to make Todd believe the entire thing is *his* idea, and that there is nothing on earth he wants more than to take advantage of *us*. We don't lure him into a poker game and take all his money in one sitting. We want him to beg us for a game, and we deliver. And we let him win."

Asprey sat up. "That's right. The first game is the bait. The second game is the take."

"Spare us the pseudo-heist-movie talk, Asprey, please." Graff wasn't nearly as excited about all this as his brother. "Who lays out the money for this win?"

Poppy stared at Graff straight on. "I told you I couldn't do this without the money from the necklace. This is why. I need to set up the game, and I need him to walk away from the table considerably richer."

"So it's our responsibility," Graff muttered.

"If you want to back out, say so right now. I'll walk away, and we can part friends."

Graff snorted. "Friends. Right."

Asprey waved his hand in the middle of the table, drawing both Poppy and Graff from their locked glare. "If you two are done, can we move on, please? The money isn't a problem. I'll fund it myself. It's not a big deal."

Poppy tried not to let the sudden wash of emotion running through her show. Yes, chances were that a few grand was pocket change to Asprey, and he'd eventually get it all back plus some, but he didn't hesitate to lay it all out on the line. People didn't really do that kind of thing for her.

She touched her hand briefly on his arm, just enough to show her gratitude, but not so much that he could mistake it for anything else. It was becoming increasingly important to draw a firmer line between them. It was a bad idea to get involved before. Now that money was on the table, it was even worse.

People didn't act at their best when money and sex were involved. And where the two intersected? She might as well slip on some handcuffs and go turn herself in. *Again.*

"I get that this guy is a dirt bag, so I'm willing to capitulate—*a little*," Graff persisted. "But I don't like it."

"Name me five things you do like, Graff," Asprey replied. "And making small children cry doesn't count."

Graff opened his mouth.

"Making Winston cry doesn't count either."

Graff's mouth snapped shut again.

Poppy let out a soft laugh, settling back in her chair. If nothing else, working with this group was going to provide plenty in the way of entertainment. "So what's the job you have planned? What am I going to do for you in return?"

Graff studied her for a moment before giving in. "There's a painting we need to get at before the end of the month. It's a painting by Jackson Pollock—a huge one. Eight by ten, and it's currently hanging inside a private residence on the twelfth floor of an apartment building in Bellevue."

"The apartment Asprey was staking out." That made sense.

Graff nodded his confirmation. "We need to find a quiet way in *and* out with the painting in tow."

Poppy swallowed. "You mean breaking and entering."

Graff didn't miss her reaction, and an almost genuine smile played on his lips. "It's the one area we don't have much of in the way of expertise. But you do. Is that going to be a problem?"

It was one thing to target a guy like Todd for her last, high-stakes take. He had it coming, and her motives—though not exactly pure—at least had ties to something honest. This was for Grandma Jean, and it was for Bea and Jenny too. A small, persistent voice spoke up. *And you. You love this more than you care to admit.*

But another B&E? For these guys? If she got caught, it wouldn't be a slap on the wrist and two years in a minimum security prison this time. They were talking severe consequences.

"I'm in." The words escaped before she could stop them. If anything, the bigger consequences only increased her excitement—this wasn't just dipping her toes back in the criminal world, she was diving headfirst into the deep end. And the water felt fine.

"All right!" Asprey didn't bother to hide his excitement.

Even Graff gave in to something approaching admiration. "I think I underestimated you, Ms. Donovan." He cracked his knuckles and nodded once. "Welcome to the team."

Asprey walked her out, an old-fashioned and ridiculous observance that made all Poppy's girly parts come rising to the surface. She'd never paid attention to those things before—taken simple pleasure in having a door opened for her, or delighted over a compliment whispered in her ear. A woman could go a lifetime without sweet nothings and never know what she was missing.

Chalk that up as reason number twelve hundred why getting closer to Asprey was a bad idea. Life would be so much simpler if she went after Graff instead. The asshole with a chip on his shoulder, the guy who would take what he wanted and move on—that was what women like her needed, what they deserved. The fewer ties, the better.

But she *wanted* Asprey. She *wanted* to be walked to her car.

She also wanted to turn back the hands of time, talk her grandmother out of a bad investment. Talk to her, period. Too bad life didn't work that way.

"So we're on for Friday at the race track?" Poppy asked, darting out of the way just as Asprey's hand came perilously near the small of her back. "You know what you need to bring and everything?"

"I'm good," he said casually, pulling open her door. She started to get in, butterflies in her stomach, but he barred her with one hand, his hair falling into his eyes as he peered down at her. In that moment, he was all those adjectives her girly parts adored—roguish and twinkling and so freaking pretty it hardly seemed fair. "But there is one thing we need to clear up first."

Her heart thudded in her chest, and she had to force herself to appear calm as she said, "Oh yeah? What's that?"

"You might have won over Graff with your bad-ass willingness to break into an upscale apartment to steal a Pollock, but we haven't yet discussed *my* fee."

The quirk of his brow and the slight drop in his voice weren't that difficult to read—mostly because they were in line with all the things she felt at that exact moment. Desire was easy like that. It was all the things accompanying it that made it messy.

"Why do I get the feeling you're about to say something you'll regret?" she asked, playing along. *For now.*

He held up his hands in mock surrender. "It's completely innocent, I swear."

"Coming from you? I doubt it."

"You have to solemnly swear not to cause any bodily harm during the duration of our partnership," he said. "No dislocations. No broken bones. I want everything to stay intact."

"I'm not so sure I can promise that." Their eyes met, and she was once again struck by how bright and clear his were. "I play hard, Asprey. I always have. You either get in the ring, or you stay home."

He wasn't fazed. "How about you at least warn me first?"

"That I can promise," she said. "Before I do anything to you, you'll have a clear five-second window in which to escape."

Asprey offered his hand to seal the deal.

Poppy didn't believe in handshakes. She also didn't believe in promises, verbal agreements or even contracts chiseled in the flesh. Words—even when signed and sealed—were just words, and trust took a heck of a lot more than that in her book.

Yet she still took the proffered appendage, running her thumb lightly over the back of his hand. He didn't look away, and neither did she, both of them locked in a kind of stalemate to see who would be the first to back down.

He let her win, eventually replacing his stare with a grin and a slight bow of his head.

"As you wish," he finally said. "I know we're asking a lot out of you, and I know you could kick my ass in about six seconds flat, but I believe this is going to work. Trust me."

"I do," she said, surprising herself by how much she meant it.

Asprey smiled then, a wide and genuine movement that folded the lines of his face into an irresistibly charming mask. "Thank you. People don't often do that."

"What?" she quipped. "Kick your ass?"

"No. Believe in me."

Poppy relaxed. It was funny how much simply being in this man's presence put her at ease—when really, she should have been running in the opposite direction. As fast as her feet would take her.

"See, Graff?" Asprey said, returning to the hangar feeling triumphant and aroused and more content with the world than he'd been in a long time. He was really beginning to like that woman. "I told you we have nothing to be afraid of. Poppy is the perfect partner in crime. She has something we want; we have something she wants. It's win-win."

Graff shook his head and pushed Asprey aside, making sure to lock the door securely behind them.

"I'll admit—I had Tiffany look a little more into Todd Kennick's financial records. Poppy is right about his side schemes. That guy has been ripping people off for years, cleared several million in investment scams. It's the only reason I was willing to consider this trade."

Asprey paused in the act of setting the alarm code. "I know how much you love to fight on the side of justice."

"That doesn't mean I like this," Graff added. "But at least now we can keep her close, watch her for signs of trouble."

"You're being paranoid, as always."

"And you're being an idealistic idiot, as always. Trust me, Asprey. She's after something bigger than cash."

"What do we have that's bigger than cash?"

The look Graff gave him was one Asprey recognized well, casting him firmly in the role of underwhelming and continually disappointing youngest brother. "We have family. And I get the feeling she knows a lot more about ours than she's letting on."

Chapter Ten

"What's the huge emergency?" Poppy strolled up to the three-story brownstone, an address Asprey had texted her with the brief but compelling message, *Meet me ASAP*. Unlike most of the brownstone houses she was familiar with, this one went beyond the skinny one-car length in width and spanned almost a quarter of a block. The neighborhood, all leafy trees and happy dogs, matched the grandeur of it. "I was supposed to meet Todd to get him to come to the racetrack tomorrow."

Asprey, clad in dark jeans and a French blue button-up that fit snugly across his shoulders and chest, ignored her remark and surveyed the house with detached interest. "I need your help with something."

"An emergency, right?" She fought a wave of irritation that had more to do with how charming he looked set against the upscale city sidewalk than being forced to delay her dinner with Todd. "That's why you called me all the way out here?"

"Well, it's not an emergency according to the standard definition of the word." As he spoke, Asprey at least had the decency to look sheepish, rubbing his finger along the side of his nose.

"Really? What definition would you use?"

"Think of it more like a strong urge."

She laughed. "I imagine you've had a lot of strong urges in your lifetime, haven't you? And you're the exact type of person who gives in to each one."

"You think I have no self-control?"

"I think you're used to people giving you what you want. Money has a way of opening doors and pandering to strong urges." His eyes flashed a warning, but Poppy ignored it. "Am I wrong?"

"Nope—you're completely right." Asprey crossed his arms and nodded up at the house. "I'm a spoiled, selfish reprobate who doesn't know how good he has it. I should be living it up in a palace like that instead of sleeping next to Graff in an airport hangar with no heating. It's my birthright. I deserve it."

Dammit. She'd hurt his feelings. Lifting a hand to his arm, she said, "Hey—I didn't mean it like that."

"You did, and it's okay."

"No, it's not okay." In the distance, a dog barked, and an elderly couple strolled by, nodding a friendly greeting toward Asprey as they went. She waited until they passed before speaking again, glad for the chance to gather her thoughts. It had been a mean thing to say, and if there was one thing Poppy strove for in all of her endeavors, it was to avoid cruelty. Maybe she didn't always do the right thing in terms of society's views, but she always did the right thing for *her*. "I'm sorry. If anyone knows how unfair it is to judge someone based on their situation, it's me. It was a crappy thing to say, and I take it back."

He studied her carefully before finally settling into a small smile. "Apology accepted and appreciated—you have no idea how much. So does that mean you're willing to help me with my, ah, emergency situation?"

Poppy was so grateful to see the smile back on his face she didn't hesitate. "Absolutely. What are we doing?"

"There is something I need inside that house, and you look like you could use a little fun. So I propose we go in there and get it."

"Oh yeah? This is your idea of showing me a good time?"

"Yes, it is." He looked supremely proud of himself. "I spent most of the day debating between this or letting you try to break my arm again. I'm not ashamed to admit I chose the former."

She rolled her eyes and scanned the building's exterior, looking for clues. Based on the size and location, she'd say they were looking at five million dollars in real estate, easy. Whoever these people were, they had money and weren't afraid to announce it to the neighborhood.

Her pulse picked up and she felt the familiar mounting thrill that always accompanied this kind of activity. Damn him for knowing exactly what got her excited. "Why not a walk on the beach or dinner at the pier? You didn't even bring me roses."

"I have something better." He pointed at the house. "In there."

"Do you want to go grab some priceless art? Maybe the family's most prized heirloom?"

Asprey shook his head. "An espresso maker."

"Great idea." She laughed, sure he was joking. "Breaking about twelve laws and endangering our lives is the only way to enjoy a good cup of coffee. Seattle's Best has it all wrong."

"What if I told you there are no consequences?"

That was absurd. How could there be no consequences? She shook her head. "Too dangerous, and the risk-to-reward ratio is ridiculously high—that is, unless we're talking about taking the espresso machine prototype that spawned all other espresso machines in the world."

"Nah. This one's from Sharper Image."

Poppy let out an inelegant snort. "So tempting, and yet…"

"What if we amped up the reward a little?" he persisted. "Con versus theft—winner takes all?"

Her heart picked up as she caught the heady inflection in his tone. Even though she'd sworn kissing him—twice—had been a reckless, glorious mistake, her body had a hard time following along. And there were too many ways Asprey could demand his winnings—too many ways she could triumph over him in return—to pretend a little friendly competition wasn't incredibly alluring.

"What is your definition of all?" she asked. "And what are the rules?"

He shrugged, but it was a studied movement. He'd considered this before. He knew exactly what he wanted from her. She suppressed a delighted shiver.

"I propose that we both attempt to get inside the house and extract the espresso machine," he said. "I'll use stealth; you'll use cunning."

"Why are you narrating this in a Morgan Freeman voice?"

"Are you going to ask questions, or are you going to accept the challenge?"

Poppy scanned the street, getting into the spirit of it. Since it was early evening, there were a few people milling about, a car pulling up across the street and a pair of teenage girls tumbling out. "You're sure this is what you want to do?"

Asprey made the motion of an X over his chest and held up his hand. "Absolutely."

"Why do I get the feeling this is a trick? This is probably the mayor's house or something, and you guys golf together on Sundays."

"You either accept or you don't." Asprey waggled his eyebrows. "But to make it fair, I won't talk to any people—it'll be a straight heist, in and out undetected. You, on the other hand, can do whatever you want."

"As in, I can knock on the front door and offer to buy it?"

"Well, yes. If you want to suck all the fun out of it."

She laughed. This was, at once, the strangest and most exhilarating date she'd ever been on. "And what is the outcome of this challenge?"

"That's easy." He crossed his arms and looked smug. "If I get the machine first, I get to ask you any question I want. If you win, you can ask me anything about what Graff and Tiffany and I are doing."

That was almost too good. "And you'll tell me the truth no matter what?"

"Unless you'd rather do something else," he offered. "Drink a nice Pinot and discuss French cheeses."

"Oh, I'm in." There was no use pretending this wasn't exactly how she wanted to spend the evening. Her, Asprey, a good challenge, better stakes. "But if I find out you cheated, I get two questions."

"Done."

She checked her watch. "Let's give it three hours. We'll meet two streets down at that martini bar at eight."

Asprey cast a look up at the house, his eyes riveted on a second-story window. "Better make it seven."

"You're not telling me something."

"Of course I'm not," Asprey said with a smile. "That would make it too easy. On your mark?"

"I'm ready when you are."

"Hit it." With those words, Asprey gave her a cheerful wave and trotted around the block, to where the house turned the corner and continued its impressive takeover of the whole neighborhood. He obviously knew where he was going and had his plan all mapped out, but she wouldn't let that faze her. Thinking on her feet was part of being a con woman. She could still win.

She made a quick scan of the street, searching for something that could get her through the front door. She wasn't dressed for a delivery or door-to-door solicitation or even a respectable emergency use of their phone, and chances were good that they were the kind of people who had a housekeeper or butler who could efficiently turn her away.

She knew firsthand that the best way to be successful with a con was to offer the person something they wanted with a limited window of opportunity. It was the same motivation that drove people to take advantage of Act Now gimmicks on infomercials and door-buster sales that required you to get up at four o'clock in the morning. If marks thought this moment would be their only chance to take advantage of a good deal, they had a much better likelihood of taking it without first weighing all the options.

Unfortunately, she had no idea who these residents were or what sort of weaknesses they had. The bland exterior, devoid of any plants or decorations or open windows that would allow her a glimpse inside, didn't provide any clues. It wasn't at all like the house next door, which, even though it rose just as impressively into the partly cloudy sky, had a toy castle with a slide in the yard and a wagon with a one-eyed teddy bear slumped over the side—items that said something about the family living inside. Kids, not enough time to always clean up after them, enough money to live in a place like this...*that's it.*

She had her in.

Poppy wore a loose tunic-like top over ripped leggings, which suited her purposes just fine. She adjusted her shirt so that the neckline swooped all the way over one shoulder and pulled her hair up into a ponytail high on her head, securing it with a rubber band from around her wrist. She trotted up the steps to the Asprey House of Wonders and, without allowing herself to overthink the issue, knocked on the bright blue door.

It was answered by an older woman who, though not exactly decked out in a crisp maid's apron, still bore the appearance of hired help in elastic-waist pants, sensible shoes and an industrial fabric on her scrub-style shirt.

"Can I help you?" she asked, somewhat taken aback.

"Oh, hi!" Poppy extended the syllable in a high-pitched, breathless tone commonly adopted by girls with fewer years and a lot less drama in their lives. "I'm so sorry, but could you grab a ball from your backyard for me?"

The woman's eyes, a kindly hazel, flew open. "Excuse me?"

Poppy thumbed over her shoulder. "I'm the nanny next door. We were playing soccer earlier, and we kicked a ball into your backyard. I was just about to get off shift, so I thought I'd swing by to grab it."

"Oh, you're with the Parsons!" The woman opened the door wider and gestured for Poppy to come into the house. "I'm sorry I haven't met you before, but I'm only here Tuesdays and Thursdays. I'm Rose."

"Poppy," she replied. No need to lie on this one.

Before she got much farther than the foyer, Rose held up a hand to stop her. "Oh, just a moment. I need to grab the alarm if we're going to be coming in and out the back door."

She reached toward a small white box on the wall. With a total disregard for common sense, she punched in the numbers so that Poppy could clearly see each one. Poppy had just enough decency to feel guilty about taking a kitchen appliance on this kindly, if misguided woman's watch, when her eyes ran from the alarm panel along the wall, which extended into a slightly recessed living room done up in a familiar pattern of glass and metal.

What was it with people and that design aesthetic? She could almost understand it at a place like Charles Appraisals and Insurance, but at someone's home? It was hardly inviting. She'd rather live in an airport hangar.

Wait a minute...

"Do you know, I've worked next door a whole month now, and I still haven't met the family that lives here?" Poppy said, doing her best to sound like a twenty-year-old nanny. "Are they nice?"

"Oh, it's no family." The woman motioned for Poppy to follow her through the impressive living room into an elongated hallway that had been half-tiled in iridescent gray, which moved in waves as if to propel them straight through. "It's just Mr. Charles these days."

"Asprey Charles?" she ventured. *That sneaky bastard.* If this was seriously his house, she was taking a heck of a lot more than the espresso machine, that was for sure. She'd spied a really nice television on the way in.

The woman laughed. "You young girls are always zeroing in on him first, aren't you? No, it's the oldest one, Winston. Used to be the whole family lived here, but it's grown quiet of late. The rest of the kids don't come around much anymore. Now, where did you say the ball went?"

They'd reached the kitchen, an oversized vault of a room that looked more like a morgue than a place to prepare meals. At the far end, a sliding glass door looked out over the patio. To her left, Poppy caught a glimpse of another large window, this one above a set of black barstools and a long wet bar. Neither one of these would have been terribly exciting except for a French blue flash of color and the telltale click of the latch moving at the side window.

Asprey was planning on coming in that way.

"Why don't I go get it?" Poppy asked. The second Rose left the kitchen, Asprey would be in and out while she was still struggling to come up with a plan that didn't involve grabbing the oversized espresso machine that sat against the metallic backsplash and making a break for it. "I'll be just a sec."

"Sure thing. Would you like something to drink?"

"A cup of coffee would be lovely," she said, not losing a beat.

Despite the grandeur of the house, the backyard wasn't all that big, the perimeter taken up primarily with overdone landscaping. She trotted down the steps of the cedar patio to make a convincing show of looking for the nonexistent ball when a hand reached out from one of the bushes and pulled her into the shrubbery.

"Thanks for getting the alarm turned off for me." Asprey's arms moved around her waist, his words a low whisper in her ear. She shivered, his nearness and the damp foliage working double time on her nervous system.

"I can't believe you're breaking into your brother's house to steal his coffeemaker. Your family is so weird."

"Every time I take one of his espresso machines, he steps up the security. It's getting really difficult," Asprey explained. The vibration of his voice against her earlobe did strange things to her sense of equilibrium. "I needed the help of an outside professional like yourself."

She pressed her hands against his chest, curling her fingers a little as she forced space between them. "Geez, Asprey. How many times have you taken it?"

He thought for a second. "This will make six. He had the security system added a few weeks ago, and I haven't been able to find a way around it."

"Couldn't you just walk in the front door and say hello?"

He released her and pushed farther back into the bushes. "You're missing the point."

"And what, exactly, *is* the point?" she asked, growing exasperated. He was like a twelve-year-old, playing spies with his brothers and sister for a lack of anything better to do.

He let out a soft tsking noise. "I don't think so. You only get to ask that question if you get to the espresso machine first."

She let out a grunt of irritation and amusement—two emotions that often sprang to the forefront whenever Asprey was around—and trotted back up to the house. She could hear Asprey rustling along the outer edge of the yard, making his way back to the kitchen window with virtually no stealth at all.

"Did you find it?" Rose asked. "You look like you had to tackle the tree back there."

Poppy pulled a few twigs from her hair. "It was in that row of bushes near the back—I had to dig a little deeper than I expected. I tossed the ball back over the fence. I hope that's okay."

"Of course. Did you still want that cup of coffee?"

She hated to play into Asprey's neurotic games any more than she absolutely had to, but she really wanted to ask him a question. Besides, the second Rose showed her the door, Asprey would swoop in and take the machine. She needed to take advantage of the situation while she had it.

"That sounds great, thanks. If you're not too busy," she hastily amended.

"Oh, it's no trouble. I was just finishing up for the day. I could use a few minutes to unwind."

Poppy slid onto one of the barstools so that she blocked the window. "You're sure I'm not in the way? The owner won't mind?"

Rose began pushing buttons on the espresso machine, which was big enough to be in a coffee shop and really did look like it came from Sharper Image. "Mr. Charles never gets home until a little before eight o'clock."

Of course. That would explain Asprey's time constraints. She put her feet up on the opposite stool and leaned back, hoping to peek out the window. Asprey was there, sitting on the outer windowsill. He waved.

He was waiting her out, was he? She'd see about that.

"So have you always worked here?" Poppy asked as soon as a tiny white ceramic cup was placed in her hand. She took a sip but wasn't all that impressed. Coffee was coffee.

"Oh, fifteen years or so," Rose replied. "I bet that seems long to a girl your age."

Poppy accepted the compliment with a wave of her hand and tried not to appear too interested. "So you were employed when the rest of the family lived here. I mean...like you said before, when it was more than just the one owner?"

"I was." Rose peered at her over the cup of coffee. "Why?"

Poppy shrugged. "Just curious. I haven't lived in Seattle very long, but I've heard the Charles name mentioned a few times. They're kind of a big deal, aren't they?"

If Rose thought it was odd to be suddenly grilled by a nanny about her employers, she hid it under her obvious love of company and chatter. "Oh, you know these old families. We all like to pretend that things like money and lineage don't matter in this day and age, but when you start talking about the people who founded our city, it's hard not to pay respect where it's due."

"They're *that* big of a deal?" Poppy asked, settling into her seat.

"They used to be." Rose set her cup down and gestured around the kitchen. "When I was hired here, it was a different place. Dinner parties every weekend, all the kids living at home—it was like one of those movies where the women always wore heels and perfume, the men in tuxedos. So glamorous.

Mrs. Charles died when the children were very young, but Mr. Charles—their father—was a huge patron of the arts and the house was filled with people who shared that love. Did you know there's a wing at the art museum dedicated to him?"

Poppy shook her head. *A whole wing? Like the kinds of people who had hospitals named after them?*

"I told you." Rose smiled. "They were a big deal, but it hasn't been like that in a long time. When Mr. Charles died, the parties stopped. So did the donations and the people coming over. They're still rich as you please, don't get me wrong, and Asprey—he's the one you girls are all sweet on—still does the parties and glamour. But it's not the same, and I don't think Winston has any intention of trying to get things back the way they were."

Rose stopped, and it was obvious she expected Poppy to say something, but the words were difficult to find. "They don't do anything illegal, do they?" she asked. Clearly the family dynamics went beyond espresso-machine pranks, but she was having a hard time seeing where forgeries and robberies fit in.

Rose laughed. "Not that I'm aware of, sweetie. But I will say this. Someone has it out for Winston these days. That espresso machine we're drinking from? Every few weeks it disappears, and in its place there is always a black mask."

Poppy snuck a peek out the window. Asprey was still there, lounging like he hadn't a care in the world. "A black mask?"

"Winston treats it like a personal threat, but I'm pretty sure it's one of his brothers playing a trick on him. You wouldn't believe the pranks they used to pull on one another when they were kids."

Um, yes, actually. That was one thing she could readily believe.

But all she said was, "Oh?" politely over the rim of her cup.

"You name it, they did it. Buckets of water on top of doors, bicycles hidden on the roof, magic tricks."

"Magic tricks?"

"Graff was always excellent at sleight of hand."

Good—that's one thing I'm definitely counting on. "Sounds harmless enough," Poppy offered. Remembering she was supposed to be playing a role, she added, "I've seen quite a bit of that myself. You know, being a nanny and all."

Rose nodded. "In my experience, bright children left unsupervised turn out one of two ways. They either get into a little harmless mischief, or they become criminals. I'm glad the kids chose the first path, though you'd think they'd have grown out of it by now." She shook her head, more amused than regretful. "But boys will be boys."

Poppy almost shot espresso out her nose. Rose obviously didn't know her beloved charges enough. Without saying a word, she grabbed Rose's empty cup and began rinsing the dishes in the sink. She needed a second to process.

For reasons she couldn't even begin to understand—at least beyond his generally unappealing personality—Winston was yet another victim of the Graff-Asprey-Tiffany robbery scheme. But why? And what good did it do to take the same piece of equipment over and over again?

"You don't have to do that," Rose protested, but she didn't get up. The poor woman probably needed a break. Working for this family, even just a few days a week, had to be a strange and trying experience. Poppy had been around them all of two weeks and had never been so confused.

All the more reason to get that espresso machine out the door and into my care.

"You know, now that I think about it, there *was* a guy with a black mask in the neighborhood today. He parked over on the other side of the block and took about a ten-minute stroll. I thought he was one of those weird hipster types." She placed the cups on the dish rack next to the sink.

"You don't say?" Rose didn't seem surprised.

"But I jotted down his license plate number just to be sure—safety is so important when you work with kids. I have the number in my purse, which I think I set down by the front door. Do you want me to grab it? Let me just finish these last few dishes and dry my hands..." She let the words trail off and tackled the sink with renewed interest.

As expected, common courtesy won out, and Rose offered to grab the bag herself. It was the exact thing Poppy needed. Just a few seconds, nothing more. The moment Rose was out of sight down the hallway, she grabbed the machine and gave the cord a yank. It was heavier than it looked, and the residual heat from the nozzle burned sharp and painfully against her upper arm, but she lugged it out the door and tossed it over the fence into the neighbor's yard. The crash of a hundred plastic and metal parts hitting the ground couldn't be helped. For the rest of it, well... *He didn't say it has to be functional.*

Before she could be spotted, Poppy ran to the back fence and climbed the bottom foothold, peering over as if looking for someone in the alleyway.

Rose emerged from the back door about thirty seconds later. "I couldn't find your purse. What are you doing out here?"

Poppy turned. "I heard something. It sounded like garbage cans crashing, but there's no one here. Weird."

"Well, no worries. It was probably the Parson's cat. What's its name again?"

Poppy pretended not to hear. She wasn't about to give her cover up now over not knowing the name of a silly pet. She was too close. In fact, this was the part where an exit strategy made all the difference.

"Now that I think about it, I might have left my purse next door. I should probably go."

"I'll walk you out."

Poppy hid a frown and followed Rose back into the house. She'd been hoping to escape through the yard, but there was a gentle firmness to the woman that brooked no argument. Hopefully, they could make it through the kitchen without taking stock of the inventory.

Luck, however, was not on Poppy's side. She shouldn't have been surprised—luck had long since given up on her, just like the rest of the world. As they ambled through the kitchen,

Rose happened to glance over to the countertop, where instead of the gaping hole left by the stolen espresso machine, there sat a simple black mask, velvety and banded, very much like the one Poppy had seen Asprey wear the night they met.

Does he carry them around in his pants?

"Oh dear," Rose said and covered her mouth. Poppy felt a twinge of guilt until she saw that Rose wasn't covering her horror—in fact, it looked very much like she was smiling. "I guess that was the sound you heard. It was a distraction to get you out of the kitchen."

"But how did he get in?" Poppy asked, whirling around the kitchen. It was all for show, of course. Asprey had left the window open on his way out. "Oh, Rose. I'm so sorry. This is all my fault."

Rose laughed and pulled the window frame down, careful to latch it. "Nothing you could have done, short of tying Asprey to a chair. You tell him I said hello, by the way, and that next time he can just knock on the door and I'll give him the darn thing. I'm too old for these games."

"You *knew*?"

"Sweetheart, the Parsons have had the same lovely British girl as their nanny for ten years. And their cat's name is Reginald."

Poppy couldn't help but laugh with the older woman. This had to be one of her least successful cons of all time. "I think it might break his heart if he knew you were on to him. What will you tell Winston?"

"Nothing." Rose led the way to the front door, opening it for Poppy. "I'm locking up and going home. They don't pay me enough to deal with their sibling rivalry—and I've long since given up trying to figure them out. Winston can find the mask when he gets home. It was lovely to meet you, dear. I hope to see you again someday under less clandestine circumstances."

There was nothing else to say, so Poppy trotted down the stairs and made her way to the next-door neighbor's yard, peering in the foliage for signs of the espresso machine. As she suspected, it had been cleared away, and except for a lingering steaming cup that rolled next to a rock, Asprey had made away with the bulk of the goods.

Asprey was already at the martini bar, a dark stretch of a room done up in wine-red paint and neon lighting, when she arrived. He'd even had the audacity to bring the broken machine in with him, a pile of plastic and metal parts on display like they were wares for sale.

"You're lucky your brother didn't come home while I was in there. He would have recognized me as Veronica Maxwell in a second."

"Hello to you too." He got up and pulled out her chair, waiting until she seated herself before pushing it back in. Wooing her with manners—and succeeding at it. The jerk. "You forget that I'm protected by the powers of reconnaissance. If there's one thing we can count on, it's people doing exactly what they always do. And Winston never comes home before eight."

"People change. People get sick. Sometimes they want to get home early to snuggle with a teddy bear and eat Thai takeout."

"You snuggle with a teddy bear?"

"Hey—I have bad days just like everyone else," she protested. "But we aren't talking about me. I said *people*. If you let them, people can surprise you."

"*You* surprise me."

She narrowed her eyes. "Are you trying to flatter me?"

He reached across the table and grabbed her hand, seemingly impervious to the fact that they embraced just a few inches above a burning candle. "When will you learn? It's not flattery if it's the truth. What did you and Rose talk about ?"

"The espresso machine," she said truthfully. "And you."

"I bet it was all good things. Rose always loved me best."

"Is there anyone in the world who hasn't fallen completely under your spell?"

"Just you." The grin that spread over Asprey's face was irresistible and cheeky and so completely him Poppy couldn't help but join in.

"You didn't win, by the way. I got the espresso machine out of the house. You just picked up the broken pieces and left a stupid mask behind. That makes me the winner."

"Technically, I'm the one who currently has the stolen goods. Isn't possession nine-tenths of the law?"

"I refuse to concede the win on those grounds."

"And I refuse to concede to your refusal to concede."

"What would you ask me?" Suddenly, that seemed more important than their ridiculous circular argument. "If—and we're talking hypotheticals here—*if* I said you won, what would you ask?"

He paused for a moment, considering her. When he looked at her like that, as though he could sit there for hours and never tire of it, she found it hard to sit still. It was the same squirming sensation she got whenever she felt trapped, as though the walls were closing in and she was swelling out, but without any of the fear. In fact, this was the opposite. She could fill the room, expanding into infinity, and still not be big enough to live up to whatever it was he saw in her.

"That's easy. I would have asked what I had to do to kiss you again."

She licked her lips slowly, watching as Asprey's mesmerized gaze followed the path of her tongue. *Nothing. It would take nothing.*

She knew it. Asprey knew it. Hell, the people the next table over probably had a pretty good clue.

Which was why she leaned over the table and grabbed the front of his shirt, fisting the material and pulling him close. Over the top of the espresso machine, the candle and the mountains of lies that lay between them, she forced his lips to meet hers. And just like that, the details melted away. Who cared about life and responsibility when she could lose herself in a pair of lips as demanding and insistent as his? Who cared about anything compared to the scratchy surface of Asprey's always-present stubble and the ferocity of his teeth as they pulled at her lower lip?

She did. She cared.

She pulled away and, as soon as her breath resumed a normal pattern, let loose a shaky laugh. "Now can we call it even?"

"No way, Poppy." Asprey fell heavily to his chair, his own breath coming short and fast. He recovered sooner than she did, though, eventually signaling for the waiter to bring them some menus. "Now's when things are starting to get interesting."

Chapter Eleven

Asprey sat, pretending to read a newspaper. A complex string of horse-racing odds covered the front and back of the pages, and he leaned casually in his chair, pretending to take a profound interest in a picture of a thoroughbred horse being brushed by his jockey. For good effect, he stroked his fake mustache a few times.

A sharp stab in his shin made him drop both efforts.

"Ouch!" he hissed, reaching down to rub his leg. Poppy had very pointy shoes on—they were probably going to leave a mark. "We had a deal about you warning me first. What was that for?"

"Don't overact. We're supposed to be two people having an enjoyable afternoon at the racetrack—not some kind of cartoon villain and his sassy accomplice. You need to look natural."

"Says the woman in a Marilyn Monroe wig."

The platinum blonde hair was back on her head, matched by several tantalizing feet of red Lycra that seemed to exist solely to support a shelf of massive, overflowing breasts—ones he could have sworn weren't there yesterday. The sight of them was almost enough to make Asprey feel sorry for Todd. There couldn't be a man alive who was impervious to those—

"Ahem."

Asprey glanced up, grinning sheepishly. "Sorry. It's hard to look away. They're right there. How do you get them up so high?"

"Rubber inserts and duct tape," she said, laughing when she saw his reaction. "And if you're going to be my distant cousin, you'll have to rein in the urge. We're not that kind of family."

"I had a kissing cousin once," Asprey said. "She could do the most amazing thing with her tongue."

"That's disgusting."

"So is taping your boobs up so high you could probably motorboat them all by yourself." He lifted a brow. "*Could* you?"

She swatted at him playfully. "Just keep your attention where it needs to be, okay? We have one chance to make this work before it starts to look like we're trying too hard."

"How did you find this guy, anyway?" Asprey asked. It was a question that had been lingering in the back of his mind for a while now. "Is there a database of Men Who Steal Things and Deserve to be Tricked somewhere that you have access to?"

The playful laughter in her eyes closed off. He wished she wouldn't do that. Her eyes—so large and expressive—were the best part of her. Followed immediately by her smile. He couldn't forget the legs. And then...well. Taped up or not taped up, her breasts were rather tempting.

"Well, why are you after that Polka painting or whatever it is? I'm sure you didn't pick that at random, either."

"It's Pollock," he corrected her. "And no, it's not a random heist. Is that your way of telling me you don't want to talk about it?"

"Consider it my way of reminding you I'm not the only one with secrets here."

Asprey hated secrets. He always had. If people didn't like what he had to say or how he lived his life—in the skies and on the prowl—that was their own fault. All these secrets he was entangled in now—they belonged to someone else. Winston. Graff. Now Poppy. It was difficult to know which way was up anymore.

"How about this? We can extend our little espresso-machine game. I'll give you one of my truths in exchange for one of yours."

She narrowed her eyes. "And I can ask anything?"

"Why not?" He leaned back and spread his arms. In keeping with the racetrack setting, he wore a black polo shirt open at the collar, several chains of gold hanging at his neck. Not normally his style, but he kind of liked the clink of all that jewelry. It was sparkly. "Any question you want."

She paused for a moment, her lips pursed as she considered his offer. "Okay. This has been bothering me since day one. Why did you steal the necklace from me and Todd if you already knew it was a fake?"

Damn. That was a good question—and one that opened the door for a lot more. Graff had made him promise not to divulge more than was necessary, but even though Asprey might defer to his brother in matters related to theft, he was still capable of making decisions on his own. And this—trading truths—was something he wanted a lot more than a stupid oversized Pollock.

"Because everything we steal is a forgery."

Her mouth parted, her lower lip falling in surprise. He had to restrain himself from reaching across the table and taking that mouth, forgeries and fake mustaches and kissing cousins aside.

"All of it?" She shook off her initial surprise, the cascades of blonde hair tumbling around her shoulders. "The big table of loot? The painting you guys need help getting?"

Asprey nodded and offered an apologetic grin. "Don't let Graff know I told you. He's likely to dislocate my other shoulder."

"But that doesn't make any sense."

"Actually, it does," he countered, "but that would cost you another question. Now it's my turn."

She scowled. "That seems like cheating. You didn't explain your answer. You just gave me the bare-bones version."

"Haven't you ever played twenty questions before? It's called strategy."

"Fine," she hedged. "What's your question?"

He gazed up at the sky, pretending to be pensive. There shone another rare patch of sunshine in the Pacific Northwest, making it a great day to be pretty much anywhere but a rickety iron table in the defunct bar of a horse-racing track that had long since seen its heyday. He brought his gaze down to land on Poppy's half-scowling, half-laughing face. The company, at least, he could find no fault with.

"Why are you always wearing those teal boots?" he finally asked.

She blinked. "What?"

"Every time I see you—the *real* you, not some made-up persona—you have those cowboy boots on. They obviously mean something to you. What is it?"

"I don't understand." Her forehead and nose crinkled. "You don't want to ask me why I targeted Todd? Or something about life in jail? Or why I turned myself in?"

Asprey shrugged. He did want to know all those things, but not nearly as much as he wanted to know *her*. "That's work stuff. I'm not wasting any of my questions on work stuff."

She glanced down at her feet, as though she wasn't wearing hooker heels in spangled silver, instead walking comfortably along in her favorite crazy footwear. "They were a gift."

"The boots?" he urged gently.

When she looked up, her eyes were larger than usual, brimming with emotion. "Every Christmas for ten years I asked—begged—for a pair of boots just like them. And every Christmas I got a pair of sensible Keds from Kmart. I know my grandmother meant well, but I vowed that when I was grown up, I would never wear anything but those teal boots."

"You mean to tell me you've been wearing those shoes for the past decade or so?"

She shook her head, laughing sadly. "They're pretty new, actually. I forgot about that promise to myself until quite recently. The boots were waiting for me when I got released from jail, a gift from my friend. A thank-you of sorts for something I did for her."

Her mouth turned down at the corners, and it was all Asprey could do not to chuck the table aside and take her into his arms. The sight of a man in creased khakis and a billowing

Hawaiian shirt in the distance stopped him from doing anything of the sort.

"Target at three o'clock," Asprey called, returning his attention to his newspaper.

Poppy seemed grateful for the distraction. "Just remember not to touch your mustache, and we'll be fine, okay? There's no need to draw any more attention to it. It already looks like something out of a bad seventies porno."

"That's exactly the look I'm going for. I don't know how many underworld mobsters *you* know, but I believe the pornstache comes standard."

"I know underworld mobsters," she countered.

"You do not." He laughed. "You picked the first gambling-slash-mafia cliché you could think of and ran with it. Me? I would have gone for something more subtle and culturally sensitive. Like high-profile politicians getting together for a weekly poker game. Or city cops playing fast and loose with their pensions."

"Very funny." She was forced to swallow the rest of her retort, since her suitor chose that moment to approach the table, taking note of Poppy-as-Natalie's cleavage with a leering twist to his lips that Asprey would have liked to smack right off his face.

"Hey, Todd," she cooed, reaching up to receive a quick kiss. Asprey forced himself to watch with a bland, almost detached interest. He was supposed to be Rufio. Rufio didn't flinch at public displays of affection or disgusting men taking up with women practically young enough to be their daughters. Rufio was jaded and worldly and sparkly.

"And who is this, Natalie?" Todd asked as soon as they separated. "You haven't introduced me to your friend."

"I'm so sorry. This is my third cousin, Rufio. I used to work with him at the Tea Room—he got me the job there, actually. Rufio, this is my special friend, Todd."

Todd murmured a distracted hello, and it was clear the wheels were turning inside his head. He seemed like one those men for whom heavy thought required intense focus—it was amazing how many people Asprey knew who were like that. Winston, for example, always looked constipated whenever he worked through a conversation of any complexity. To some extent, Graff was like that too. He had a tendency to withdraw when he needed time to think through a problem.

Asprey preferred the quick back and forth of reactionary wit. He might not be able to conquer worlds, but at least he could hold his own at a cocktail party.

"Rufio happened to walk by and offered to keep me company while I waited for you," Poppy said. "I don't know why I was so surprised to run into him. You can always find my cousins milling around this place. Sometimes it feels like we grew up here."

Asprey stood and gestured for Todd to take his spot, careful to let the newspaper fall open to the horse races, where he'd made a few random marks in red.

"Don't let me keep you from your lovely companion," he said, adding just a touch of a European accent—enough to sound tough, not so much his authenticity could be questioned. *See?* He shot Poppy a pointed look. Like Graff, she'd had her doubts about his acting abilities—neither of them realized exactly how much of his life was spent pretending. "I was on my way to an appointment anyway."

"No, please stay," Todd urged. He grabbed a chair from a nearby table and pulled it over, metal scraping the concrete. "I've been dying to meet some of Natalie's family."

Asprey met Poppy's eyes and swallowed a laugh. No man said that unless he either wanted to get married or was looking for a high-stakes mafia poker game.

"I don't know why you haven't introduced me before," Todd persisted.

She let out a peal of laughter and toyed with a strand of her wig. "Oh, Todd. You're funny. I've mentioned my parents at least ten times. They're just the start. Between the two of us, Rufio and I must have almost a hundred aunts and uncles milling around. We're one of those big, well-connected families. A finger in every pot, you know?"

Todd nodded eagerly, and Asprey couldn't help but be impressed by it all. For weeks she'd been sowing the seeds, and now the pieces fell into place around them. A nice, big family. Vague references to money and politics. Ties to an underground gambling ring straight out of a Rat Pack movie. He was tempted to beg entry to a quiet, family game of indeterminate stakes himself.

"We have at least a hundred," he agreed breezily. "I'm supposed to meet a few here in a short while."

Poppy ran a finger negligently up and down Todd's arm. "Oh, are you going to see Drago? You must give him my love."

"I'll try, but it's not your love he wants." Asprey frowned and stabbed at the paper. "What he wants is *my* money. My stupid horse lost again. Lucky Seven? There's nothing lucky about him."

"You'll win it back," Poppy said confidently. "You always do. Don't forget—I've seen you walk away from the tables a very rich man. Well, right before you lose it all again." She turned to Todd with a laugh. "It's the family luck. We never seem to land a winning streak for long."

Todd's throat worked up and down, signaling his greed.

"But I don't want to bore you with all my family details. Rufio really should go."

"There's no need to hurry," Todd insisted. He turned his chair so it faced Asprey, Poppy all but wiped from the situation. "Let me buy you a drink."

"Well..." Asprey checked his oversized gold watch—yet another piece of Rufio's sparkly bits.

"I insist." He flicked a hand up, as though they were at a restaurant that catered to douchebags rather than a run-down bar with two types of beer on tap. But they must have known him here, because a man in a blue T-shirt came right out to take their order. "Two Buds," Todd commanded.

"Um...three?" Asprey suggested, nodding his head at Poppy.

"What was I thinking—three, please," Todd amended. "This is great. You, me, Natalie...where was it you said you all worked together? The Tea Room? I've heard they sometimes set up private poker games. Is that true? Natalie is damnably mum on the subject."

"Oh, you know how it is," Asprey hedged. He dropped his voice a notch. "There's been some heat lately. We've got a floating game. Invitation only."

"What are the chances of a guy like me getting one of those invitations?"

Asprey studied the man carefully, pretending to take his measure. "That depends, my friend, on the kinds of stakes you're willing to make."

"I make them all, Rufio. I make them all."

Across the table, Poppy bit her lip to keep from smiling.

Asprey shared her enthusiasm. This was exactly how they needed this to go. Todd was practically chomping at the bit for more information, struggling to play it cool but falling short in his Jimmy Buffet outfit and eager lean over the table.

It was strange, coming face-to-face with a mark like this again—and on purpose. Most of the time, Asprey ran from his victims as fast as he could, getting in with the job and out again before he made the kind of human connection that would allow him to feel actual remorse.

What Poppy did, the long con, was scary. She sat across from this man more than once, sharing meals, swapping spit. She looked him in the eye and made dates she actually intended to follow through with. And by her own admission, she'd spent six weeks building up her game, gaining Todd's trust.

Asprey suppressed a shiver. For the first time since he and Graff and Tiffany had started this robbery stuff, he realized the situation might be out of his reach. That *Poppy* might be out of his reach.

But he'd made a deal, and she trusted him to make this work.

Asprey liked that feeling more than he cared to admit.

Chapter Twelve

"You're going out again."

Poppy shoved her wig and shoes into the gym bag and zipped it before turning to face her friend, a cheerful, yogurt-covered Jenny resting on Bea's hip as she stood in the doorway to the spare bedroom.

"Yep, I sure am," Poppy confirmed brightly, even though Bea hadn't posed her words as a question. "I joined a gym." She pointed at the bag as if to confirm the statement.

"And that's what you're doing on a Saturday night? With all that make-up on?"

Shoot. She'd forgotten she already shellacked on ten layers of foundation and mascara, hoping to save time before she met Todd at the strip club.

"Um, yes?" Even though lying came naturally to Poppy in all other areas of her life, she had a hard time not being straight with the people she cared about. "Look, I know it's a bit odd, me looking all made up." She searched for an appropriate excuse, landing on the handiest one—and the one that wasn't a total lie. "...but there's this guy."

That got her. Bea bounced Jenny and let out a contented sigh. "I knew it! I knew something was going on with you. Don't play with Mommy's earrings, honey." She set the toddler down. Jenny, true to the title, toddled on her unsteady feet toward the bed and started playing with a pile of Poppy's numerous lipsticks and giant blush brushes, which were spread out over the multicolored patchwork quilt Grandma Jean had made out of all Poppy's childhood clothes. "Who is he? Where did you meet? Please tell me he has a nice, normal job."

Poppy stepped back. "Whoa, Mama Bear. Slow down there."

"No way." Bea put her hands on ample hips. "You've been running in and out of this apartment for weeks, never mentioning where you're going or why. I'm trying to respect your privacy and everything, but I've been worried about you. Is he cute?"

Before she could stop it, an image of Asprey flitted through her mind, all the lean muscles of him folded into carefully tailored clothes, the easy laughter that rose to his unfairly full lips. "Yeah. He's really cute." A sigh from somewhere deep inside her chest escaped. "Polished. Fancy. Not at all like the guys I normally go for."

Bea didn't blink as she pulled an eyebrow pencil from out of Jenny's mouth. "You think he's got money?"

"Yeah, I do," Poppy said truthfully. "But it's not really something we've talked about. He's nice, but it's not like we're to the point where we're spilling all the deep, dark secrets, if you know what I mean." More like they were dancing around the secrets, whirling against one another until she had a hard time holding her balance.

"Taking it slow." Bea nodded firmly. Hoisting Jenny into her lap, she sank to the bed. This time, her gaze wasn't direct, and she busied herself with lining up the pots of make-up. "So he doesn't know about your past, then? About your grandmother? About jail?"

Poppy closed her eyes. There was no easy way to answer that question.

When Bea first offered her a place to live after she'd been released from jail, Poppy had been seconds away from turning her down. There was too much between them, both said and unsaid, to make life very comfortable. And that was all she'd really wanted—not the kind of comfort that came from a penthouse with a view or bubble baths every night, but the kind that could only be offered through a clean slate. She'd wanted anonymity. She'd wanted the freedom to come and go according to her own schedule, no questions asked.

Jail hadn't been *terrible*, at least not in the way the movies taught her to believe. There had been a surprising amount of opportunity inside—books to read, classes to attend, time alone to think about her life. A straightforward plea of breaking and entering hadn't made her worth much notice to anyone, and she'd done her best to keep things that way by putting her head down and staying out of everyone's path. In terms of life experiences, it wasn't the worst thing that could have happened.

But living that lifestyle for two whole years, the staying quiet, the not making waves—it wasn't *her*, and that was where the real cost had come in. The old Poppy would have told Bea every last secret, spun her around the room and mimicked the warden's New Jersey accent, which all the women in her block had decided was adopted solely for show. The old Poppy would have admitted how she'd purposefully antagonized the other women to avoid unwittingly forming alliances, and how lonely that had made things.

The new Poppy found it easier to keep her secrets close and comfortable—and she wasn't sure that feeling would ever go away.

Which was why it was so hard to be here now. Bea was constantly searching for the girl she knew and remembered, and her disappointment as each day passed and old Poppy was nowhere in sight drove them further apart. And it *hurt*, knowing she constantly let her friend down. If Poppy had anywhere else to go, she would.

Everything came at a price. Even home.

"He knows some of the details," Poppy replied, taking Bea's hand and giving it a squeeze. "So far, it hasn't scared him away."

Bea glanced up at the shelves on the bedroom wall, where Poppy stored the few personal effects she had. The wobbly brackets held a worn copy of *The Count of Monte Cristo*, the only book she'd been able to actually finish in high school, and a framed photo of her ten-year-old self smiling into the warm, weather-beaten face of the woman who'd raised her. There was also the conspicuous wooden box containing all that remained of that warm, weather-beaten woman. *Ashes to ashes, dust to dust.*

"You have to talk about it sometime," Bea said softly. "I just wish…"

"What is it?" Poppy faced her friend then, exhausted with the talking and the tiptoeing and the monumental struggle to get through each freaking day. She leaned down and gave Jenny a kiss. She loved the way the little girl smelled, like baby shampoo and candy. "Do you wish we could go back and undo the job? Do you wish you hadn't gotten pregnant? Do you wish I'd kept my mouth shut and let you have Jenny in a jail cell so she could be taken away and raised by foster parents? We made our decisions, Bea. I know you want us to go back to the way we were, but I'm not sure the person I was exists anymore."

Bea's face crinkled with unshed tears and the stoicism of a woman who'd made hard choices and had to live with them.

"I just wish you'd had a chance to say good-bye to your grandmother before she died."

"Well, I didn't." Poppy's words were harsher than she meant, but she had to get out of there. She was going to be late for the poker game—and she was going to ruin her make-up.

"Are you at least going to do something with her ashes?" Bea asked. "It's weird, Poppy, leaving them up there like some kind of shrine. What are you waiting for?"

"I have one little thing I need to do first," Poppy promised. She forced herself to smile brightly as she grabbed her gym bag, once again resorting to half-truths. "Grandma Jean invested some money before she died—did I tell you that? I'm working with the financial broker right now to get the returns she's owed. Then I can give her a proper sendoff."

Bea lifted a brow, but she busied herself scooping up Jenny and clearing away Poppy's make-up. "No. You never mentioned it. How much did she invest?"

"About eighty thousand dollars." Poppy slipped on a pair of tennis shoes and ignored the way Bea's eyes grew wide.

"Holy crap, Poppy. You're serious?"

"She was a wily one, Grandma Jean," Poppy agreed. "I'm guessing most of it came from all those bridge games she played down at the senior's center. She went there for, what? Twenty years? And she almost never lost. That'll add up after a while."

"You know she cheated, right?" Bea asked.

Poppy laughed. "Everyone knew she cheated. But no one cared because it was worth it to have the privilege of playing with her."

"'It's not right to steal, but if you do, make sure no one can fault you for your technique'," Bea said, quoting Poppy's maternal grandparent.

"'And you give it back if it turns out they need it more than you'," Poppy added. Even if it meant losing two years of your life.

"Growing up with that woman was a trial."

"Maybe. But it was also never dull." Poppy waggled her fingers at Jenny. "You listen to your mommy, okay? Go to bed without a fight for once. And don't wait up, Bea. It'll be a late night."

"Buh-bye, Pop," Jenny said, waving good-bye by opening and closing her fist as quickly as she could. It was all the sendoff Poppy needed. She would see this job through to the end, and then she was out of it for good. Just like Bea wanted.

Yeah right.

Poppy had been to one or two strip clubs in her lifetime.

It wasn't a fact that filled her with pride, and she would have been thrilled to say she never gave in to the catcalls of a raucous crowd and hopped up on stage for her turn at the pole. But her life was nothing if not a warning to all the wayward youth of the world.

Finish high school. Get a real job. And for God's sake, leave your pants on.

"Bouncing Booty." Todd craned his neck to read the marquee, which boasted not just one but two neon signs flashing the surprisingly mobile rear-end of a woman bent at the waist. "This place seems nice."

She wished he were kidding. "It does the trick," she offered, moving out of the way so he didn't get any funny ideas about the bounciness of the booty nearest him at the moment. Thank goodness for chasteberries—if they didn't finish this soon, she'd have to suggest an increase in his wheatgrass regimen. "But we have to go in the back door. They run the game out of one of the storerooms. You know, to keep things quiet."

It didn't really make sense to her—if *she* was going to run an illegal poker game, she'd do it somewhere no one suspected, like a bingo hall or a roller-skating rink or somewhere else with windows and clearly marked exits. But Asprey had insisted this was the most authentic place. Also, he claimed to know a guy who could get them in for cheap.

She rapped the secret knock, Morse code for booty, on the back door, another of Asprey's many ideas for making the night feel more authentic. A rough-looking cook with a greasy apron and even greasier face opened the door. As she stepped through, his gaze wandered over every inch of her like she was a rack of lamb he was about to hack into tiny pieces and roast.

The cook thumbed over his shoulder to a door near the far end of the kitchen. It was shut, but there was a hole punched at about face level. "It's through there. You sure you ain't here to take a turn on the stage, honey?"

Poppy smiled sweetly and tugged on Todd, moving in the direction of the poker game. "Isn't that nice, doll? He thinks I could be a dancer."

They picked their way carefully past fallen, slimy pieces of lettuce. While the cleaning left a little to be desired, the total effect worked. In fact, the closer they got to the door, the less interested in her Todd got. He was like a kid dragging an unwilling parent to see Santa Claus or the Easter Bunny—eager and excited and clueless that none of it was real.

This time, he took the reins, tapping on the door in the same ridiculously long and drawn out booty beat from before.

"Enter."

They did.

The space they'd rented for the evening was little more than a pantry off the kitchen. Windowless and small, it had been cleared of the metal shelves and food, but the unmistakable scent of rotting produce still filled the air. If they were going for authentic backroom gaming according to every bad movie ever made, which seemed about right, they'd definitely hit their mark.

The room swirled with a smoky haze that made it difficult to draw a deep breath and obscured the already dim lighting from a single overhead bulb. A banged-up poker table stood in one corner; the other held an old meat counter covered with a broken television set, a handful of gold jewelry, and various dusty knickknacks that might have come from either a 1960s kitchen or a modern-day torture chamber.

About ten bottles of alcohol sat in a red crate near the door, and there were also a few cardboard boxes clearly labeled with a biohazard sign. Overall, the effect was one of absolute depravity—the kind of place only the bravest soul would take a black light to. Poppy almost felt home again.

"Rufio!" she cried warmly, offering Asprey her arms. He rose smoothly, taking her hands and planting a kiss on either cheek. She saw his eyes flick quickly over her—she wore a tiny silver dress this time—before settling on her face. *Good boy.*

"Thank you for squeezing us into your game. It means a lot to us."

"There is always a place for you." Asprey ignored the *us* part of the comment and zeroed in entirely on her. She'd have been lying if she said the words didn't make her feel surprisingly buoyant and tingly.

She forced herself to look away and examine the room's inhabitants. The mobster persona wasn't that much of a stretch for Graff, who pretty much played his normal surly self, though with a slightly more sinister air.

There were two other men there, and Poppy instantly approved. Asprey had promised he had a few friends from college who would unquestioningly follow him through the pits of hell and into any illicit activity in which breaking the law played a primary part. If Poppy had her doubts, she released them now. The two men he'd recruited were youngish, average guys who looked like they lived off trust funds, the kind of guys sinister gangsters might invite to a friendly game of poker in order to fleece the wool from off their backs.

She met Asprey's eye, nodding just once to note her approval. This might actually work.

Then she saw Todd, and doubt settled firmly in the pit of her stomach.

She knew quite a bit about this man—much more than she cared to, really. He seemed to lack the basic understanding of how lips could be put together to share a kiss that curled a woman's toes. He rarely talked about work but loved to mention money—especially how much he had of it and what famous people he'd encountered along the path to riches. His huge house reeked of ecologically destructive hardwoods, and mirrors seemed to appear on every other wall, but there were no indications that his house was anything approaching a home. And unless you knew what he'd done to people like her grandmother, he seemed like every other bland, middle aged man who knew finance but lacked intelligence or skills of any other kind.

But Todd at a poker table with two supposedly notorious mobsters? He looked like he knew more about this than the rest of them combined.

"Thank you," he said coolly, taking Asprey's hand and giving it a firm shake. "As Natalie says, it was generous of you to allow me in. I take it you men are regulars here?"

"It's no problem," Asprey returned, not the least bit ruffled. "We love new faces, don't we, Drago? Please, let's make the introductions."

"I'd rather we didn't, if you don't mind." Todd took the seat offered to him—to the right of Graff, a spot that had been prearranged so Graff could keep an eye on the older man's movements. "I believe the less we know about one another, the better. Am I right, gentlemen?"

Asprey's two friends nodded and murmured noncommittal responses, both of them looking a little wide-eyed at the way Todd appraised the pair of them. Poppy strove to make up for his rudeness, smiling warmly and offering her hand.

"Are you playing, Natalie, or are you just going to stand there and get in the way?" Todd interrupted.

Startled, she looked to Graff. Since he was the one rigging the deck to make sure Todd won, it was up to him whether or not she needed to add to the numbers at the table. He shook his head briefly.

"Little old me?" she asked, adding a throaty laugh and tossing her hair. "You men are far too much for me to handle on my own. I'll be the good luck charm—and you let me know if one of you gets thirsty."

"Why don't you sit by me, gorgeous," one of the extra players said, patting the folding chair next to him. The way he waggled his eyebrows at her indicated he meant no harm. "I always appreciate a chance to get lucky."

She peeked through lowered eyelashes to see if Todd cared whether or not she abandoned him to the game, but she might as well have ceased to exist, for all he noticed. He'd even pulled out a pair of dark sunglasses and was testing the light.

"Thanks," Poppy said gratefully. She took the seat, her back to the wall so she could at least *see* the door, as Graff gruffly called out the stakes.

"We'll keep this simple, yes?" Graff asked, looking to Todd. The latter man was busy arranging the enormous pile of colorful chips that Asprey placed in front of him in exchange for a fat roll of bills. A fat roll of bills that probably equaled a *real* pearl-and-diamond necklace, thank you very much.

"Buy-in is ten thousand, minimum bet is set at a hundred. The game is five card stud—no exceptions."

The men murmured their consent.

"This is my game, and we play by my rules. You want to stake against Drago, you keep your mouth shut and your hands up. Got it?"

Even Poppy found herself nodding in agreement. The only sounds beyond the distant shouts of drunken revelry inside the bar were the clack of the clay chips and the soft rustle of the worn felt-top table. She wasn't sure where Asprey and Graff had gotten all the props, but now that it was night and the poker chips fell, the room really looked and felt like the kind of place where men lost fortunes and possibly their lives. Goose bumps—the kind that sprang of a spooky awareness that she was nearer her goals than ever before—made an appearance on her arms.

Graff laughed then, a rough bark that made all five of them jump. "And relax! This is a game for family and friends. Have fun."

Asprey moved to sit next to him, clearly flashing his piece as he went. Poppy prayed it was yet another prop. She seriously didn't trust those men around guns. They'd probably shoot their feet off if given half a chance.

The message was pretty clear, though—she would at least give them that. Have fun...but not too much. And keep your hands where they could see them.

Poppy might not have been there, for all she played a role in the proceedings over the next few hours. She watched for a while, but there was only so much a person could take of men swelling up in their own egos. Because that was what they did— all of them. Asprey and Graff barked out orders and insults, while the other two men tried to one-up each other with their bluffs.

Todd, at least, played it cool. He'd started winning almost from the start, growing quieter and more intent with each chip added to his stack.

If she hadn't known Graff was signaling with Asprey through the placement of their chips on the table, there would have been no way to tell the game was rigged. When Graff dealt, his hands moved swift and sure, not once faltering over the cards he pulled from the bottom. From the looks of things, he and Asprey also fell back on soft play every now and then, betting heavy and then letting Todd take the pot.

She got up a few times to pour drinks and check the exits, and once even got up the courage to explore the main bar area of the club, ironically, for some air. The dank aura of decades of piss and sweat was better than that back room, but once the stripper, who looked to be all of eighteen years old, started flossing with her thong, Poppy gave up. Some things couldn't be unseen.

Asprey's friends drank too much and slipped out of their sleaze-bag characters a few times, but the real winning moment of the night occurred when Asprey's mustache fell into his glass. It was his own stupid fault—one second, he was fondling it like some sort of old-time villain, and the next, it had plunked into a glass of the watered-down scotch she was serving, bobbing there like a drowned caterpillar.

Asprey clapped a hand over his face, his gaze meeting Poppy's over the heads of the poker players. *Do something,* he seemed to say. *Save me.*

So she screamed.

"What?" The two extra men shot up out of their seats, ready to come to her aid. Graff reached for Asprey's gun. And Todd put his hands over his chips, protecting them from whatever it was that had caused Poppy to release such a bloodcurdling sound. Only Asprey remained unmoved, flashing a grateful smile as he fished the mustache out of his glass and excused himself from the room.

"A rat!" she cried, jumping onto the nearest chair. "In the corner—he was as big as my head. Kill him. Kill him!"

"For Christ's sake, Natalie," Todd said, not moving from his protective huddle over the table. "Control yourself."

"Did you see where he went?" one of the other men asked, preparing to come to her aid.

"I hate rats," she wailed, ignoring them both and shuddering dramatically. "Those eyes. Those *tails.*"

Her rescuer made a big show of looking for the rat, using the long end of a dirty mop to poke in the corners for any sign of the creature. Poppy was pretty sure he dislodged about ten actual rats in the process, but she allowed herself to be helped down on shaky, feminine legs.

"You're sure it's gone?" she asked, feigning disgust.

"Sit down," Todd barked.

Asprey chose that moment to breeze back into the room, mustache fully attached, if a little askew. "My cousin, she overreacts." He shrugged and smiled, like a parent apologizing for a temper tantrum in the grocery store. "Shall we continue?"

"Yes," Todd said firmly.

The game didn't last much longer after that. Poppy worked at becoming Most Annoying Woman ever, dropping wide hints about the Bubonic Plague and fleas and the scientific likelihood of rats acting as carriers for the zombie apocalypse.

"I once heard the chupacabra is actually a breed of rat that has mutated and grown to be the size of a dog," Poppy added, rattling off facts that existed only in her imagination. "People sometimes mistake them for pets, and there have been three cases this year alone of owners getting their faces eaten off while they slept."

Across the table, Asprey choked on his drink.

"Todd, doll, do *you* think a rat would eat a human face? Or are they mostly vegetarian?"

When he turned to face her, there was a snarl on his lips. "Do you want to go wait in the car? Where it's safe?"

She smiled brightly and hugged his arm. "That's a good idea. I think I'm ready to go home."

Taking the cue, Asprey rose from the table, kicking at an empty cage with little white feathers poking out the bottom. "Natalie is right, as always," he said. "The night grows late, and my luck strikes again. I'm going to walk away with nothing."

He whirled on Todd, his eyes narrowed and intense for a beat too long. Then he smiled and stuck out his hand, all icy cool and polite. Even Poppy got a little shiver, watching him. "It was good to play with you. You get to take my luck, my cousin and my money home with you. I think this means you win. For today."

Todd made a big show of getting up from the table and thanking each man individually for a great game. When he reached Graff, he nodded once, as if that that motion contained some meaning beyond I'm-a-middle-aged-jerk-who-thinks-he's-badass.

"We will meet again soon, I think," Graff said vaguely, motioning for Todd to join him at the meat counter. Poppy could hear their low murmurs as Todd's winnings were counted out.

"How much did you let him take?" Poppy asked under her breath, watching the two men make their transaction.

Asprey thought for a moment. "Probably close to thirty, by my count. I lost track there at the end, though. You don't want to know what the stripper out front gave me to hold this mustache on."

Poppy laughed softly. "And by thirty you mean..."

"Thirty thousand. Give or take a few g's."

Say what? That couldn't be right. "Are you kidding me? Not in real money?"

"No," Asprey replied. "In Monopoly money. Hopefully he won't notice that most of it is bright orange."

She nudged him with her hip, but she was far from feeling playful. That was way more than she'd expected them to lay out. "You can't really let him walk out the door with that. What if he bolts?"

"Then I guess you're in trouble." Asprey grinned as he said the words, his eyes flashing. Poppy had the distinct impression that he might be willing to lose that kind of money just to have the upper hand.

"And Graff is okay with this?"

"It's not Graff's decision to make." He shrugged. "I can be very convincing when I need to be. Don't tell anyone—it's my superpower."

That's one hell of a superpower. Thirty thousand dollars dropped like it was nothing, like he picked it up with his dry cleaning.

What a luxury that must be.

"Don't worry, Poppy," he added, his hand coming up to brush her cheek. It was a quick movement, almost hidden, a stolen caress in the middle of a dung heap of a room with her mark just a few feet away. "We'll get it back. It's just the bait. This is only the beginning."

The beginning of what? she wanted to ask, but there wasn't time. Todd and Graff completed their transaction, the latter moving to stand menacingly by the door, the former taking his place at Poppy's side. Her conversation with Asprey would have to wait.

For the first time that evening, a worried look puckered Asprey's brow. Like all of his facial movements, it was heavily lined and emphasized, a map of emotions he neither attempted nor cared to hide. "Should I walk you out?"

Her heart sputtered.

He was worried about *her*. Asprey Charles, a man she had no doubts she could take out in less than ten seconds, felt concerned she might not be able to handle herself on the way to the parking lot with Todd, a man she had no doubts she could take out in less than five seconds. These men had no idea who they were dealing with.

She smiled brightly, latching on to Todd's arm, trying not to notice the bulge in his pocket. She knew that bulge. It was wads of cash. "No need. I'll see you around, Rufio. If I were you, I'd take care of the rat situation."

At her mention of the rats, Todd stiffened, remembering the role she'd played in bringing the evening to an early end. He didn't mention it as they moved through the kitchen, though, instead giving her hand an almost paternal pat.

"I think they liked me. Do you think they liked me?"

"They don't like anyone," Poppy said, waving a cheerful farewell to the surly cook as they left. "Especially when they lose."

"The one with the face—that Drago character—said we'd meet again. I think he wants me to play another time. Do you think you could get them to invite me?"

"I might," Poppy replied, feigning thoughtfulness as they reached the parking lot. It was probably close to three in the morning, but this part of town was full of outdoor activity—the kind that involved slinking along the streets in search of the darkest alley. "But it's not a good idea. You don't know these guys like I do—they don't take losing lightly. If you play again, it'll be higher stakes and a lot more competition. It's not just a game with them."

As she expected, Todd practically vibrated with excitement. "Do it for me, Natalie, please? Just drop a casual word when you can." He paused and offered her a kiss. She accepted it, but it was obvious neither one of them felt anything as lips met lips, so far from a sizzle they might have been shaking hands. It was a comforting sensation. Any sexual promise Poppy contained just hours earlier had been replaced by the high of the poker game and the promise of things to come.

It was a promise Todd was desperate to cash in on. He lowered his voice and added, "I think we have a good thing going here, you and me."

The words carried the kind of meaning every woman dreamed of. A good thing. A future together. Untold riches. Even better, someone to share them with.

Too bad it was the wrong man—and the wrong woman. Poppy didn't want any plans for the future beyond her own freedom.

She smiled and said a vague good night, slipping into her own car, which she'd insisted on driving to the game. She'd have bet the full thirty thousand dollars that she'd have a text from him in the morning, asking her to contact her cousin for the higher-stakes game.

This was it—her break. She was in.

She rolled the windows down, letting the night air blow in and cool her skin. It was effective in cleaning off the stink of the strip club and Todd's cologne—but not in wiping off the smile that worked its way across her face, ear to ear and soul-deep.

Grandma Jean would have been proud.

Chapter Thirteen

Poppy drank the last of her coffee and shook the cup, determined to get every drop of caffeine she could out of the damn thing. Her throat hurt from working so hard to breathe clean air the night before, and her five a.m. wake-up call wasn't doing the bags under her eyes any favors. Todd and Graff and Asprey and the stripper might have been able to spend the entire day recovering from the smoke and depravity in the comfort of their own beds, but until the con was all the way complete, Natalie had her usual yoga class to teach.

Besides, Poppy figured the extra income couldn't hurt. There was every chance she'd end up owing Asprey thirty thousand dollars when all was said and done. She needed a getaway fund.

"Good morning!" she called with a brightness she didn't feel, greeting her students at the door. "Nice to see you again."

Most of them were regulars, the same dozen women who got their morning calm on before heading off to high-intensity jobs as surgeons and professors and account executives. There was an eerie similarity to each one, with their sleek ponytails and name-brand gear, but Poppy liked them. They were the kind of women who had purpose and drive, willing to get up early five days a week to stick to their goals.

Kind of like her, if you didn't count their college degrees and intrinsic value to society.

"I thought we might work on our flexibility today, so we're going to start with some intense stretches to loosen everything up."

As one, all twelve women followed her to the ground, their legs spread as they reached slowly toward each foot, toes pointing and muscles awakening.

"Is there room for one more?" a deep male voice asked, materializing at the door.

Poppy looked up from her stretch to find Asprey with a rolled blue yoga mat under one arm, dressed the most casual she'd ever seen him in loose gym pants and a gray T-shirt. Instead of making him look grubby, as it would most people, the informal look suited him. His dark hair was adorably rumpled, pieces of it falling into his eyes, and he exuded a refreshing energy she could feel from all the way across the room.

In fact, he looked fantastic, not at all as though he'd spent most of the previous night twirling a fake mustache.

She couldn't compete. Not at six o'clock in the morning. Not when there was a good chance her hair was on crooked and there were coffee grounds in her teeth.

All heads turned toward the interruption, more than one of the women straightening her posture once she noticed what—or rather, who—caused it.

"Come on in," she said, motioning with one hand and allowing her middle finger to shoot clearly up as she did. Asprey noticed it and smiled wider, beaming as though he'd gotten a full eight hours of sleep.

Of course he'd be a morning person on top of everything else.

"Set up anywhere there's space. I hope you're more limber than you look, because we're getting really deep today."

"I can go deep," he promised, trotting into the small studio, which was set off from the weight room by a mirrored partition wall. "'Scuse me. Pardon me." He touched the shoulder or back of every woman he passed as he made his way to the exact center of the room, asking politely if a few of them would scootch over just a touch so he could squeeze in.

Dead center. Right in her line of vision.

She stabbed the MP3 dock behind her and cranked up the sounds of the surf as they went through the regular warm-up, trying her best to remember to breathe. That tiny act, so integral to yoga, seemed beyond her in that moment. It didn't help when Asprey looked up from a pelvic tilt, his pants stretched tight across the crotch with all his manly, unapologetic parts right there for her to ogle, and gave her a thumbs-up.

"Let's all move into Downward Facing Dog," she called. She would *not* pay attention to Asprey's unapologetic parts. "I'll come around and help you extend your legs one at a time to add a challenge. I want to see straight lines and tight cores."

At least with this pose, she wouldn't have to look directly at him. Besides, in her experience, men couldn't handle the dog. They got distracted by all those yoga-tight asses in the air and moved into a trance. She was pretty sure that was why yoga had been invented in the first place.

The women shifted into rows of human molehills, so Poppy started at one end, checking form and technique as well as she could, given her lack of any actual training in the field. When she got to Asprey, she lost her footing a little, and only caught herself from toppling into him at the last minute. He had good form. *Great* form, actually, and he didn't seem at all distracted by the woman in front of him, whose incredibly trim glutes were on his eye level.

She would never call Asprey an athletic man, and she doubted strength competitions were where he got even a portion of his monumental arrogance. But his lean build was never more appealing than at that exact moment, his limbs long and firm as he held his body stable, a Greek statue molded by reverent hands.

Poppy grabbed his right calf and lifted his leg to waist-level, exerting none of the gentle pressure the other women in the class got. He grunted but didn't falter, exhibiting more flexibility than she thought possible. And still he didn't waver. He looked like a man with great staying power. Stamina.

Oh, man. And his ass was yoga-tight. She felt a trance coming on.

"How am I doing, teacher?" he asked, turning his head to watch her. She dropped his leg with a heavy thump. "Do you give out gold stars for good technique?"

Poppy let out a half-snort, half-snuffled sound. "This is basic stuff. If you'd ever taken my class before, you'd know it gets a lot harder than this."

She clapped her hands, ignoring the five women she had yet to get to. "Okay, guys. I want you to break off into two groups. Half of you take a breather by the back wall. The other half I want spread out on the floor. I doubt we're there yet, but let's go for full Warrior."

Warrior Pose III was one of her favorites because of its simplicity. The stance pretty much required a person to make the shape of a T with one leg flat on the floor, the other extended at a forty-five degree angle behind her and the upper torso bent at the waist. It was easy enough in theory, but holding it still for any length of time required supreme balance and control.

She hadn't been able to successfully do it until recently. She hadn't been able to do any poses at all until recently, if she was being honest. There had been a Kundalini yoga program offered at the jail. She'd taken the classes hoping to alleviate some of the monumental boredom that assailed her inside there, and found she liked the calm focus of it, like martial arts while taking a nap.

And she could use the classes to her advantage now, especially since most of the poses she taught were made up on the fly. It was a different kind of training, keeping her con mentality primed and ready to go.

Asprey shook his arms and legs, rolling his neck quickly. "Stay right there," he said to Poppy. She paused in the middle of switching off the music. "I need you to be my focus."

She remained in an awkward hunched position near the front while Asprey set himself and extended his leg. His front half bowed before her, though he kept his gaze trained on her as he bent to become a flat plane. His T-shirt slipped up as he reached his full length, enough so that she could see the flash of skin above the waistline of his pants. Hard, lean, tan—all those things a man should be if he could possibly help it.

And he didn't waver or wobble once. There was even a moment when he winked at her.

The class broke out into applause as he resumed a normal standing position.

"Do the Crane!" someone called from the back of the room. Just last week, they'd discussed the possibility of learning the two-handed stand that forced you to curl your body entirely up in the air—but Poppy had no idea how to do that advanced of a technique, so she'd distracted them with some basic splits.

"Oh, come on," she tried. "Let's not put our new student on the spot."

"I wish I could," Asprey said, his eyes laughing, "but I recently underwent some trauma to my arm and it's not quite back to normal yet. I can probably do a one-legged squat, though."

Before Poppy could say anything in protest, he fell into a squat and lifted one leg so that he balanced on the ball of just his right foot. With an otherworldly and strangely masculine kind of grace, he squared his back and brought his palms together in front of him. It was mesmerizing, how much concentration it took him to remain there with his entire body focused on one task, all of his muscles working together to accomplish their goal. The rise and fall of his chest in a perfectly even pattern was the only sound in the room.

The goal of yoga was to create a sense of inner balance bred of the mastery of one's own body—that much she knew. But as Poppy blew out a long breath, striving for some of that inner balance, the room spun, Asprey as the irresistible and unquestionable center. Her body felt each turn, hot and cold at the same time, her skin pricking to life as if after a long sleep.

This wasn't mastery. This was desire, plain and simple—and it moved in lopsided revolutions that shook and expanded by the second.

She wasn't alone.

As Poppy took in the sight of all the women trained on the exact same phenomenon created by Asprey and the air around him, she coughed loudly. It was successful in getting Asprey to unfold himself and stop the one-man show-off exhibition, but the applause only grew in enthusiasm.

"Thank you, thank you," he said with a laugh, holding up his hands as if to ward off the ministrations of his new fan club. "I'm a little out of practice these days."

"That was amazing!" a blonde in bright blue bicycle shorts said, coming up to touch him on the arm.

"Where did you train?" a redhead added, sidling up on his other side.

"Yeah," Poppy added, curiosity getting the better of her. "Where *did* you train?"

"Are you asking me a personal question?" Asprey straightened and looked her firmly in the eye. "An...exchange of truths, perhaps?"

Damn him. She'd forgotten about their deal. "I retract the question," she said hurriedly.

He ignored her, and even though he addressed the room as a group, it was obvious he spoke only to her. And the worst part was that she *wanted* to know. How did an over-privileged trust-fund baby turned jewelry thief who took nothing seriously in life master the kinds of techniques that took years of dedication and training? Who *were* these people?

"It's not that exciting," he apologized with a schoolboy smile, his blue eyes twinkling. "I spent a year in India in my early twenties. It was one of those find-yourself-in-third-world-hostels sort of trips that I took right after I graduated from college. There was this popular ashram in Chennai—near the south coast—and I stayed there for a while, working with the yogi and kind of hanging out."

"Third-world hostels?" She doubted it. Where would he have ironed his vests?

He grinned sheepishly, clearly caught with his hand in the cookie jar. "Well, sometimes. There might have been a few five-star hotels booked during my trip to break things up a little. Also so I could shower. But the ashram was real. I stayed there for a few months, even slept on a pallet on the floor, if you can believe that."

The other women jumped all over the idea, peppering him with questions about his spiritual journey and whether or not he'd read *Eat, Pray, Love.* Poppy tried to be angry at him—after all, he was hijacking her yoga class just like he was hijacking her con.

But it felt good to see a friendly face, especially when it came accompanied by a fluttery feeling that started somewhere near her chest and worked in tumbled circles down to her stomach. As much as she might not want to admit it, trying to do this all on her own was lonely work. She was tired of being lonely. She was tired of feeling isolated. She was tired of being locked up, even if it was just inside her own head.

They eventually got back on track, and it was the hardest Poppy had ever been on her poor students, moving from gentle morning yoga to sets of crunches that left them all sweaty and heaving. If she could have gotten away with it, she might have even suggested they break up into sparring partners. Then they could see who was better at showing off—even if they didn't all have fancy overseas experiences to back it up.

"So," Asprey said, as Poppy stood at the door, bidding farewell to the students one by one. He was the last in line, and he made no attempt to exit the premises in a timely manner. "That was fun, wasn't it, *Natalie?*"

She threw a towel at him and glared. "Some of us have to preserve our cover for a few more days. It was a stupid idea for you to come here. What if Todd had come in?"

"Todd wakes up every morning at seven-thirty. On a good day, he's out of the house at eight, at which point he stops for a coffee at that lingerie barista stand over on 129th before heading to work. He's an evening gym patron, stops by on his way home for the night. That is, unless he opts to stop at the bar around the corner, which he typically does on Thursdays and Fridays, because those are your days off."

"You really *are* the accomplished stalker, aren't you?"

He threw the towel back at her. "I'm not accomplished at anything. People are predictable, and anyone can figure them out. It takes nothing but time."

She wasn't so sure about that. Asprey had an uncanny way of putting a person at ease, stripping her of defenses carefully wrought over years of hard use. "You came here on purpose to aggravate me, didn't you?"

"Not at all. I came here to make sure you're okay."

She stopped in the process of gathering her things to clear the studio for Zumba, which started in fifteen minutes. "Why wouldn't I be?"

He helped her lift the stack of yoga mats and pile them in the corner. Before she could step back, he placed a hand on her arm. "I didn't like letting you walk out with him last night."

She let out a short bark of a laugh, but the hand remained. "I've been walking out with him for weeks, Asprey. That's kind of the point."

His eyes flashed, the blue deepening to an almost twilight hue. "I know it is. But that was before you met me."

"Are you sure that is what's really bothering you about me and Todd?" She held her breath, waiting for the explosion. *This* was why it was a bad idea to let feelings take over in the middle of a job—it clouded judgment, made them second-guess the kinds of decisions necessary to pull things off successfully.

"I just want you to know I'm here to help, that's all," he said quietly. "I know you're a lone wolf and you can take care of yourself, but if this arrangement of ours is going to work, I reserve the right to be concerned when we leave you in the hands of a criminal in the middle of the night."

Her hand moved to his cheek, acting as if of its own resolution, taken in by the moment and the unexpectedness of his reply. His face was scratchy, just like she expected, the stubble grazing her palm almost like a caress. "I *am* the criminal in the middle of the night, Asprey." Before she could think better of it, she added, "And I don't sleep with my marks. I'm not that kind of con artist."

"I never thought you were."

"I know. That's why I wanted to make sure you heard it from me."

Asprey released her then, and they moved toward the door, side by side but not touching. When he turned to face her, the smile once again played on his lips. "Speaking of truth, does this mean it's time for *my* question? Seeing as how I divulged the roots of my training in the manly art of yoga?"

The breath she released was both a laugh and a cry. They were treading on dangerous ground, and she didn't mean the overly waxed studio floors. Right here, right now, there was every chance she'd feel compelled to tell him whatever it was he asked—and there wasn't anything that existed that could be so disastrous to her sense of self-preservation.

When he hesitated, she used the moment to her advantage, angling for a distraction. "That's not fair. You came here intending to goad me with your superior yoga skills. Let me guess—you learned them to impress a woman."

"That's only partially true," he protested. "I journeyed to the ashram for a woman. I stayed for me."

It was getting uncomfortable being trapped in the tiny studio, especially since he blocked the only exit, all six feet of him. She moved so that she stood between Asprey and the door, and relief compelled her to capitulate.

"Fine. You win. What's your big, important question?"

He steepled his fingers and pretended to think about it, not giving in until Poppy let out an exasperated sigh and made a motion at her wrist. She was technically at work, and it wouldn't help matters any if word got back to Todd that she spent fifteen minutes chatting up her hot new male student.

"Where did you learn to fight?"

Once again, he managed to topple all of her expectations with one simple question—and she could see what he was doing, sneaking under her layers of protection, chipping away at her façade one personal fact at a time.

"I have to man the juice counter until this afternoon," she said, her mouth taking over her common sense. "If you want to pick me up three blocks west of here, by the newspaper stand that sells those weird sock puppets, I'll show you."

To his credit, Asprey didn't let his surprise show beyond a quick widening of the eyes and the grin he'd never be able to fully eliminate because his laugh lines ran too deep. "Three blocks. Sock puppets. Got it."

As he made to leave, Poppy gave in to one more impulse. "Oh, and Asprey?"

He turned back. "Yeah?"

"Thanks." She squirmed a little, unfamiliar with what came next. "For being worried enough to stop by and make sure I was okay."

"Of course," he said lightly, but by that time, he'd turned away, his head slightly bent as he made his way out of the gym.

"Thus the Prodigal returns." Tiffany pushed open the back door to the hangar, watching as Asprey parked his bike and pulled the helmet off his head. They switched the license plates when on a job requiring mobility, which meant he could take the motorcycle out for regular errands like the one to Poppy's gym with no criminal investigators being the wiser.

His feet crunched loudly on the gravel as he hung his helmet on the back peg pounded into the outer wall and stretched. He was taking his time, and Tiffany knew it.

"What happened? She skip town just like Graff said she would?"

"No. Graff was wrong."

"Graff begs to differ," his brother said, coming out to join Tiffany in the doorway. He bit into an oversized sandwich, chewing loud enough that he could have probably covered the sound of an airplane taking off, had the airport still been fully

151

functional. "There's plenty of time for her and Todd to pocket that money and run."

Asprey was very careful to pay attention to each movement of air through his body, in his nostrils and out his mouth. He would not let Graff goad him. He would not let Graff get to him.

"The amount of planning and foresight that would have to go into a con of that magnitude wouldn't be worth the thirty thousand," Asprey said. "Not when we offered her two-thirds of that free and clear last week."

"So that's it? We trust her?" Tiffany didn't seem too concerned one way or the other. Asprey's indifference in general life activities was nothing compared to hers.

"Yes. Absolutely," Asprey said, just as Graff barked out a sandwich-laden, "No."

"Cool." Tiffany nodded and turned back to the hangar. "I like her—and not just because she's tough. She doesn't ask questions or make demands. Or whine. You guys whine."

Asprey decided to follow Tiffany's path of retreat and brushed past his brother, allowing their shoulders to meet in a solid whump.

"Hey." Graff grabbed him on the shoulder and squeezed. Other than a slight flare, the pain was almost gone now. "Don't be like that. We talked about this—that woman is a professional at what she does. You don't do two years in adult detention and walk out with pure motives. I'm just taking the necessary precautions."

Asprey didn't like the direction his brother was headed. "A professional at what she does? You mean robbing people of their hard-earned money, right?"

Graff maintained his grip. "Yes, there's definitely that. But you also have to consider her methods—she knows how to use her looks to her advantage. Don't be that guy. Don't let your dick get in the way of what's really important here."

Asprey shook him off. He already felt like a dirt bag for lying to Poppy about why he'd stopped by the gym that morning. He didn't need his brother making it any worse with flippant remarks. Graff hadn't earned that right.

"I mean it." Graff pointed the remains of his sandwich at him. "You might have been able to convince me that her ex-con status is a good thing, since she has a lot more at stake if we were to get caught or an anonymous tip was whispered in the right ear, but the fact remains that you aren't in charge here. *I* am. I can't even imagine what kind of trouble we'd be in if we let you call the shots for a change."

That did it. Asprey whirled. "Why am I here? If I'm such a fuck-up, if I can't even be trusted to control myself around one woman, why do you want my help getting the company back from Winston's evil clutches?"

"Now you're being stupid," Graff muttered. "This is as much for you as it is for me."

"Is it? Really? Because from where I stand, your biggest goal is to divide the family, and I put the numbers on your side."

"It's not dividing the family, Asp. It's doing what needs to be done." Fury made Graff even gruffer than usual. "Winston can't keep stealing from innocent people under *our* name. Something has to give."

"So turn him over to the police and let them handle it," Asprey returned. "Besides, it's only a matter of time before Winston discovers that we're the ones behind all the thefts. What happens to your grand plan then?"

"He won't figure it out." Graff's lips were white and tense, and he'd given up the pretense of nonchalant eating. That was Asprey's line anyway, that of the careless rogue. "He's a man with enemies, especially in the world of business. You know he was the one who convinced Dad to take the company deeper into the insurance side of things, and that's not a move anyone makes without a hell of a lot of greed at his back. I could name half a dozen men who would be happy to bring him to ruin."

"So let them."

"No." Graff released Asprey with a shove. "This is our responsibility. Five years he spent making those forgeries, handing off the fakes to clients and selling the real thing to God-knows-who. Jail time won't get people their valuables back—and you know Winston would probably hire some lawyer who could get him off with a slap on the wrist. This is the best way. It's our mess, our responsibility."

"And it has nothing to do with you wanting control of the company, does it?" Asprey asked bitterly. He knew Graff was right, knew that at least this way they could compensate people for the damages Winston had done.

"Of course it does," Graff said coolly. "I'm not afraid to admit that we're the victims here too. With each successful forgery, Winston methodically chipped away at everything Dad and Grandpa and Great-Grandpa built. He also stole the Charles family legacy—and that belongs to all of us."

Asprey threw up his hands. "And when have I ever cared about the stupid Charles family legacy?"

Graff laughed, though there was no real humor in it. Asprey couldn't remember the last time he'd heard his brother give in to real mirth. "Don't kid yourself. You care every time you pull out your credit cards, every time you roll out of bed in the afternoon and decide you'd rather take your airplane for a spin than go to work. Maybe our motivations aren't the same, but you need this as much as I do."

Asprey's chest tightened, and he stepped aside to let his brother pass him into the hangar. Experience told him not to let his brother go, that his words, which sprang more out of his deep-seated sense of self-loathing rather than any intention to hurt Asprey's feelings, were a gateway to something more.

But he let Graff go, failing like he always did.

It was kind of his thing.

Chapter Fourteen

"Here." Asprey extended a plastic bag, swinging it casually between his fingers. "I bought you a sock puppet."

Poppy laughed. She still had on her Natalie gear, her hair pulled back in a springy blonde ponytail, matched by the tightest pair of yoga pants he'd ever seen. They were his favorite pants. They made everything bounce.

And while the bounce was good—the bounce was *great*—it couldn't all be attributed to her attire. Natalie was a naturally springy person. He could see that now. She walked differently than Poppy, with an extra sway to her backside and a jiggle to her step not unlike that of a sorority girl. Her mannerisms were different too, her hands more fluid as she spoke, her facial expressions exaggerated to the point of cartoons. Regular Poppy was a lot more controlled, and she had an uncanny way of sizing up both a person and a room at a glance. She always positioned herself defensively when she entered a new situation, her back to the wall so she faced the exit, never quite letting her guard down around the other people in the room.

Outside, on the sidewalk where a group of teenaged skaters whizzed past, leaving the earthy scent of pot and coffee in their wake, she seemed a little more at ease. He wondered if it had anything to do with him.

He hoped so.

She peeked into the bag and smiled. "A ninja. How cute."

"It was either that or the fairy princess." He shrugged. "I took a stab."

Her laughter sprang forth, both a validation and a promise. "Thank you. A girl can never have enough ninja paraphernalia." She cast a quick glance around. "But I should probably get off the street until I get a chance to take off the Natalie gear. I don't want to risk being seen. You parked nearby?"

"Yeah. Right there, actually." He pointed at his motorcycle a few car lengths down, the front wheel turned into the curb.

She swiveled to face him, one of her Natalie-darkened eyebrows raised in a question. "Seriously? You drove your getaway vehicle to a centrally located public place? And you want me to hop on?"

He tossed her his extra helmet. White and baby blue and covered in dainty swirls, the helmet had originally been purchased for any female riders he might pick up along his general cruise through life. Those moments were fewer and further between than he'd hoped, although Tiffany had been grateful to use it the few times she'd been out with him. "What can I say? I like to live on the edge."

"That's not it," she said, pulling the helmet over her head, expertly tucking in her ponytail and buckling the chin strap. This clearly wasn't her first time on a bike.

"How do you figure?"

She flipped up the face guard and studied him. "You don't live on the edge. You live in the land of privilege. You think things can't touch you."

He flipped her face guard back down.

He hadn't told Graff or Tiffany about this particular errand—mostly because both of them would approve of it, assuming he meant to build trust and break down walls. Well, that was what he intended, but not in the way they would have imagined it. For the first time in months, there would be no thinking about theft or family or the next big heist. He was back to thinking about himself.

A selfish and vain bastard that might make him, but even Asprey of London closed its doors for business every now and then.

"Just hold on," he commanded, pulling his own helmet down. He swung his leg over the motorcycle, stabilizing it while Poppy moved into place behind him. Even through the thick leather of his riding jacket and the extra one he'd brought for her, he felt a surge of pleasure at the swell of her chest against his back. She didn't hesitate to press firmly against him, slipping her arms around his waist and tucking her hands inside the flaps of his jacket, palms flat against his stomach.

He didn't want those hands to stop moving, could already imagine how they would feel moving lower, her long fingers swift and sure as they sought a place to land. *Ninja legs and pickpocket hands.*

His groin tightened, his cock responding the only way it knew how to such an unlikely combination of attributes. It was going to be hard to concentrate on the road.

Fortunately, he found a kind of balance between speed and sensation as he started the motorcycle and turned the throttle. Women didn't normally clamor to take place in this part of his life—they preferred the Charles family soirees or a candlelit dinner for two over a chance to zoom astride his high-speed Ducati through the city streets. The woman he'd gone to the ashram with had been like that. When the facility turned out to be a sprawling un-air-conditioned hovel on the outskirts of a slum instead of the luxury yoga retreat the brochure had led her to believe, she couldn't pack her bags fast enough.

But he'd liked the balance between the turmoil around them and the quiet of their centuries-old courtyard. The bike, well, that wasn't nearly as noble. Mostly he liked the way it made him feel, like he was still in touch with his admittedly juvenile, adventurous side—if only for a little while.

With every corner he took at a too-sharp turn, Poppy signaling where to go with the tap of her hand as they approached each intersection, she moved into him like someone who knew what she was doing.

That was when it hit him. Poppy was *from* the admittedly juvenile, adventurous side. Her life experiences—as a con woman, as a prisoner, as someone who looked a cheating gambler in the eye and went all in—trumped his in every way possible. There was something to respect in that. There was something to *desire* in that.

They drove for a while, much longer than he'd expected, moving south out of Seattle until they hit I-5 through a tunnel of greenery headed for the coast. The freeway winds whipped around them with a forceful, frigid hand, and it didn't take long for his entire body to numb to the constant pressure and cold.

He welcomed the feeling. One of the reasons he loved this bike—why he missed his Cessna so much—was the way the thrill of speed soothed him. No thoughts other than what lay before him on the stretch of road entered his mind, and he didn't have to play a role. Not son, not brother, not lover, not anything.

It was just him, and he was enough. That was a feeling he didn't get to experience very often.

They hit Aberdeen, a small coastal logging town, as the sun began to set over Gray's Harbor. It was one of the duller sunsets Asprey had seen in a while, dark and muted with the bulbous clouds that signaled an oncoming storm.

He thought they were headed for the city center, but Poppy gave him a few more signals, leading them past the populated area and into one of the more rural settings just north of town. The houses grew fewer and farther between, the leafy undergrowth taking over the empty spaces, until they finally stopped in front of a long, winding dirt road that led up into a wall of evergreen trees.

Poppy dismounted quickly, ripping off the helmet and shaking her head. Before Asprey could offer to help, she yanked at her wig, sending hairpins flying in all directions.

"We should have stopped along the way so I could take this thing off," she offered by way of explanation as she tossed the hair into her bag. "Wearing it feels like someone is trying to shove my brain in a jar."

"Here. Let me." Asprey reached up and began extracting the remaining pins—dozens of them, it looked like, picking them off one by one and tucking them into his pocket. When he was sure they were all out, he moved his hands gently through her hair—her natural hair, those dark, loopy curls that ran through his fingers like silk.

She let out a low moan. "Let me guess—scalp massage was part of your advanced Eastern training?"

He let out a chuckle, the intimacy of the moment catching him off guard. "Nope. General life training."

"I see." She stepped away. "Lots of experience helping women to relax?"

Shoot. That wasn't what he meant. He just knew what it was like to feel trapped in a vise, pressured on all sides. But it was too late to retract so he just smiled good-naturedly. "Any time you want a personal demonstration, just ask."

"I'll keep that in mind," she said drily. "So...you want to see where I learned to fight?"

He perked up. "Here? In the middle of the woods? Please tell me there's a hidden cave and a secret ninja brotherhood. I'll give you anything you want if there's a secret brotherhood."

She laughed and shook her head, her hair regaining a little bounce with each movement. "I think you watch too many action movies. This is Aberdeen, not some Tibetan refuge. Come on. I'll show you."

On foot, they wound up a long driveway about a quarter of a mile in length, the deepening dusk making it difficult to discern any details other than lush greenery in all directions. Asprey would never have admitted it out loud, but there was a moment when he realized this would be the perfect place for her to lure wealthy, unsuspecting marks to be tied up and ransomed.

The possibility that Graff might be right—that Poppy was indeed playing a game so twisted it was impossible for a guy like Asprey to see his way out of it—settled uncomfortably in the air, blanketing him as much as the darkness.

He fought it. Asprey might not have Graff's natural leadership abilities and innate sense of justice, and he might not be as valuable in a heist as someone with Tiffany's computer skills, but he wasn't an idiot. He knew people, and, more specifically, he knew Poppy.

Or he was trying to, anyway.

The line of trees broke to reveal a crumbling house slumped in the distance, the rustic décor set with an overgrown yard and a broken-down car in the dirt driveway. It had obviously never been a grand building, as evidenced by the decaying boards of negligible quality, and the roof, which sagged under layers of moss and poor craftsmanship. But there was an underlying charm to it just the same, like x-raying a mediocre painting to reveal a masterpiece underneath.

Poppy took a deep breath. "Here it is. The secret ninja training center."

"You're right. That isn't at all like the movies. I expected there to be at least one giant stone staircase for me to run up."

"To where? The top of that hill?"

"No," he corrected her with a grin. "To a wise old man who smells like incense and has the answer to the question buried deep inside my heart."

She snorted and cast an incredulous look at him over her shoulder, playing along. "When you find out what that is, I'd love to hear it."

He paused, watching her. Poppy's brown eyes were warm and expressive, miles from what he expected of someone with a criminal record. Her crooked smile made it even harder to believe she possessed the ability to knock a man flat.

Or did it?

"Sometimes," he said simply, "I think I might already know."

Her smile faded, and she quickly turned away. "You're only looking at the outside," she said. Asprey couldn't tell whether they were still talking about the metaphoric wise man or the house. Or her.

"Am I?"

"Of course." She snapped right back into Poppy mode, efficient and cool, and thumbed at the house. "The real training ground is out back. I used to spend quite a bit of time inside there, though."

"Does that mean I get the grand tour?"

"Ew—no way. It's a local hangout for teenage kids, probably full of discarded condoms and used needles and a dead body or two. I haven't gone inside in years."

"Sounds lovely."

"You're in the backwoods of Aberdeen. This is as good as it gets." She nodded toward the side of the house. "Come on. I'll show you around the back."

If the front of the house was in disrepair, the back was even worse, with decades of undergrowth taking over what must have once been a serviceable porch. Again, the underlying appeal was there, what with the breathtaking views of the trees set against the deepening twilight sky in a one-hundred-and-eighty-degree rotation. Poppy brought his notice to the ground as she pointed out a huge concrete hole in the shape of an Olympic-sized pool.

Into which she promptly dived.

Okay, she didn't exactly dive—it was more of a jump, but Asprey was still taken aback. He got closer to the edge and peered in. It was exactly what one would expect from an empty, decaying swimming pool, cracked and dirty, with huge chunks of concrete broken off the edges. But the area had also been recently cleared of debris, and there were spatters of rust near the drain in the center, which didn't showcase the usual collection of leaves and dead things.

Poppy shrugged out of her jacket and tossed it up onto the pool's edge, shaking her limbs and falling into a fighter's stance. "Welcome to the Pit. Hands up."

Asprey laughed for a few seconds before he realized she wasn't smiling back. Once again, he tamped down the niggling voice telling him that Graff was right about Poppy and her true motivations. He wondered if that feeling would ever go away—if he would ever be able to let go and truly trust this woman.

"You want me to get in there and fight you?" he asked warily.

"Calm down, Asprey. I'm not going to take advantage of you." Was it his imagination, or was there a note of disappointment in her voice? "You wanted to know where I came from. Well, this is it. No ninjas. No secret brotherhood. Just a bunch of lower-class kids with too much time and aggression on their hands—and not nearly enough adult supervision. Throw in a few cage-fighting DVDs we stole from the video store in town and this is what you get. Me."

As if on cue, the clouds overhead broke open, dumping huge splatters of rain on them both. The rust, which Asprey suspected now might actually be blood, swirled before beginning to move down the drain. He lowered himself to the pool's shallow end, taking it all in.

"It's gruesome. Kind of like the Colosseum at Rome."

"A fight to the death." She paused thoughtfully. "That's not too far off. I broke a total of three bones in the Pit. Lost my virginity here too."

"Not at the same time, I hope."

She laughed. "No one would have dared. I was a fast learner."

"So...are you some sort of mixed martial arts specialist?" he asked, not moving as the rain dripped down his face, obscuring his vision. That would explain the *MMA* magazine subscription—as well as his inability to stand his ground whenever she was around.

"Not even close. You've watched me teach yoga, seen me deep in the con—I know a few basic principles, and the rest I make up as I go." She shrugged, but it wasn't quite the nonchalant brush-off she was obviously going for. "I never learned how to learn. I just *do* things."

Asprey wasn't sure what came next. When he'd asked Poppy where she learned to fight, he'd expected a flippant reply about prison weight rooms, maybe a website address for a Jiu-Jitsu class somewhere in the Greater Seattle area. Not this. Not an intimate slice of her past.

It wasn't that he couldn't handle the truth. He just wasn't prepared for it.

"Is this the point where you school me in the ways of the street?" Asprey asked, only partially kidding.

"It probably wouldn't hurt you to have a few lessons," she admitted, wiping some of the rain from her mouth and leaving a grin in its place. "You know, in case you need to take down a rogue woman in the middle of a necklace robbery."

"Oh yeah?" Asprey was more amused than annoyed. He was man enough to admit that he preferred peace to combat. Graff and Winston were the fighters in the family, always grappling when they were younger, an assortment of black eyes between the two of them as they fought over things that mattered to no one but them. They could have that dubious honor all to themselves. Asprey had learned early on that it was just as effective to diffuse a tense situation with humor as it was with his fists. "What would you teach me?"

She cocked her head and studied him. Asprey did his best not to move or breathe or otherwise mar her appreciation of what she saw. The rain was doing wonders for her—her sports-bra top clung even tighter to her breasts, the outline of her nipples too taut and conspicuous to ignore. Even her yoga pants seemed to grip tighter, clinging to the curve of her hips as though they might slide off if they let go for a second.

Vanity compelled him to hope he stood up just as well to her scrutiny, though he doubted such a thing was possible.

"You have unnaturally long limbs," she finally said.

That wasn't exactly the approval he'd been going for. "Thank you?"

She laughed and dropped into a fighter's stance, legs spread with one in front of the other and hands in fists at chin level. "That's a good thing—it means you can use reach to your advantage. If you do it right, reach can be better than strength."

"Are you saying I don't have any strength?" he asked playfully, mimicking her movements.

"I saw you showing off at yoga today. Don't worry. I'm appropriately in awe of your physique."

"That's better. Now what?"

"A sweep kick. You'll like that one—it's showy. Turn on your front foot so that you face your opponent, and then drop like this." She twisted her body around and fell into a squat, bringing one hand down to stabilize her body, the other reaching under her right leg.

He knew Poppy was flexible—the yoga class had pretty much confirmed that suspicion and provided him with enough fuel to fantasize for a lifetime. But the way she bent and twisted now? She was practically a contortionist, all bendy and open limbs. Despite the rain, Asprey's mouth went dry.

"Then put all your weight on your right leg, push the left one out and pivot." She demonstrated the move, her leg sweeping a wide arc before she rose effortlessly to her feet again and bounced back into fighting stance. "See? It's easy. Try it."

He did, and, as promised, the move was fairly simple, though it felt a bit like break dancing. He wore his regular clothes, so he didn't sweep nearly as fast as she did, and his hand slipped on the wet concrete once or twice, but it wasn't all that different from a squatting yoga position, except that his goal was to maim.

"You're a natural," she said, watching him. He expected her to be smiling, but her face had taken on an intent look, and she licked her lips as he stretched his arms up, preparing to do it again.

He paused, lowering his arms with infinite slowness, sucking in a sharp breath when her eyes shot down to the line where stomach met the waistband of his jeans. He *knew* that look. He felt it down to his cock.

"We should do a defense technique too," she said, her voice coming as if from the end of a long a tunnel. "So you can throw off your attacker long enough to flee."

"That's what you think of me?" Asprey asked, his own voice raspy and low. "My only hope of survival against you is to run away?"

In retrospect, Asprey should have been prepared for it. They stood, after all, just a few feet from each other in a rain-slicked pit that had probably seen its share of loose teeth and looser morals. But the strangely confiding atmosphere of the moment caught him off guard, and Poppy had his feet out from under him before he had a chance to do more than notice a blur of movement as she closed the gap between them.

He hit the ground with a thud, his back flat, his lungs sucked free of air. There was probably pain involved, but all he noticed was the sudden lack of everything. He lost focus and the ability to breathe, the sensation of both the cold and the wet. All that remained was a supremely freeing sense of nothing.

"See?" Poppy's face appeared above him. Sensation came roaring back then, primarily because she straddled him, her hands pinning his arms to the ground, her thighs clamped on either side of his body. "You don't have a chance of escape now."

A small part of him—the proud, manful part—wanted to show her just how wrong she was. Even though he wasn't a fighter by nature and she seemed trained to kill, he wasn't weak. He'd been in this position enough times in his life to know that he could flip her expertly beneath him, take all the strength of her and reduce it to a feminine pliancy.

Not because he was a man and she was a woman, but because he began to suspect that her toughness was a kind of protection. Some women hid behind outrageous flirtation or a succession of crappy boyfriends. Others, like Tiffany, immersed themselves in an alternate universe made up of complex layers of code. Poppy's cover seemed rooted in this strange, archaic place, where past battles had to do with a lot more than the outcome of a single fight.

"Why would I want to escape this?" Asprey asked, meaning it. The rain sluiced down Poppy's face, dripping over her upper body, which had to be freezing. Her nipples, outlined and erect, seemed to agree with him. "I already told you my safe word—and I'm nowhere close to needing it yet. I trust you, Poppy."

She leaned in, her lower half pressing more firmly into his groin as her lips came perilously close to his own. Asprey bit back a groan. "You shouldn't," she murmured. Her eyes searched his, but he didn't know what they were looking for. "I'm strong, Asprey, in more ways than you realize. You and your family might have tons of disposable cash, and I might stand in your debt right now, but in a fight—fair or otherwise—I'll always come out ahead. You need to know that."

"Is that a threat or a promise?"

"It's both."

A drop of rainwater collected on her lower lip, and it fell to Asprey's waiting mouth, tasting of the sky. For one long, tense moment, neither one of them moved or breathed, the whole world suspended until an overhead rumble of thunder signaled a kind of starting bell.

Their lips met then, in a furious kiss that Asprey seemed unable to control. There was no finesse about it, no sign of the gentle seduction he normally enjoyed when kissing a woman. She released none of the strength of her grip on his arms as his tongue swept into her mouth, and she ground her hips into his even harder when he refused to reduce any of the urgency.

Poppy might have him pinned to the ground, and the kiss was hers to initiate or break off as she chose, but Asprey yielded nothing.

The kiss continued with that kind of strength much longer than Asprey thought possible, none of the passion spent as she eventually let up her hold on his biceps. The freedom meant he could wind his arms around her body, pull her so close she almost completely protected him from the heavy drops of rain. One hand made its way to the back of her head, forcing her to stay close—to stay his.

The thunder once again rumbled its timeless warning. And once again, they both heeded its call. The abruptness with which they separated was almost painful, leaving him feeling oddly bereft. Still, she remained on top of him, looking down as if waiting for him to respond.

"So," he said, unable to resist the pleading look in her eyes. They begged him to make this normal, to make this okay. "Lost your virginity here, eh?"

It was the right thing to say. With the same strangled laugh that only he seemed able to elicit, she swatted playfully at his head, which he covered with his hands. She swung her leg over him and helped him to his feet. They were both drenched from head to toe, clothes and hair slicked to the skin. "Don't get any funny ideas. It wasn't my most glamorous moment."

"The first time is always unglamorous," Asprey protested, glad they were back to normal footing. Well, normal-*ish*. There was no way to undo a kiss like that. "It's one of the cardinal rules."

"You think so?" Poppy leaped nimbly up the side of the pit, watching with a smirk as he struggled to do the same. He got up, but not nimbly, the edges slippery in the rain. "Where did you lose yours?"

"Not too much of a departure from this, actually. It was at a pool house with Mrs. Garrison, my friend Peter's mom. We spent the whole summer doing cannonballs into a pool about the size of this one, Mrs. Garrison watching from her chaise lounge in this tiny gold-and-black bikini." He paused. "Do you know, I don't even remember her first name? She was always Mrs. Garrison. Before, after...*during*."

"That's disgusting on so many levels."

"You're freezing." He scooped up their jackets, but they were logged with water and cold to the touch. With a glance at the decrepit house, he said, "Do we brave it?"

She shook her head firmly and looked at the house with a kind of loathing that made Asprey long to take her in his arms. "No. Absolutely not. I'd rather die a long and painful death of pneumonia than ever set foot inside there again."

The path leading back to the motorcycle was slippery and muddied, and more than once, Poppy reached out to grab Asprey's arm to keep from falling flat on her face. He was happy to be her support—if only for the brief moments of weakness she allowed herself.

"I'm not sure we can ride very far," he said doubtfully, surveying the road as they approached. "If we don't slide off into the wooded abyss, we run the risk of turning into human popsicles after about five minutes with this weather and these jackets."

Poppy frowned as she followed the line of the road, one side leading back to the semi-civilization of Aberdeen, the other going farther up into the wilderness, where bears and hypothermia awaited.

"When I was a kid, there was a bed-and-breakfast about two miles up the road. The lady who ran the place used to call the cops on us at least three times a week."

At the mention of a bed and food, Asprey felt the full effects of their current state of exposure. It was cold and wet and only growing more so by the second. "You think it's still there?"

Poppy wrapped her arms around her midsection, hands rubbing her exposed forearms. "I think it's worth a shot."

He tossed her the jacket and helmet. "Then suck it up and hold on tight."

Chapter Fifteen

"Are you here for the Chaucer-Jones wedding?" The woman at the counter looked over the top of her glasses at them, one eyebrow raised in disbelief. She had the worn, kindly look of a grandmother, but Poppy recognized her and knew she was nothing of the sort. Well, she was probably a grandmother, but not a kindly one. More than once, she'd tramped through the forest toward the Pit with a shotgun, shouting statistics about how likely the police would be to believe she'd mistaken a juvenile delinquent for a black bear.

Poppy squirmed in her too-wet, too-revealing clothes. "No. We just need a room. Two rooms," she hastily amended, refusing to look at Asprey. She'd already made the mistake of following him into the B&B. There wasn't a dry patch of him left. Even though he wore his signature layers of preppy clothing, it wasn't difficult to make out each twitch of muscle under his clothes, his dark jeans heavy enough to hang a bit lower on his hips than they normally did. When he'd leaned in to help her off the motorcycle, she could actually see the line of his tan, where golden skin met the chalky whiteness of an ass whose rounded deliciousness she couldn't stop imagining between her teeth.

She took a deep breath and forced herself to think beyond the body to the meaning below the surface. People in Seattle did not have tans. Asprey Charles, the thieving playboy son of a renowned art appraiser, probably got his sun-kissed glow from jet-setting around the globe on someone else's dime.

That tan line drew more than boundaries in the skin—it separated worlds.

"Unless you're with the wedding party, you're out of luck." The woman—Norma, she remembered now—tapped at her keyboard, though Poppy was pretty sure she gleefully pushed random letters. "They've booked through the weekend. Such a nice young couple." She stared harder at Poppy, who quickly turned her head to avoid recognition, though she was a far cry from the gangly semi-Goth teen she'd once been. "He's a doctor, and she works in interior design. Isn't that lovely?"

Poppy opened her mouth to voice her opinions on interior design as a profession, which in her eyes was almost as bad as being a con artist, but Asprey placed a hand on the small of her back to nudge her out of the way.

She sucked in a sharp breath. What was it with him and that spot? He had to be doing it on purpose—had to be willfully sapping her of her resolve to keep him at an arm's length. *Remember the rules, Poppy. Never get involved.*

"I can't tell you how much we'd appreciate it if you could find a place to squeeze us in." Asprey clicked easily into smooth-talker mode even with his soaking wet, muddied clothes and their leather jackets hanging over one arm. Poppy might have been amused if she wasn't so freaking distracted by his hand. "I know we look like drowned rats, but we got caught on our motorcycle tour of the coast, and could really use some shelter from the storm."

Norma sniffed loudly. "And if we weren't hosting a wedding this weekend, I'm sure I'd be delighted to accommodate you. You understand. *Dr.* Chaucer and Miss Jones have requested a private party."

"Oh, we'll keep things private, I promise." Out of the corner of her eye, Poppy saw Asprey wink. What was it with that man and winking? "Surely you have a bat-room hiding around here somewhere. I'd be happy to pay for the privilege of using it."

"Bat-room?" Norma's look of disdain only deepened.

Asprey let go of Poppy then, freeing her from the naughty-doe-in-the-headlights position she'd been stuck in. He leaned on the counter, a lock of his dark hair falling into his eye. He couldn't have oozed sex appeal any harder if he tried.

"It's not as strange as it sounds," he said, flashing his signature smile—the one plastered on a hundred Internet photos. "A friend and I once rode our motorcycles up through Glacier National Park—it's an incredible trip if you ever get the chance—and we got caught in a storm just like this one. The only place to stay was this big, old hotel with no vacancies left."

"Except the bat-room?" Norma guessed. There was a definite thawing going on over at the other side of the counter. Asprey was using his powers for good. For once.

"Exactly!" Asprey cried. "Apparently, there's this small opening in the side of the building where bats get in and nest. They never used the room right next to it, since the little buggers fly in and out all night long—sounds like you're sleeping on a bed of newspapers. No matter how many barriers or traps they put up, the bats always come back. They like it there, and they've become something of a fixture."

Norma smiled. *Smiled,* for crying out loud. "We don't have any bats up here, mind you. Skunks on the rare occasion, but if there's one thing we know, it's how to get rid of pests."

Easy for Norma to say. She never had to deal with one like Asprey before.

Asprey put his hand over Norma's. "I think I'm going to like what you say next."

She let out a sigh they all knew was just for show, and this time when she typed, she pushed actual buttons. "It used to be the woodshed, so don't expect anything too grand. We had it made up into a cozy room when my husband's mother, may she rest in peace, came to live with us."

Asprey beamed. "You're an angel."

"I'll have to bring your breakfast to you in the morning, so you don't get in the good doctor's way. There's no shower or bath in there—just a toilet and sink, and you have to be careful of the hooks in the walls. And there's only one full-sized bed, but I'd avoid the right side if I were you."

"It sounds perfect. I'll pay double," Asprey promised. "And I don't want to hear any objections."

Poppy had an objection—she had several of them, actually, almost all of which stemmed from her dislike of being cast aside while decisions were made for her. But Asprey must have anticipated her mood, because he moved in front of her, effectively shutting her off from Norma's view as he whipped out a credit card and chatted about airline mileage plans.

"What do you think you're doing?" Poppy hissed after Norma drew them a quick map to what sounded like a miniature murder-house.

"My first objective was to find us someplace dry and warm," he returned, lifting a hand. She ducked and weaved out of the way before he could get it near her lower back. "Then I was thinking food."

She stalked a good three feet ahead of him, following a series of circular path stones into the darkness. "Maybe I don't want to share a room with you—did you ever think of that? And I'm paying for my half."

He laughed and jogged to catch up. Thankfully, he'd tucked his hands in his pockets, so there was no imminent danger of an x-spot landing. "You're worried about giving me a hundred bucks? I don't know if you remember, but you're currently in the hole to the Charles family to the tune of around thirty-two thousand dollars."

She whirled. "That's kind of a crappy thing to rub in my face right now. When we finish the job, we'll be more than even—I'll make sure you and your family get your fair share of the takings. Unlike some people, I have principles."

"You think I'm worried about my principles?" Asprey let out a soft laugh. "I passed caring about that long before I ever became a thief. You're going to have to do better if you want to insult me."

"A miserable thief," she added helpfully.

He bowed his head. "Of course." Then, "I think it's right through here." He let out a low whistle as the woodshed came into view.

Poppy couldn't help a laugh from escaping as she peered over Asprey's shoulder, inhaling the scent of him—rain and leather and the subtle mint of whatever shampoo he used.

"She's got that entire house full of rooms and *this* is where she stashed her mother-in-law? Norma's worse than I remember."

He turned, their lips a fraction of an inch apart as they came face-to-face. Poppy did her best not to move, not to let him know how much it affected her.

But it did affect her—even more since she'd brought him to this place, where memories loomed larger than life. She hadn't been to Aberdeen since her release.

She hadn't expected to ever come back.

Just as she was about to lean in, he reached around her to open the door to the shed, which wasn't even locked to protect against invaders. One look at the interior and it wasn't hard to see why. You'd have to be pretty desperate to call a place like this home.

As Asprey's hand came away from the door, he pulled it across her lower back, fingers dragging and lingering. She shivered. *Desperate.* That seemed about right.

But if he noticed the effect he had on her, he didn't let on. He flipped on the lights, illuminating layers of dust, the basic details of a bare-bones hotel room and, as Norma had promised, about two dozen coat hooks hanging off the walls in a haphazard pattern.

"What do you think the mother-in-law *did* in here?" Asprey asked, taking it all in. He tossed their wet jackets and helmets onto an overstuffed floral chair.

"HolyshitmotherofGod!" Poppy screamed. She leaped a good three feet into the air, not landing until she was safely on top of that chair, her arms wound around Asprey's chest where he stood next to it. "Get it out. Get it out. Get it out."

"What are you freaking out about?" he asked. She wanted to smack the calm right out of him, but he noticed it then, the bundle of mangy white fur and red-devil eyes ambling like it hadn't a care in the world. He twitched a little but didn't lose his footing. "Is that a rat?" He leaned down, taking Poppy with him. "Or that chupacabra you were talking about before?"

Poppy squealed and wrapped one of her legs around him, far too shaky for her own peace of mind. But adrenaline had taken over the rest of her limbs, and instead of turning her into the militant ninja Asprey loved to joke about, she was dissolving into a gooey, feminine mess. "Don't get any closer! It's a possum. It could have rabies."

His laughter rumbled from somewhere deep in his chest, and if Poppy didn't need him as an anchor to keep her from hitting the floor, she'd have let go. "That's the least rabid-looking animal I've ever seen."

She closed her eyes. This wasn't funny. Asprey might have grown up with an oversized mansion and all the vermin of the world a safe distance away, but opossum had been as common as dogs around here. And they *bit*. She'd been only eight years old when it happened, when the neighborhood boys had dared her to pet a stray mom living under her grandma's trailer. It was one of the many initiations that resulted in a trip to the free clinic.

The rabies shots had taken weeks to get over. The memories...they lingered.

"Would you please get it out of here?" she asked, unable to stop a shudder from running through her. "Rats I can do. Jail I can do. Todds and Graffs and Winstons I can do. Opossums I cannot."

Asprey complied, gently disentangling her arms from around his chest and grabbing hold of a ceramic cat that doubled as a bookend. With a quick jab, he waved the cat like it was some sort of lance. The opossum blinked twice before taking the hint and scampering out the still-open door.

Her adrenaline hadn't yet had a chance to fully abate when Asprey turned to confront her, the ceramic cat in one hand, his smirk undeniable. "Your foe has been vanquished, my lady."

"Check under the bed for babies."

"What?"

"If that *thing* has any of its demon spawn under the bed, it'll be back. Trust me."

He stared at her for a full thirty seconds, where she remained safely perched on the chair, as if waiting for the punch line. "I don't know that I'll ever figure you out."

"I'm glad my justifiable fear of rabies-infested vermin amuses you," she countered. "But I will not hesitate to stab one of those coat hooks in your eye if you don't check under that bed."

With a long-suffering and totally fake sigh, Asprey dropped to his stomach, peering under the bed for signs of mammalian life. Poppy used the moment to check out the rest of the room—and definitely *not* the way his ass twitched as he looked this way and that.

In addition to the numerous hooks hanging from the walls, there were several pieces of cat decorations, ranging from ceramic statuettes to framed pictures that looked like they came out of a paint-by-number box. The room was narrow, no more than two Asprey-lengths across, with a quilt-covered bed right in the middle. A single desk stood behind her, holding a ten-inch television, and a door to the back led to what must have been the bathroom.

It wasn't much, and it was dusty, and there were probably opossum droppings in all kinds of awful places. And the only window was a shoebox-sized one next to the bed, looking, from Poppy's current angle, like it had been painted shut.

She couldn't tell what was worse—the lack of exits and open air or the fact that the bed was awfully small. Single-old-lady-living-alone small. Newlywed small.

Asprey leaped to his feet, wiping his hands on his pants, seemingly unconcerned about what kind of sleeping arrangements might exist in this twelve-by-twelve space. "Unless you count about twenty dead beetles, there's no sign of anything approaching life under there. I think we're safe."

He held out a hand to help her down from the chair. Other than a slight wobble to her legs, Poppy felt like she did passably well.

He didn't let go right away, rubbing his thumb along the back of her hand as he asked, "Any other fears I should know about? Snakes? Roller coasters?"

"I'm not keen on the lack of exits in this place," she confessed. Might as well get it out now—in a few hours, she might very well be rocking back and forth in a ball in the corner, broken out in a cold sweat and mumbling incoherencies.

He studied her, his eyes darkening. "We'll sleep with the window open, if that helps. And you can be closest to the door."

He let go and turned his back to her. She thought he was going to leave, but he lifted off his shirt, revealing a lightly muscled back she had a sudden and profound urge to lick.

She whirled around instead, fixating on the pattern of wall hooks. "What are you doing?"

"We have to get out of these wet clothes, fear of tiny spaces and marsupials aside. I don't suppose you have anything dry to wear?"

"I have a ninja sock," she offered.

He snorted. The sound was accompanied by the fall of a zipper, and Poppy's head whirled as she realized he'd removed his pants. Her own pants were soaked well beyond her underwear. *Please let him still be wearing his underwear.*

"I never would have taken you for a prude, either," Asprey said, amusement in his voice. "This trip is turning out to be quite enlightening. Here."

"What?" She turned, just catching sight of seemingly endless expanses of perfectly molded skin, before a quilt fell over her head, smelling of old age and what she swore had to be opossum droppings.

"Undress and wrap in that. It's the best we have under the circumstances. I'll hang our clothes up to dry."

Under cover of the quilt, she wriggled out of her wet clothes, which were already a pain to get in and out of because of their high spandex content. She balled them into a wet, steaming bundle and handed them to Asprey out a fold in the blanket. By the time she was able to get her head out without flashing all her goods, Asprey had tied a towel around his waist and already created some kind of efficient laundry line that strung between two of the hooks using floss, his lithe body moving efficiently, as though he had no idea he was the most beautiful creation in the world.

She loved his chest.

There. She admitted it.

Poppy was a strong, independent woman who had faced her own failings as a human being behind a locked door for two straight years. She'd proven on the ultimate battle ground that she didn't need anyone to hold her up or hold her hand.

But she was still *human*—and that man, with his natural grace and seemingly endless lines of lean, tantalizing flesh—he was something else entirely.

She watched for a minute, flustered and impressed by his easy maneuvering. "You're almost self-sufficient," she said wonderingly. "Like a real person."

"Strange as it seems, I *am* a real person, and you'd be surprised what tricks I know. In addition to India, I also spent time in Thailand, Indonesia and Australia—took the grand Pacific tour. I even did a two-night stint in an island jail in Bali, cots and public urinals and all." He thumped his chest. "Made a man out of me."

The walls swelled and started moving in.

Poppy brushed past him and tried to work the window. Fortunately, the paint had chipped away over the years, and she was able to get it to slide down. Cold air washed over her, and even though she shivered, it was a welcome sensation. She breathed. *In and out. Honest and clear.*

"It just slipped out." Asprey's hand was heavy and warm where it came down on her shoulder, even through the layers of blankets. "I'm sorry. I wasn't thinking when I mentioned Bali."

She shook her head and sniffled. The cold and wet must have been working against her body's immune system already. "It's not a big deal—you don't have to censor yourself for my sake. We should probably get some sleep. I need to be back tomorrow pretty early."

Bea was going to have a heart attack when Poppy didn't come home tonight, and she had a meeting with her parole officer at ten the next morning at a nondescript office full of inspirational posters better suited for corporate drones. Asprey might like to joke about what was probably a misunderstanding over a bag of weed in a Bali customs office, but her reality was a little bit harsher.

And even though the worst of it was behind her, Poppy wasn't exactly free. She couldn't leave the state on a whim or fall into bed with the first handsome face who rented her a ramshackle bed-and-breakfast room in her hometown. All actions had repercussions—even the ones she made with good intentions.

In her life, it seemed to be *especially* for the ones she made with good intentions.

"Where will you sleep?" she added, looking purposefully at the bed. They'd stripped the blankets off, and, true to Norma's warning, the right side of the mattress sagged heavily, and a rust-brown stain extended up from the bottom.

"I don't know," Asprey said carefully. "On the creepy side?"

Before she could stop herself, a laugh escaped. "Don't worry. I'll take it. I've slept in worse places."

"Are we talking about the house by the Pit or jail now?" Asprey's hand wound up the back of her neck, his fingers weaving through her hair. She leaned into him, her eyes closing sleepily, and did her best to ignore the blinking red warning sign in her brain.

"Jail wasn't too bad," she said, aware she was crossing a line but unable to stop herself. "Don't get me wrong—there were definite bad parts. It's a really dehumanizing experience, being put in a tiny room, told when to eat and what to wear. I promised myself when I got out that I'd never let anyone dictate those things to me ever again."

"That explains your odd taste in clothes."

"Watch the judgment, Vest Boy."

His hand moved in a gentle pattern along her spine as Poppy let the quilt fall over her shoulders. She could feel the weight of it on every inch of her skin, the fabric worn and weary, scratching against her nipples as it slipped lower.

"But it's the feeling of being *trapped*—that's what I can't seem to get over. I didn't become a con woman and a pickpocket because I like following other people's rules." She paused, breathing deep. "The point has always been to live my life the way *I* want to—which is exactly what they take away from you the moment the key turns in the lock."

"Yet you're back at it."

In any other situation, those words would have had her back up and fur flying, because they were the words of her parole officer, of Bea, of society. It was hard to be the one person who dared to defy all that.

"I've *tried* being other people," she said. "There were some fairly long stretches when my conscience got the better of me, and I always thought that I could make it, transform the error of my ways and start paying dues to Uncle Sam."

"But no dice?" Asprey's hands moved lower, slipping over her shoulders, continuing to rub a pattern of warm insistence that made her long to stop talking and just *feel*. But the momentum of her confession felt too good to ignore. If she didn't say this now, she wasn't sure she ever could.

"I don't *mean* to be the bad guy," she said. "I know I shouldn't take what isn't mine—believe me, I *know*. But there are so many different shades of right and wrong. No matter how many times they might throw me in jail, no matter how many times I might look in the mirror and wonder what kind of future is out there for a woman like me, I know I'm being true to myself. And in all honesty, I think burying that part of me— pretending she doesn't exist—would be worse than jail."

"Hey." Asprey turned her so that she faced him. His hand came up under her chin, forcing her gaze to meet his. His eyes blazed a vibrant blue. "You do realize you're talking to a guy who's also chosen to walk that shady line? I'm the last person in the world who has the right to judge you for the decisions you've made. Life is messy. Relationships are messy. And the things we do—you and me and Graff and Winston and even Todd—they don't come with a handbook. The best we can do is take each difficult decision as it comes and follow our instincts. And you know what? My instincts tell me that you're a good person. No matter what else happens, you have to believe that."

"So it's all okay? Because *the* Asprey Charles says so?"

"No. It's all okay because *you* say so."

She lifted a hand to his brow and wiped away a lock of hair, tracing the firm lines of his cheek and jaw as her hand trailed lower. "I appreciate the sentiment, but if you want the opinion of a professional, you're better off not being on my side. You're not nearly strong enough and way too pretty to end up in jail. You wouldn't last a day in there."

He pulled her tighter. "You think I'm pretty?"

"I also said not strong enough," she pointed out, her smile lifting.

The humor wasn't reciprocated. In fact, Asprey looked almost angry as he said, "Strength isn't just about being able to take people down, Poppy."

She would never know exactly what Asprey meant by those words, because he chose that moment to lift her up, tilting her mouth to meet his. All of the fight from the kiss in the Pit seemed to have left him, because this one was as gentle as it was strong, and, despite the fact that her body was clammy from the rain, searing in its heat.

As she lifted her hands to pull him closer, the quilt fell to the floor in a heavy slump. Her bare chest hit his, the tips of her nipples flecked with overwhelming sensation as they brushed against the rough smattering of hair on his lovely, perfect chest.

"You're still freezing," he murmured against her mouth, his hands moving over her body, palms flat as if to achieve maximum skin-to-skin ratio. "We should probably pick up that quilt."

"I've always heard the best way to avoid hypothermia is to get a naked body as close to yours as possible," she breathed back, her words interrupted by a series of moans she couldn't seem to control. One of Asprey's palms moved up her belly to cup her breast, his thumb rubbing against the nipple in slow, agonizing circles.

"Feel free." He stepped back and lifted his hands. Bereft of sensation, Poppy used the moment to drink in the sight of him, her eyes greedy as they roamed over the long torso marked with just a hint of musculature and the flat plane of his stomach with its line of dark hair, which dipped to the towel just resting on his hips.

"Do you know," she said slowly. "If we do this, you'll be the first man I've slept with since I got out of jail."

Asprey licked his lips. "Isn't there a name for that?"

"What do you mean?" She trailed her fingers on his skin just above the towel, her whole body responding with a jerk when Asprey sucked in a sharp breath. "Like a freedom fuck?"

He laughed, a sound that got cut short when her hand dipped just below the towel's edge. "I meant something more along the lines of a release party."

"I don't care what we call it, as long as it happens soon." No use pretending this wasn't exactly what she wanted. There would be time tomorrow to regret crossing the line, to pay for her mistakes. Wasn't that what she did? Barreled headfirst into danger, paying the price later?

Impulsivity had its benefits. Her legs quaked and her back arched, her entire body thrumming with pleasure. There was a reason her weaknesses always won.

She tugged at Asprey's towel, whipping it away with something approaching triumph.

Triumph was a good word for it. Asprey's cock leaped at its sudden freedom, the wide, hard lines of it almost too good to be true. It really had been a long time. Too long. *Much* too long. She let out a sigh.

"If you don't stop looking at it and *do* something with the damn thing, I refuse to be responsible for what comes next."

She wasn't sure which one of them moved first. One second, they were little more than two bodies, and the next, they were a whirl of limbs and heat and sensation. They kissed and growled, Asprey's hands roaming in all the right places. But no matter how much time he might spend with his arms wrapped around her or with his hands moving deftly between her legs, Poppy never once lost track of his cock. Pressed against her belly, shifting smoothly through her fingers, a hard promise of things to come—the dull ache in her core yearned for that part of him.

"Please, Asprey, just fuck me," she begged when it became too much. She wasn't a woman given to begging, but there was almost nothing she wouldn't do to feel him inside her.

He shifted only slightly away, bending to retrieve his leather jacket, which had fallen to the floor. "Just a second," he called, fishing in the pocket for a familiar foil square. Even then, she couldn't take her eyes away from him. "Got it."

"I'm not going to question why you're carrying protection in there," she said. "Let me."

She took her time rolling the condom over the length of him. This was always one of her favorite parts, the slow, sensual act of her hands working his length. Her dedication was rewarded with a low groan and Asprey's head tossed back, a man given over wholly to the pleasure of the moment.

The temporary distraction gave her time to back against the wall, where several of the bizarre coat hooks protruded. Using one to secure her leg and two as handholds, she lifted herself off the floor, her body angled to receive him.

"So *that's* what the hooks are for," Asprey said with a low laugh. He might have had more jokes to crack, more observations to make, but they got tossed aside for more urgent matters.

As he slid into her, her body stretching in that familiar and glorious way, she stopped supporting her own body and anchored herself completely to him. She couldn't think of a better place to be. He plunged deep and hard, taking her without apology but with extreme consideration for her satisfaction.

It didn't take long to reach it. In another lifetime, she might have been ashamed for succumbing so easily to a man's ministrations, for taking pleasure with the kind of selfish speed that signaled inexperience. But Asprey felt so good and so right, and his own growl of release came not long after hers.

They took a moment to regain their breath, forehead to forehead, neither one talking but communicating through the pounding of twin pulses. She was the first to break away, sliding through his arms, coming to rest on the floor on unsteady legs.

"I don't feel cold anymore," she said, testing her voice. It still worked.

"No, you really don't," he returned, pressing a soft kiss on her lips.

They fell to the bed in a jumble of limbs and blankets, both of them careful to avoid the creepy spot, choosing instead to wedge their bodies as close as possible on the left side.

"I don't feel hungry anymore either," she murmured, as they nestled into a comfortable spoon, his cock still semi-hard against her backside.

"Eating is overrated," Asprey agreed, biting softly into her neck.

She arched into the graze of his teeth, sure he would leave prints, oddly thrilled at being thus marked.

"If I fall asleep, will you still be here when I wake up?" Asprey's mouth was still buried in her neck as he spoke, his breath a hot whirl against her skin.

"Afraid I'm going to run off in the night with your wallet?" she asked, laughing softly.

"No." Tongue replaced teeth against her neck, and this time when she arched, it was with her whole body. "I'm just afraid you'll run off, period."

She slowly lengthened her right thigh, pressing it between his legs as though she intended to rub and grind and put a man at his ease. As soon as he let out a low, guttural noise that indicated such ease was on its way, she used the lock of her leg to immobilize Asprey's lower half. Caught off guard, he was easy to flip from there.

She ended up on top of him, kneeling on either side of his ass as she forced his face and stomach to the bed. Laughing, she leaned down and laid a series of kisses along his shoulder blades, tracing the lines of his muscles with her teeth and tongue. He tasted of salt and skin and bergamot. "Believe me, Asprey, when I say that if I wanted to run off, there would be nothing you could do to stop me. I told you once—when I play, I play hard. And *I* decide when the game is over."

He angled his head just a little, enough so she could see the damnable smile of self-satisfaction that never seemed to fully disappear from his face. "Could you work my rotator cuff while you're back there? I haven't had time to visit my regular masseuse since you've been around."

Her body shook as she bit back a laugh. How was she supposed to prove her point if he kept making her laugh? "Do you visit her between trips to the manicurist?"

"One should never neglect one's cuticles," he replied primly.

"I bet you exfoliate too." She loosened her legs enough so that he could flip over. When he settled once again between her legs, this time on his back, his dick had become fully erect and pressed insistently against her belly. Grabbing hold of his length, working him gently with her palm, she leaned in and added, "Just so we're clear—I don't date business partners."

A groan escaped his lips. "Is that what this is? A date?"

"No. This is a freedom fuck, remember?"

"Yes, Poppy." He grabbed her free hand and pressed a soft kiss on the palm. "I remember."

When he once again entered her, she was careful to remain on top, working up and down so that she and she alone determined their pace, decided when she would come. She was in charge. She was in control. She called all the shots.

But when she threw her head back and cried, no longer able to resist the insistent pull down, down toward the meeting of their bodies, control was the last thing on her mind.

And that was something she feared even more than being trapped.

Chapter Sixteen

Poppy woke and dressed well before dawn, wakened by the soft sound of Asprey snoring. Such an inconsiderate sound, snoring, yet it fit his personality to a tee. He slept like a child who had spent a long, hard day at play, sprawled out over the entire bed and flush with the heat of his own exhaustion. He lay on his stomach, his naked ass framed by a twist of sheets, his hair adorably rumpled and falling into his fluttering eyelids.

It was a sight that filled her with longing and lust and the feeling that the night before had been a big mistake. She was attached now—not just involved on the job, but *attached*. It didn't get much worse than that.

"Good morning." Asprey rolled over and greeted her with a smile. *Morning person.* She'd forgotten about that. "Did Norma leave us a stack of hot pancakes, as promised?"

Poppy chuckled and tossed a miniature box of Raisin Bran at him. "This is as good as we're getting. She also left us a few packets of instant coffee but nothing to make them with. If we want caffeine, we're going to have to snort it."

He sat up further, undismayed by this news. Fortunately for them both, the sheets fell naturally across his lap, though they didn't do anything to hide the breadth of his chest, naked and gleaming and hairy in all the right places. It was amazing how well-crafted the male form was, she realized as her eyes naturally following the path of his chest hair from its widest point down along the crested planes of his abs to where... She looked away. She was supposed to be *un*attaching herself here, not getting lost forever in promises of the flesh.

Although the glint of humor in Asprey's eyes indicated he hadn't missed her appreciation, he busied himself ripping open the box of cereal and popping a few raisins into his mouth.

"Sit," he said, patting the bed next to him. "Have breakfast with me."

She *was* starving. And they *did* have to ride all the way back to Seattle together. "I kept the Lucky Charms for myself," she admitted, taking a seat near the foot of the bed. In the clear light of day, the creepy side looked even more like the site of a recent murder. "I told you I'm trouble."

"You're right—cereal hogging is kind of a deal-breaker for me. Why are you sitting so far away? I promise not to bite."

"It's not the biting I'm worried about." She held out a blue marshmallow diamond. "It's all that other stuff."

He took the marshmallow from her and offered a sad smile in return. "We're back to where we started, I see. I guess that means it's your turn."

"My turn?"

"At twenty questions. So far, we've each asked two. That means you're up."

"I'm not playing this game with you, Asprey. What's the point?" Other than making things even more complicated than they already were.

"So you can ask me anything you want about our scheme— don't pretend you aren't dying to know why we steal forgeries. I promise to hold nothing back, and I won't tell Graff if you don't."

Curiosity had never been one of her besetting sins before. Sure, she had her vices, most of them bad enough to outweigh any pretense at virtue, but she was generally content to let people be—if they wanted to ruin their lives with drink or sell homemade soap at street fairs or listen to country music, it wasn't her place to critique the choices they made.

Unfortunately, there was no use pretending that the Charles family rulebook wasn't a proverbial carrot dangling constantly overhead.

"Okay." She shifted so that she faced Asprey head-on, even managing to keep her eyes above his waist as she did. "So, I know that Todd's necklace was a fake, and I know you guys stole it for that specific reason. But I don't know why."

Asprey made a buzzer sound. "That was not in the form of a question."

Oh, geez. He was turning it into a game show now. "Fine. Why do you steal forgeries?"

"Because the owners don't know they're fake, and we don't want them to find out. My turn."

Her head spun. "Wait a minute—that's barely even an answer. What do you mean they don't know they're fake? Are you telling me Todd thought he was giving me a real necklace that whole time?" The news hardly made him a prince, but it meant *something.*

Asprey kicked back a handful of cereal before aiming the empty box at the nearby wastebasket, hitting the plastic bag with a neat swish. "The owners don't know, as in they think they're in possession of the genuine article—a belief they continue to hold long after we relieve them of their goods. And yes. Todd had no idea it was fake. That's three questions for me."

"You're cheating!" She jumped off the bed. "Those were follow-up questions."

"It's not my fault you aren't any good at this game. Hand me those coffee packets, will you?"

Poppy tossed them over and made a face, but he didn't eat them in crystal form. Instead, he unfolded himself from the bed and stretched, showing her the finely chiseled cheeks of his ass as he padded into the bathroom to—hopefully—collect his clothes. There was only so much morning nudity a woman could take with only a box of Lucky Charms to keep her mouth busy.

Asprey leaned his head out the doorway. "What's your favorite color?"

"Seriously?" He was doing his questions all wrong again.

"Yes, seriously," he shouted over the sound of running water. "I'd guess teal, but that seems a touch too obvious."

There wasn't anything to do but play along. "It's pink."

His head popped out again. "You're lying."

"I like pink," she insisted. He was going to ask stupid questions and then not believe her when she answered them? "It's pretty, and it makes me think of cotton candy."

When he emerged, it was with his jeans slung low on his hips and his hair slightly dampened, his smile so bright it was unseemly for this hour of the morning. Two ceramic mugs containing what looked like muddied water inside were unseemly too, but lukewarm tap-water coffee was better than nothing. He handed her the mug with a picture of Garfield and an I Hate Mondays logo.

"Pink, huh?" Without spilling a drop of his coffee, he tossed himself onto the bed, his legs extended in front of him and crossed at the ankle, a god on rumpled sheets. She wished he'd put a shirt on. It was distracting. "You're full of delightful surprises. How about this one—if you could travel anywhere in the world, money is no object, where would you go?"

"Well, I can't go anywhere in the world because I'm on parole and probably will be for the next few years. You know—for that crime you refuse to ask me about."

He waved his hand. "Let's pretend you're going with someone who has political connections and can get some of those pesky red tapes waived."

Her heart thudded heavily, and she forced herself to focus on her mug. That wasn't a promise. It was hypothetical. Things like that didn't happen in real life.

"I never really thought about it," she said, buying time while her pulse slowed. Worldwide travel had never been in her playbook before—she dreamed of getting out of Seattle, sure, maybe moving south, a grifter on the run. But if money wasn't an object? "Somewhere I don't speak the language. Lots of open sky. Electrical storms would be a bonus."

"Why wouldn't you want to speak the language?" he asked. "And yes, I'm aware that counts as question three."

She studied the cracks in the ceiling tiles. "I don't know. It seems like a really good way to be alone without being lonely, if that makes any sense. And I get so tired of talking about things all the time. It doesn't accomplish anything."

"Is that a hint?"

She smiled. "No. Just an observation. Now it's my turn. How does stealing forgeries tie in to your family business?"

He released a long sigh. "That's a huge question."

"It's your stupid game."

Asprey must have realized he was trapped, because he set aside his cup and swung his legs off the bed, his body hunched, arms on his knees. He tilted his head to look at her. "The quick and easy answer is that every single thing we've taken—and it's a lot—is insured by Charles Appraisals and Insurance."

Poppy swallowed her mouthful of coffee. A lump in her throat made it oddly difficult. "As in, you guys have to pay out the insurance claim? For things you stole? Things that aren't even real?"

Asprey nodded.

"That doesn't make even the smallest bit of sense."

"No, it doesn't," he agreed. "Neither does turning yourself in to the police for a robbery in which they didn't have a scrap of evidence that pointed to you as the culprit. Did you turn yourself in because you were guilty of the crime, or because you were protecting someone?"

Both those things. All those things. Once again, it was so hard to see her way through the fog of right and wrong. "Yes."

"Just yes?"

"Just yes."

"Okay, Poppy." He got up and wrapped his arms around her, dropping a soft kiss on her hairline. It was undemanding and sweet and the move of someone who was also growing dangerously attached. "Are we done playing for now?"

She nodded. *We're done playing for good.*

Chapter Seventeen

"Is this some kind of joke?" Poppy took a step back, her hands up. "Why would I want to take her home with me? I can barely keep plants alive."

"This is your new best friend," Asprey offered. He unclipped the leash and set the wriggling animal on the ground. "But it's not a her. His name is Gunner."

The scrawny, tufted dog skittered across the cement floor of the hangar, its nails making a louder clacking than Tiffany's endless work at her computer. It was some sort of hairy, ferocious Chihuahua mix, the only dog at the pound small enough to work for their purposes. One look at the tiny thing in its cage, teeth bared and leg poised to launch a urine attack on the first person who dared try to get in, and Asprey had known he was the right dog for Poppy.

"I thought you said you were going to borrow one, not buy one." Poppy tilted her chin up at him and scowled. "I'm not really a long-term commitment sort of a girl. People or pets."

Real subtle, Poppy. That woman had serious intimacy issues—and Asprey would know. It was an accusation leveled at his head more times than he cared to admit. "We can always take him back to the pound when we're done."

Poppy's mouth fell open, her lower lip a testament to her indignation. "You will *not*. You can't let him out of puppy jail just to shove him back in when he's done his job. That's mean—we aren't running a chain gang here."

As if to punctuate her statement, Poppy squatted to the dog's level and extended a hand in greeting. Asprey couldn't help but smile. After her reaction to the opossum, he'd been half hopeful that the sight of another undersized creature would send her catapulting into his arms. Only half hopeful, though. Those brief minutes when she'd wrapped herself around him, begging him to save her, were probably something of an anomaly.

Still, it had been a nice change, being the kind of guy a woman could count on, to have someone believe him dependable and capable and all those other adjectives that had eluded him for years. Not to mention finding out firsthand that there was something in this world that broke down Poppy's ninja façade and allowed a glimpse of her soft, mushy insides. Asprey had a feeling that experience didn't happen very often.

Though he was going to do his damnedest to get a repeat performance.

"I hate dogs," Graff muttered, interrupting the moment with a heavy tread and huge sneeze. He handed Poppy a paper bag of supplies with one hand, holding a tissue to his nose with the other. "Food, water bowl, leash and a ridiculously small toothbrush the lady at the store says is important for oral hygiene. You don't have any cats, do you?"

"No, why?" Poppy looked up from her spot on the floor, where Gunner made wary circles around her. "Are you allergic to those too?"

"Yes, he is," Asprey said. "But he doesn't like to talk about it. He thinks the sniffles are beneath him."

"Apparently, that thing"—Graff let out another sneeze, loud and rumbling—"will attack anything of the feline nature."

"Got it. No cats for my new partner in crime." Poppy got as far as getting her hand under the dog's nose before giving up and getting to her feet. She took the garment bag Asprey held out. "What's this?"

"Your clothes. No offense, but you need to be an uptown professional woman. This should do the trick a whole lot better than..." He paused. How did one glibly describe a bright red halter sundress with yellow polka dots, once again paired with the cowboy boots that wouldn't die? Charming? Strangely irresistible? Hot as all hell? "That."

Poppy ignored him as she peeked in the bag and appraised its contents with cool efficiency. "I'm going to need nylons and pearls too. Also a shoulder bag—big, leather, no knockoffs, please. And sunglasses. Preferably Gucci."

"What are we, a fucking department store? Make it work with what you have." Graff blew his nose into the tissue and stormed off, casting one last, contemptible look at the dog before he went.

"What crawled up his nasal cavity and died?" Poppy asked.

"Graff hates anything warm and fuzzy. It's in his nature. Also—between us? He's nervous." That was a huge understatement, but it was as close as Asprey was going to get to an explanation. Graff didn't like giving up power over anything—especially things as big as the VanHuett job—and he had trust issues growing over the top of it like mold. "Graff likes to share his emotions by making other people feel small. It's his way of showing he cares."

"How noble of him." Poppy rolled her eyes. "But you can tell Graff to relax. I've got skills he's never even heard of."

Asprey knew she was talking about the con, but still, his body reacted. She might be willing to pretend the other night in Aberdeen was a one-time lapse of judgment, and Asprey was willing to play along for now, but that didn't mean the rest of him forgot. His dick had a long memory like that.

"Now, me?" he added. "I show I care by placing complete confidence in my criminal partners." He squatted and put a hand out, intending to give Gunner a pat. The dog bared two vampire-sized fangs and lunged. "If I didn't know any better, I'd swear this dog graduated from the Poppy School of Social Interaction."

"Very funny." Poppy leaned down and scratched behind the dog's ear. Finally sensing her kindred spirit, Gunner promptly fell to the ground, legs up, his tongue slavishly lolling up at her. "Maybe he can smell your ego and takes it personally."

"Egos have a smell?"

"Yep. Smells like Ed Hardy cologne most of the time. Yours has more of a Calvin Klein feel to it."

He laughed, happy to be falling into playful banter. Familiar, neutral territory was better than retreat. "I'd offer to keep Gunner myself, but our personalities are too similar. He thinks I'm the competition."

"Similar how?" She quirked a brow and watched as the dog began to circle the leg of a carved medieval chest—fake, of course—looking for a place to mark. "You both destroy fine art?"

Asprey looked up, his gaze running the length of her leg. And while he appreciated the view, he didn't stop until he reached her smile, which began to falter with the sudden shift in intimacy. "I'd say I'm more of a preservationist at heart. But we do both like *you.*"

She busied herself with pulling the respectable baby blue tweed skirt set from the garment bag. It was upscale and untouchable and not at all what Asprey was coming to associate with Poppy.

"I'm happy to keep the dog," she said. "He might not be very big or very menacing, but he *is* pretty to look at."

Asprey couldn't resist. "And he can probably save you from opossum attacks."

Her laugh escaped in a tumbled breath as she moved toward a screen in the corner of the hangar. It was a silk Chinese affair hand painted with giant red cranes—one of their first jobs, an easy one since it literally fell off a truck when a roadway obstruction they'd set up stopped it en route to the owner's house.

He could see flashes of Poppy's skin as she stripped and did something quick and twisty with her hair. There was enough to whet the appetite as she wriggled and squirmed far more than seemed necessary, the shadowy outline of her ass as she bent almost enough to make him go crashing through the screen to feel it in his hands once more.

"Your new mommy is a tease," he mumbled to the dog.

When she reappeared, Asprey almost started clapping. Gone was Natalie's suggestive swagger; nowhere to be found was Poppy's decisive, athletic step. Lucy Higgenbottom—Tiffany picked the name—with her vintage suit and sleek French twist, adopted the tight, mincing gait of a woman who would rather kiss her dog than a hot-blooded man.

"How do you do that?" he asked wonderingly. "How do you change so easily from one person to another?"

"What?" she asked, looking at her suit as if seeing it for the first time. "They're just clothes—nice ones, I'll admit—but they're only trappings. I feel like the First Lady."

"It's more than that," he said. "The second you change your outfit, it's like you actually become the person inside them. You're not just wearing that suit—you're part of it. No one would mistake you for Natalie right now, even if you added a blonde wig to the mix."

"That's because Natalie relies heavily on manufactured looks. She's a sucker for supportive undergarments—you have no idea how much a good pair of Spanx transforms a woman."

"And Poppy? What makes her the way she is?"

"You've been to the Pit, seen her police record," Poppy said quietly. "You tell me."

Caution warned Asprey against his natural instinct, which was to swoop Poppy into his arms, refusing to let go until she realized that a person was so much more than the sum parts of his or her upbringing. But he had the feeling such obvious tactics would cause immediate—and potentially permanent—damages. "You've been to the house I grew up in, seen me at the offices of Charles Appraisals and Insurance," he finally responded. "Is that all I am?"

She stepped back and took him in, from the top of his head—yes, he was willing to admit, with a little product in his hair—to his feet, which boasted a pair of gray suede dress shoes. His brothers had always called his careful grooming shallow and self-serving, and maybe it was. But if Poppy could be more than teal cowboy boots dreamt of since girlhood, then so could he.

"I guess not."

"Thank you," he replied, although he wasn't exactly sure what he was thanking her for. For agreeing, maybe. For being the first person who didn't laugh him out of the room when he admitted he wanted to be seen as more than a nice pair of shoes. "Now—are we ready to go lure Cindy VanHuett into our trap?"

"I'm ready if you are." Poppy straightened and buttoned up the suit jacket, falling once again into her Lucy Higgenbottom role. She scooped up the dog, not the least bit ruffled when he let out a low growl. "I'm going to use my natural charm and this lovely little guy to earn her trust."

"Yes."

"So we can find a way into her apartment to steal a painting that isn't actually worth anything because it's a forgery."

"Yes."

"That your company will then pay out a huge lump sum to cover, because you are responsible for insuring it."

"Until the end of this month, yes." He nodded firmly. "And just because you aren't phrasing these as questions doesn't mean they don't count."

She ignored him, but he was keeping track. Oh yes—he was keeping track. "Didn't Graff say that painting is worth like ten million dollars or something?"

"Thereabouts."

"I'm no business expert, but won't that kind of damage ruin your company? I know you guys are rich and all, but when thrown on top of all the rest of the thefts, that's an awful lot of money. Wouldn't it make more sense to steal the painting *after* you don't insure it anymore?"

"Yes, it would," he agreed. He was absurdly pleased at how close she was to figuring him out. All the secrets were beginning to chafe. "Yet here we are, getting ready to launch the final stage of our plans."

He could see the last of the pieces clicking into place, her large, expressive eyes growing even larger, her smile crooked and charming even in the Lucy Higgenbottom disguise. "You guys are ruining your own company on purpose."

He gave a slight bow. "And that, Ms. Higgenbottom, is all you're getting out of me today."

Poppy held both dogs by the scruffs of their necks, her arms flung wide. For such tiny animals, the dogs packed a powerful punch as they wriggled and strained to attack, Gunner's teeth bared as he fought to defend his new mistress against a larger foe.

The dog was scrappy. Poppy was already well on her way to liking the little guy, but now? *Love.* Gunner had her back.

"Oh my gosh, I'm so sorry!" the woman, Cindy VanHuett, cried. She clipped forward at the pace perfected by women in tight skirts and high heels, her arms outstretched. "I don't know what got into Jasmine. She's normally so sweet."

Poppy surveyed the yappy puff of fur, which wriggled in its attempt to continue devouring Gunner's flesh, and forced herself to smile. "I'm sure it's just her natural instinct. Say what they will about pit bulls and Rottweilers, there is no dog more loyal to her owner than a Bichon."

Poppy had no idea if that was true or not, but Cindy beamed as if she'd given birth to the creature herself. She gathered up her dog with a coo, soothing it as only a mother could.

Poppy thought about offering the same maternal comforts to Gunner, but his enormous eyes warned her against that kind of emotion. He was full of opinions, that dog. She'd tried putting him in a cute miniature bomber jacket earlier, but he would have none of it. No sooner had she gotten one leg in the tiny, stitched jacket hole than the other three popped out and he let out an almost maniacal bark, daring her to try again.

"It's okay, little man." She set him near a rock instead, which he took a profound interest in circling and smelling. "We'll do it your way."

"I'm Lucy," she said, addressing Cindy and sticking out her hand. "And that down there is Gunner."

"Cindy," the other woman said. She was younger looking than Poppy had expected. According to the eerily detailed dossier Asprey had given her, she was thirty-eight, but in the clear light of day, she had the flawless skin of a much younger woman. It probably had something to do with all the tension holding her together, like her limbs were attached to a demanding puppeteer who kept her in a constant state of readiness. "And my precious is called Jasmine."

"Hello, Jasmine," Poppy said brightly, giving the dog her hand to sniff. It wasn't impressed, watery eyes examining her for flaws and finding plenty.

Knowing that winning over the dog was secondary to winning over the woman, she backed away and offered Cindy an apologetic shrug. "Maybe she doesn't like my scent." She could see Asprey off in the distance, doing a fairly convincing job at watching a pair of blue jays flirting in the trees, and added, "I use a strawberry shampoo I've been told is rather overpowering."

"That's...nice," Cindy said unconvincingly.

Poppy was beginning to see why they brought her on for this job. Cindy VanHuett was a tough nut to crack, and they were looking at a pretty short timeline to build her trust and find a way inside her private residence. If this was *her* mark, she'd have started having these chance meetings weeks ago, made it less obvious that she wanted inside and near that painting, more like a normal relationship between two women with a shared love of tiny canines.

But Cindy wasn't her mark. She was just a pawn in an attempt to bring a century-old, multimillion dollar company to its knees.

What the hell had she gotten herself into?

For the first time, her attraction to Asprey wasn't the biggest problem here. This whole thing screamed of run-away-and-don't-ever-look-back, made her feel like the heroine in a horror movie everyone knows at the outset is going to get killed by the end of the first act.

And if it wasn't for being so close to finishing Todd, she might just do that—run away, offer up a bloodcurdling scream and make her grand exit.

No you wouldn't. You love this.

Cindy frowned as Poppy continued warring with her conscience, so she jumped back into action, peering close to the dog's face and asking, "Oh dear. Is Jasmine supposed to be eating that?"

"What? What is it?" Distracted, Cindy turned the dog to face her, whisking a finger inside the animal's mouth like one of those saving-a-baby-from-choking videos. "Did she swallow it?"

"Here. Let me." Poppy stabilized herself with a hand on Cindy's arm and pretended to examine between the Bichon's teeth, which looked to be in much better repair than most human's.

"Oh, good. It's just a twig." She pretended to flick something to the ground.

The deception worked. Cindy hugged the dog closer and flashed Poppy a grateful smile. The woman wasn't exactly *thawing* to her, exactly, but at least her face wasn't pulled in that unhealthy-looking pinch anymore.

"I'm sure I seem really silly..." Cindy began.

Poppy waved her hand. "Not at all. Gunner once had a gum infection and I had to chew up all his food for him. It's what we parents do."

Too much? Cindy didn't seem to have a reply to that admittedly bizarre statement, and she checked her watch nervously.

"I'm so sorry," Poppy said quickly. She'd done all she could for the time being, and it was better not to overplay her hand at the start. "I'm probably keeping you. Gunner and I just moved in to an apartment across the way, so I foresee quite a bit of this park in our future. Maybe we'll see you around."

"I'd like that," Cindy said slowly. "Have a good day, um, Lucy, right?"

"That's me!" Poppy called brightly. She waved her fingers in a gesture of farewell. "Toodles."

She watched the woman rush away, her head bent over the dog and a hesitant hitch in her step. That woman had enough money to hang a ten-million-dollar painting—albeit one that happened to be a fake—in her apartment, yet she looked a lot less happy in her own skin than anyone Poppy knew.

"Well, Gunner, that wasn't so bad." Poppy let the dog finish investigating his rock before tugging his leash in the opposite direction. "But that woman is going to be harder to soften than Asprey thinks."

She felt for her pocket and smiled. Good thing she always had a back-up plan.

"What was that all about?" Asprey asked later, meeting her at their rendezvous spot. Instead of a sock-puppet vendor, they'd opted for a hot-dog stand on a rotating schedule this time. It was the kind of place no one ever knew how to find in advance, but all it took was a few questions and you could make your way there. The hot dogs were supposedly that good.

Poppy wouldn't know—Gunner had eaten every last bite of hers.

"I thought the plan was to make contact with Cindy," he added. "Not to sic your dog on her."

"Maybe you should have chosen a more personable pet, then," Poppy replied. She tugged on the leash as they rose and began walking a few blocks to the parking lot where they'd left the car. No motorcycle this time—just Graff's sensibly overpriced Lexus. "And relax. I grabbed Cindy's wallet out of her purse. I'll stop by her apartment to return it when you guys are ready to launch the next phase. We'll be BFFs in no time."

Asprey stopped in the middle of the sidewalk, studying her. "That's so simple it's almost genius."

She kept walking. "It's not genius, Asprey. It's one of the oldest cons in the book. A returned wallet—with all the money intact—builds instant trust. It's way more effective than a series of lunch dates and chance meetings walking the dog in the park like you guys had planned, believe me."

He let out a low whistle and shook his head. "I think maybe bringing you onto our team was the smartest thing I've ever done."

Poppy laughed, absurdly pleased by the misdirected compliment. "You won't get an argument from me on that one. But let's not forget—I'm not on your team if I don't know all the facts. Including *why*." Why did their company insure forgeries? And why, unless it was part of their perverse sibling rivalry against Winston, would they try to ruin their own company?

He shoved his hands deep in his pockets and cast her a sidelong look. "It's my turn to ask questions. Remember?"

"Thin-crust pizza with pineapples and green peppers," she announced, resigned. "Chocolate-covered strawberries. Virgo. Yesterday I was a cat person, but Gunner might have changed my mind for good on that one. I can't swim, but I love the ocean. You've seen me around an opossum. What am I missing?"

"I think you know."

She halted. *Damn him.* "The jail situation was complicated, Asprey, and it's not just my story to tell. If it were only me..."

"Then don't tell me." He shrugged and kept walking. "We can go to the ocean instead. And not swim."

But the second she started walking again, she knew it was already too late. Every day spent in this man's company pushed her guard down a few more inches, made her feel a little bit more like an abandoned airport was close to home. She was breaking all the rules. *Worse*—even knowing that trust was the one thing she couldn't afford, she continued to slip further and further under his warm, magnetic, impossibly delicious spell.

Never get involved on the job.

One of these days, she'd be smart enough to take her own advice.

Chapter Eighteen

"Holy shit, Poppy—are you dating an actor?"

"What? No." Poppy watched Asprey, who crouched on the ground jiggling a stuffed bunny to make it look alive, and frowned. Jenny was eating it up, her giggles muffling the conversation she and Bea shared across the room. "Why would you think that?"

"That's the guy, the one you were looking at online a few weeks ago."

Damn. She'd forgotten about that. "Yeah, um, I might have been lying about that."

"Poppy..."

"I know, I know." She raised her hands and shot her friend a beseeching look. "I promised you I wouldn't lie and that we would take some time, just the two of us. But I wasn't ready to talk about him yet. I wasn't ready to talk about jail yet."

One of Bea's brows rose. "And now all of a sudden you are? Because of him?"

Poppy took a deep breath and examined the man in question. He glanced through a fallen piece of hair and smiled at her, and her breath caught before she could finish. Squatting on the dinged apartment floor in part one of a three-piece suit, the glinting watch on his wrist worth more than Poppy's car and all of Bea's worldly possessions combined. On any other man, she'd have called it overdone and ridiculous—but on Asprey? It was just who he was. Money and ease and charm and high-class heists that revolved around painters whose names she could barely pronounce. *Why him? Why now?*

"I'm not sure I have a choice." She softened. She'd already come this far—there was another Grandma Jean maxim for the records. *No use doing something half-assed. Ain't no one attractive with half an ass.* "I know I haven't been a very good friend since I got out of jail, but I'm going to try better, I swear."

"I know why you're afraid to be around here all the time."

Poppy forgot that she'd fallen into the habit of denying Bea's accusations and gave in to the impulse to ask, "You do?"

"Of course. You aren't the only one who had two years of nothing but time to think, Poppy. I know I'll never be able to understand what you went through in there, but it was just as hard for me on the outside, knowing what you'd sacrificed. Even with Jenny to take the edge off."

"I'm so sorry, Bea," Poppy said, her nose feeling tingly and sharp. "I never thought about it that way."

"Don't apologize to me," Bea said sternly. "You have every right to your feelings, and I'm not about to tell you that you have to forgive me or even that you should be able to be my friend again the way we used to be. But you have to confront your loss sometime. If you can't do it with me, then I hope you can find someone who makes it easier." She looked pointedly at Asprey. "That one looks like he might do the trick—a face like his? Good for you."

Poppy laughed softly. Bea always did have a thing for the pretty ones. "He wants to know why I went to jail—and he has this persistence I can't seem to shake off. But I don't want to say anything that will put you and Jenny in danger."

"You trust this guy? He looks like someone we would have used as a punching bag back in high school."

Poppy glanced over again. Asprey lay on his back, his legs in the air, thrashing as Jenny pretended to tickle his stomach. He *would* be good with kids on top of everything else. "I dislocated his arm the day we met."

Bea laughed, a low rumble that Poppy hadn't heard in so long she'd forgotten such a sound existed. "Only you could do that to a guy and turn it into a date, Poppy. Only you."

"Bea used to work the cons with me," Poppy explained, settling at the square dining room table with a mug of tea in her hand. Asprey had one too, but he was a lot less interested in refreshments than he was in hearing what she had to say.

The woman named Bea—the roommate—and her daughter had gone for a walk with Gunner in tow, even when Asprey pressed them to stay. He couldn't imagine anyone walking a kid around in this neighborhood.

But Poppy had just laughed at him. "Bea used to train with me at the Pit, Asprey. We don't intend to set up shop here forever, but for now, she can walk in the broad light of day— especially with Gunner standing guard. I promise."

He took in Bea's attire, which was like Poppy's if she opted for more hardware and leather, and nodded. Women who could hold their own in a street fight were an anomaly where he grew up, but that didn't mean he wasn't growing to like them. A lot.

"She's tough," he offered.

"She has to be," Poppy replied in a steely, defensive tone. "Where we're from, girls have two options in life: learn some street smarts or get knocked up by the first jackass with a compliment dangling from his lips. Forgive us for choosing the former."

"I wasn't judging. I was observing."

She didn't appear convinced, but she wrapped her hands around her mug and continued, her gaze pinpointed somewhere a few feet above Asprey's head.

"It happened about two and a half years ago." Her voice took on a lyrical quality, and Asprey fell into the sound of it. He tried not to appear overeager, but he had never been more curious. Poppy's truth. Her deep, dark secret. "The job was easy enough—we'd recently come across a half dozen baseballs signed by Mickey Mantle. Fakes, of course, but pretty decent ones. I played the girlfriend of a cheating scumbag, selling all my ex-boyfriend's stuff to the first buyer I could find, as is only due a woman crossed."

"Noted," Asprey said with a smile. "Not only can you demolish a guy, but you'll sell all his stuff when he's down."

Her lips lifted at the corner. "He was supposed to be a cheating scumbag. Did you miss that part? Anyway, we had a whole box of convincing stuff. Men's shirts, some Blu-Ray Schwarzenegger movies, cuff links, baseball paraphernalia. I'd run into my target on the street, the box's contents spilling all over the street in the process."

"Of course," Asprey murmured, following along. "At which point your target just happened to notice the signed baseball."

Poppy nodded. "A good, clean con—one of our best. You wouldn't believe how nice the guys got once they realized I was looking to dump the stuff at the first pawn shop I could find. They listened to me rant and cry and rave for as long as I wanted."

This plan was even better than pickpocketing Cindy to build trust—Poppy had a natural eye for this sort of thing. "And immediately offered to buy the whole lot from you for a generous sum, right?"

"Like you wouldn't believe."

"Not one of them thought to give you fair market value or suggest you consult someone first?"

"Of course not. The best cons work because they take advantage of natural greed. Guilty men never press charges. They know they can't."

His criminal knowledge was expanding every minute. "Like Todd and his gambling addiction."

"Exactly."

"So what went wrong?"

She frowned. "We were off on one of the marks. We did a little research first, found guys who carried a lot of cash and were always on the lookout for a bargain, and who knew baseball but weren't fanatic about it. But we got one of them wrong—he wasn't a bad guy, just down on his luck. It turned out the five hundred he offered for the box was a last-ditch effort to turn a quick profit and get his rent covered for the month."

"Sounds like a lesson well learned to me."

"It would have been, if he didn't have a kid."

Oh. "Oh."

"Tell me about it." Poppy released a long sigh and finally looked him head-on. Her eyes had lost most of their sparkle, and there was a firm set to her mouth he hadn't ever seen before. "It was lazy researching on our part, but we were having such easy luck with the con we got careless. Taking that guy's money went against our code."

He raised a brow.

"Give it back if it turns out they need it more than you." She took a deep breath. "It's not much of a code, but it's ours. Once we figured out that the money had to go back, I called the guy up and asked him to meet me. I pretended to want his advice about the breakup, but it was really an attempt to keep him away from home long enough for Bea to break in and trade the baseball for the money he'd paid us. We didn't want to leave a trail."

"It didn't work?"

"Not entirely. The ex-wife had a key to the apartment, and she came in as Bea was going out the window. She caught a glimpse of the license plate as Bea drove away and called the police."

"So Bea was looking at third-degree felony breaking and entering." A minimum two-year sentence.

"Yep."

"Yet you took the fall."

"Yep."

He was about to ask why, but that was when realization struck. It was an uncomfortable sensation, one that made him feel equal parts in awe of her and ashamed of himself. While she was in jail for a five hundred dollar act of kindness, he'd been spending five hundred dollars a day on gasoline for his private plane. "How old is Bea's little girl?"

"Twenty-two months."

He did the math in his head. Two years of jail time plus five months since her release. Subtract nine months of gestation.

"She was two months pregnant when I turned myself in," Poppy said quietly, saving him the trouble.

For what had to be the first time in his life, Asprey was at a loss for words. There were a hundred things he *could* say, things he might offer any other woman on the face of the planet—the soft, fluffy ones who were Virgos and loved pink but who hadn't spent two years paying for a crime that wasn't, in his eyes, much of a crime at all.

"So there you have it." She threw the words at him with something approaching triumph. "We made a mistake, and we both paid for it ten times over."

"I'm sorry," he said simply.

"And that's not the worst part."

He didn't move. There was something worse than two years in jail?

She pushed back from the table. "Give me a minute."

Asprey wasn't sure what he expected when she returned from the back of the apartment—if maybe an orange jumpsuit or leg shackles or a mug shot would have been less surprising than the small plywood box she placed unceremoniously on the table. When she didn't say anything or move to sit down, he assumed he was supposed to lift the lid.

"I wouldn't," she warned. "It's my grandma."

He pulled his hand away as if burned. "You keep your grandma in a box?"

She smiled tightly. "Until I have the money to make alternate arrangements, yes. We don't all get limos and black hearses and front-page obituaries, you know. A wooden box— *this* wooden box—is the only option when your last living relative is in jail and you've invested every penny you have with a scam artist who preys on the elderly. Grandma Jean was lucky to get this."

Todd Kennick.

She sat, leaving the box there, glancing at it with a mixture of loathing and sadness. "This is life and death, Asprey, the way it exists down here in the real world. But you wouldn't have any idea about that, would you?"

She might as well have launched herself across the room and pulled his shoulder out of its socket again. He almost wished she *had*—that pain, the searing, physical kind with a beginning and an end—was something he knew how to handle, had experience handling with regard to this woman in particular.

"I never thought I'd see you without a smart-ass comment, Asprey," she added, a cold smile playing on her lips. "I guess I've finally shocked you with my sordid past. I was beginning to think that wasn't possible."

"No." He let the word sit there a moment.

Her smile faltered. "No?"

"No," he repeated firmly. "You haven't shocked me."

"If you could see your face right now, you might be willing to rephrase that statement."

"This isn't shock, Poppy." Was she being this obtuse on purpose? "I'm sorry that your grandmother died. I'm even more sorry that Todd took advantage of her—and that you have to go to such lengths to get her money back."

If anything, the knowledge only served to make her more appealing. She'd once said this whole thing was a mission of justice, and all he could think now was *good for you*. It would take a lot more than a few years in jail to stop this woman from doing what she felt was right.

"Thank you," she replied.

"I'm not done yet." Asprey leaned over the table and didn't speak until her eyes met his. "I will do everything in my power to help you vindicate your grandmother, and I'll do it with a smile. But if you think having a limo and black hearses and front-page obituaries make death any less painful, you're not only being stupid, you're being mean."

She shot up from the table, her hands gripping the edge of the yellow Formica. "Excuse me?"

"That's what you were trying to say here, wasn't it?" He gestured at the box. "That I can't possibly know what that sort of loss feels like because I have money? That the regular human emotions driving you to act don't apply to my kind? You know what that makes you, right?"

"Don't you dare say it."

He dared. "A snob, Poppy. You're a snob. The moment we met, you took one look at my clothes and my lifestyle and decided you know exactly who I am. A piece of society fluff. An easygoing rich boy who's only up for a good time." He laughed bitterly. It was all coming out now. "Of all the people in my life, I thought *you* would understand."

A man like him couldn't possibly know what it was like to struggle. Silver spoons and Cessna planes rendered him useless for any function but decoration. It was the same story he'd heard his whole life, but this time, the storyteller had the potential to crush him. And she didn't seem to care.

"Oh, I understand, all right." Poppy crossed her arms. "You talk big, but your vision of the world is filtered through the huge, rose-colored bubble where you live—where you've always lived. As soon as this job ends, I'm going to bury my grandmother and go back to being an ex-felon with no prospects, and you're going to...what? Stay in the hangar with Graff forever? Take over Winston's house and drink espresso all day long? Roll around on your bed with millions of dollars and a bevy of well-bred socialites? I'm a criminal, Asprey. I've always been one and, despite promises to Bea and my parole officer, I'll most likely stay one. And you..."

"I'm just a playboy millionaire who will never amount to anything?" he offered, finishing her statement. "Is that it?"

"If the shoe fits," she replied. Her lips curved in a humorless smile. "I'm glad I finally gave in and told you about Grandma Jean. I thought it would make things clearer between us, and it has. It's high time we both see this thing for what it really is."

His chest grew tight. "And what is it?"

"A business relationship. A means to an end. Nothing more." She nodded toward the door. "And I think it's best that we treat it that way from here on out. See you at the hangar tomorrow, Asprey. It's been fun."

There didn't seem to be anything left to say.

Asprey grabbed his keys and moved to the door, but there were about eight locks and he couldn't figure out the pattern to get the damn thing open. Wordlessly, Poppy came up behind him, expertly flipping each one. She lingered so close he could feel the warmth of her breath on his neck.

But it wasn't close enough.

Chapter Nineteen

"We need to shift the timetables." Graff strode into the hangar apartment with his chest out and his frown on. "Can you get Poppy to postpone the poker game with Todd and work on Cindy this afternoon instead?"

Asprey looked up from his bowl of Frosted Flakes and jabbed his spoon at Graff. Great. Graff was on his high horse, Poppy had pretty much slammed the door behind him yesterday, and no one seemed to notice or care that Asprey still existed. It was going to be a hell of a day. "Good morning to you too. I see the sun has risen up your ass this fine June morning."

"Save it, Asprey. You were right about the VanHuett job."

Asprey almost dropped his spoon into his milk. Had his brother just told him he was right about something? He cupped his ear with one hand. "I'm sorry—can you repeat that last bit? My brain must be playing a trick on me."

"Very funny." Graff fell into the chair on the other side of the massage table, a hand to the bridge of his nose. "That guy you saw coming in and out of Cindy's apartment a few weeks ago? I had Tiffany do a check, and it turns out he works for Winston."

"Winston's on to us?"

"Not us." Graff shook his head forcefully. "But he obviously knows the painting is our last target, and he posted the guard to prevent us from getting in before the policy expires. We're going to have to get Poppy in there as soon as we can—we're running out of time, and increased security is only going to make it harder to get in."

Asprey let out a low whistle. "I guess that means it was a good thing I took the time to watch Cindy's apartment, huh? I told you it's dangerous to rely on data alone. Why—you'd almost think I know what I'm doing, sitting outside all day pretending to watch birds."

"Are you done?"

"I will be once you tell me I'm right again."

Graff grunted. "Don't push your luck."

"You should go lie down."

Graff's eyelid twitched.

"I mean it." Asprey resumed his breakfast with a cheerful aplomb he was far from feeling. "If you don't take it easy, you're going to get one of your migraines—and it's not going to do us any good if you're throwing up in bed, pretending to be fine."

"I'm glad it's that easy for you to sleep at night," Graff responded through dangerously thin lips. "But forgive me if I can't fall into the dreams of a baby each time my head hits the pillow like you can. Between trying to find a way inside Cindy's apartment building and the extra plans I have for Todd…"

That was new. Asprey nudged his brother's leg under the table. "What are you talking about? I thought we had things all settled for the Todd situation. It's just supposed to be one more poker game. We cheat and take him for the full hundred-thousand buy-in, recouping Poppy's money and ours in one fell swoop. And then the world is right again."

"See? That's what I mean," Graff said. "You think everything is that simple—that a few dollars thrown at the right problem will guarantee happiness. When will you learn that things are more complicated than they look on the surface?"

"I don't think that," Asprey said, his voice low. He pushed his bowl away, no longer hungry. "And if you want Poppy to put her job aside, you talk to her. I'm tired of doing everything you demand just because you demand it."

Graff looked up sharply. "What's your problem today?"

"Nothing," he lied. "But if you're going to barge in and change the game plan with Todd, I think it's something we all need to sit down and discuss."

"It's not important." Graff got up from the table and pointed a warning finger at Asprey. "But since you're being so stubborn, I'll get Poppy to switch her appointments. I'll pick up the slack, like I always do."

"Oh yeah," Asprey muttered. "*You're* the one doing the heavy lifting around here."

Graff ignored him. "Don't quit on me now, Asprey. We're almost done. We're so close."

Close to what? he wanted to ask. But he kept his mouth shut. When it came to important issues, that was all he was good at anyway.

"I suppose it's too much to ask to know why we're suddenly shifting things around?" Poppy crossed her arms and looked up at Graff. He was probably an inch shorter than Asprey, but something about the way he glowered made him seem taller. "The last time I checked, this wasn't an autocracy."

"I don't answer to you."

She was so not in the mood for this. "Well, I don't answer to you either. Whoop-dee-freaking-do. That doesn't mean I get to make overbearing demands and expect them to be carried out— especially since I'm the one who's going to have to keep stringing Todd along until you deem us ready. He's gross, Graff. And I don't like working at a gym."

This was the first time she'd ever been alone with Graff, the pair of them toe-to-toe in the center of the hangar. If she had anything to say about it, it would also be the last time they'd be alone together. He was too secretive, too controlling, too much aware of the role he played in the lives of others. That was probably what kings were like in the days of old—the asshole stamp a necessary evil to get things done.

Which was why Graff's next question caught her so off guard. "What are your plans when we're finished with the job?"

She mirrored his stance, feet shoulder's width apart, arms crossed. "I don't see how that's any of your business."

He laughed then, and Poppy saw a flash of Asprey in his face, the same laugh lines making their presence known, though it was obvious Graff didn't wear them quite as often. Asprey hadn't worn them quite as much yesterday, either, but however much her stomach might knot at the thought of how he'd looked when he left the apartment, her more sensible parts congratulated her at every turn. Better to sever the ties now. Better to move on while she could still hold her head up.

"You're a smart woman, Poppy," Graff said carefully. "And we both know you're in a pretty enviable position right now."

"I have a criminal record and you for a partner," she countered. "Find me one person willing to change places."

"Touché." He flashed his teeth and gave a slight bow, which should have been ridiculous, considering their current situation, but seemed to fit him. "You get bonus points for lowering yourself to work with me. But I'm talking about tomorrow and the next week and the week after. You'll be sitting pretty comfortably, don't you think?"

"Oh yeah," she said, not even bothering to hide her sarcasm. "I plan to take my eighty thousand dollars and enjoy a grand lifestyle for the rest of my years. I'll practically be a Hilton. I might even buy a hotel."

"I don't mean the money."

She knew that. "Just say it, Graff. What is it you're so afraid of?"

"Asprey trusts people too easily. He always has."

"Some people might consider that a virtue."

"Some people might," he agreed. "But I'm not one of them." For the first time, he relaxed, blowing out a long breath and weighing his next words. "Look, I'm not trying to accuse you of anything, and I don't have any qualms about going after Todd on your behalf. But to Asprey, this whole thing is a game, a way to pass the time and irritate his brothers in the process. Sometimes I don't even think he realizes what kind of trouble he could be in if we got caught."

In a way, that was the exact same thing she'd said to Asprey the day before. His world was one in which consequences were pesky flies to be swatted away, and he had the attitude to prove it. But hearing it from Graff's lips only made her angry. If anyone was supposed to be on Asprey's side, it should have been his big brother.

"I'm not going to take advantage of him. Or you. Or Tiffany. Strange as it may seem, I *like* your family."

"So you're going to walk away when it's all done, just like that?"

She shrugged. To be honest, every day was a lesson in trying not to think about what came next. The original plan had been to take care of Grandma Jean's ashes and set aside some money for Bea and Jenny and then to disappear. She didn't know where she'd go, and she had no idea what she wanted to do when she got there, but at least it was something.

"I can promise to stay out of your way. How's that?"

"Is that some sort of prison code?"

"Seriously?" She cocked her head and blinked at Graff, waiting for the joke. It never came. "It was women's detention, Graff, not San Quentin. Most of the time I sat in my room and read outdated magazines."

He paused for a long minute, watching her—though for what, she couldn't say. Apparently she passed muster, because he finally nodded once. "I'm sorry for changing the timeline without telling you. But there are a few more complications than we originally planned for, and we need to get things going with Cindy. How about you visit her tomorrow and we'll plan Todd for this weekend?"

"Are you asking or telling?" It didn't matter at this point, but the distinction seemed important.

"Please?" he managed.

"Oh, look—I think Asprey and Tiffany are back with our lunch." Poppy smiled brightly. "You're just in time, guys. Graff said the word 'please'."

"Oh, crap. That makes me out ten bucks." Tiffany tossed the pizza onto one of the worktables and began digging into her purse. She fished out a bill and thrust it at Asprey. "I don't know how you always call it, Asp. I was sure one of them would end up at the hospital."

Poppy avoided Asprey's gaze and prepared herself to smile through the family lunch. But her hand froze when she saw what was inside the box—pineapple-and-green-pepper pizza. Thin crust. Her favorite.

Poppy's throat closed, and she slammed the box shut again, her appetite gone in the clench of her stomach and heart and every internal organ that pumped blood through her cold, hard system. It was going to be a lot more difficult than she thought to walk away when this job was done.

Good thing she already knew how to fight.

Good thing she already knew what it felt like to never get a chance to say good-bye.

Chapter Twenty

Poppy took in the apartment without blinking, but it required most of her self-control to keep her eyes from popping out of her head.

She'd seen money before, of course. Todd had it. Asprey had it. It was one of those things that rich people could never completely separate themselves from, like a lifetime of luxury seeped into their pores and became a part of their DNA.

It seemed like it would be nice to live that way—to never question whether or not they belonged somewhere. Upscale boutique? Watch them buy a jacket without even looking at the price tag. Sidewalk? Sure, as long as it was clear of litter and near a good parking spot. Grocery store? Yep. Even there, looking over the persimmons like they actually knew what those things were for.

Poppy's people slunk a little closer to the ground, always wary, never at home.

She would definitely never be at home in a place like Cindy VanHuett's apartment. No one could be.

Even though it was technically an apartment building, the ceilings were high—loft high—almost like she lived in an upscale version of Asprey's airport hangar. Floor-to-ceiling white hit her in the retinas, with lush carpets underfoot and sleek white leather upholstery everywhere else. Cindy seemed to be allergic to color, except for a few dramatic splashes in strategic locations, like the bowl of green apples on the dining room table and an orange goldfish swimming in a clear tank built into the living room wall.

If anyone asked her, Poppy would fiercely claim loyalty to hand-knitted colorful afghans draped over every surface and a giant, worn picture of the Virgin Mary staring down at them from above the dining room table. Secretly, though, she kind of liked the stark elegance of all that white. It was like walking through a work of art.

"Please make yourself at home," Cindy said, wringing her hands as she nodded toward what was probably a couch but looked more like a long, puckered ottoman. "I feel so stupid for dropping my wallet in the park—I've already cancelled most of the cards in there, and I hate having to explain to everyone what happened and why a grown woman could be so careless."

"Don't mention it," Poppy said warmly. "It happens to the best of us."

"Say, do you want a drink? I know it's early, but I can mix up a pitcher of gimlets. I usually have one before dinner. Cocktail hour, my mom always says, though sometimes I think the whole day is cocktail hour as far as she's concerned."

Cindy was nervous. It didn't take a psychologist to realize that the mile-a-minute talking was one of many signs that Cindy wasn't exactly happy to have her new friend Lucy Higgenbottom drop by.

Poppy lowered herself to the couch—surprisingly comfortable—and smiled. "A gimlet sounds wonderful." And it did, even though she had no idea what it was.

The skittering of tiny nails on expensive hardwoods filled the room. It made sense now that the dog was white. Any stray hairs would blend.

"Hello, Jasmine, baby," Cindy cooed. The only time she seemed comfortable was when talking to the dog.

"Is she named after the tea or the Disney character?" Poppy asked casually, grabbing a women's magazine from a carefully arranged arc on the coffee table. It promised to teach her how to *Catch a Man between Your Legs*, but that was silly. She already knew how to do that—it was called a flying scissor kick.

"Oh. Um. No." Cindy was having a hard time deciding on a syllable.

"She's such a sweetie," Poppy cooed, her voice raising several octaves. She reached down to pet the dog, its fluffy white fur like cotton balls underneath her fingers. Jasmine bore it patiently but was clearly tolerating her out of form rather than kindness. At least Gunner's emotions—full of bite—were real. Bea and Jenny had immediately taken to the little dog, and he'd taken to them right back, thank goodness. Asprey might be willing to shove the poor thing back in a cage at the pound, but that just showed how skewed his version of the world was. All it took was a good home and some consideration to show Gunner's good side. Just like every other scrappy mongrel roaming the streets.

"Do you give her free rein over the apartment while you're gone, or do you kennel her?" Poppy asked, forcing herself to focus on the task standing literally in front of her. *The sooner it's over, the sooner I can move on.* "I can't leave Gunner alone for a second or he gets into my shoes. I don't know what it is about him and Jimmy Choo, but I suspect the two of them have a love affair going on behind my back."

"Oh, I let Jasmine have the run of the place." Cindy moved in the direction of the kitchen, throwing open a set of french doors—all in white, of course. "She's a surprisingly good guard dog. She might not look like much, but if she suspects anyone is here without my invitation, she'll bark long and loud. Once, my cleaning woman came in when I wasn't home. Jasmine cornered her in the bathroom until my next door neighbor, Mrs. Partridge, heard the commotion and thought someone was dying. She's really sensitive to loud noises."

"The dog or the neighbor?"

Cindy gave a nervous laugh, thawing a little. "Mrs. Partridge. I had to give her a key to the apartment so she can come over and calm Jasmine if she gets too worked up."

Good to know. Poppy absorbed the information like a sponge. Guard dog, guard neighbor, and so far, no painting in sight.

"Where *is* your dog, by the way?" Cindy asked, looking around as if she'd somehow missed his entry.

"Oh, I remembered how he didn't get along with Jasmine and decided to leave him with my boyfriend today."

Where had that come from? Technically, Bea had to work, so Gunner *was* with Asprey, but that was taking the whole half-truth-is-better-than-a-straight-lie thing too far. She needed to get a grip on herself. And soon.

"Aww, that's so sweet. I love a man who's good with animals. Does your boyfriend like dogs?"

"Not really. But I think Gunner is growing on him."

"I wish I had that," Cindy said.

"A boyfriend who's willing to dog-sit?" Poppy crossed her legs and tried to look unconcerned, even though her whole body flushed with heat. "I'm sure you'll find one someday."

"No...just one who makes me light up like you do."

The fire blazed higher. She needed a distraction before she blew her whole cover.

"Do you mind if I..." She let the words trail off and looked toward the hall.

"Of course. Bathroom is the second door on the right."

Poppy waited until Cindy got swallowed by the massive french doors leading to the kitchen, thankfully followed by Jasmine, before she got up. Moving swiftly, she headed in the direction of the hall, her legs only wobbling with every other step.

The hallway spread out long and wide, with rooms leading off every few feet. Most of the doors were closed, which probably meant that they were bedrooms or offices—hardly big enough to showcase a piece of art like the kind Asprey had described.

"Giant. Splotchy. Unless she's got an entire museum in there, it shouldn't be hard to find."

She'd assumed the painting would be in the living room, based on the size of the thing, but so far it was nowhere to be seen. Where else did one hang an enormous piece of colorful art if not the living room? Was it even here?

She pushed open the bathroom door for form's sake, taking in the blank walls, metal accents and white plush bathmat at a glance. The light in there had to be amazing for doing make-up—and for obsessing over pores. She thought of the bathroom she and Bea shared, with their tweezers out on the counter and little notes they wrote to each other on the mirror in lipstick and eyeliner, and shuddered. No way could she live under a microscope like this.

The next room was some sort of guest bedroom, evident by the fact that there was a splash of color in there, though mostly in shades of muted gray and slate blue. No artwork, though, unless you counted the framed black-and-white photo. She peered closer and made out a signature with a pair of giant sloping As. The picture looked expensive.

The next room was a sleek, modern-looking office furnished with a huge frosted-glass desk that probably showcased fingerprints like crazy. On the other side of the hall stood Cindy's bedroom, which didn't look at all like a human female lived there. Where were the discarded clothes and dirty panties balled up in a corner? Where were the spots of spilled nail polish on the carpet? How did a person move through life without making any marks?

There wasn't enough time to explore Cindy's house further, so Poppy hightailed it back to the living room. Cindy stood next to the couch, a martini glass in each hand, one of them emptied almost to the bottom.

"I guess I was thirstier than I thought," she said, forcing a laugh and thrusting the full glass toward Poppy. "This is okay, isn't it?"

Poppy sipped at the drink—lime and pine trees and antiseptic, the upper-class version of gin and juice—and forced a smile. "Yes. Delicious."

"Oh no. I meant that I had the doorman buzz you up. You probably just wanted to drop off the wallet and go home. I sometimes forget that people—"

"Are you kidding?" Poppy asked, taking a deep drink and smiling warmly at Cindy, trying not to notice how warmly the woman smiled back. Cindy was nice, if slightly awkward. That complicated things. "You're doing me a favor. This is exactly what I needed. I don't know very many people in town, and it's nice to get away from all the unpacked boxes at home."

"I should give you the number to my organizer." Cindy shot to her feet, what remained of her drink sloshing all over the floor in the process. Jasmine chose that moment to skitter around the corner of the couch, sliding in the turn with the kind of expertise it took NASCAR racers decades to perfect.

"No, Jasmine! Bad precious!" Cindy reached for the dog, but Jasmine was too fast, angling her body to evade capture while she lapped hungrily at the mess. Cindy slipped and landed on her butt, her legs skewed in what had to be the least ladylike position she'd ever adopted in her life.

Poppy thought about helping Cindy up, but there was such a look of misery on the woman's face that the only thing to do was make a fake lunge for the dog and crash to the ground next to her, which she did, a telltale rip on the back of her skirt adding a splash of authenticity.

Jasmine glanced calmly at them both and continued lapping.

"I'm so sorry—I'm such a mess when it comes to things like this." Cindy sniffled, struggling to right herself. Poppy put a hand on Cindy's shoulder, refusing to let her up. The poor woman wasn't cold or standoffish like Asprey had suggested. She was lonely.

"You think this is bad?" Poppy giggled. "You should see what lengths Gunner will go to over a little pâté."

Cindy sniffled. "Really?"

"Really," Poppy said firmly.

Cindy's smile was small, tentative—but real. Poppy's stomach twinged. *Guilt.* She felt it every con, even with Todd. There were a few times over dinner when she'd caught Todd staring at her—not with lust but with sadness. She didn't blame him. No matter who you were, it would be depressing to know that you were out with a gorgeous, empty woman who only wanted you for your money.

Cindy grabbed Poppy's hand and gave it a squeeze, tentative but warm. "I hope you don't think I'm a total idiot—I'm just not used to people, to women, coming over to hang out. You know, here. At my house."

Jasmine barked loudly, the sharp raps echoing through the apartment so that the sound magnified about ten times. No wonder Mrs. Partridge protested the noise.

"Oh dear. How much of that did she drink?"

Poppy looked around, her own glass now empty. "I think she polished off mine too."

Cindy let out a giggle before clapping a hand over her mouth, almost as if trying to press the sound back in. "Poor Jasmine has a weakness for gin."

Poppy got to her feet as elegantly as she could in her tight skirt, one hand holding the rip together, the other helping Cindy up. "Is Mrs. Partridge going to come yell at us?" she asked conspiratorially.

Cindy giggled again. "Probably."

"Then we should go make more gimlets. You know, in case we need the liquid courage."

"I like that idea."

Their bonds of friendship now forged in the kind of steel crafted from high-priced liquor, Poppy followed Cindy to the kitchen, a huge, oversized space that was obviously where she the bulk of her living.

She didn't get much beyond taking in the warm tones and fresh-baked bread on the counter before she stopped, her head spinning. There, on the far side of the attached dining area, hung the world-famous painting Asprey had assured her was a one-of-a-kind masterpiece.

White canvas. Big painting. Splotches—most of them red and blobby. Even though she knew it was technically a forgery, it was the closest she had ever been to real art, the first time she'd come face-to-face with the kind of object people would risk their lives for.

And all she could think was, *ten million dollars for that?*

"How did it go?" Asprey let go of Gunner's leash, unable to suppress a smile as he bounded across the hangar to whine and paw until Poppy lifted him up. For the entire time they'd been waiting, the dog had let out a sigh and moan every five minutes, awaiting his mistress's return.

"Me too, little buddy," he'd said more than once, throwing a scrap of leftover pizza to the dog. Food was a poor substitute, and Gunner knew it. "It's just not the same without her, is it?"

Poppy had changed out of her Lucy Higgenbottom clothes and into her cowboy boots, this time paired with striped tights and an oversized off-the-shoulder tunic. Even though Asprey strove to be detached and uninterested, he loved that tunic, the way the slope of her shoulder was unbroken by anything but the play of light and the promise of silk against his tongue.

She plopped to the chair opposite him, the dog in her lap, completely oblivious to the effect she had on him.

"The painting is there," she announced coolly, doing her best to avoid meeting Asprey's eyes. That was her thing now. Avoidance. "But it's inaccessible."

"What do you mean inaccessible?" Graff asked. He hovered behind Asprey's chair. He'd been hovering there all day, paranoid and full of angst and driving him crazy.

"I mean inaccessible. Stuck. Impossible to get at."

"What?" Graff repeated.

Asprey twisted in his seat. "Sit, Graff, and calm down. Yelling at her isn't going to help."

"He can yell," Poppy said. "It's better than taking nothing seriously."

Asprey slapped on the most dazzling smile he had in his arsenal and leaned back in his chair, nonchalant and uncaring as he had never been before, even though his heart felt like lead. After everything they'd been through, he was still a big, fat nothing in her eyes.

"Life is so much easier when you let someone else carry the weight of the world," he said. "You both should try it sometime."

As predicted, the blasé statement made Graff let out a strangled semi-roar. Poppy just narrowed her eyes and pulled out a notebook and pencil. With a deft and sure hand, she mapped out the floor plan of the apartment, pointing out key areas of interest.

"It's a pretty basic layout, longer than it is wide. Living space is near the entry, and most of the rooms are down a hallway to the right. To the left is the kitchen, which is where you'll find the painting."

Asprey sat up. "Wait a minute—the kitchen?"

"That's what she said." Graff tapped on the drawing. "There aren't any windows in that room?"

Poppy shook her head. "Just a tiny one above her dining area. Apparently the entire room was remodeled around the painting, so the only way it's getting out of there is if you bring a chainsaw—which Mrs. Partridge will be sure and object to, I can tell you that."

"Mrs. Partridge? Chainsaws?" Graff scooted closer to Poppy. Asprey might as well have been out taking the dog for a walk for all anyone cared whether or not he helped.

"The ridiculously nosy neighbor. And what you'll need to get the painting out the door. It won't fit otherwise."

"Is the painting really in the kitchen?" Asprey persisted. "Are you sure it was the one we want?"

She stopped sketching and stabbed her pencil his direction. "Big painting. Lots of globs. I may not have a fancy art degree, but I'm pretty sure I got the right one."

"I've never heard of anyone putting millions of dollars' worth of artwork in a kitchen before," Asprey persisted. "Stuff like that is usually under temperature and humidity controls—not in the middle of a house's warmest, most often used room. Even da Vinci's Last Supper started to flake after less than twenty years because it was in such a high-traffic place. You can't put oil-based paintings in a place like a kitchen. It's ridiculous..."

He let the words trail off. Poppy was looking at him with a mixture of irritation and curiosity.

"Well, that's where it is. And there's no way to get it out the doorway—believe me. I checked while Cindy was in the bathroom."

"Oh, yeah? You had a tape measure handy?"

"I have arms, Asprey." She held them out. "The height of the painting is about two feet more than my arm span. The doorway is about six inches less. You do the math."

Graff let out a chuckle designed, Asprey knew, to set up his back. *Glad someone's enjoying this.*

"Also, I asked," she added. She cocked her head and opened her eyes wide. "Gee, Cindy, your Pollock is huge. How did you get it in here? What will you do if you move?"

"Okay," Asprey capitulated. "I bow to your superior knowledge."

"Thank you. I accept."

Graff grabbed the notepad and studied it for a moment. "Well, the good news is that we don't have to get the painting out whole. We can just cut it out and roll it up. What I'm worried about is access. How close are the neighbor's doors?"

Poppy frowned. "That's the other thing. She's really close to the old woman next door—it sounds kind of like she takes care of her, sharing casseroles and Saturday nights and stuff. And the neighbor hears everything that goes on in the apartment. Especially the dog."

"And?" Asprey prompted. Something else was bothering her.

"Well...Cindy's a really nice woman," she admitted. "I don't think she has very many friends, Asprey, and she seemed kind of sad."

"I'm not surprised. In all her carefully scheduled plans, there didn't seem like a whole lot of girls' nights out or hot dates listed."

"I don't like it."

"You of all people should know that some women are natural loners," he said gently.

"I don't like it," she repeated. She turned her attention to Graff. "I know I'm not supposed to know about the insurance stuff, but Asprey told me about the forgeries. I know the painting is fake."

To any other person in the world, it would have looked as though Graff merely got up to stretch and consider his options. Asprey wasn't fooled. The spring in his brother's step was pure tension.

Poppy shot Asprey a brief but apologetic look. "I'm sorry to let it out like that, Asprey, but she loves that painting. The kitchen is the only personalized space in that entire apartment. She bakes in there. Lives in there, really. Taking the painting from her—even if it's not real—is going to break her heart. There's got to be another way."

"Well, since you apparently know everything, you also know that she'll get her ten million dollars back," Graff interrupted, growling. "She'll be fine."

She whirled to face him, and Asprey was glad to see that her irritation landed right smack dab on his brother's shoulders. "Did it ever occur to either of you that instead of money, the people you steal from would rather have their grandma's cameo back? That painting was a gift from her husband. Who *died*, Graff. Ten million dollars doesn't bring people back from the grave."

"We would if we could, Poppy," Asprey said gently. "But the real items are long gone. Winston sold them off years ago."

"Asprey," Graff warned, his meaning clear. This was the last piece of the puzzle, the one thing he'd held back from telling her. Maybe that had been a mistake—maybe it would have been better to lay it all out on the line from the very first day. *Probably not.* The truth didn't make any difference if Poppy refused to see him as anything more than the playboy sidekick to Graff's carefully laid plans.

Besides—no matter what else Graff and Poppy might think, he was dedicated to this job. He *did* care about the outcome, and not just because Winston had left a message that morning notifying him that Ruby had been repossessed.

"He sold them off?" Poppy echoed. "What do you mean?"

Asprey looked at his brother and shrugged. *Too late now.* "She deserves to know the whole story, Graff. She's risking a lot for us. She might as well know why."

"Fine. I obviously have no authority here." Graff agreeing— it was turning out to be quite a strange day. He turned to Poppy. "About five years ago, Winston must have hit a rough financial patch, because he launched a huge forgery scam—the kind most people couldn't imagine. Almost half of the pieces that went through Charles Appraisals and Insurance during that time were sent out to a company I've never heard of and can't seem to find any information on. A front."

"Nearest we can tell, they were the ones who forged the items for Winston," Asprey added. They still didn't have a ton of information, but what they did know wasn't good. "Winston passed the forgeries on to the clients and had the fake appraisal company sell the real things—presumably on the black market—so he could pocket the money himself. And until Graff stumbled on some of the records, no one was any the wiser."

Poppy looked back and forth between them, disbelief momentarily taking the place of her other, less Asprey-friendly emotions. "That's huge."

Graff tilted his head in agreement. "Which is why we would be very grateful if you helped us with the VanHuett job *without* getting emotionally attached."

Poppy turned unnaturally still. "I don't get emotionally attached."

As there was no mistaking her meaning, Asprey pushed back from the table and turned, walking slowly and casually toward the stairs to the hangar apartment.

Let Poppy and Graff debate the merits of crime and the drawbacks of human emotion. Let them make lists of all the reasons why a guy like Asprey—who *did* get emotionally

229

attached—wasn't suited for that particular line of work, why he wasn't suited for any line of work except self-indulgence and profligacy. He didn't need to sit there and hear that conversation again.

Once had been more than enough.

Chapter Twenty-One

Poppy dangled her shoe from her toe, trying her best to look playful and interested in Todd's running dialogue on a racecar that had recently lost him quite a bit of money. Apparently, he blamed a bookie for misunderstanding his bet, his hands flying as he explained the delicacy of long odds.

"Are we going anywhere today, doll? Like...lunch?" She scanned the kitchen for signs of lunch being made, ordered or even thought of. Her stomach growled at the lack of anything edible in sight. She'd rushed from the gym, where she'd spent the morning teaching two yoga classes and one self-defense aerobics class, for this supposed date. If Todd didn't stop talking about the benefits of deep braking and provide her with a meal, she was not going to be responsible for blowing this entire operation with one swift kick to the kneecap.

Todd shook his head. "I ate at the club."

She paused, waiting for the rest of the statement, but nothing came. The man's interest was definitely on its way out—he wasn't even willing to *feed* her anymore. "What was your mother like, I wonder?"

"My mother?" Todd's neck did a full swivel her direction. "What do you mean?"

Poppy swallowed a sigh. "Nothing. I just find parental history interesting, that's all. How it is a person becomes the way they are... I bet your mom was really pretty, wasn't she?"

Todd must have partially gotten the hint because he stood, grabbed a sparkling water from his refrigerator and offered it to her. *Better than nothing.* "She was beautiful."

He let the statement sit there, and Poppy thought it would be an easy jump to finish the rest of the description. Beautiful, expensive and most likely not around much.

She knew guys like Todd—had grown up with guys like Todd. They were the ones who lived with single mothers and their endless string of boyfriends, who felt the only way they could compete for her attention was with either money or meanness. Some boys became overachievers and opted for both.

Todd was one of them.

"Speaking of families," he said, inserting a casual note into his voice. "I got a call from Drago. The game's been moved to tonight."

Aha. That was the real reason they weren't going out. He wanted to discuss the poker game. The plan was to end things this evening. They'd increased the buy-in so that Todd would arrive with at least a hundred grand in tow. As before, they'd lull him into a belief he was doing well, only to start hitting hard as the night wore on. As soon as they had their take, Poppy planned on starting an argument with him to end the game.

By the time he left, Todd Kennick would be broke and alone. *Just like Grandma Jean.*

"Ohh, that's good." She came up behind him and wrapped her arms around his midsection. It was hard not to make the comparison between that embrace and the ones she'd lately shared with Asprey. It wasn't just their physiques that were different—it was the way two bodies molded together.

Natalie, with her mile-high breasts and tight clothes, would have felt awkward pushed up against anyone, let alone a man who never appeared to be at ease in his own skin. But Poppy, naked Poppy, stripped-down Poppy—she seemed to melt into Asprey's arms without even trying.

She pulled away. That was a bad comparison to make. She wasn't going to end up in any man's arms.

"It's good, it's good." Todd grabbed his comb from his back pocket and ran it through his hair. "But I need to make some, ah, arrangements with my money guy."

His money guy? Todd wasn't doing as well as she'd thought lately if he had to scramble to come up with the hundred grand. "Is everything okay?"

"It's fine," he rushed. "But you know guys like this. They upped the stakes a little, made it clear this is a private game. They're part of a rough crowd, Natalie. A man has to be able to handle himself."

He really *was* nervous. "You'll be great, doll," she said, her tone low and soothing. "As long as you have me with you, there's nothing to be worried about. Those guys are like brothers to me."

For the first time since she'd forced their meeting, Todd looked at her with wariness. Gone was the greedy glint in his eyes. Nowhere to be seen were those initial throes of lust. He looked kind of like that little boy who was still working so hard to impress his mother.

Bam. There was her con guilt again. These jobs were always so much easier when her marks didn't let those rare glimpses of humanity through.

So she did the only thing she could in a situation like this—closed her eyes and thought of Grandma Jean. Almost as much as she wished she'd been able to say good-bye to the old woman, Poppy wanted to know why she'd trusted a man like Todd with her money.

She had a few guesses as to her grandmother's motivations, not the least of which was the promise of a quick payout. *Like grandmother, like granddaughter.* They were the type of people who always looked for a shortcut, always wanted to get more for less. Bargain shoppers with criminal intentions.

Not at all like Asprey. Of all the information thrown at her over the past few days, Poppy could process only one thing: he wasn't really a thief. Those fleeting, criminal ties that bound the two of them existed only in her imagination.

The glitz and glamour of his high-brow life, the art museum in his name and the trips to Bali—that was his world. Not the art and jewelry thefts. Not the underworld poker. He righted the world's wrongs, made up for Winston's criminal activities, gave people their money back because it was the right thing to do.

He's one of the good guys.

And Poppy, who in all this time was only out to get her own money back from Todd, was not.

"I can call them right now and cancel." She looked at Todd, her guilt still in place but with a firm set to her jaw all the same. She'd already invested the time and energy and heartbreak. *Once a thief, always a thief.* "Don't you worry, I can take care of this for you. Those boys won't think any less of you for having a change of heart. I'll make sure of it."

As expected, Todd's pride shot straight up his spine, and he loomed close. "I can take care of this myself," he muttered. "I don't need you getting in there and messing things up."

"Sure thing," she cooed. Whatever it was going to take. Less than twenty-four hours and she'd be done with this man for good. "Why don't I go get myself freshened up for this evening and let you handle your business?"

"Yes. Good." Todd had moved on and checked a text on his phone. He waved his hand in a negligent farewell. "I'll see you tonight."

She was grateful to leave. If she was going to spend the rest of the evening facing Asprey, feigning indifference and keeping her focus, she needed food, a nap and eighty thousand dollars.

In that order.

Graff moved Louis into the back room at Bouncing Booty, setting the chair up at the head of the poker table as though reenacting a scene out of the Godfather.

"Are you sure that's a good idea?" Asprey asked, shaking his head. His brother was really getting into the second leg of this plan. "You sleep with that chair next to your bed at night, and don't think I didn't notice when you sent it away for cleaning last month. You timed it exactly for your weekend trip so the chair wouldn't be left alone with me. Yet you'll slum it up enough to bring it to the poker game?"

"I thought it added a nice touch."

"You're obsessed."

Graff ran his hand over the carved woodwork with its original stain worn but intact. "This chair has been in the Charles family for centuries."

"I'm not sure if you remember, but I'm actually a part of the Charles family," Asprey pointed out. "In fact, I've heard it mentioned once or twice that we might be brothers."

"Ha-ha." Graff's tone lacked its usual bite. "I know you and Tiff think I'm ridiculous, but Louis is the only thing I have left of Dad's. It's one of the few items that Winston didn't sell when he took over the company."

Asprey was acutely aware of the chair's successive lines of ownership. He had fond memories of their father sitting in the chair, pushed up to an equally ornate desk that had once belonged to an obscure nineteenth-century German philosopher. Even though the family business had shifted by then, as much about insuring jewelry and art as it was about appraising the items, Manchester Charles had held fast to the ideologies that founded the company. Beauty and preservation, true appreciation for the artistic capabilities of mankind.

There was even a picture of their grandfather in that chair floating around somewhere. Asprey remembered him grinning at the camera with three pairs of glasses pushed up on top of his head, holding an enormous champagne diamond up to one eye.

"I'm just surprised you're willing to sacrifice Louis to this scheme, that's all," Asprey said, giving voice to none of the memories he was sure Graff shared in that moment. "Seeing as how it's for Poppy's benefit rather than ours."

"It's symbolic, Asp." Graff avoided him, adjusting the chair one last time before stepping back to survey the scene. "Leave it alone."

He didn't, of course. Asprey launched himself into the chair, dangling his legs over one of the arms. "Poppy's starting to grow on you, huh? You're such a softie, Graff, always happy to help a lady in distress."

Graff smacked Asprey on the back of the head and hefted him out of the chair. "I don't like this Todd guy, that's all. We'll take care of him tonight."

Asprey laughed. "You make it sound like we're going to force him to sleep with the fishes."

Graff examined a seam in the chair with intense interest.

"Graff?" Asprey asked, inserting himself into his brother's line of vision. A sudden empty buzzing filled his head. When Graff got all quiet and vigilante, Asprey's life had a way of getting turned upside down. "What do you mean, take care of him? We have a plan all worked out. Deal the cards. Cheat. Look intimidating. Repeat as needed."

"Don't worry about it, Asp. I've got it taken care of."

Don't worry. Like all it took for Asprey to slap on a smile and move forward was a cursory command. He gripped his brother's arm, forcing him to look up. "What did you do?"

"I had Tiff look a little bit more into Todd's financial records, that's all," Graff said. "I wanted to make sure Poppy was telling us the truth about him scamming all those people."

"And?"

Graff's lips thinned in a tight grimace. "And she was."

Instinct warned him that the dark glimmer in Graff's eye was incentive enough to pull the plug on the entire evening's plan, but the familiar knock on the door sounded at that moment. Asprey had no choice but to shake himself off, loosening his limbs and falling into his role as Rufio.

"And don't do anything stupid," Graff said, almost cheerful as Asprey pulled open the door to reveal Poppy and Todd, arm in arm. This time, Todd had dressed to rival them all in a dark suit layered over a red silk shirt, once again in sunglasses designed to shade his eyes.

But it would have been ridiculous to pretend that it was Todd who caught the eye first—or that he even existed in a world that Poppy shared. She wore the barest scraps of white fabric with strategic cutaway parts, not so much a dress as a shrine to her sexual energy. Hips, waist, shoulders—her flashes of skin were blinding, God playing tricks with mirrors and light. Asprey forced himself to appear unmoved and greet Poppy with the same Euro-kiss from before, but it was difficult, not only because she looked incredible but because he felt an overwhelming urge to protect her from whatever crap Graff had planned.

Then he remembered. Poppy didn't want protecting. She didn't *need* protecting. She'd made it very clear what kind of a role he was allowed to play in her life. In her eyes, he was just a pretty toy.

"Be careful," she whispered, her words barely more than a breath against his cheek. "He's packing."

Asprey pulled away, smiling and ebullient on the outside, his stomach like molten rock on the inside. This had better be part of Graff's master plan or they were all in trouble.

"It's wonderful to see you again so soon," he said and meant it. He turned to Todd, all feelings turned off. "And you, of course."

Todd flipped off his sunglasses and stuffed them in his pocket, where a red silk handkerchief that matched his tie rested. He dropped a briefcase fairly bulging with the promise of money at his feet and shook Asprey's hand. The appendage was cold and clammy. *He's nervous.* "Always a pleasure."

"I hope the higher stakes aren't a problem," Graff said, pushing himself forward and flashing his teeth. "I fear Rufio doesn't take losing well, and he's fairly keen on recouping his losses."

Todd cast a wary glance Asprey's way, and he remembered just in time to straighten and look intimidating. Mustering those feelings was difficult when all he really wanted to do was to grab Poppy by the hand, pull her out the door and never look back.

"It's nothing I can't handle," Todd replied. "Although I will say your request was highly unorthodox—at least in my experience with this sort of thing."

Graff flashed his teeth again. "If my game is too much for you, you are welcome to go. We hold no man against his will."

Asprey turned to look at Poppy. Her eyes widened, and she shook her head, just enough to signal that she was as clueless as him as to what kind of requests and conversations had passed between the two men.

"I think we could all use a drink." Asprey strove to stay neutral as the men settled around the card table. "Natalie—will you oblige us?"

"None for me, thanks," Todd said, accepting the pile of chips Graff pushed across the table. "Too much smoke and liquor make it hard to concentrate."

Asprey made a quick, furtive motion to his hip in what he hoped was a readable gesture that Todd had taken a few security measures this time around, but it was hard to tell if Graff saw. His brother was tense and taut, power practically thrumming around him.

"I begin to like our guest." Graff dealt the cards with a deft and sure hand. "He understands that when men meet to play cards, they aren't just matching skills—they match wits. Dealer takes two. Rufio?"

"Um...three," Asprey blustered. Graff's eyes glittered as he tossed the cards down. *Damn.* He'd somehow missed the signal to only take one.

The situation coursed downhill from there.

It didn't take long for Graff to notice Asprey's inattention, and he began dealing him mostly number cards and failing to bother with cues at all. Nothing Asprey could have done would have allowed him to stay in the game for long, and his chips continued to dwindle until he had no choice but to go all-in on a pair of jacks.

He lost, of course, to Todd, whose own pile of chips grew steadily in front of him, far surpassing the original dollar amount they'd agreed upon—they were now talking hundreds of thousands of dollars, not tens. Something was off.

"What is Graff *doing*?" Poppy hissed when Asprey took a seat next to her, their backs against the wall, their eyes never straying from Todd's hands. "At this rate, he's going to let Todd walk away a very rich man."

"I don't know," Asprey returned, watching his brother for any clues. Always a close, unreadable man, Graff was a virtual stone wall now—and that scared him. Since Asprey was out of the game, they couldn't rely on whipsawing to trap Todd between the two of them, making the opportunities to rig the outcome that much scarcer.

"We can't afford to let Todd walk away again." Poppy played with the hem of her dress nervously. "He's already losing interest in me—I doubt I can wrap him around my finger anymore. I don't like where Graff is going with this. I don't like not knowing what comes next."

"We can trust him," Asprey assured her, though he failed to convince himself. "He knows what he's doing."

"He better."

"I begin to see your strategy, my friend," Graff murmured after Todd took a spectacularly dazzling win with a full house of aces over queens. "I commend you on your gameplay."

Todd took out his handkerchief and wiped along his brow, which beaded with the sweat of exertion. "Thank you. I was fortunate to pull the ace of spades at the last minute."

"Yes," Graff replied, smiling widely. "You were."

Asprey was missing something. He had to be.

Neither he nor Poppy moved much as they continued watching the two men play, and Asprey had lost track of the time when he felt warm fingers slip into his. His heart picked up at the sudden contact, but he didn't dare look over at Poppy for fear he'd do something to ruin the whole thing. He squeezed.

"Oh no." Poppy dropped his hand. "I know what Graff is doing."

Asprey watched as Todd took another big win, stacking his chips slowly and with a furrow in the middle of his brow. For the first time, he looked his age. For the first time, he looked scared.

"Stop him, Asprey. Stop your brother."

"I can't." It was one of the many things that fell outside Asprey's area of expertise. If it were possible to make Graff focus on anything outside of his own obsessions, the person responsible for such a thing had yet to make an appearance. Most of what Asprey did anymore was damage control. "Let him finish. He'll turn the game around."

"He *won't*." Poppy's voice rose, and she had to clamp her lips shut to stop from making a scene. "He has no intention of making Todd lose," she added with a hiss.

Poppy's prediction came to fruition much sooner than either of them anticipated. With a crash, Graff stood and knocked Louis to the ground—a move that meant a lot more to Asprey than it did to Poppy. He loomed over the head of the table, intimidating even to Asprey as he placed either hand on the surface and leaned down, carefully and with infinite control.

"Show me your hand," Graff growled.

"Ex...excuse me?" Todd also rose to his feet, but clumsily, his face growing red.

"*Show me your hand!*" Graff pounded the table with his fist. Chips flew and clattered to the ground, a few rolling until they reached Asprey's feet.

Without thinking, he rose and placed a restraining hand on Poppy's arm. None of his thoughts were coherent or even recognizable beyond the overwhelming urge to keep her from getting hurt.

Poppy took one look at Asprey's arm and stilled. They both knew she could throw him off, that she could aim one of those long, perfect ninja legs at his head and be freed to go wherever she wanted. But she remained seated.

"I want to see your cards," Graff repeated. He reached across the table and grabbed Todd by the tie, pulling him closer. "And I want to see up your sleeves."

The insult hit home. Todd turned an alarming shade of red, probably unable to breathe because Graff pulled his tie so tight. Understanding hit Asprey at the same time.

Graff isn't just going to win the hundred grand from Todd. He's setting him up so he can walk away with the entire briefcase.

"Are you calling me a cheat?" Todd managed, his words croaked and hoarse.

Graff pulled tighter. "It's been bothering me for days—how you managed to win so much in a single night's game. I even sat up a few evenings, replaying the hands, watching you with my mind's eye. It's very detailed, that eye."

Todd regained some of his breath then, and if Asprey hadn't seen the slight motion of the man's hand to his hip, he might have called it heroic. "I don't take being called a cheat very lightly."

"And I don't take cheating very lightly. How many kings are in your hand?"

"That's *not* the kind of game I play," Todd spat out.

Todd and Graff made a kind of stilled portrait as they sized each other up, neither one willing to back down. Graff finally turned to acknowledge Asprey standing there. He was alert and ready and still holding Poppy from tackling the lot of them.

"Oh, I know exactly what kind of game you play." That was Graff's voice. His real voice—his hurt voice. "I'll start. I have two kings. Hearts and diamonds."

Todd made a strange choking sound.

"Rufio? Please have the courtesy of flipping our guest's cards." His voice rumbled a warning. "*Now*, Rufio."

Asprey flipped the cards one by one, trying not to be dramatic but finding it difficult to be anything else in that moment. The cards hit the felt in a slow, almost otherworldly succession—three kings and a pair of deuces.

"No!" Todd cried, the syllable drawn out like he was shouting at a horror movie whose denouement was already written across the floors in fake blood.

"You dare to cheat Drago?" Graff roared.

The gun came out. Asprey hurtled forward to get to it in time, but he was knocked off his feet by Poppy, who had sprung into action the moment Todd's hand moved for his hip. Instead of moving toward Todd, as Asprey expected, she moved in front of Graff, her hands raised in supplication.

"That's enough. Both of you stop."

The twin clicks of two guns cocking filled the air, both of them pointed right at Poppy. Graff's gun was one Asprey had never seen before, a high-tech Glock-22 that he'd pulled from a shoulder holster. Todd's was a wood-handled revolver, which looked more like a showpiece than anything the least bit functional.

Asprey didn't like the look of either one. They had guns in the hangar, of course, and Asprey had handled his fair share. It was impossible to accomplish as many successful heists as they had without invoking the use of some kind of force. He didn't always like it, but arms were one of the several necessary evils he'd come to accept as part of their trade.

This, though—it went too far. Graff didn't get to point a gun at Poppy without his permission. He didn't get to endanger a life that was rapidly becoming to mean more to Asprey than his own.

"Move, Natalie," Graff ordered. "I know you're dating this scumbug, but no one cheats against Drago and lives to tell the tale. No one."

"She doesn't move an inch, or I'll blow her head off," Todd warned, his voice shaky.

"Todd! Drago!" Poppy sounded more like a schoolteacher than a woman with one gun pointed at her chest and the other at her back. "Both of you put the guns down right now. This stupid game isn't worth anyone's life. *Drago—that includes you.*"

"You guys have the wrong idea. Natalie, I need you to reach down, grab my briefcase and hand it to me very slowly." When she didn't move, he added, "Do it, or I will shoot you."

Asprey could hear the same fear in Todd's voice from the day of the necklace heist, and he felt jolts of warning move through his spine. What had he thought then? That all Todd's heroics were misplaced, at getting the gun pointed anywhere but toward himself? That Todd seemed like the type who would have gladly thrown Poppy into harm's way if it meant saving his own skin?

Not if Asprey had anything to say about it.

He moved.

With a quick jab that was more of an automatic reflex than anything else, he hit the gun with his fist. It hurt, a lot more than he expected it to, what with the cold metal against bone and a lot more force than he thought he was capable of, but it had the bonus of sending the gun flying out of Todd's hand and across the room. Away from Poppy, which was the only thing that mattered.

But gravity was a law even they had to adhere to, and the gun continued flying until it hit the far wall, firing once in a loud burst. The whole room stopped, suspended in time as they watched to see where the bullet tore through. The whole room, that was, except Asprey. Using the momentary distraction to his advantage, he fell into the squat he and Poppy had practiced at the Pit, his right leg shooting out to sweep a wide arc in Todd's direction.

There was no finesse to it, and there was a second there when Asprey almost lost his balance and toppled sideways to the floor. But it worked, damn it, and Todd fell to the ground in a heap, grunting as he hit his head on the side of the table.

And just like that, it was over.

"Holy shit." Asprey lifted himself and moved to Todd's side, placing a hand on the older man's leg. The body was warm and solid, but it wasn't moving, and dark, viscous blood slugged into a pool beneath his head. "Did I kill him?"

"For fuck's sake, Asprey!" Graff cried. "What is wrong with you?"

"What's wrong with *me*?" Adrenaline coursed through him, hot and insistent. "Todd had a gun pointed at the woman I l—" He broke off, quieter this time, though his fury was still very much intact. "Excuse me if my first instinct was to knock the guy over."

"He's breathing and has a good pulse, thank goodness." Poppy looked up from her squat near Todd's neck. Her eyes, when they met Asprey's, were shuttered. "That head wound's not going to stop any time soon, but we're lucky it's not worse. That was a good sweep, by the way."

A short bark escaped Asprey's throat, a combination of fear and laughter. "I learned from the best."

"No," she said, so quiet he had to strain to hear her. "You learned from the worst."

Graff pushed Asprey out of the way and used his sleeve to pick up Todd's gun, which he tossed into the empty poker-chip box. "We're going to need to clear out—the props, the body, all of it. This isn't how I wanted it to go down, but I think we can make it work."

"What are you talking about?" Asprey crossed his arms. "Todd needs an ambulance."

"What he needs is a good lesson—and that's exactly what I intend to give him. You think he's going to stop stealing from people because he loses in a poker game?" Graff laughed bitterly. "That's just like you, Asprey, seeing only what's right in front of your face. Poppy, I'm going to need you to wipe up his blood and spread some of it along your chest and back—make it look like the bullet hit right to your heart. The messier, the better. Even put some on your shoes if you can. We're going to have to dispose of you no matter what, and if we can set it up so it looks like Todd was the one who killed you, we'll have a better chance of him staying quiet about this whole affair."

"You had no right to do that," she said, and even though her words were harsh, they were cool and almost detached. "We had an agreement. My eighty grand and your thirty, and everyone walks away happy."

Whereas Asprey had suddenly heightened emotions, senses, *everything*, Poppy looked as though she were seconds away from shutting down altogether.

Asprey stepped in front of her, wrapping one hand carefully around the back of her neck and pulling her close. Her body was so tense he could practically feel her vibrating. "Hey. You okay?"

"No, I'm not," she whispered. "No one was supposed to get hurt. Not for me."

"Asprey—we don't have time for this." Graff nudged him with the toe of his sneaker. "Get moving."

Asprey ignored him. It was the only option that let him hold on to the last of his control. "What can I do, Poppy? What do you need?"

"I'll tell you what *I* need," Graff interrupted. "I need you to get out and ask the kitchen staff to take a small break out front. I'd rather they didn't watch us move a body out the back door."

Asprey turned to him and snarled. "Give me a minute to make sure she's okay. I don't know if you noticed, but a gun went off very near her head just a second ago."

Graff snorted. "You think an ex-con is afraid of one measly bullet?"

That was *enough*. He swiveled until he was right up in his brother's face, the two of them meeting on common ground, even though Graff had the advantage of him in terms of strength. Asprey wasn't sure what he would have done if not for Poppy's voice materializing gently at his back.

"He's right."

Asprey faced her. The dead, scary look was still in her eyes—but this time, parts of it were directed at him. "A bullet isn't going to stop someone like me. We need to get out of here."

Graff didn't question it and busied himself flipping open the shiny gold panels on Todd's briefcase and pulling out a stack of hundred dollar bills. He smacked them into Asprey's chest. "Get the guys out of the kitchen. That should be persuasive enough."

"Jesus, Graff—how much money is in that briefcase? How much did you tell him to bring?"

Poppy made a quick assessment of the contents. "I'm guessing near half a million—is that about right, Graff?"

Graff growled a few incomprehensible syllables and motioned for Asprey to continue doing his bidding.

Asprey looked at the money and back at Poppy. "You're sure about this?"

"What other choice do we have right now? Todd is going to wake up considerably poorer and with one hell of a grudge to repay. The more scared of us he is, the better everyone's chances. Graff is right."

"No thanks to you two and your ridiculous heroics. I had it covered." Graff began tossing their props into a few of the empty boxes piled in the corner. "Just clear the back and try not to look so panicked. We're going to have to get him into the trunk and find somewhere to dump him."

Who are you? Asprey wanted to ask. They'd bent quite a few laws to steal the forged items from the clients Winston had cheated, but they'd never hurt anyone before. Something inside Graff had shifted, and Asprey had no idea how or when it happened.

He took a deep breath, flipping through the pile of hundreds and invoking whatever was left of Rufio.

"My friends!" Asprey called, moving out the door, his arms raised. Only two cooks sat in the kitchen, both of them smoking over a pot of what had equal chances of being soup or human remains. They'd obviously heard the gunshot, because they both reached for their belts. "It seems my guests have a powerful hunger. No, no—the lady is very particular. If you don't mind, I'd like to rent these kitchen facilities for the next hour or so."

The older of the two cooks took a long pull on his cigarette before flicking the ashes on the floor. "We hafta finish this stew. It's Brunswick."

That was definitely not what it smelled like. "I'll stir it faithfully, I swear." Asprey tossed the stack of bills on the counter. "I've always wanted to try my hand at being a cook. I can't tell you how much I appreciate the opportunity."

The younger cook—who looked halfway normal in a chef's jacket layered over loose-fitting pants—pocketed the money with a cool efficiency. Without batting an eye, he turned and moved through the swinging doors to the front.

"Take the green pepper out at half past," the older cook ordered. He handed Asprey the spoon. "Don't throw it away. I need it for later."

"Noted. And thank you."

"Just clean up when you're done." He wasn't talking about the kitchen.

Asprey returned to the back room to find Poppy with the top half of her dress pooled around her waist, her back to the door.

"Um, Poppy?" He took in the soft taper of her back, broken only by the band of her tan strapless bra. "Shouldn't you, ah, put something else on?"

"We don't have a whole lot of options, Asp," Graff said, busy tossing their gangster decorations into boxes. "If we're going to make Todd think she's dead without supplying him with a body, he needs something else to convince him. A dress with a bullet hole and plenty of blood should send the right message."

"But it's *his* blood," Asprey protested. "That won't hold up in a court of law."

Graff snorted. "You think Todd's going to take a bloodied dress with a hole supposedly ripped by *his* firearm, a gang of underground mobsters and a missing briefcase of stolen money to the cops? No. That bastard is going to leave town as fast as his legs can carry him."

Asprey blinked. It was a good plan. It was a *great* plan—
and one that fell way, way outside the bounds of what they were
used to. Hell, this even had to be a bit of a stretch for Poppy.
Forged baseballs weren't quite the same as making a man
believe he'd murdered someone.

Poppy must have agreed because she turned her head a
little and paused in the act of removing her dress. "Did you just
call him 'that bastard'?"

"What?" Graff's voice was rough. "You think you're the only
person he's ripped off in the past few years? You failed to
mention that Washington has been just one of the many stops
along his tour. Alaska, Oregon, California, Texas...he left a
nasty trail behind."

Poppy turned in surprise, dropping her hand from where
the barest scraps of fabric remained pressed up against her
chest, exposing the swell of her breasts over the top of her
banded bra. That was the last straw. Maybe it was a ridiculous,
last-ditch effort to gain a semblance of control over the
situation, but Asprey wasn't about to let her stand there half-
naked while Graff steamrolled everything.

With a possessive growl, he tugged the button-up black
shirt out of his pants, quickly working the row of buttons and
shrugging out of it.

"Here. This should be long enough to cover most of you."
He handed the shirt to Poppy, his hand brushing along her bare
shoulder, trying not to notice the way her skin moved under his
fingertips, like ripples of silk. He could have kept going, except
he caught a glimpse of blood swiped on her arm—Todd's blood.

What have we gotten ourselves into?

Poppy's eyes met his, and there was still a strange dearth
of emotion to them. "Thank you."

Asprey nodded once.

"Can you two speed things up, please?" Graff's bark caused
both of them to jump. "Todd's starting to come to, and I don't
want to have to hit him again. Asprey—you grab his legs.
Poppy, start grabbing boxes. We'll load him in your car, the
stuff in mine. And be careful with Louis."

There didn't seem to be anything to argue in that, so Asprey left Poppy to make what she could out of his shirt and leaned down to take Todd's feet. Graff took the helm, hoisting Todd's arms and shoulders.

Moving a body was a lot harder than it looked. They shuffled him through the kitchen as quickly as they could, but the dead weight multiplied the strain of Todd's already solid form. They dropped him twice in the parking lot, and it took several attempts to swing him up before they finally got him inside the trunk.

"Are we sure he's going to be okay in there?" Asprey asked, adjusting Todd's head so that it rested on a slightly dirty picnic blanket rather than the jack.

Poppy materialized behind him, a few boxes in her hand. She set them down to study Todd, and the way she looked down on the body in the trunk, without so much as a blink, filled Asprey with a strange sensation. The sensation wasn't fear, and it wasn't judgment—both of which seemed reasonable, given this situation. He mostly wanted to give her a hug.

"Always give it back if it turns out they need it more than you do, Todd. Always." She slammed the trunk down. The shirt he'd worn hit her just at the top of her thighs, and she'd rolled the sleeves up, looking sexy as hell in all the wrong ways. It wasn't a good time to admire the view. They had a half-dead man on their hands and Asprey was the only one who seemed to have a problem with it.

"I should never have involved you in all this," she added, her quiet voice offset by a desperate kind of urgency. Her eyes flicked down as she took in Asprey's bare chest, propelling his body backward in time, to the safety of the bat-room and the passion of two people who were just people—not thieves or con women or millionaires or ex-felons. "We need to get the rest of the boxes and go."

It only took a few trips to clear most of the stuff out, since they decided no one would care if they left the television set or other large items. The hardest task was cleaning up the blood, but Asprey stood firm and wouldn't budge until Graff got down on his hands and knees and sopped it up with a load of greasy kitchen towels. This was *his* mess, after all.

On their way out, Asprey paused a beat. "You'll have to give me just a second," he said. He ignored their protests as he ran into the kitchen. Graff might be able to run a backroom poker game and nonchalantly shove men into trunks, but he wasn't about to desert that green pepper so it continued bobbing in the Brunswick stew.

He wasn't leaving anything to chance. Not anymore.

Chapter Twenty-Two

Someone needs to give Asprey a shirt.

The scene spread out before them, a perfect tableau taken from a crime scene drama. Todd slumped in an inert heap underneath the docks, the moon barely a glimmer through the clouds. No sound other than the lapping of waves on crusty shores filled the night air, and the unmistakable scent of rotting seaweed surrounded them.

Graff had chosen an isolated spot near a collection of industrial warehouses, so there was no one about—and anyone who might have chanced by would have kept going, head bent, no questions asked.

Farther off, closer to the receding water's edge, crumpled what remained of Poppy's white dress, soaked with blood and with a hole clearly ripped open on the chest. One high heel lay spike up; the other bobbed in the waves. As a final touch, Graff tucked the gun—Todd's own—into the bastard's hand, so that the first thing he would see when he came to was evidence of his crime.

And yet, with all those touches, almost cinematic in their execution, Poppy couldn't stop looking at Asprey and his stupid bare chest. He was eerily beautiful in the moonlight, his torso seeming to extend for miles to where it trailed into the waistband of his slacks, each movement an education in masculine grace.

"What?" Asprey asked, kicking some sand around to cover their footprints. "Why are you looking at me like that?"

"It's cold," was all she said. No need to let him know how that young, ripped Abe Lincoln look was working on her. She crossed her arms over her chest. "And late. Graff? Are we ready?"

"You guys take your car and head back to the hangar." Graff jogged up, looking flushed and, dare she say it—happy? The sense of criminal purpose suited him. "I'm going to hide out down by the pier and watch. I want to make sure he understands the full severity of what he's done when he wakes up."

"I think you covered it." Poppy didn't harbor any illusions about Todd Kennick's sense of right and wrong. He wouldn't make a push to see if Natalie was okay, wouldn't try to contact the gangsters to issue a formal apology. He'd run—fast, and as far as his legs would take him.

And there it was, all cleaned up in a tidy bow. Natalie would no longer be showing up to work at In the Buff. The backroom poker game was cleared and gone. The three of them would disappear, all of Todd's money in hand—well beyond the eighty grand she'd set out to recover.

The question was *why*?

Looking over at Graff, pride and maliciousness warring for supremacy in his face—that face so like Asprey's but without a tenth of his humanity—she was almost afraid to ask. The half million? Simply because he could? Or was it that maybe, just maybe, he wanted to return the money to its rightful owners?

Either way, he was far too secretive about it.

"Don't you think you've done enough for one night?" she asked Graff coldly. "We should all head back to the hangar to debrief. I'm very interested in what the hell that was all about."

"Just take Asprey home, will you? I think he might try to strangle me if he stays here any longer." The look Graff settled on Asprey was almost gentle. "I'm sorry things had to turn out this way."

He tossed her the keys, but Asprey intercepted, catching them easily. "I can drive," he muttered. "But before we go, I want you to give me your gun."

"Excuse me?"

Asprey extended his hand. "You heard me. I'm not leaving you here with Todd and a gun. Is it loaded this time?"

Asprey still sucked at having a staring contest, blinking several times as he met his brother's eyes and refused to back down, but Poppy couldn't help a tick of pride from beating in her chest. Graff needed taking down a notch. Or twelve.

"Jesus, Asp. I'm not a murderer."

Asprey's hand didn't move.

"Fine." Graff reached into his waistband and handed the gun to Asprey, but not before pressing the magazine catch and pulling back the slide. "See? There were never even any bullets."

For some reason, that fact only served to make Asprey angrier. She'd never seen him like that, the finely chiseled angles of his face hard and resolute, the laugh lines all but disappeared. He snatched the gun out of his brother's hand and tossed it into the trunk of Poppy's car, the dark stain of blood a testament to the night's activities.

"Come on, Poppy." Asprey moved his hand on her lower back as he helped her into the car. Always the gentleman, even in the face of spiraling criminal intent. "There's not much more we can do here."

She slid into the passenger's seat, careful to keep her shirt-slash-dress from riding too high up her legs. The last thing either one of them needed was to be reminded of their current state of undress.

Not that it would have mattered. Asprey stabbed the keys into the ignition and forced the stick into reverse, his foot heavy on the pedal as he spun the car out of the empty parking lot. His eyes didn't once stray from the road. She could have been sitting there naked and he probably would have remained at ten and two, fury rising from the surface of his skin in a smoldering combination of hot and cold.

"You probably shouldn't drive so fast," she murmured after a few minutes. They took the freeway onramp at a good eighty miles per hour, traffic being almost a negligible entity this time of the night. Or morning, depending on which way you looked at it.

"This isn't fast." He passed a car with a sharp turn. "This is efficient. The less time I spend on the road, the more time I have to devote to plotting Graff's demise."

Grumpy Asprey sounded so much like his brother she had to laugh. "Try explaining that to the cop who's bound to pull you over. You don't think that driving a car with a large amount of blood and a gun in the trunk might call for a little more moderation?"

He let out an irritated growl and lifted his foot from the pedal. Instead of slowing to a more reasonable speed, as she expected, Asprey took the nearest exit and pulled into the parking lot of an abandoned gas station.

"I don't think loitering in this part of town is very smart either." She peered out the window. Darkness enveloped the fifties-style building, the ancient pumps standing like stone relics to a simpler era. "Even in this crappy old car."

"A carjacking is the least of my worries right now."

"Oh yeah. I'm always forgetting—money is like a toy to you. Lose a car, buy a new one. Run out of funds, take a man's briefcase full of blood money."

"Why are you taking this out on me?"

Irritation slammed into her. "He's your brother! You're the untouchable thieves, rolling in trust funds and only out for— what? Fun? Is that what this is supposed to be?"

"That was *not* my idea of fun." His voice was very near a growl—the good, protective kind. His hand gripped the back of her neck with intensity, forcing her to meet his gaze. "You could have been seriously hurt back there at the poker game. I swear to you, if I'd had any idea he was going to pull something like that... It's not okay with me, Poppy, endangering your life."

"Well, Graff seemed to be enjoying himself." She tried not to notice how his sudden burst into heroics affected her, like she wanted to curl up in a ball and let him ameliorate every problem she'd ever had. First tackling Todd, then demanding the gun from Graff, now this smoldering, protective anger. She wasn't the type of woman who needed rescuing, but that didn't mean she couldn't appreciate a man who wanted to try—especially when he wasn't wearing a shirt.

"Graff is a sociopath."

"And yet you take all your orders from him," she countered. "How comforting."

Asprey gave a reluctant laugh and lowered his hand from her neck, letting his fingers fall softly through her hair. "He's a sociopath with an innate sense of right and wrong—he always has been. He was the type of kid who saw a bully knock someone down on the playground and fought back, no matter how much smaller in size he was. I never knew if it was because he loved to beat the crap out of people, or because his moral compass was just that rigid. These days, I think it's a little of both. If what he said is true—that Todd's been cheating people across several states—then this is exactly the kind of vigilante justice he'd go for."

Her breath caught in her throat. "What about you?"

"What about me?" Asprey's voice was hoarse—raw and resigned. "I was the kid on the playground who stood near the monkey bars to watch the girls swing upside down in their dresses."

"You never helped him fight?"

Asprey smiled tightly, etchings of sadness along his eyes. "He wouldn't let me. But I always helped him get home afterward. Which is why—"

She didn't wait to hear anything more. Leaning in, a hand flat on that gloriously bare, hair-smattered chest, she kissed him.

Asprey was hesitant at first, as though he wasn't finished with their conversation and planned on fighting the baser urges that held her in their fiery grip. But her persistence won out, and his lips parted to allow her entry.

The victory of it was short-lived.

"I never thought I'd say this, but maybe we should save the kissing for a later date." His mouth pressed gently against hers as he spoke. "We need to talk."

She pulled away just enough to see his face, but not so much that the connection between them was lost. She'd almost *died*, and the need to feel connected to something, to someone, was stronger than any presumption at common sense. Especially since the morning was likely to bring with it the realization that she had officially ruined her chances of getting out of this unscathed. "I don't want to talk, Asprey. I don't want to think about Graff or Todd or jail or Bea or even what I'm going to have for breakfast in the morning. I just want you."

Snagging his lower lip with her teeth, Poppy resumed their kiss, refusing to hold anything back as she climbed out of her seat and into his lap, reaching down to push the driver's seat back as far as it could go. It wasn't far, but by that time, she had either leg straddling his lap, their bodies a jumble of half-clothed limbs, so it didn't really matter.

"We should get you home." Asprey's words carried no meaning, as he'd completely fallen into the kiss, his mouth hot and searing where it landed—on her lips, along her jaw, at the open collar of her shirt—causing her body to respond with shivers of pleasure.

"Absolutely," she agreed, arching her back as his lips slid even further under the collar. "But if you're going to sit there all night without a shirt on, I refuse to be responsible for my actions."

Asprey's hands moved to her bare thighs, running up the length of them but stopping before he got to the good parts. She grabbed the headrest to give her leverage and ground her hips against his. He groaned, and his grip on her tightened.

She undid the top two buttons to the shirt she wore, which smelled like Asprey. Everything smelled like him, the crisp, clean scent of bergamot and mint. It filled the air and her senses, making it easy to conceal herself in the moment. She wasn't covered in Todd's blood. She wasn't parked in the lot of a gas station that probably housed an entire family of opossums. She wasn't falling headfirst into a situation that was so far outside her plans it might as well have been on the moon.

There was just that smell and his lips and the hot, steady pulse of desire that she felt in every place their skin touched.

"In all my years, I don't think I've actually steamed up the windows before," Asprey murmured, using a momentary pause to catch his breath and adjust her hips so that she could feel the entire length of him pressing against her. The shirt had hitched up enough so that the only thing separating the two of them was the thin cotton of her panties and his dark slacks. The direct pressure was enough to send mounting pleasure to every nerve ending she had.

Using one hand on the ceiling to steady herself, Poppy let out a low moan. "Asprey, if you're paying attention to the windows right now, I'm doing something wrong."

His laughter shook the car, the vibrations working a number on her body. A strong arm wrapped around her waist, pulling her back down into a kiss that stretched into the night as an explosion of bright lights and flashing colors.

Until the lights dimmed and the colors stopped flashing and a heavy knock on the window startled them both.

Poppy scrambled off Asprey's lap and into the passenger seat, her fingers working quickly at the open buttons of her shirt, but it was a severe case of too little, too late. A second knock sounded, this time accompanied by the all-too-familiar rap of metal on glass, of flashlight meeting window. Like the ubiquitous crash of a domestic squabble next door, it was a sound that took Poppy right to her youth.

"You decent?" Asprey asked, a wry twist to his smile.

"As decent as it's gonna get," she managed, tugging the shirt down her legs. It was a silly attempt, seeing as how Asprey was shirtless, sweating and had an undeniable and substantial swelling in his pants. "It's not like we have much in the way of options, and they don't like waiting long."

"I see you're an old hand at this." He rolled the damp, murky glass down. The look he gave her was wary but confident. "And look natural. This, at least, is something I can do."

Poppy wished she had a tenth of his reserves of charm, able to be conjured at a moment's notice. She'd bottle it up and keep it stashed in her bra for just such an occasion.

"Hullo, Officer," he called. "How can I help you?"

"This is a No Park zone," the officer said, clearly not as impressed with Asprey's nonchalance as she was. The officer's head moved down into Poppy's line of vision, and she was able to breathe when she saw the pinched, weathered face of a complete stranger. It wasn't like she knew all of the Seattle cops, but it only took one of the many officers who'd processed her to turn this evening into a nightmare beyond her worst imagination. "That means you can't park here."

Another big sigh of relief. He obviously wasn't the brightest cop on the beat.

"We were just on our way," Asprey said, not once losing his smile. "I guess we got a little caught up in the moment, if you know what I mean. We're newlyweds, heading to the airport right now for our flight out. I've always wanted to show the little woman Bali. She's never been, but there's this incredible place in Denpasar I stayed once. Small but cozy."

Hilarious. Asprey was cracking inside jokes about Balinese prisons now, of all times.

The cop moved his flashlight around the inside of the car, lingering a bit too long on their attire—or lack of it—for Poppy's comfort. "You lose some clothes on the way?"

Asprey looked down, as if seeing his state of undress for the first time. "Well, look at that. I guess we got a little more carried away than we intended. Honey, have you seen my shirt?"

"I'm sure it's around here somewhere," Poppy managed, pretending to rustle around the floor of the car.

It must have been a convincing show, because the cop pulled the flashlight far enough out of the car they were no longer spotlighted. "You seem like decent folks, but this isn't a good part of town, so you'd best be on your way."

"Of course, Officer," Asprey agreed. "Couldn't agree more."

They might actually get away. She might actually end the night without handcuffs on her wrists, Nancy the parole officer's wrath upon her head and years more of regret. Hope, an ever-elusive prankster as far as Poppy was concerned, reared her bright head.

"I'll just need to check your IDs."

And then it disappeared.

"Just as a precaution, of course." The cop ran his gloved hand over the door.

Asprey reached across the car, presumably to grab identification, though he used the moment to look at her and offer a reassuring smile. "I got this," he mouthed.

She smiled tightly. He had no idea how close they were to the precipice—how close they were to losing it everything. It was like he was incapable of understanding that not everyone had a wink and several thousand dollars at the ready to emerge unscathed from every situation. There was blood in the trunk, for crying out loud.

"This isn't normally my kind of car," Asprey said casually, handing over his driver's license. "It's my wife's, but since we're parking at the airport, it seemed safer to leave this one. I'm more of a speed man myself, though I shouldn't be saying that to you."

"Oh yeah?" The cop peeked in. "Your wife there have ID?"

"Not on her," Asprey said calmly. "Most of the time, I reserve my speed for the skies, so you don't have to worry about pulling me over. Once you hit the clouds at a good two hundred mile an hour pace, no car can compare."

"You a pilot?"

"Amateur stuff, mostly. I used to fly with my dad when I was a kid, and he bought me my first Cessna the day I turned eighteen. I'm pretty sure my grandmother didn't talk to him for a month after that. She was sure I'd crash the damn thing into Mt. Rainier or something."

"But you're still here."

Asprey spread his hands. "Ten crash-free years and counting. What's the fastest your patrol car hits?"

"Highest I've ever gotten her is ninety-two, chasing down a drunk teenager in a stolen Miata." The cop handed back the paperwork. "How is it your wife expects to get through airport security without any identification? Or pants?"

Poppy gripped the door handle so tightly she almost lost feeling in her fingers. For a second there, she thought Asprey had it covered, what with his tales of a rich snob childhood and manly pursuits of velocity. He was a definite people person— hitting all the right notes, engaging the officer in conversation as though they'd been golf buddies for years.

"Oh, I'm flying us out," Asprey said easily. "Didn't I mention that? We shipped most of our stuff ahead of time—Ruby, my plane, she's great with a tailwind and a lightweight like the little woman here, but she can't handle the long-distances with a ton of luggage. And between you and me? My wife packed twelve suitcases for our two week trip. Twelve, and I swear most of them are full of shoes." Asprey reached over and patted her leg.

The cop chuckled appreciatively. "You two kids have fun on your honeymoon—and try to keep it all buttoned up until you get there, okay?"

Asprey nodded and winked, waving a cheerful good-bye. They waited until the cop car pulled out of the lot before daring to move.

"That was close," Poppy said. She clamped her hands in her lap to keep Asprey from noticing the way they shook. "It's a good thing you can think on your feet. That cop was about to offer to take my place on the honeymoon."

He started the car. "I do have my occasional uses."

"Hey," she began. Her initial urge was to protest the bitter note in his voice, but a sinking feeling took the place of anything warmer or fuzzier. His privileged roots were showing again—a strong reminder of the places they needed to maintain. "Is there anything you can't talk your way out of? Any situation that doesn't naturally work out in your favor?"

Confidence Tricks

He cast her a sidelong look so full of meaning she squirmed uncomfortably. "There is one thing I have my doubts about. But I think our first task should be to demolish my brother."

"Which one?" she asked wryly, playing along.

"Honestly?" He cocked his head her direction, and this time, his smile seemed genuine. "At this point, I'm not so sure I care."

"He'll be here." Asprey sat on one of their folding chairs, a bowl of Rice Krispies balanced on one knee. The act of bringing spoon to mouth was doing wonders in helping him keep his calm. "He's probably just running late."

"Six hours late?" Poppy, on the other hand, paced the floor of the hangar at an almost frantic pace, Gunner on her heels. "I don't like it. He should be here by now."

She came to a halt in front of him. Under any other circumstances, the sight of Poppy in a leather bustier over faded, form-fitting jeans would have him dreaming of spaghetti westerns and saloon girls. But even though he wouldn't have minded wrapping his arms around her and forcing her to sit still, she had a point. It wasn't like Graff to be late.

"We probably shouldn't have left him alone with Todd." Asprey gave voice to the worst of his concerns.

"We shouldn't have left him alone with that money. It looks an awful lot like Graff took that briefcase and skipped town."

Asprey couldn't help the laughter from rumbling through his chest.

"What's so funny?" Poppy leaned in, and might have been menacing if the curve of each breast wasn't exactly on his eye level. Those were not the parts of her that scared him the most. "I'm glad this is all such a nice joke for you."

"Poppy, stop." He placed the cereal on the floor for Gunner to lap. "I'm only laughing because that is the exact same thing Graff said to me the day after the first poker game—only *he* was talking about *you*."

"What?" Some of her stiffness gave way as she searched his face.

"He was sure you were going to skip town with Todd and our thirty grand." He shook his head. "You're both so afraid of getting cheated—haven't we been through enough yet to earn a little trust?"

"Wait a minute. That was the day you stopped by the gym to show off your yoga skills."

"Ye-es." He didn't like that flash in her eyes. He recognized that flash.

She strode forward, but there was nothing welcoming in her approach. "The day you said you were checking up on me to make sure I was okay."

Oh, crap. He knew where this was headed. "And I was so glad you were?"

"You were checking to make sure I was still there!"

He spread his hands helplessly. "Can you blame me? You've said it yourself countless times, Poppy—that's what you do. And you have to admit, getting us to offer up that kind of cash...it would have been one hell of a con."

"You lied to me."

"I lied to Graff. He wanted me to make sure you didn't leave," Asprey countered. Feeling brave, he added, "Me? I just wanted to see you again."

A resounding yap from somewhere near their feet and the slam of a door stopped Asprey from making the mistake of following that declaration with action. *Graff.* He was finally here.

"We have a problem."

Asprey and Poppy both whirled to face Tiffany, who stalked into the hangar, her laptop bag in hand. She used it as a shield to prevent Gunner from attacking her ankle. Poppy took the hint and gathered up the dog, settling him carefully in the area they'd set up near the entrance, a playpen full of squeaky toys and bones that were bigger than he was.

"Graff didn't show up for the rendezvous this morning," Tiffany announced, skipping the preliminaries. "What the hell happened last night?"

"You mean you haven't seen him either?" Asprey and Poppy shared a worried look. The thought of Graff skipping town with the money was ridiculous—and not just because it was a drop in the bucket compared to the company's value. There was also the small matter of Graff bringing Winston to justice. A man didn't spend years of his life plotting the downfall of his nemesis only to give it all up for half a million dollars. For a woman, yes—Asprey could understand that rationale all too well. But money? Not a chance.

Tiffany pulled out her laptop and booted it up. "Last I heard from him, Graff was heading out to the poker game. He and I planned to meet back here early this morning, but he never showed. And his cell phone must be either destroyed or the battery was taken out, because I can't even track that."

Asprey frowned. "Why would his cell phone be destroyed?"

Tiffany's pointed stare would have put Graff's to shame. "Because he's in trouble. Walk me through the exact steps last night. What happened in that strip club?"

Asprey did his best to lay out the night's events, beginning with Graff's change of plans regarding Todd and their own bewilderment when it turned out things were much deeper than either of them knew. Tiffany didn't seem at all surprised to hear that Todd had been asked to bring more money, or that Graff intended to cheat him out of every last penny.

"I know. We were going to send it back."

"What do you mean, send it back?" Poppy spoke up for the first time.

For Poppy, Tiffany took the time to actually look up from her computer and address her. "There wasn't even close to enough money to pay back everyone Todd ripped off, but we were going to send as much as we could."

"Why didn't you tell us about the plan?" Poppy sounded hurt. "We could have helped."

"Graff doesn't trust easily," Tiffany said lamely, looking to Asprey for help. It was a look he knew well, the pleading mixed with expectation. *Handle the messy human stuff for us, will you, Asp? Transform the grand decisions the rest of us make on a whim into something acceptable.*

"Let me guess," he said drily. "He thought that if Poppy knew we could take Todd for more, she'd want a bigger cut. So he decided to go all dark and rogue and do it on his own."

Tiffany squirmed uncomfortably. "He didn't think that *exactly.* He just thought the less you guys were involved, the better."

"It's fine," Poppy interjected, her voice flat.

"No, it's not," Asprey protested. He was tired of this role, tired of being the clown carrying the bucket and a shovel behind a parade of high-stepping stallions. "Graff is an overbearing jerk who thinks he gets to make all the rules. And it's my fault because I never tried to stop him. It was easier to let him call the shots, make all the difficult choices, leaving me blame-free and responsibility-free. I should have paid more attention to what was going on with him, should have forced him to include us in that plan, if only because then we'd at least have an idea where he might be right now."

Poppy watched his speech closely, her shoulders falling with each sentence. "I think his motivations had less to do with you and a lot more to do with me. What reason does he have to trust me? What reason does anyone?"

"I think you've more than proven yourself here."

"But that's not really the point, is it?" Poppy countered. "The point is that we need to find where he is—and fast. I think I should come back from the dead to find Todd, see if I can talk a little sense into him." She pounded a fist into the opposite hand.

Tiffany shook her head resolutely. "It's not Todd. *His* cell phone is on and working just fine." She whirled the laptop so the screen faced them. A map of the southwestern United States popped up. "Right now he's headed due south—I'm guessing Mexico."

"He could have Graff with him," Poppy insisted.

"And he smashed Graff's phone to keep us from triangulating his location, but left his own intact?" Tiffany shook her head. "Todd even has the GPS on—most middle school students with Internet access could find him with that. It doesn't make any sense."

"You said Graff's car is missing too?" Asprey asked. Something about this scenario didn't make sense. "It wasn't by the docks?"

"Not by the docks, not at any of his regular spots, not in impound."

"All the stuff from the Bouncing Booty was in that car."

"So?" Poppy asked. "It could be at the bottom of the ocean by now. Todd looks benign, but he's not. Believe me."

"That's not it—Louis was in that car."

Poppy shook her head. "I still don't follow."

"If he left the docks after Todd fled, there's no way he would go anywhere but this hangar afterwards. Not with Louis in the car. He had to have been stopped sometime between leaving the docks and heading here."

"So?"

"He probably left between three, when we were there with him, and, what, six? When the sun came up?"

Tiffany nodded. "We were supposed to meet here around seven. That makes sense."

Asprey pushed the laptop closed. His heart had picked up to the point where he could feel his rib cage reverberating with each beat, but the rest of him clicked smoothly into action. "Then I know where he is."

"Where?" Poppy and Tiffany cried at the same time, the latter rising to her feet.

"Poppy, you're coming with me. Tiff—you stay here in case anything goes wrong. There's only one place Graff goes every morning, without fail, Louis and Todd money be damned."

"Oh no." Tiffany dropped her head in her hands.

Poppy whirled on him. "What? Where?"

"Charles Appraisals and Insurance," he said firmly. "Or rather, the coffee shop across the street. He's been going there since long before any of this started happening. Jalapeno bagel, cream cheese, black coffee. Sits by the window on the right, under that picture of the dancing scones. He'll leave a five-dollar tip to make up for the fact that he won't begrudge the waitress a single smile."

"You don't think..."

"I do think. If he's not still there, someone will have at least seen him." Asprey nodded once. "Suit up, Veronica Maxwell. We're headed to the office."

Chapter Twenty-Three

"You are such a wimp. Thirty-three flights are not that many."

Asprey leaned over, his hands on his knees, breathing deep. "Elevators were invented for a reason."

"Elevators are windowless, airless boxes of doom." Poppy rubbed her hand in circles on Asprey's back, moving lower and lower until he shot straight up. That got him moving again. "I promised myself I would never have to be trapped anywhere like that if I could possibly help it."

"What happens if you go to jail again?"

"Why would I?" she asked breezily, even though her whole body clenched at the thought. "I'm with you. You'll never get caught—it's that charmed life you lead."

He stared at her a moment too long. "You call this charmed?"

She nodded at the placard above the door, his surname in large, expensive lettering. "I do. Now here's hoping that waitress was right and Graff is still here."

Before Asprey could say anything else on the subject, she pulled the door open and let out a peal of false laughter. Making a grand entrance was a great way to force him to comply.

"And then the president told me it was a goose the whole time! Can you imagine?" Poppy linked her arm in Asprey's and pretended to be perfectly at ease. She nodded politely to the receptionist, Tracy.

"I'm still on the lookout for that old, ugly yellow chair for you," she quipped, remembering their conversation from before.

Tracy laughed. "You're off the hook for that one, Ms. Maxwell. We had one go rogue for a while but it's back now, none the worse for wear. Good afternoon, Mr. Charles."

Asprey's grip on her arm tightened. "Hey, Tracy. Is my brother in?"

"He should be in his office. Did you want me to buzz him?"

"No need. We'll show ourselves in."

"Was she talking about Louis?" Poppy hissed as they moved through the fish-tank maze toward the executive offices. "What is it with you guys and that chair?"

"Think of it this way—if we were playing chess, Louis would be the king. It belonged to our father." It was all the explanation she was going to get. Asprey stalked ahead of her, not stopping until he stood in front of a heavy steel door that looked like it led to a vault.

Please don't let it be a vault.

It wasn't. Yet another huge office with windows up to the ceiling and decorated like it was cut from sheets of stainless steel, it was almost identical to Asprey's office, though a bit bigger and with a familiar and elaborate wingback yellow chair behind the desk. *Louis.* And Graff was nowhere to be seen.

Poppy had to admit the effect was chilling.

"I wish I could say I'm surprised to see you here, Asprey." Winston looked up from his seat on the chair, missing only a cat in his lap to make the perfect villain. "But since most of the accounts have been of not one, but two masked crusaders, I knew he had a partner. Or are there three? Veronica from Vancouver, right? How lovely to see you again. I can't tell you how happy I am to find my original assessment of you was correct."

"Do you want me to take him out?" Poppy asked, glancing sideways at Asprey, her body tensed. She didn't have a whole lot of love to spare for Graff, but he was their partner. And the way Winston looked at Asprey, as though he was an insignificant worm, made her want to punch something—preferably a squishy body part. "Just say the word."

Asprey shook his head just slightly, enough so that she knew he needed some space. She took a literal step back, giving him the floor but letting him know she was there for him. *Not for him. For Tiffany and Graff and their entire cause.* It was an important distinction.

"What did you do to Graff?"

"You think I don't know he's been watching me from that coffee shop every morning?" Winston let out an almost silent laugh. "I just needed his guard to be down—and taking Louis out of his car was the perfect bait. *He* came to *me*, blazed right up here like he owns the place. I expected him to be a lot tanner, having spent all that time in Hawaii."

"Where is he?"

"Don't be stupid. This isn't some game—it's not one of your pranks with my espresso machines. Which, by the way, I want back. All of them."

"I've always loved a good cup of coffee," Asprey returned. A strange calm had descended over him, and he even took a seat on the other side of Graff's desk, hitching his pants and propping one leg on the opposite knee. If Poppy didn't know better, she'd think he was preparing to chat about the weather or next season's Mariner's line up. But she *did* know better— and Asprey was far from calm. This false serenity was a hell of a lot more dangerous than Winston knew.

She flanked Asprey's chair, arms crossed, legs wide. She was also a lot more dangerous than Winston knew.

But Winston's gaze barely flicked over her. "Don't be flippant. This is real life, Asprey—you've heard of that, right? This whole, big, grown-up world where people make hard decisions and live with the repercussions? Dad didn't do you any favors growing up, letting you always have your way, indulging your little art hobbies."

"At least he saw to it that I have manners."

Poppy snorted. Winston obviously didn't appreciate the interruption, his face growing purple in that way Graff had when pushed too far.

"You let me know how those manners work out for you when I find a way to cut off your trust fund. Like it or not, this is *my* company, and now that Graff and I have reached an understanding, there's not a whole lot you can do to change that."

"An understanding?" Asprey sat up, dropping some of the pretense at relaxation. "You and I both know that's the last thing Graff would ever offer you. What have you done to him?"

"Calm down, Asprey. Whatever you may think of me, I'm not going to hurt my own brother." Winston stood, pushing back from the desk so that the chair grated across the floor. Even Poppy winced, knowing what that was doing to the delicate wood surface of Graff's prized possession. "All you need to know is that he's not hurt, and he will continue to stay unhurt until—"he paused to check his calendar sitting open on the desk "—Friday at nine a.m. Pacific Time."

"What happens on Friday at nine?" Poppy couldn't help asking.

"That's when all of this becomes irrelevant, isn't it, Asprey?" Winston smiled and tapped the calendar. "All your hard work, all your careful planning. The moment that insurance policy expires, you have nothing left."

"That's four days from now," Asprey said tightly. "What's to stop me from waltzing in there right now and taking the painting tonight?"

Winston spread his hands in a gesture of generosity. "Certainly not me, though my guards might have something to say about it. But let's not kid ourselves. You and I both know that you would have never been able to do any of this on your own. This is Graff's grudge, and it has his stamp all over it. Oh, wait—I know what this situation needs."

He held up a finger and moved to his desk drawer, rummaging around until he found a stack of papers. With a smile, he held them extended, his arm unwavering. "Go on, they won't bite."

"You know how I feel about heavy reading," Asprey said, not moving to take them. Unable to help herself, Poppy grabbed the proffered item.

"It looks like some kind of title and registration," she said, flipping through the several pages of legal jargon. "For something called a Corvalis?"

Asprey took the papers then, and without glancing at them, ripped them in half. "You think you can bribe me with my own plane?"

"Yes, I do. The plane and everything that comes with it. You're as much a part of this company as any of us. I don't know what Graff promised you in exchange for your help, but I'll double it."

There was a long pause in which Poppy thought Asprey might actually accept the deal his brother laid out on the table, that the promise of money might win out in this strange power struggle.

But he didn't. Even though she'd refused to see it for so long, Asprey was stronger than a simple promise of dollars and cents.

"Thanks but no thanks." Asprey smirked. "Your generosity moves me, but I'm going to see this through to the end. You better beef up security, Winston. I'm taking that painting."

They turned to leave, but Winston stopped them with one hand on the door. "This is your final chance. Don't be stupid. Don't throw your life away on another man's dreams. Hell, I'll even give you the damn chair back."

"I don't want the chair, Winston. I've got my eye on a Pollock."

Winston stepped back. "If you were any other man, Asprey, I'd consider that a threat."

"And if you were any other man, Winston, I'd consider *you* one."

Dinghies and Donuts seemed like the most appropriate place to plan the heist. Call him sentimental, but there was something about being in charge that made Asprey want to pull out all the stops. If he thought he could get away with asking the waitress at the diner to put on some Dubstep, he'd have done it.

"Why are we here?" Poppy asked warily. "Can't we just do this at the hangar?"

"This is probably the only time I get to be in charge, and I intend to enjoy it." Asprey put his hand on Poppy's back as he led her inside, nodding at the waitress to bring them a pot of the diner's infamous coffee.

Poppy didn't know it, but she had this thing about him touching her in the small of her back. Her body went completely tense for a fraction of a second, and then a low hum escaped her throat. That hum told tales, gave him powers—he probably could have directed her over a cliff's edge, lemming-style, and she would have purred contentedly as she fell.

"Well, this works for me," Tiffany said. She lifted the ubiquitous laptop out of her bag and set it up on the chipped, wood-grain surface of the table. "Chances are Winston isn't watching the hangar, and I did a sweep for bugs, but we can't be too careful."

"Speaking of bugs, um, did you take care of the one...?"

Tiffany laughed. "That we stuck on Poppy's boots? Yes."

"Seriously, you guys?"

Asprey offered an apologetic smile, though judging from Poppy's frown, it didn't stick. "It was when we first met, I swear."

She threw up her hands in a gesture of surrender. "I'm so tired of playing spy games with you guys. You win. Every time. But I will say this—if you dare to track me after all this is said and done, I will make you drink an entire gallon of this coffee. No more bugs, no more secrets. Promise me."

Asprey made the signal of an x over his chest and leaned back in the booth, his arm draped just over Poppy's back. It was a studied calm. He had no idea where Graff was, no idea if they could successfully pull this off and no idea what Poppy intended to do when all this was "said and done". He'd have even been hard-pressed to pick which one of those worried him the most.

Tiffany began tapping at the keys of her computer. "So, as near as I can figure it, Winston has three guards posted at the apartment. One is working as a doorman and the other two rotate between watching the front entrance and the fire escape out back." She looked up from her computer. "That's in addition to the building's regular security."

"Why only three?" Poppy asked. "If he knows we're coming and he knows when, shouldn't he pull out all the stops? Or call the police or something?"

Asprey shook his head. This, at least, was something he could focus on. "He can't risk it. He's not supposed to know what's being stolen next. That would be admitting there something unique about all the items, which would point a big finger in his direction. It's why he hasn't come right out and warned Cindy."

"So it's easy, then." Poppy let out a huff of air. "We're just going to have to let me do it. I can get an invitation from Cindy to get inside. I'll have to—what? Tie her up or something? Then I can grab the painting and we go."

"No way." Asprey refused to even acknowledge that idea. "She can't know you're part of this. Not with your record. One police sketch or fingerprint and you'd be sunk."

Poppy smacked the table. "So? I'm just a petty thief, a small-time con woman. You saw the trouble I had with Todd. Bigger jobs aren't my thing."

"You must have some ideas," Asprey suggested.

"You're the one who loves all this heist stuff," Poppy countered. "Not me."

Tiffany snorted. "All Asprey knows is the clichés. If it's been done, overdone and turned into a sequel, he has the answers. Otherwise? Nothing. Face it, guys. We need Graff."

They all slunk a little farther in their seats, feeling the truth of that statement. A gang of thieves without their leader was just that—a gang. They could smash things and run amok, but the intricacies of this kind of operation were just too much.

Poppy was the first to shake her head. "I refuse to believe that. Asprey—you and Graff have taken dozens of items, and even though I know Graff likes to bark orders, he can't possibly have come up with all that on his own. He's militant but not clever. Not like you."

She thought he was clever? "That sounds an awful lot like a compliment," he said.

Her eyes sparkled warmly. "As someone clever once told me, it's not a compliment if it's true."

"She's right, you know," Tiffany added. "Graff once told me that he hated having to rely on you so much to get things done, but that there was no way he could come up with half the things you did. Of course, he didn't mean it as a compliment— he said it was all thanks to the hundreds of heist movies you watched as a kid."

"That's it." Asprey sat up straighter, even dared to take a sip of the coffee sludge. It tasted like dirt smoldering over an open fire, but he welcomed the burn of it. "We're trying too hard to make this something Graff would do—polished and professional. This is our chance to do things my way, which means we need to rely on the clichés. *All* of them."

Poppy's brow knit. "Are you serious?"

He leaned over the table, pointing to Tiffany's computer. "Bring up every heist movie ever made. I want to know what they did to get inside a building, what tricks they pulled to confuse the bad guy."

"Do you have a plan?" Poppy asked. When their eyes met, Poppy's sparkled with appreciation and something warmer, but the look turned off before he could do much more than register its presence, which he did on a fully visceral level, stored for future use.

"I'm starting to," he admitted, blowing out a long breath. He might be able to pull this off after all. Maybe he could be more than just a pretty toy. "Now...who do we know who can rent us some scaffolding?"

Chapter Twenty-Four

They parked the van outside Cindy VanHuett's apartment building at dawn on Thursday. Even though the vehicle was already ominous, what with the black paint and the darkened windows and all, they tricked it out even more. Asprey screwed mesh-type bars over the back window, and Poppy installed a giant antenna to the top that looked like it might be able to reach the moon, had it not been superglued on.

Poppy was responsible for putting the vehicle in place and plunking in enough quarters to keep it there all day. One of the guards posted by Winston, a flat-faced man with the widest shoulders she'd ever seen on a human being, noticed her and reached for his hip—for a Taser or a gun or a walkie-talkie, she'd never know, since Asprey pulled his motorcycle up just then. She hopped on, her helmet already in place to serve as a face mask to avoid recognition.

The deliveries started around eight. Asprey had asked Tiffany to make untraceable calls to virtually every delivery company in the greater Seattle area, placing orders almost at random. Cookie bouquets, flowers, pajamagrams, a singing clown, no fewer than ten sandwich-shop orders, over a dozen pizzas and even the stripper from Bouncing Booty had been bought and paid for. Together, they created a steady stream of various uniformed professionals moving through the building doors, and not even Poppy—who had the master list of their times on a spreadsheet in front of her—could keep track of who was coming and going.

The scaffolding was set to go up around ten. They'd opted to hire the job out to a professional window-washing company, using layers of Tiffany's encryption to make the arrangements without being tracked. Because of Asprey's continued insistence that she be seen as little as possible, Poppy was only able to catch a glimpse of the huge wood and metal structure going up along the backside of the apartment building as she and Tiffany drove by in her car. At least they also had the fortune of seeing the other guard, a smaller man with a pointy goatee, arguing with the workers putting it up.

The power started cutting out around noon. Tiffany had the power grid for the entire block set on a random and automatic rotation so that the guards couldn't predict when or how the building would go dark. Five minutes here, thirty seconds there—but never on the elevator, which Poppy had insisted would continue running no matter what.

"I don't want people getting trapped in there," she'd said. "I'm not budging on that issue."

Asprey had his own issues he refused to budge on.

"That is *not* a cliché. Name one heist movie that includes ninjas," Poppy had protested when he pulled out the costumes, black harem pants and face masks that left a slit for the eyes.

"The iconic ninja," he'd retorted, his eyes sparkling, "invokes fear like no other symbol. You of all people should know that."

Fear was not the emotion she saw reflected in his eyes at that moment. "You're just putting them in there to get a rise out of me."

He'd stood up and straightened his vest. "Is it working?"

Yes. But she wasn't about to say so. "I'll let you know. So what are Tiffany and I supposed to do exactly—run around the park in ninja costumes? What if someone asks us what we're doing?"

"If that someone is a little old lady with a cane, tell her you're rehearsing for a play. If it's one of Winston's security guards, run like hell."

Poppy grabbed the costumes from him forcefully. The whole plan was ridiculous and juvenile and so much like him she had a hard time keeping a straight face.

Asprey stopped her before she turned away. "We don't have to do this," he said. "If you want to stop right now, Tiffany and I can manage. This isn't your problem, and you shouldn't put yourself at risk for us."

She smiled with a brightness she didn't feel—not because she was afraid of what was to come but because she felt fantastic. A person shouldn't be excited about breaking into a woman's heavily guarded apartment to steal her most prized, albeit fake, possession—especially not when the consequences of getting caught were so high. Like Asprey, she delighted in the ninjas and the over-the-top ludicrousness of it all. But while his motivations were rooted in good, hers were simply part of her criminally bent mind. She was seriously disturbed.

"I wouldn't miss this for the world," she said. "After all, I'm an old hand at breaking and entering. The question is...are *you* ready?"

His eyes deepened in color. "I'm beginning to think I was born for this."

Getting in was easy.

Even with the circus going on all around the building—one security guard bouncing between circling the window washing scaffolding and checking the exits every time the power went out, the other with his eyes trained on the van and the flashes of black that wove in and out of the park—Asprey still had to get past the guard stationed out front as well as the regular front desk clerk.

So he did the last thing anyone expected.

He walked right in.

Asprey waited for a lull in the mayhem, when the ninjas disappeared into a pair of portable toilets in the park and the power was all the way on. The van and window scaffolding sat untouched for hours. It was the first time all day that the guards felt sure nothing was going to happen.

"Afternoon, Greg," he called cheerfully to the front desk clerk. Asprey had dressed in an understated suit and tie, a briefcase in one hand, and otherwise did nothing to hide his appearance. If the guard had been paying the least bit of attention, he would have recognized Asprey and immediately stopped him. It just so turned out that, today of all days, a man walking casually through the door was the last thing on the guard's mind.

He sauntered to the elevator and pressed the Up button.

"I'd take the stairs if I were you," the guard called out. "The power's been cutting in and out and we don't have time to bail you out if it gets stuck. Oh, shit—is that another flower delivery coming in?"

"Thanks," Asprey called back, swallowing a laugh. "I will."

The power cut just as he hit the twelfth floor. He couldn't have timed it better if he'd tried.

Using a hand-crank awl, Asprey began boring a hole in the wainscoting outside Cindy's apartment, moving through the layers of wood and drywall at a fairly quick rate. The sawdust and other debris collected in a small pan he laid out on the floor, filling up twice. He had to empty it into his briefcase, which was already crowded with various tools needed for the job.

The awl moved almost silently through to the interior of Cindy's apartment, and when he finally felt the giving way as he punched through, Asprey leaned down and blew the rest of the dust away. He was left with a clean hole, into which he peered to catch a glimpse of miniature bared fangs and the guttural growl of a dog who suspected danger but wasn't quite sure of it.

"Here, doggy, doggy," he called. "That's a good doggy. You're a thirsty girl aren't you? Aren't you?"

The dog barked a negative reply.

"Not yet," Asprey hissed, glancing up and down the hall. So far, it was all clear. Hopefully, it would stay that way long enough for him to finish. "You can bark in about two minutes. Three, depending on how fast I can move."

Next, he pulled a long, clear plastic tube out of his briefcase and slipped it through the hole. The dog almost immediately began tugging on it, and Asprey was about an inch from losing the whole thing before he caught the stubby end.

"Next time, extra tubing," he muttered. "Check."

He affixed a bright red funnel to his end, securing it swiftly with duct tape—a beer bong of the finest craftsmanship known to mankind. After taking a long pull from the bottle of gin he grabbed from the briefcase, he began slugging the alcohol through to the other side.

"Vile stuff," he said, wiping his mouth with his sleeve. "I don't know what is wrong with you, dog. At your mommy's income, at least have the decency to prefer a nicely aged scotch. Or even a stout ale."

The tugging came a little fiercer now, which Asprey could only assume meant the dog was chugging the stuff fast enough to make his frat brothers proud. About half the bottle in, he stopped, not sure if the dog would continue lapping it off the floor until he fell into an alcoholic stupor—also much like his frat brothers—or if it preferred a nice ceramic bowl handcrafted from Spain or something.

A noise from the end of the hall startled Asprey into shooting to his feet, yanking the gin bong with him. He'd just tucked it behind his back when a door pulled open and shut again, a newspaper making a quick disappearance from the doorstep.

Crisis averted.

But that was only the first one. From inside the apartment, a series of sharp yips signaled that the plan was already working. Asprey grabbed the wooden plug Poppy had whittled down to size and stopped the hole, careful to cover it with another plug they'd cut out of wainscoting of a similar hue.

He kicked at the carpet to brush away the last of the debris and stood. It looked pretty good.

With a cheerful hop and a whistle, he made his way to the end of the hall. The plan was working.

He hid himself on the far end of the floor, in a small, offset bay window that looked out over the park. Anyone paying attention would see a man in a suit taking in the sights of the round of deliveries and security guards arguing down below. But he was counting on no one paying attention—at least not right away. He needed to use the flexibility garnered through his years of yoga to wedge himself up against the window when—plan willing—Mrs. Partridge came out to inspect the noise.

That happened exactly six minutes later. It was a wonder it took that long—he could hear the dog barking from all the way down the corridor. Poppy hadn't been lying when she said that creature had a voice.

After stepping carefully onto the window frame, Asprey flattened his body against the cool glass, using his arms on either side to stabilize him. His face pressed against the window, increasing his range of vision enough so that he could see the window washer's scaffolding set up outside, the frame of it set within reach of Cindy's window. If he strained just so, he could also see a streak of black moving through the far end of the park. Poppy. There was no way in hell Tiffany had that kind of speed.

"Jasmine, precious!" Mrs. Partridge's shrill cries were almost as bad as the dog's. "Are you having a bad time, little dear? Did Mommy go out and leave you all day for her big office downtown?"

The jangling of keys and some low mumbling were like music to his ears. Thank the gods of robbery for good neighbors and single women. And for Poppy laying all the groundwork.

Asprey's neck was getting a kink, so he adjusted it a little. The dog's barks had lost some of their volubility, and he could no longer hear Mrs. Partridge cooing, so he carefully lowered himself to the floor, being careful to grab his briefcase. With a quick, furtive glance, he scanned the hallway. It was empty.

But not for long.

The original plan had been to walk by the hopefully open door to the apartment and slip a cover over the deadbolt frame so that it couldn't fully lock when Mrs. Partridge exited with or without the dog. It was risky, and there were quite a few things that could go wrong with that plan, but the fates that ruled over heists must have been smiling down on them. Just as Asprey was about to get the deadbolt cover in his palm, Cindy's dog dashed out the door and made a beeline for the elevators on the other end of the corridor.

Mrs. Partridge followed at a clipped pace, her arms outstretched.

Asprey moved, unwilling to lose the moment. He ducked into the open door of the apartment and took a quick survey. All but a few drops of the gin remained, the dog having done a fairly good job of cleaning up. There was a fairly substantial pile of sawdust, and Asprey took a moment to scoop it up and kick his foot over what remained.

The bedroom seemed like the safest place to go, so he followed the mental map he'd created from Poppy's blueprints. Dropping to his stomach, he slid underneath the bed, tucked his briefcase by his side, and prepared to wait.

"You naughty little puppy." Mrs. Partridge's voice returned to the apartment, and Asprey could hear the keys jangling again. "We'll keep you cozy until Mommy gets home, how about that?"

The door slammed shut, and the lock clicked. It was almost too easy.

It *was* too easy.

Asprey knew the painting was in the kitchen, and he made his way there as soon as the coast was officially clear. As Poppy had described, the rest of the apartment was almost sterile in its cleanliness and lack of décor, but life actually touched down in the kitchen's interior. Some kind of half-eaten, freshly baked pie sat on the counter next to an empty plate and a cozy mystery that bore the inevitable creases of use. The smell of morning coffee still filled the air, and a table with hand-woven placemats stood at a half-cocked angle under the enormous Pollock.

He stopped.

He'd seen a Pollock before, of course. And Caravaggios and da Vincis and Monets and Manets and any number of modern artists who had yet to reach the same kind of distinction. It came with the art appraisal territory and with the life of privilege Poppy liked to constantly rub in his face.

But this painting was something else—it was something more. Maybe it was because most of his experience of fine art was in museums and the sterile homes of the wealthy, not unlike the rest of Cindy's apartment, but the warm kitchen, with one wall almost entirely taken up in the dizzying pattern of reds and browns, rendered him speechless.

So that's why she keeps it in the kitchen. It felt like home here.

Swallowing his pang of regret, Asprey pulled out the razor blade tucked carefully in his back pocket and stepped up to the painting, running his hands along the outer edge.

Even though he knew the painting was a fake, it seemed wrong to stab the blade into the canvas. The only way he could get it out of there was to shred it in a series of ten one-foot strips. He'd roll each one up as tight as it would go and toss them down the garbage chute on his way out. If all went well, they could get to the garbage dumpsters to collect and hide the evidence before anyone caught on.

Bracing himself for the first rip, Asprey took a deep breath, allowing himself to take in the painting one last time. The colors were typical of Pollock in the forties, bright but also muted, the fractal patterns providing most of the brilliance, the colors secondary to the technique. On a fake like this one, the colors were probably pigments that hadn't existed prior to 1950, and the layers of carefully controlled paint splatters not quite the mathematical genius that had made Pollock so famous.

It was an incredible forgery, though. Asprey leaned closer, allowing his fingers to graze over the painting, the raised surface of decades-old oil paint grounding him to the spot.

Something isn't right.

He peered closer. Although he didn't have any of his equipment on him, there was a telltale crackling to the paint, where time and age had broken down some of the largest raised surfaces. It was possible to fake that, of course, especially with a high-end forgery that applied heat in the right proportion— and even more easily here in the kitchen, where additional moisture would do its damage. But that kind of warping was always too systematic, too controlled, a lot like a Pollock in its own right.

This was natural warping. This was too close to similar paintings he'd examined in the past, always looking for signs of authenticity.

This wasn't a fake.

Asprey tucked the razor away, surprised to find his hands were shaking. He couldn't be a hundred percent sure, of course—not without a lab and a thorough examination somewhere with better lighting. But if he was asked to make an initial guess, stick with his gut reaction, he'd say this was the real thing.

Reading people, reading paintings—those were the two things he could do.

Or so he'd always thought.

Asprey reached for his cell phone, unsure who, exactly, he was supposed to call. Cindy? Winston? The college professor who had first introduced him to the postmodern abstracts? For some reason, the voice he most wanted to hear at that moment belonged to Poppy, a woman who knew nothing about art but who could make him feel a thousand times better about his unerring faith in humanity.

"I'm so sorry, Asp." A familiar voice behind him caused Asprey to whirl, his phone clattering noisily to the ground. "I didn't think you'd get this far. You're better at this than I thought."

The last thing Asprey thought before a heavy cudgel came crashing down on his head was that surprise was an emotion they both shared in that moment. Probably the only one.

Chapter Twenty-Five

"It's taking too long."

Poppy and Tiffany watched the apartment building from the far side of the park, using their ridiculous twin ninja suits to blend into the shrubbery. Heavy rain clouds obscured what was left of the setting sun, replacing the gray sky with an encroaching, inky blue.

At least that's one benefit to dressing up like kids at Halloween. Unless someone was looking explicitly for them, they were hard to spot.

"Maybe he had a hard time getting into the apartment or something," Tiffany suggested. She scanned the park, and Poppy could see the other woman's doubt in the small opening where her eyes peeked through. "We haven't seen any cops or heard sirens yet, so no one has called the police. That's a good sign."

Poppy shook her head and ripped off her mask. It was getting suffocating in there anyway. "Cindy will be home any minute—we can't risk her walking in on him in the middle of the job. I think I should go in. The doorman knows me. I might at least be able to get up to the floor, find out what's going on."

"No way." Tiffany tore her mask off too, offering Poppy an apologetic smile. "Asprey made me promise that no matter what else happens, you're not allowed to go inside. I'm supposed to use force to restrain you if I have to."

Poppy couldn't help laughing. "What kind of force did he have in mind?"

"He didn't get that far. But I'm pretty inventive. I think I saw some poison ivy over there."

"I'll be good and save you the trouble," Poppy promised. "I just wish there was some way to know if he was still inside or not. I'd try calling his cell, but for all we know, he left the ringer on. That wouldn't go over well in a compromising situation."

"Well..." Tiffany's face flushed and she wrinkled her nose. "There might be one thing we can do."

Poppy grabbed Tiffany by the shoulders, stopping just short of shaking her. Maybe she was more wound up than she realized, but she hated being so ineffective. The last time she'd let her partner go in on the job alone, things hadn't ended well—and Bea was a professional.

"What is it?" Poppy asked, reining herself in.

"You know how you got all mad the other day and said we couldn't bug you anymore without your permission?"

She didn't like where this was going. "Ye-es."

"Well, Asprey might have asked if maybe I'd do it one more time. Just to keep you safe during the heist. You know, in case something happened."

"Where is it?"

Tiffany pointed at Poppy's wrist. "He had me sew it into the hem of your ninja suit."

"Fucking Asprey." Poppy ripped at her sleeve, not stopping until a tiny round piece of metal not unlike a watch battery fell out. She was about to drop it and crush it under her heel when Tiffany plucked it out of her hand.

"It's a really nice bug. Please don't."

Poppy crossed her arms and did her best to look intimidating. "I can't believe you let him talk you into that—I thought we were *friends*. And how is my being bugged going to help us right now?"

Tiffany smiled and inclined her head to the back entrance of the park, where they'd parked Poppy's car with all their equipment. "I thought it wasn't very fair, us keeping tabs on just you—especially after you asked us not to. So I planted one on Asprey too. To make it even."

Poppy could have kissed her. "Are you serious?"

Tiffany sprang to her feet and began climbing out of the bushes. Poppy followed suit, and they both tried to appear normal as an elderly couple took one look at their strange, unmarked clothes and veered the opposite direction.

"It won't give us all the answers, but at least we'll know where he is."

Poppy breathed a sigh of relief. She didn't need all the answers—she'd probably never have those. She just needed to know that Asprey was safe.

Asprey had only had two headaches in his lifetime that competed with the one currently threatening to split his skull in half. The first was the direct result of an overconsumption of alcohol when he was thirteen, before he knew that too much of a good thing was painfully, palpably real. The second occurred in his favorite Balinese prison. It was a good story, and he loved dropping that term around whenever he could, but the truth had been that there was a lot of pain, not a lot of healthy air to breathe and a prison guard with a grudge against rich American tourists.

Still. He'd have taken either of those situations with a glad heart in place of the one currently keeping him bound to Louis. To *Louis*, of all chairs. His brother should have just dug up their father's bones and done a voodoo dance through town with them—it would have been less disrespectful to the dead.

"It's your own fault, you know." Graff looked up from the opposite side of the room. "If you'd just taken the painting without examining it first, I would have let you walk out of there." Asprey was having a hard time getting his line of vision to clear up and stop making multiples of everything, but he would have known this place even if he'd been blindfolded.

Home.

His loft, smelling of leather and the potted rosemary he kept above the sink. Of all the places they could have dragged his limp, lifeless form, they had to choose the one that made his head reel with more than pain.

"I can forgive for you a lot of things, Graff," he said, managing a small grin. "But letting me butcher a genuine Pollock would have been too much."

Graff snorted. "How ridiculously noble of you."

"I wish I could say the same of you."

Graff was on his feet in seconds, across the room and crouched in front of Asprey so that he had no choice but to focus his gaze on his brother. *Brother.* That seemed an awfully dirty word these days. "Don't. You can't even possibly begin to understand my motivations, so don't judge me."

"Where's Winston?"

"He's heading here from work—you know, the place that even now doesn't occur to you? The place the rest of us have spent years of our lives trying to keep afloat while you've been off playing airplanes with your friends?"

Asprey winced. He was pretty sure a cut tore apart the better part of his forehead, since that small movement had blood dripping in his line of vision. It *hurt*, but not nearly as much as the knowledge that he'd been so blind for so long.

"Considering I spent the last six months helping you try and save the company from Winston, doesn't that seem a little harsh?" Asprey asked, striving to keep his tone light. He wouldn't let Graff see his pain—either kind. "Talk about judging others."

Graff laughed and rose to his feet. There was no humor in the sound, no joy in his movements. "Don't kid yourself. You were helping me save your portion of the profits."

"Oh yeah? And what were you and Winston doing?"

"Saving your portion of the profits." Graff checked his watch. "Winston should be here any minute—he's as much a part of this as we are."

"Did you give him all of Todd's money too? Or was that part of some other plan?"

Graff's eyes softened. "Todd Kennick had it coming—I wasn't lying when I said he had a string of robberies at his back. He would have only used that money to hurt more people."

"You're in a funny position to play jury."

"I'm doing the best I can, Asp. I don't like it—any of it. I never have. But put a man between a rock and a hard place and give him a brother like you to look out for, and this is what happens. I had to smash my way out."

"Don't pin this on me. I never said this was what I wanted."

Before Graff could say more, a lock sounded at the front door, and the familiar form of the eldest Charles brother moved smoothly in. "He's up," Winston said unnecessarily. He flipped the dead bolts and secured the chain on the door. "That was some kind of stunt you pulled today, Asp. I didn't think you had it in you."

"Your problem is that you've always underestimated me," Asprey returned. Taking a gamble, he added, "Tiffany too. What makes you think she's not going to the police right now?"

"To say what? That her brother went missing while breaking into an apartment to steal a ten-million-dollar painting?" Winston dropped himself onto Asprey's favorite recliner. "You can do better than that."

"So you're going to keep me here?" He was rapidly losing some of his cool. It felt like Graff had used zip ties to secure his hands behind the chair, and the plastic dug painfully into his wrists. His shoulder too didn't particularly like the angle it was forced into. "Until...what? Nine o'clock tomorrow morning? Or my untimely death?"

Graff and Winston shared a glance that didn't add to his comfort. They didn't know the answer to that question any more than he did.

"You have to understand, Asprey," Graff said, his voice low. "We didn't have a choice."

"There's *always* a choice." It wasn't necessarily easy, and right and wrong weren't always laid out as clear options. But if there was one thing he'd learned from Poppy over the past few weeks, it was that a person could always choose between better and worse. This was worse. "The Pollock was real—I know that now. But the other stuff we took was fake. I saw it with my own two eyes. What gives?"

"Dad didn't exactly leave us a booming company," Graff said. Winston tried to shush him, but Graff shook his head. "We have to tell him, Winston. It's the only way."

"You were sure he wouldn't be able to find his way into Cindy VanHuett's apartment either. Look how that turned out."

Graff ignored Winston and kept talking. "Dad was all about the people, like you, about discussing painters and donating to the arts community. About making himself look good—which seems fine on the outside, but all that schmoozing hid some really messed up finances. We were facing bankruptcy even before he died."

So? Asprey wanted to say. Lots of companies had ups and downs—especially around that time. They wouldn't have been the first business to need a helping hand. But he doubted his opinion was being solicited right then, so he kept his mouth shut.

"It wasn't our finest hour, but Winston and I knew someone who dealt in forgeries, who might be able to help us out selling some of the higher-end pieces that came through."

"That part I know already," Asprey said. "It's what you told me to get my help with stealing all the forgeries. But if the company is so broke, how can we afford to pay out all the insurance claims?"

"We're not." Graff let out a long sigh. "That's what I told you was going on, but the truth is that we've been stealing the forgeries whose claims have expired and not been renewed. We can't risk the new insurance providers finding out they're fake. It would only take one or two before all the signs started pointing at us. And it's not all bad, you have to admit—the owners are still getting their full dollar value for the insurance. Just not from us. We did the best we could, Asp, given the circumstances. You have to believe that."

"And the Pollock?"

"It was our exit strategy. I'd disappear, you and Tiffany would fail to get in, and Winston would win. The end—until you actually found your way in there."

Winston sat up. "Tell me, Asprey...was it you who planned that heist or was it Poppy? The three-ring-circus act smacked of your style, but I'm guessing she did quite a bit of the real work. I knew we should have gotten rid of her while we had the chance."

"It was rather clever of me, wasn't it?" Asprey said, playing dumb. He didn't like where this conversation was headed.

"That's it!" Winston shot to his feet and pointed at him.

"What?" Asprey and Graff asked at the same time. But Asprey was afraid he already knew.

Winston turned to Graff, his brows lifted in excitement. "You said that woman is an ex-con, right? It's easy. Asprey will keep his mouth shut about this whole thing and maybe even do some recovery work for us in the future."

"Or else what?" Asprey was inches away from going full-Hulk on his brother and busting out of those zip ties. He just needed about fifty more pounds of green muscle to do it.

"Or else we hand her over to the police with information on the several dozen robberies around town lately. I bet they'd love to pin it all nice and clean on a woman with a chip on her shoulder and a criminal record."

"You wouldn't dare."

"That might actually work." Graff turned to face him, leaning in close. "Asprey has a little crush on that woman, don't you, little brother? What do you say—we'll keep our mouths shut if you do the same? We can go back to the way things were. You can keep not showing up to work; we can keep paying you for the privilege. Even-steven," he added, using a favorite term from their boyhood.

It was a tempting offer. Life before all this had been pretty nice, if he did say so himself. Sleeping until he felt like getting up, parties every night of the week, Bali and India and Australia with any woman he chose.

But he didn't want that anymore. Not at this cost. Not without Poppy.

"Patio door open," he announced.

"What?" Graff turned. "I'm not opening the door. Come on, Asprey. Please just take this offer. I don't like this any more than you do, but life means having to make hard choices sometimes. You'll learn that someday."

"I think he already has."

As soon as he heard Poppy's voice, Asprey snapped his head up so fast it caught Graff's chin, sending his brother flying backward. The pain reverberated inside his own skull tenfold, but he'd have done it again in an instant. It was that cool.

"How did you get in here?" Winston demanded.

"Voice-activated control panel," Asprey offered, but his words were lost as Poppy fell into her favorite tuck-and-roll maneuver, moving quickly across the room and behind Winston's still-bewildered form. And even better—she was in the ninja costume. If he didn't think his head was going to explode right that moment, he might have tried to take a picture.

Asprey would have been hard-pressed to name half the things she did to Winston over the next twenty seconds, but he did know they involved a kick to the head, a punch to each kidney and some kind of weird Vulcan death grip that had him falling into an inert heap on the hardwood floor.

Graff, watching the exchange warily, equipped himself with a large vase—not Ming but still one of Asprey's favorites—and prepared to meet Poppy head-on. Since Asprey had always been her target in the past, Graff had no idea what he was up against. It was almost enough to make Asprey smile. *Almost.*

But then she stopped and studied his brother carefully, her head at a slight tilt. "It was you all along."

It was an odd time to start a conversation, but when Asprey felt a tug on his arms, he realized Poppy hadn't come alone. Tiffany used a knife she must have grabbed from the kitchen to free his bound wrists before moving on to his feet. The return of blood to his limbs hurt even more than his head, pins and needles stabbing the surface of his skin. He shook loose the worst of it, determined to come to Poppy's aid, but Tiffany placed a finger to her lips in a gesture of silence as she jerked her head toward the door.

They were here to rescue him.

It was both the most touching and the most emasculating gesture anyone had ever made on his behalf. Which was why he planned on ignoring it.

"This doesn't have to be a bad thing, Poppy," Graff said carefully, not moving. "I'll give you all of Todd's money back, I swear. You can go your way and we can go ours—there's no reason for our paths to ever cross again."

Tiffany gestured again, but Asprey shook his head firmly, even though each movement hit him as a wave of nausea. Moving as stealthily as he could, he crept up behind Graff. He could have tried another one of those cool leg sweeps, or even kicked the vase out of his brother's hand...but he didn't. He was tired of fighting.

With a heavy sigh, he dropped his hand to his brother's shoulder. Graff whirled, the vase poised over Asprey's head. But he caught sight of Tiffany standing near the door and lowered his arms. At least all that stuff about protecting their sister hadn't been a lie.

"You know Poppy can take you out in five seconds flat. You're outnumbered and outmaneuvered. Why don't we skip this part for once?"

"So what?" Graff said, a sneer twisting his lips. "It's *your* turn to lead *me* to an untimely death? Is that what you're saying?"

Asprey didn't lift his hand. "No. I'm saying maybe it's time we all sit down and have a nice, long talk about the family legacy."

Graff snorted. "What family legacy?"

This time, Asprey did give his brother a little shove. Directing him toward the couch—that long, L-shaped, rich leather seat he'd been dreaming of for months—he and Graff moved as one.

It was probably the first time that had happened in a long time. And, based on the aching hole in his chest, right where his favorite brother had once held a crowning seat, Asprey realized it was also probably going to be the last.

Chapter Twenty-Six

"Ashes to ashes, dust to dust." Poppy took a long pull from a fifth of Jack Daniels before wiping her mouth on her sleeve and handing the bottle off to Bea. If either of them thought it was an odd sendoff, guzzling whiskey and scattering Poppy's grandmother on the front lawn of the Aberdeen Bingo Hall, they didn't mention it.

Neither did Asprey.

He stood as unobtrusively as he could on the outskirts, drinking when the bottle came his way, otherwise nothing more than an observer, a man holding a little dog with quiet stoicism.

It seemed wrong to intrude on Poppy's grief, somehow. He hadn't been invited to this funeral, but he hadn't been *not* invited either. It made for an interesting memorial dynamic—a situation not exactly helped along by Poppy's mourning clothes, which were composed of a short, tight black skirt, gray striped tights and, of course, her teal cowboy boots.

"What are you kids doing out on that lawn?" An overlarge matron in a floral blouse and a navy skirt hiked up to her armpits appeared on the steps of the bingo hall. "You can't loiter here."

Poppy held up the box of ashes like it was a trophy. "It's Grandma Jean. We're bidding her farewell."

"Grandma Jean? Jean Donovan?" The matron lumbered down the steps. "You her granddaughter?"

Poppy nodded and offered the woman a drink, which she promptly declined with a whole list of dietary restrictions.

"I heard she went real quiet," the woman said kindly, flanking Poppy as the last of the ashes fell onto the grass. It wasn't a very windy day, so most of it clumped in little heaps on the ground. "We miss her."

"Me too," Poppy said. Unable to help himself, Asprey put an arm around her waist. She tensed but didn't push him off, so he stayed there.

"She owes me about two hundred bucks," the woman added. "She cheated at bingo, you know. We didn't even know a person *could* cheat at bingo until she joined the club. Made her own score sheets at home."

Poppy laughed, her smile misty. "Everyone knew that." She jerked her head toward the south side of the street and added. "I opened a tab at Ludwig's Hole. You and everyone else she owes money to can feel free to drink every last penny she cheated you out of. Just say a few toasts for her while you're in there. Please?"

The woman gently pushed Asprey out of the way and engulfed Poppy in a swell of pink chiffon. He couldn't hear what the woman whispered, but it must have been the right thing because when she pulled away, Poppy had abandoned the misty stage and fallen into a laugh-sob.

"What do you suppose she said?" Asprey asked Bea. Poppy's roommate and friend was a hard woman to read, but if he had to guess, he'd say he was begrudgingly accepted by her. That seemed pretty par for the course, though. Begrudging acceptance from these women seemed to be the most he could ever hope for.

Bea eyed him warily. "Probably that there isn't enough booze in the world to cover Grandma Jean's outstanding tab. Good thing Poppy was able to recover that eighty grand her grandmother invested."

Asprey nodded, not sure how much he was supposed to divulge of Poppy's exact recovery methods.

"What's not going to Ludwig's Hole is yours," Poppy said, interrupting their conversation. "I mean it, Bea. It's for you and Jenny—it always has been."

Bea's mouth, already scarily firm, grew even tighter. "Absolutely not. There's no way you're giving me money in addition to everything else. I won't take it."

"Then it's a good thing I had a lawyer friend put it in a trust fund in Jenny's name, huh?" Poppy asked, triumphant. "You can't get around this one, Bea. I know fancy people now."

Asprey set Gunner down so he could put his hands defensively up. "It's not me. The only thing I know about a trust fund is how to spend one."

Bea snorted. "I can believe that."

"It's all I've dreamed of since I walked through those doors out of jail," Poppy said. She forced her friend to look at her. "It's the one thing that kept me going after I found out Grandma Jean died—knowing that I might be able to make some good come out of all this. Take the money, Bea, please. Give Jenny a home like we never had. Make it all worthwhile."

"But what about you?" Bea cast a suspicious glance over Asprey.

He straightened. "I'll handle Poppy. In fact, I've come to make an offer I don't think she can refuse..."

Poppy scowled, taking him in for the first time since he rode down for the impromptu funeral. He had on a leather jacket over a suit—not his finest look in the world, but he'd been spending a lot more time at the office lately than he cared to dwell on. Graff and Winston hadn't been lying when they said things were a financial mess.

"If you're about to offer me a job at Charles Appraisals and Insurance, I'll have to ask you to meet me at the Pit."

"Considering what happened the last time we were there," he said, his voice low, "I accept."

She didn't miss the reference, and, with a brief flash in her eyes, she grabbed him by the front of his jacket and dragged him away from the rest of the group. Bea scooped up Gunner before the dog could follow them. It was the first time in days he and Poppy had been alone together, and he couldn't help but be grateful, even if they stood outside a small-town bingo hall.

Poppy wrapped her arms around her midsection and offered him a pointed look. *Strictly business*, it said. "How are things with the family? Is running a company as much fun as you expected it to be?"

Asprey didn't let her icy exterior ruffle him, even though he couldn't remember the last time he'd felt so nervous. Not even being tied to a chair while his brothers threatened to turn her in compared to this. "It's *exactly* as much fun as I expected it to be," he admitted. "Which is to say none at all. That's why I quit."

Her eyebrows shot up, and Asprey had to restrain himself from reaching out and tracing the path of them. More than anything, he just wanted to *feel* her—but even with her daring rescue the other night, she showed no signs of wanting to resume their intimacy.

He didn't blame her. Now that the job was done and their roles were complete, she probably thought he'd retreated right back to being a fluffy, useless trust-fund baby.

But he wasn't going back there.

"How can you just quit? It's your family's company—we practically forced Graff to draw up the papers signing everything over to you and Tiffany. All that stuff we did, all those laws you broke, those people you robbed...what was it *for?*"

He shrugged. "I kind of suck at being people's boss. Yesterday, I gave them all a half day. There was a parade downtown—it seemed as good a reason as any. Today I told them not to bother coming in at all."

She let out a strangled laugh but cut it short when he let himself fall into a wide grin of his own. "What are you doing here, Asprey? I appreciate you coming for this...thing to say good-bye to my grandma, but I'm not sure this is a good idea. Now that you convinced Graff and Winston to tuck their tails between their legs and disappear, you have your big, fancy, crime-free world to live in. And I'm still me—can't leave the state, can't get a job, not sure I care on either count. Leaving your company isn't going to change things between us."

He stilled, his heart in his throat. "So your only objection to me is that you're an ex-con and I'm not?"

She spread her hands helplessly. "It's not just the ex-con stuff, Asprey. All that time I was breaking laws, breaking the conditions of my parole, so close to losing everything and heading back to jail—the only thing I could think of was how great it felt to be alive again. You hate your job, but that's all it is for you. A job. You can go home at the end of the day and eat your expensive dinners and fly your plane and still get to be *you.*" She let out a sigh and looked away. "But me? I *am* the job. More than anything, these past few weeks have highlighted that I'm not cut out for anything else. I have to find a way to exist in this world, and that doesn't leave a whole lot of room for anything else."

He pulled her into an embrace then, expecting a battle but not getting one. She sagged against him, her whole body limp. That softness—such a contrast to the exterior she normally presented to the world—almost made him lose his footing.

"It was fun while it lasted, Asprey. Can't we just leave it at that?"

"No." He spoke into her hair. "I refuse to leave it at that. Flee the country with me."

She pulled away and looked up, an adorably puzzled look on her face. "What? Are you insane?"

He shook his head. He'd never felt more sane in his whole life. Maybe he wasn't going to devote his life to art like his dad or build a company with his own two hands like his grandfather. Maybe he'd always have to rely on buckets of family money to get by. But that didn't mean he couldn't make his own contribution to the world. That didn't mean he couldn't choose between better and worse.

Poppy was better.

"Tiff and I sat down. We think it's best to close the company down. Neither one of us loves it the way Graff and Winston did, but there's no way in hell we're giving them a chance to do any more damage to the family name. It's time to say good-bye."

"You can't do that! What will you do? How will you make a living?"

"Well, we're not *destitute*." He laughed softly. "We can sell off the company's assets. I can rent out my loft. We have Todd's half of a million, though we should probably try to give that back to the people who lost it. And if that's not enough, I hear there's good money in the confidence trade."

She snorted. "You're not becoming a criminal, and that's final."

"That's too bad," he said, shaking his head with mock sadness. "I was really hoping I could convince you to help me. I'm not sure I can steal all that stuff alone."

"Steal?" Poppy's eyes lit, and he realized she hadn't been lying. This stuff really did bring her to life. And that was okay with him. The way he figured it, getting all the original paintings and pieces of jewelry and heirlooms back from the black-market buyers would take at least two decades. After that...well, they could figure it out later.

"Someone once told me I was a selfish prick, that maybe instead of the insurance money, the people we stole from might rather have Grandma's cameo back."

"Asprey Charles, are you saying what I think you're saying?"

His smile threatened to crack his face, and he dropped to one knee. The wet grass soaked through the fabric of his two-thousand-dollar suit, and he would have gladly rolled in the mud if it would make her smile again. "Poppy Donovan, will you do me the very great honor of fleeing the country, thereby breaking your parole, only to embark on a life of crime with me by your side?"

She paused, not breathing, not moving, not doing anything to end Asprey's agony.

He knew, coming here like this, that he risked breaking something more than society's stupid laws—his heart was on the line too. But he had to *try*. He'd spent far too many years letting his brothers call the shots, in believing the world when it said he was only good for a fun time.

"Five," she said, staring at him.

Asprey looked around, wondering what she meant, but the grassy clumps of dirt yielded no clues.

"Four."

"Are we negotiating something?" he asked. "If that's the case, I want twenty. No, thirty."

She smiled, and that tiny action lifted a huge portion of his agony away. He knew that smile. He loved that smile.

"Three. And you're running out of time. I only promised you a five-second window in which to escape."

"Poppy." He didn't need a warning. There was nothing he wanted more than to be sent hurtling through this world at her hands.

"Two," she said.

"One," he finished for her.

She squealed and tackled him, sprawling him flat on his back, knocking the wind out of his lungs and the last of his common sense out of his head. "Do you mean it?" she asked, lips parted, hovering over him like some strange angel-demon creature he had no power to resist. "This isn't just a game?"

"Of course it's a game." Asprey reached up and brushed the hair behind her ear, pausing to gently cup the side of her face. His heart soared. "It's life. It's you and me. It's doing what we should, black and white and right and wrong be damned. We make a good team, you and I."

He didn't get a chance to hear her response. There were words, he was sure, and maybe even an insult or two, but all Asprey knew was that the moment her lips met his and they tumbled through the grass, he finally found his higher calling. It was loving Poppy.

And he knew, without a doubt, that he'd be excellent at it.

About the Author

Tamara Morgan is a romance writer and unabashed lover of historical reenactments—the more elaborate and geeky the costume requirements, the better. In her quest for modern-day history and intrigue, she has taken fencing classes, forced her child into Highland dancing, and, of course, journeyed annually to the local Renaissance Fair. These feats are matched by a universal love of men in tights, of both the superhero and codpiece variety.

Visit her online at www.tamaramorgan.com or come say hello on Twitter at @Tamara_Morgan.

It's all about the story...

Romance

HORROR

www.samhainpublishing.com

CPSIA information can be obtained at www.ICGtesting.com
Printed in the USA
BVOW02s0457191213

339207BV00002B/13/P